THE TIGER ⌐

THE TIGER'S WRATH

MARC ALAN EDELHEIT

Book 5
Chronicles of an Imperial Legionary Officer

This book is a work of fiction. Names, characters, places, and incidents are either the product of the author's imagination or are used fictitiously. Any resemblance to actual persons, living or dead, or to actual events or locales is entirely coincidental.

The Tiger's Wrath: Book 5, Chronicles of an Imperial Legionary Officer
First Edition
I wish to thank my agent, Andrea Hurst, for her invaluable support and assistance. I would also like to thank my beta readers, who suffered through several early drafts. My betas: Jon Cockes, Nicolas Weiss, Melinda Vallem, Paul Klebaur, James Doak, David Cheever, Bruce Heaven, Erin Penny, April Faas, Rodney Gigone, Tim Adams, Paul Bersoux, Phillip Broom, David Houston, Sheldon Levy, Michael Hetts, Walker Graham, Bill Schnippert, Jan McClintock, Jonathan Parkin, Spencer Morris, Jimmy McAfee, Rusty Juban, Joel M. Rainey. I would also like to take a moment to thank my loving wife who sacrificed many an evening and weekends to allow me to work on my writing.
Editing Assistance by Hannah Streetman, Audrey Mackaman, Brandon Purcell
Cover Art by Piero Mng (Gianpiero Mangialardi)
Cover Formatting by Telemachus Press
Agented by Andrea Hurst & Associates, LLC
http://maenovels.com/

Author's note:
Writing *The Tiger's Wrath* has been a labor of love and a joy. I have long wanted to tell this story but getting here took some time. I would like to take a moment to explain. To keep my writing fresh and original, I take a break between books in the CILO series and work on other stories. This also gives me time to better plan and prepare. I know it can be difficult waiting for the next book... However, I feel my process vital to delivering the high-quality writing you have come to expect. That said...with luck...you will not have to wait that long for the next CILO book.

You may wish to sign up to my newsletter to get the latest updates on my writing.

http://maenovels.com/

Reviews keep me motivated and also help to drive sales. I make a point to read each and every one, so please continue to post them.

I hope you enjoy *The Tiger's Wrath* and would like to offer a sincere thank you for your purchase and support.

Best regards,
Marc Alan Edelheit, author and your tour guide to the worlds of Tanis and Istros

The Mal'Zeelan Imperial Legion

Pre-Emperor Midisian Reformation

The imperial legion was a formation that numbered, when at full strength, 5,500 to 6,000 men. The legion was composed of heavy infantry recruited exclusively from the citizens of the empire. Slaves and non-citizens were prohibited from serving. The legion was divided into ten cohorts of 480 men, with First Cohort, being an overstrength unit, numbering around a thousand. A legion usually included a mix of engineers, surgeons, and various support staff. Legions were always accompanied by allied auxiliary formations, ranging from cavalry to various forms of light infantry. The imperial legion was commanded by a legate (general).

The basic unit of the legion was the century, numbering eighty men in strength. There were six centuries in a cohort. A centurion (basic officer) commanded the century. The centurion was supported by an optio (equivalent of a corporal) who handled minor administrative duties. Both had to be capable of reading and performing basic math.

Note: Very rarely were legions ever maintained at full strength. This was due primarily to the following reasons: retirement, death, disability, budget shortages (graft), and the slow stream of replacements.

The most famous legion was the Thirteenth, commanded by Legate...

Post-Emperor Midisian Reformation

Emperor Midiuses's reforms were focused on streamlining the legions and cutting cost through the elimination of at least half of the officer corps per legion, amongst other changes.

The basic unit of the legion became the company, numbering around 200 men in strength. There were ten twenty-man files per company. A captain commanded the company. The captain was supported by a lieutenant, two sergeants, and a corporal per file.

TABLE OF CONTENTS

Stiger

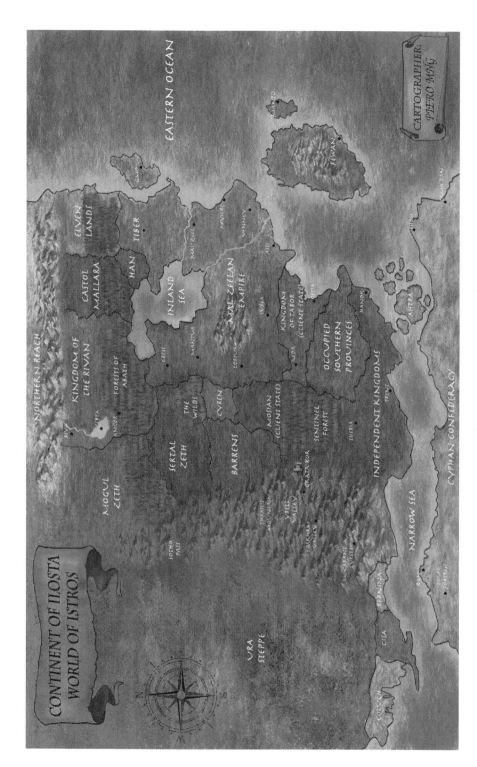

ONE

The gust of mountain wind was strong, powerful and bitterly cold. Powdered snow swirled around Stiger in a cloud that stung the exposed skin of his face and neck. Clearly unhappy about being out in such conditions, Nomad jerked his head up and down. The horse sidestepped, whinnying. Until the wind and blown snow subsided, Stiger held up a hand before his face as a shield.

"Easy, boy," Stiger said as he pulled the heavy bearskin cloak closer about himself. "There's a warm stable waiting for you at the castle and some tasty oats too. If you're lucky, perhaps there'll even be an apple."

One of Nomad's ears gave a twitch and the horse whinnied again. Stiger nudged Nomad back into a walk. As he did, a cheer rose up on the air. Ten yards ahead, men from Third and Fourth Cohorts spilled out of their tents and lined the snow-packed road that climbed steeply on a winding path up to Grata'Kor. The mighty fortress, better known as Castle Vrell, blocked the only pass leading in and out of the Vrell Valley. It loomed high above, dwarfing the single road that passed through its gates, a silent sentinel, just one component of the elaborate defenses guarding the World Gate hidden within the valley.

The cheering grew in enthusiasm as Stiger and his party entered the camp. This was the fifth camp they'd ridden through since setting out for the castle earlier in the morning. At each one, he'd been greeted in the same manner.

Stiger raised a gloved hand and gave a wave. Then abruptly, as if his wave had been the catalyst, the men pushed forward. They pressed in close, on either side of his horse. They reached out eager hands, seeking his, a touch to his horse, or simply a pat to his leg. Their enthusiasm surprised, overwhelmed, and embarrassed him. He had never experienced anything like this, the unfiltered adoration and love freely given. He felt undeserving of their affection and guilty for permitting it.

Officers and optios shouted, ordering the men back, but it did no good. Their effort was futile and, for the most part, their calls were drowned out by the cheering. The men of the Thirteenth Legion loved their legate, some of whom, despite Stiger's revelations to the contrary, were still convinced he was Delvaris reborn, beloved of the gods and an instrument of destiny.

Dog was several yards ahead of Stiger's horse. The animal received pats, much neck scratching, and occasionally a treat of bacon or jerky, which he greedily wolfed down. His tail wagged madly as the men showered almost as much attention on him as they did upon Stiger.

The animal had become the legion's unofficial mascot. At night, he was known to wander the camp, visiting fires in search of food or attention. Just as Stiger had done, the legion had come to adopt the sad-looking, shaggy dog. Stiger wondered if Dog was more popular than he was, for the men always seemed to go out of their way for the animal, sharing their meals, offering a treat or a bone that had been saved just for him. They spoiled him shamelessly.

Stiger turned in the saddle and glanced back at Eli, who had dropped back a few yards. Taha'Leeth was riding alongside Eli. Both elves had their eyes upon him. The hood of Taha'Leeth's cloak was pulled up against the cold. What he could see of her face was an unreadable mask.

Eli's eyes sparkled with amusement. He clearly understood Stiger's discomfort. Stuck for five long years in the past, Stiger had missed his friend's company. After so long an absence, it felt good to be back with him. Stiger had no closer friend than the elf, unless one counted Dog.

Therik and Stiger's aide, Tribune Severus, came next, along with two full troops of cavalry led by Lieutenant Lan. The cavalry, riding in a column of two, trailed behind, snaking back down the road.

Eli turned his attention to the lieutenant, who had just ordered one of the troops forward to push the men back. The elf spoke briefly and shook his head in the negative. After hearing what Eli had to say, the lieutenant raised a gloved hand and countermanded his order. The troop dutifully fell back into line.

Nomad sidestepped skittishly and whinnied in near panic. Stiger returned his attention to the men gathered around him and took firmer hold of the reins.

"Easy, boy." He patted the horse's neck, which seemed to have a calming effect. Nomad was an exceptionally well-trained horse. He was able to keep Nomad moving forward at a slow, steady walk through the throng of soldiers. Satisfied the horse was under control, Stiger reached down, shaking proffered hands, as many as he could.

The cheering was so loud, it rivaled the noisiest of battles. They were treating him as if he were a god and not a man. He wished they saw him as he was, flawed, imperfect, not someone to be held up on a pedestal.

No matter how much he desired otherwise, he knew deep down it was never meant to be. The High Father had seen fit to make him special, to set him on the road of destiny. And the men knew it. Amongst other things, they had seen him take down a dragon, fight a minion of evil, and orchestrate the routing of an entire army. In short, they had seen him do what had seemed not only improbable, but impossible.

In their eyes, he was the fearless leader, blessed by the divine, who set the example for others to follow. He could lead them to certain defeat and so true was their faith, they'd follow, convinced he would somehow manage to beat the odds. And so, they cheered madly and greeted him as a beloved hero.

Despite being terribly discomforted, he tolerated their behavior. It served his purposes that they love him. And in moments like this, he readily embraced their affection. He would use their love, their adoration, and whatever else they gave freely, for he was the High Father's Champion and had a job to do. And Stiger meant to do the job right, for should he succeed, he would save the empire he loved.

He did wonder, usually at night when he was alone, if that made him a terrible, perhaps even a despicable person. Whenever such thoughts bubbled up, he forced them back down. He couldn't afford the luxury of doubt. Not now, not ever. Such thinking was self-defeating and counterproductive.

Stiger intended to use every trick, edge, and advantage he had or was given. If he failed in the task set before him, all would be lost. Darkness would sweep over this world, like so many others before it. He was not about to allow that to happen.

So, Stiger continued to shake hands and accept the well wishes of his men, legionaries of the Lost...the Thirteenth Legion. These men, those he'd brought with him from the past, were all volunteers. Every single one had come with him because they believed. They understood why they were here and just what was at stake. He had hidden nothing from them, revealing everything he knew. Well, almost everything. There were some things he just could not reveal. He had not told them about his sword and the spirit of the dangerous, evil wizard trapped within.

A small number of men from the Thirteenth and her auxiliary cohorts had elected to remain behind and make a life for themselves in the valley. Those few had become the foundation of the valley's militia and filled out the ranks of the two valley cohorts. To them had fallen the responsibility of watching over the valley and helping to protect and guard the World Gate. The rest, after what they'd witnessed and what Stiger had revealed, had readily joined him in stasis, along with most of the camp followers.

Stiger continued shaking hands, accepting the well wishes of his men. He glanced over their heads, studying the camp. Just behind the cheering throngs were dozens of women and children who had come out to watch. Along both sides of the steep and winding road were neatly ordered tents, defensive ditches, and ramparts facing outward. Smoke from hundreds of fires climbed up into the air, where the wind caught and swirled it away.

Over the last three days, the road leading to Castle Vrell had become one large fortified army encampment, which ran from the valley's base right up to the pass at the top. This was where not only his men were encamped, but also Thane Braddock's army.

With every passing day, additional dwarven forces arrived, marching out of Old City. Cragg had also called forth his masses and the gnomes had come in strength. At the latest count, which he'd seen this morning before leaving Old City, the combined army of humans, dwarves, and gnomes numbered over eighty thousand. There was the very real chance that, within the month, the army would be well over one hundred thousand strong. It was an awesome force, a mighty host. And the enemy had no idea it existed. That thought alone almost made Stiger smile, as he continued to shake hands.

Working his way through the excited throng took time, but eventually the legionaries gave over to a dwarven warband's camp. Stiger recognized the green cross-patterned colors and standard of the Rock Breakers. They were fearsome warriors, proud not only of their history, but also their clanhold, a beautiful place Stiger had once visited.

Before entering stasis to be returned to his proper time, Stiger had spent some months living and traveling amongst the dwarves, touring what they called their nations, a holdover from earlier days. Each individual clan was considered its own nation, united under the leadership of the thane.

His weeks with the Rock Breakers had stood out as memorable. In a misty valley tucked deep in the mountains, they had built their capital city, Garand Gerkane. It was one of the few aboveground dwarven cities. Theo had made a point of taking him there.

As Nomad continued to work his way along the snow-packed road, Stiger let go an unhappy breath. It seemed as if he had only just left Theo and Brogan to enter Thoggle's magical stasis. One moment he'd closed his eyes and the next opened them as if he'd taken a short nap. Over three hundred years had passed. Theo, Brogan, and everyone else he had left behind were now gone, lost to the mists of time. They were all long dead.

Stiger felt a sudden pang of loss, not only for them, but for Sarai as well. The wound of her passing hurt and some nights was still quite raw. For the most part, he'd come to terms with it. Regardless of whether he found love again, the wound would never fully heal. Within her arms, he had discovered a measure of comfort, peace, and healing. For that, he would be grateful 'til the day he died.

It had been a long, well-traveled road to get to this point. Over the years, he'd lost many friends and companions. Theo and Brogan were just two more to add to the list. Sarai's death was different...more significant. He had moved on, but her loss pained him.

Stiger glanced back again at the elves. Was this what it was like for them? He had always thought Eli's longevity a blessing, but now, he wasn't so certain. Was a prolonged life instead a curse?

Stiger steered Nomad around a rut in the packed-down snow. He knew Taha'Leeth had suffered terribly. But now he wondered...how many friends had Eli lost over the long years? How much sadness and grief had he suffered?

As he drew nearer to the dwarven camp, Stiger shifted his thoughts back to happier times with the dwarves, recalling the wonders of Garand Gerkane. Somewhat like the elves, the Rock Breakers had sculpted nature to their will and then enhanced it to their own tastes.

After Sarai's loss, he had found a measure of peace in Garand Gerkane. Stiger wondered if the city was still there and just as peaceful as he recalled. He suspected it was and hoped in the future there might be time one day to return.

The dwarves came out of their tents and into the cold. They cheered him, almost as vociferously as his legionaries. Stiger well understood their emotion. He had restored the Compact, delivered the traitor Hrove to their thane, and brought the Thirteenth Legion with him from the past to help fulfill a prophecy dear to their hearts.

For the dwarves, his actions meant the time of shutting out the world was at an end. They eagerly looked forward to what they called their return. Stiger thought perhaps the world, the Cyphan included, were not ready for them.

Tyga, chieftain of the Rock Breakers, stepped forth from an overly large tent painted in his clan's colors. It was likely his headquarters. Two guards wearing plate armor were posted before the tent. They snapped to attention as their chieftain strode past. With him came two other dwarves, likely his senior officers.

Tyga moved slowly to the edge of the roadway and there came to a stop. The two officers stepped to either side of their chieftain. Even for a dwarf, Tyga was powerfully built, with bulging muscles and a broad chest. Tyga wore a well-cut tunic and a pair of dark leather boots, which sank into the fresh snow. His forearm was bandaged, for he had taken a wound at the battle before Old City. As he waited for Stiger to come nearer, he rested his hands upon his hips.

Unlike his warriors, the chieftain of the Rock Breakers did not cheer, but instead offered a solemn nod. Tyga was the near spitting image of his father, Rohka. Stiger returned the nod and then he was past, continuing his way up the road toward Castle Vrell, its massive fortified walls reaching vainly for the gray overcast sky.

A gnomish camp was next. Braddock had broken the gnomes up, with the rationale that if they were left together there would be trouble, and not the little kind either. Having gotten to know the mean little shits, Stiger had readily agreed with the thane's thinking.

Still, he thought, even broken up, they were likely to cause trouble. Only by keeping them busy could one truly keep the gnomes from trouble, and sometimes not even then. Right now, there was little for the majority of them to do, and that worried Stiger immensely.

The gnomes, wearing simple gray tunics with black boots, did not cheer, nor did they show any emotion. They lined both sides of the road and silently watched as Stiger and his party rode into their midst.

Stiger glanced back at Therik, who was still riding at Severus's side. The orc's face was drawn. His hand rested on his sword hilt, while the other held the reins to the horse tightly. Stiger could well imagine the former king's thoughts, for orcs and gnomes did not mix well.

Something had occurred long ago between the two races that left not only hard feelings on both sides, but bad blood. What that occurrence was, Stiger did not know. The gnomes and dwarves refused to talk about it. What mattered was that the gnomes were holding a serious grudge. Despite that, they knew Therik was an ally and, as such, tolerated him, at least for Stiger's sake.

A gnome wearing a black tunic emerged from a tent identical to the others. Before the tent was a black standard.

The standard's fabric, emblazoned with the skull of an orc, rippled as the wind tugged at it. The gnome strode forward, toward the road. The other gnomes silently made space for him and drew back several paces.

Dog stopped before the gnome. The two considered each other for a long moment. Then Dog turned away and continued up the road. The gnome's eyes followed the animal before shifting to Stiger.

"Greetings, Cragg." Stiger brought his horse to a halt. He spoke to the kluge in Dwarven.

"Stiger," Cragg replied. "Is good you live."

"It's good to see you too." Stiger understood Cragg was not making a joke. He was deadly serious. Stiger glanced around at the gnomes. "Keeping your boys busy? Lots of training, I hope?"

"No," Cragg said simply. "Not much to do. They grow bored."

"I don't need trouble, Cragg," Stiger warned, hardening his voice. "You promised me you'd keep them in hand." Stiger pointed up toward the castle in the distance. "I have enough trouble waiting for me on the other side of the pass. I don't need to be worrying about your gnomes causing havoc with the dwarves or my legionaries."

Cragg showed his needle-like teeth in what Stiger supposed was amusement and then gave a shrug of his tiny shoulders. "You call, we come. We fight." The gnome gestured around at his fellows. "We no cause trouble. We wait. We bored, but no trouble. I say so. They listen."

Stiger glanced once again around at the silent gnomes. There were thousands of them. They watched both Stiger and Cragg with unblinking gazes. That Cragg wasn't keeping them busy was not welcome news. He had no idea how long Cragg's promise would hold. Really, it all came down to how long the other gnomes would continue to listen to their kluge and behave themselves. There was simply no telling. From experience, Stiger knew Cragg's reach only went so far.

"We won't be sitting here for much longer," Stiger assured the kluge. "You well know that. So…keep your boys in line."

"I do. I send Braddock help to fix roads." Cragg gave a nod of his small head. "We honor Compact. Soon, soon, yes?"

"Soon enough," Stiger said, then paused. He wasn't sure how the gnome would interpret the next part. Would he see the truth in the words? Or would he perceive weakness to be exploited? Regardless, Stiger felt it needed to be said. "I thank you for your assistance, Cragg."

"Bah…thanks not needed," Cragg said quickly and waved a tiny hand dismissively. "You hurry once work done. No keep us waiting. We honor Compact, kill enemy. No let anyone but ally to get World Gate, yes? We fight to last… keep World Gate from enemy. Yes, yes?"

"You are a gnome after my own heart. Take care, Cragg." With that, Stiger nudged Nomad into a walk again.

"You don't die," Cragg called after him, with insistence.

"As I said, you are a gnome after my own heart." Stiger resisted a scowl at Cragg's words as Nomad drew him farther away. He was about to say more when first one and then all the gnomes began to hum. Coming from thousands of tiny throats, it was an unsettling sound, almost to the point of being thoroughly unnerving. The hairs on the back of Stiger's neck stood on end. He figured it was their way of showing him some measure of respect, which was interesting because, in his experience, they respected no one.

Leaving the gnomes behind, they came upon another legionary cohort, the Fifth. These men cheered just as enthusiastically as those others he'd passed. They pressed tightly forward. Stiger was forced to pull Nomad to a halt. The men had gathered so closely around his horse, it was impossible to proceed farther without the serious possibility of Nomad injuring a man. Keeping a tight hold on the reins, he shook as many hands as he could. Then the officers began to reestablish discipline the old-fashioned way. The centurions waded into the press, using their vine canes to get their men's attention and force them back.

"Sorry about that, sir," Centurion Nantus said as Stiger started Nomad back into a walk. "They got a little excited."

"No need to apologize," Stiger said. "And no punishments for the men. Understand me?"

"Yes, sir," Nantus said.

"Carry on, Centurion," Stiger said.

Nantus saluted. Stiger returned the salute.

The road took them around a bend, the sides of which were steep, rocky, and unsuitable for camping. It provided a welcome respite from the throngs of cheering men, dwarves, and humming gnomes. Dog loped happily ahead, stretching his legs, occasionally stopping to sniff at something he found interesting, dig in the snow, or pee on an exposed rock. Then he was off again, dashing away.

Stiger sucked in a breath of cold winter air and then breathed out through his nose, enjoying the moment. Therik, riding one of the stout dwarven mountain ponies, cantered up beside him and then slowed his horse to Nomad's pace. It had taken more than a little convincing to get the orc on horseback and then even more work to get the horse to accept Therik.

Stiger glanced over at the orc, who looked terribly uncomfortable in the saddle. He clung to the reins, as if afraid he would drop them and lose control. The orc's feet almost touched the ground. Stiger grinned at the orc, for Therik's mount appeared even more uncertain than its rider. The pony walked along in a skittish manner, rolling her eyes and flaring her nostrils, as if she was working up the courage to throw her rider and bolt.

"That," Therik spoke in Common. He waved with one hand behind them, while the other gripped the reins tightly. "That is nothing."

Stiger looked over at his friend, wondering what he was getting at. Stiger had discovered Therik had an opinion on just about everything. He was sharp as a freshly honed blade. Over the long years spent in the past, Stiger had found himself coming to rely upon the orc's counsel.

"It means nothing," Therik said firmly. "Nothing."

"What do you mean?" Stiger asked, resting a hand upon his thigh as Nomad continued working his way up the snow-covered road.

"Your men"—Therik jerked his head back behind them—"they love you, yes?"

Stiger gave a nod, thinking that over the last few years Therik had become fluent with the common tongue. Though the orc's accent was a little guttural, he spoke quite well.

"I suppose so," Stiger said, after a prolonged pause.

"It can all go away like that." Therik gave a snap of his large fingers. "Do not make mistake like me. I tell you. It will not last forever. My people turned their back on me. The love of your people can be short-lived. You could lose everything."

Stiger considered Therik for a long moment. As Nomad plodded along, he looked at the road before him. The gnomes had used a horse-pulled roller to press and pack the snow down. It was quite an ingenious device and made travel easier. "I am mortal," Stiger said, in a voice barely above a whisper.

Therik glanced over at him in question.

"During the empire's early days," Stiger said, "upon their return home, victorious generals were rewarded with a triumph."

"A triumph?" Therik asked. "What's that?" "A grand parade through the capital," Stiger explained. "Prisoners, treasure, and some of the men who had been on campaign would parade with the general. For days afterwards, there would be feasts and games, mostly for the people, but always in honor of the victorious. It was a big show, a reward for exemplary service to the empire. All shared in the general's success, and in return, the general was treated, at least for a few days, as a near god."

"There are no more triumphs?"

Stiger shook his head. "Those days have passed. Now, the most a general can expect is an ovation, being honored in a simple ceremony by the emperor and senate…perhaps a party."

"Why?" Therik asked.

"Because emperors enjoy the popularity of the masses too much," Stiger said. "A popular person, especially a successful general, is a threat to their power. So, there are no more grand displays of success."

"That is wise," Therik said. "What is your point?"

"During the triumph," Stiger said, "a slave would ride in the chariot with the one being honored. The slave's sole responsibility on that triumphant ride through the capital and cheering masses of the mob was to continually whisper in the general's ear."

"What did he say?" Therik asked.

"'Remember, you are mortal,'" Stiger said and then fell silent. Everything in this world was fleeting. Having traveled from the past back to the present, that had been made only too clear. Everything changed. Nothing was permanent. The elves understood it and now so too did Stiger.

Therik was more than correct and, without realizing it, had in a way been acting the part of the general's slave. The adoration Stiger's men showered upon him was transitory, a temporary thing. He loved them and they him, but that could all change. It was quite possible, at some point in the future, he could lose their affection, their trust. It was something to remember and keep close to mind.

"Thank you," Stiger said back to the orc as the wind gusted again, blowing a cloud of snow over them both. Stiger averted his face until the stinging gust subsided. When he looked back, Therik bared his tusks back at him in what was, for the orc, an amused grin.

"You are mortal. Good that you understand." Therik pointed a thick index finger at him. "You might live long enough for me to get around to one day killing you."

Stiger gave an amused chuckle. "I would have none other do the deed."

"I will allow none other the honor," Therik said, in a tone he struggled to keep solemn.

Then, there was no more time for talk, as they had reached the next camp. Men from Seventh Cohort poured out of their tents and began cheering. As the throngs surrounded him, Stiger glanced once more over at Therik.

The big orc made an exaggerated snapping motion of his fingers, to emphasize his point. Stiger gave a nod and then turned his attention back to the men.

Another hour's ride brought them through five more camps and then finally to the massive walls of the castle, which sat smack in the middle of the pass.

Castle Vrell guarded the entrance to the valley. The gate on this side of the pass was open, with a century of men standing guard. The centurion in command of the detail, Verenus of Third Cohort, called his men to attention and saluted, fist to chest.

Stiger returned the salute as he gave Nomad a nudge to increase his pace. He passed into the long tunnel that would take them under the walls of the fortress. In the confines of the tunnel, lit only by a handful of torches, the sound of the hooves of the party were almost painfully loud as they clacked against the ancient stone paving. Then they were through, emerging out into the light of the castle courtyard.

Camp Prefect Oney, known affectionately as Salt, waited. Salt had ridden ahead to begin the setup of Stiger's head-quarters. With him was Lieutenant Ikely, along with a hand-ful of legionaries who stood off to the side. Stiger had left Ikely in command of the castle. As Stiger pulled up before them and dismounted, both offered him a salute. Holding the reins of his horse, Stiger returned their salutes.

"Gentlemen," Stiger said, "it is good to see you."

"You too, sir," Ikely said as he gave Stiger a funny look and then quickly hid it. Stiger had gotten a lot of that of late. He had not seen his lieutenant in over five years but under-stood to Ikely it had only been a handful of days. Stiger had aged a bit. There were a few more lines on his face than there had been before he stepped through the World Gate. His hair was also a touch grayer.

Another pang of loss coursed through Stiger, this time over his company. Returning to the future had not been as easy as he had assumed it would be. The boys of the Eighty-Fifth were still his men, but it was different now. The legion, the garrison, and his old company, they were all his boys now. Stiger's days as a company commander were over, and the sight of Ikely brought it all home, and hard too.

A moment later, Lan's cavalry clattered into the court-yard, crowding the space with dozens of horses and riders. The troopers began dismounting around them. The men looked cold and tired.

"Permission to dismiss the men, sir," Lan, still on horse-back, asked of Stiger.

"Granted," Stiger replied. "Thank you for the escort, Lieutenant."

"I should be thanking you, sir," Lan said, "for getting me out of that damned dwarven underground."

"Even in this miserable weather?" Salt asked.

"I don't know how the dwarves can live underground," Lan added, "with no sky overhead, no sun, the change in seasons. It's gotta be a miserable affair."

"Jenna being here in the castle," Stiger said, "wouldn't have anything to do with your eagerness to put Old City behind you, would it?"

Lan was silent for several heartbeats. He shifted in his saddle, as if uncomfortable.

"You know about that, sir?"

Stiger gave a nod. Lan's face flushed around the bruises and cuts to his face he had taken in the recent fighting. The lieutenant looked quite a sight, a battle-scarred veteran.

"Vargus mentioned it," Stiger said. "He asked me to look in on his daughter."

"I see, sir," Lan said, and then, to cover his evident embarrassment, turned his attention to his men as he himself dismounted. "Take your horses to the stable. You know the drill. See to their care before your own."

The dismounted riders began leading their horses toward the castle's stables. One of the two stable doors was open. Yellowed lantern light glowed from within.

"Severus." Stiger turned to the junior tribune. He had become invaluable to Stiger as an aide. "See to your horse, get some food, and then report to headquarters. Go through any dispatches and messages that are waiting. Set aside those you deem important. I will be there shortly."

"Yes, sir," Severus said and led his horse off toward the stables.

Dog weaved his way through the men and horses, padding up to Salt. He received a vigorous scratch on the neck, followed by a pat on the head. The animal was so large that the top of his head came up to Salt's chest. Dog tried to lick the prefect's face. With practiced ease, Salt deftly dodged the long pink tongue. Dog in turn settled for licking the prefect's hand.

Ikely's gaze fell upon the animal and he shook his head in what was clear disbelief, as the dog, with his tongue hanging out of his mouth, turned his attention to him. Stiger wondered if Ikely would take a step back, as many did when first meeting his hound. Though he appeared a little uncertain, the lieutenant held his ground.

Dog sniffed at Ikely curiously, almost hesitantly. The lieutenant's eyes went to Stiger briefly before returning his attention to Dog. He held out his hand for the animal to sniff.

"He's a big baby, is all," Stiger said. "He'll beg food from you whenever he gets the chance. I assure you, no matter how hungry he looks or how sad his eyes get...he's well fed, mostly by the men. They spoil him something terrible."

"Is that right, sir?" Ikely asked, with an amused laugh as Dog raised his head and began licking at his face. "I've always loved dogs."

The dog's long tail began wagging quite vigorously, to the point where it shook his entire body.

"I think he can tell," Stiger said with some amusement.

"He's a killer," Therik said in Common, having dismounted. The orc scowled at his horse, which had taken several steps from him and was trying to pull the reins from Therik's grasp. The orc gave a mighty tug and the horse gave up the attempt.

"A killer?" Ikely said skeptically, his attention focused on Dog. "I don't believe it."

"Believe," Therik said and gestured at Dog. "That animal is a vicious killer."

Dog looked back at the orc, tail becoming still. The animal gave Therik a sad whine, as if protesting the comment. It was moments like these that had Stiger convinced Dog understood every spoken word. The animal was special. That much he knew. Dog was a naverum, one of the mystical guardians of Olimbus, the place in which the gods supposedly resided. Stiger did not know which of the gods sent him, but whichever one it was, he was grateful. He could no longer imagine life without him, for he was not just a companion, but also had become a friend.

Dog jumped up on Ikely, placing both his paws on the lieutenant's shoulders. With no little amount of effort, Ikely forced Dog back down, then rubbed at the animal's thick neck with both hands. Dog's back right leg began to kick. "A killer? This sad thing? I seriously doubt that."

"You are a fool, then," Therik said in a hard tone. "He has heart of warrior. If you can't see it, you are blind."

The lieutenant turned his gaze for the first time to Therik. He stiffened in surprise as he realized he was speaking to an orc. The lieutenant glanced to Stiger, then back to Therik with a mixture of horror and curiosity.

"Lieutenant Ikely," Stiger said hastily. He did not want Ikely to get off on the wrong foot with Therik, for the orc tended to hold grudges with people he took a disliking to. "I would like to introduce you to my *friend*"—Stiger stressed the word—"King Therik."

"Your friend?" Ikely asked, dubious, as Dog continued to sniff at the lieutenant's hand. Ikely began absently patting Dog's head.

"My friend," Stiger affirmed. "I trust him with my life."

Ikely's eyes narrowed slightly but he gave the orc a respectful nod. "A friend of yours is a friend of mine, sir. Well met, King Therik."

"This is Ikely?" Therik gave an unimpressed grunt and turned his attention back to the lieutenant. "I thought you would be taller."

Ikely's gaze flicked to Stiger and then to Therik before returning to Stiger in question.

"Right, everyone is now acquainted," Stiger said, clapping both hands together. He was feeling stiff and cold from the ride. He stretched out his back and felt a sudden stitch of pain in his side. It caused him to wince. The old wound, inflicted upon him by the minion, occasionally troubled him, especially when it rained or snowed. It had never quite healed right.

"One day…" Therik, not one to let another have the last word, bared his tusks at the lieutenant in another amused grin. The orc pointed at Stiger with a thick finger. "I will kill him."

Ikely frowned.

"Same old game." Salt gave an amused chuckle. "It's good to see you, Therik."

"You too, old Salt," Therik said and stepped forward. The two shook hands warmly.

Salt glanced over at the waiting legionaries. They had been standing off to the side. "What are you waiting for? Get their horses."

The legionaries rushed forward. Eli and Taha'Leeth, having dismounted, handed over their reins. Therik readily gave up the reins to the dwarven mountain pony and then spat on the ground in front of the horse.

Stiger hesitated as one of the legionaries stepped up with the clear intention of taking Nomad. He preferred to see to the care of his own mount. Then, he reconsidered and gave the legionary the reins. There was work to be done.

"See that he's brushed down and fed," Stiger said.

"I will take good care of your horse, sir," the legionary assured him.

"Do you think you can find him an apple?" Stiger asked. "Maybe a carrot, if you don't have one."

"We don't have any fresh apples, sir," the legionary said, "but we do have some that are pickled."

"He's not fussy," Stiger said.

"I will see that he gets one and some carrots too, sir," the legionary said, patting Nomad's neck.

"Thank you," Stiger said.

Nomad was led away toward the stables.

Large puffy flakes began drifting downward into the courtyard. Stiger glanced up at the gray overcast sky. The clouds were almost close enough that they reached the tops of the castle walls. He could see a few of the sentries high above.

It had snowed the day before, coating the entire valley in a thick carpet of white. The base of the valley had seen four inches of snow. At higher elevations, like the castle, the snow had fallen heavier. Stiger glanced around the courtyard. The snow had been shoveled to the sides and piled high against the interior walls. Near the barred east gate, which led to the Vrell road and the other side of the pass, a detail was busy filling the bed of a wagon hitched to a team of draft horses. It was clear their intention was to haul the snow out of the castle.

Stiger took a deep breath through his nose. The air smelled strongly of another storm. The first flakes of snow were a sure sign one was on the way. Winter had finally come to the mountains and it was proving to be quite harsh. And yet, he knew that a few hundred miles to the east, at lower elevation, the weather would be much milder, drier. The rainy season would have ended and the ground become firm.

Stiger felt a sudden urgency for action. He was ignorant of what was happening outside the valley. That bothered him to no end. But one thing he did know was that the fighting season had begun.

He glanced around the courtyard once more. His eyes caught upon Taha'Leeth. She was speaking quietly with Eli off to the side. With a hand, she threw back her hood. Her fiery red hair was a shock of color set in contrast to the drabness of the day. She captured his gaze and held it for a long moment, then smirked slightly in a manner Stiger felt was almost seductive. His heartbeat quickened. She returned her attention to Eli and said something more. Eli replied with a nod. She stepped away, heading for the keep. A legionary was standing guard before the door. He opened it for her. She stepped through and was gone a heartbeat later as the legionary closed the door. With her departure, it seemed the day darkened just a tad.

Stiger blew out a breath, his gaze on the door to the keep. He wanted to warm up next to a good fire and have a hot meal before addressing the dispatches and reports that surely were waiting for him. They always were. But first, he had something to do.

"I want to see them," Stiger announced and began moving for the stone steps that led up to the battlements several hundred feet up. The wide stairs had been shoveled. Dirt had been thrown onto the steps for added traction, as there were the remnants of snow and ice on the steps. The others followed him up.

The climb was steep. Stiger made sure to use the iron handrail, for he did not want to slip and fall into the courtyard. With every step climbed, it became a more dangerous drop. At first, it felt good to exercise his legs, especially after such a long ride. But step after step steadily began to take its toll. Before long, his thighs burned, and despite the wickedly cold air, he began to perspire. Climbing the stairs in armor was not all it was cracked up to be.

Reaching the top was a relief. Stiger found his breathing coming hard and fast. Still, the exercise had felt good. He paused and glanced around. Out of the shelter of the courtyard walls, the mountain winds were intense, bitingly cold, and strong. They howled through the gaps in the battlements, sounding very much like a banshee screaming her rage at the world. Then, the wind would subside, and it would become nearly deathly quiet.

The sentries manning the walls, both legionaries and dwarven warriors, were wrapped tightly in their cloaks and furs. Their faces were completely covered over in scarves or blankets. Only their eyes were visible.

The gusts, when they came, whipped over and around the battlements. They were cold enough to burn exposed flesh. A few of the sentries glanced over in Stiger's direction and then, as was proper, shifted their gazes back outward or continued their rounds. Stiger understood it was miserable duty, but necessary.

He walked up to the east wall and found a free spot between the battlements. The vastness of the Sentinel Forest stretched outward, for as far as the eye could see. The trees were coated in white and Stiger thought it a spectacular view.

Therik chose a spot farther down the wall to look out, as did Eli. Stiger turned his gaze downward to the large encampment that had cut its way into the edge of the forest.

He felt his anger stir at the sight of his enemy, the Cyphan. He rested a hand upon his sword hilt. The enemy's camp looked like an ugly scar upon what was otherwise unspoiled land. One hundred yards from the wall, he could see where part of it had been abandoned and the bulk of the encampment moved back to the foot of the pass, the edge of which was more than a half mile distant. Smoke from uncounted campfires rose lazily up into the sky, until the mountain winds dispersed and carried it away. Below, thousands of the enemy moved about, looking for all the world like ants.

Closer to the walls of the castle, a series of defensive trenches designed to hem the castle in had been dug. Behind the trenches was a large earthen rampart, with artillery emplacements for bombardment.

The defenses appeared formidable. Their purpose was clearly to keep Stiger and the garrison from breaking out. He wondered why they had bothered. They had to know by now that he had an inferior force. Heck, they'd chased him all the way back to the castle. Unless they somehow knew the truth, that he had brought back the Thirteenth Legion and assembled an army of dwarves and gnomes.

He did not see how they could, though he did concede that they knew there were dwarves in league with him. The parley with Braddock and Lord General Kryven on the Vrell road had made that blatantly apparent to the enemy. That parley had not gone as expected. It had ended with Braddock killing the lord general and swearing to end the Cyphan.

Stiger's eyes moved away from the defenses sealing the valley in, to the main part of the enemy's camp. Though quite a ways off, he could see hundreds of tents, along with dozens of smaller buildings... likely cabins... most of which looked to have been built out of rough-cut logs, harvested from the nearby forest. More were in partial states of construction.

When the wind subsided between gusts, Stiger could hear distant hammering. The enemy was clearly hard at work constructing winter quarters for their men.

They were settling in. It was what Stiger wanted to see. For it likely meant that, with the snow, they had become complacent, thinking fighting was finished 'til spring. Stiger's gaze tracked to the enemy's siege line. He counted thirty stone throwers. Another five of the large artillery pieces were in various states of assembly. The presence of artillery told him the enemy had trained engineers.

He felt his anger go from a simmer to a slow boil. Despite the bitter cold and the brutal wind that howled and whistled through the battlements, it warmed him. He placed his hands upon the wall, feeling the cold touch of the stone through his leather gloves. They had no idea an army of humans, dwarves, and gnomes waited, hidden on the other side of the pass. Those people down there were his enemy and they had absolutely no concept of what he had planned for them. Stiger was going to bring his wrath down upon them and everyone else who stood in his way.

Ikely came up next to Stiger. "Once the weather improves, the gnomes intend on bringing up specialized machines, sir. They think they can hit the artillery along the siege line, but not much beyond that."

Stiger gave a nod, studying the distance from the siege line to the castle walls. It was a long way off. Gnomes were born engineers. If they thought they could do it, then they probably could. Still, if what Stiger and Braddock had planned worked, the gnomes would not have the chance to test their machines. They would have to settle for a little disappointment.

Eli stepped nearer and looked at Ikely. "What do you think?"

"I think it certainly doesn't hurt to try," Ikely said. "Before the weather soured, the enemy clearly planned on starting serious work at reducing the walls. They even took a few ranging shots when the first machines were completed. The walls are strong. Their shot simply bounced off or shattered upon impact." Ikely blew out a steaming breath.

"So, they turned their attention to constructing additional machines. Then the weather turned on them. We got our first real snow a week ago, and since then, they've stopped. Their focus has shifted almost exclusively over to building winter quarters. The gnomes seem to think the enemy artillery is susceptible to cold weather."

"They're right," Salt said. "In temperatures like this, there's a good chance a rope would snap or a support fail. Such a thing could see the machine destroyed, the crew killed or injured. They won't want to risk losing highly trained men and engineers, not when we're nicely bottled up and they have all the time in the world to get to us. No, the gnomes are right. The enemy will wait until the weather improves and the temperature climbs. Until then, they will sit tight and settle for keeping us from escaping."

Stiger agreed, then looked at Ikely. "How many men do you think they have?"

"I've done some counting and more than a little estimation, sir," Ikely said with a glance back down toward the enemy encampment. "I figure the enemy's strength is at least thirty thousand strong. It's possible that they have more, sir, concealed by the trees, but I doubt it."

Stiger gave a nod of agreement. That information matched the intelligence Braddock's pioneers had collected. Judging from the size of the enemy's encampment, he decided the estimate likely correct. Stiger continued to scan the enemy's camp, critically studying what he saw, analyzing it and doing his best to commit it to memory. He wondered if the defenses extended into the trees on the far side of their encampment. He could not quite tell.

If it had been a legionary camp, the planned defense not only would have hemmed in the castle, but would have extended walls and trenches completely around the legion's camp. However, he was wholly unfamiliar with the standards of the Cyphan.

Stiger felt himself frown, the scar on his cheek pulling the skin taut. He could not see any defenses facing or moving out into the forest. He realized any such defensive works could be hidden by the trees and snow. He glanced over at Eli and decided he would soon have a job for the elves, though only when the legion was ready and not before.

The wind gusted strongly again, the cold burning his cheeks and causing his eyes to water. Stiger turned his attention back to the enemy's camp. It seemed more of a jumbled mess, hastily thrown together, than an organized army encampment. The tents had been erected haphazardly instead of in orderly rows, as one would expect from a professional army. On the wind, he could smell the stench of poor sanitation too. He wondered on their discipline, suspecting it was not the best. How many of the enemy were Cyphan? How many were the rabble that were the Southern rebels? He just did not know.

"No matter how strong the walls," Ikely said, "once they get all of their artillery hammering away, I'd imagine they might do some damage."

"I don't intend to give them that much time," Stiger growled, stepping back from the wall and out of the wind. He had seen enough. "We're going to deal with them, sooner rather than later."

"You mean to attack?" Ikely asked, with not a little surprise. He waved toward the defenses below. "Is that why you and Braddock brought the army up and camped them on the road in such poor weather? Sir, I'm quite sure you know, but assaulting that defensive line will prove costly, sir, no matter our numbers."

Stiger turned and made for the stairs. It was time to find a warm fire, a jar of heated wine, and some food. He stopped on the first step and looked back at Ikely.

"Lieutenant, I have no intention of attacking that defensive line," Stiger said. "Braddock and I have something a little more elegant planned."

With that, Stiger started down the stairs.

Two

It had been four hours since he'd arrived at the castle. Leaning forward, Stiger placed both palms on the stout table. It was made of oak planking nailed together. The tabletop was scarred, pitted, and stained from heavy use. Stiger supposed it had been used for communal meals or perhaps even to prepare food.

Several wax tablets lay neatly stacked on the table. Upon his request, the legion's clerks had prepared these reports. An old oil lamp, hanging from the ceiling by an iron chain, lit the medium-sized room, as did a fat tallow candle that had been set on the table.

Severus had selected the space as a working office for him. Stiger was well pleased with the choice, for the room came with its own fireplace. After the long, cold ride up from the valley, the warmth was more than welcome. The fire crackled and popped loudly in the hearth. A clerk had recently fed it. Dog lay stretched out on his side, stomach toward the fire, sleeping.

Another smaller table that served as a desk faced the wall to the right. A half-eaten bowl of beef stew and an empty wine mug rested on the desk, along with a pile of maps that Braddock had provided and a stack of dispatches. Stiger had spent the last two hours reviewing and responding to them.

In the next room over, Stiger could hear his headquarters staff at work, the scuff of feet on stone as messengers came and went, the drone of many voices, an occasional cough or sneeze.

Salt, Severus, Ikely, Eli, and Taha'Leeth were standing around the table. At his request, they had joined him. Stiger and Salt had just reviewed and outlined the plans that they, along with Braddock, had developed for the coming campaign. They had fielded several questions before moving on to other business.

Stiger picked up one of the tablets, examining it. He handed it over to Ikely for his review. "They are seriously understrength."

"Are you certain you want to do this, sir?" Ikely asked, with a quick glance at the tablet. He tapped it with a finger. "There could be some resentment amongst the men."

"That might be," Stiger said. "However, disbanding the garrison companies makes good sense. Besides, they will be joining the Thirteenth, an elite formation. That should help mitigate any discord." Stiger picked up another tablet from the table and gestured at it. "Ninth Cohort has existed in name only for a very long time too."

"Since just before you joined the legion, sir," Salt said.

"That's right," Stiger said, suddenly reminded of the raid on the valley. The cohort had been ambushed and almost completely wiped out by orcs. He felt a stab of pain at the memory, for that had happened on the same day Sarai had been killed. Stiger set the tablet down and picked up another that showed the strength totals for the garrison companies. Ikely peered at it.

"As it now stands," Stiger said, "after the fighting retreat on Castle Vrell and the battle with the orcs before Old City, the garrison companies are badly understrength. For all intents and purposes, they are now little better than light companies. First their senior officers were killed by Captain Aveeno and then most of their sergeants and corporals were lost in the fighting that followed, which makes their condition even worse."

Stiger set the tablet back down on the table, looking over at Ikely. "I don't want to have to rebuild the command structure of each individual company. We don't have the time for that. Consolidating them into the Ninth makes it easier on us. By doing it this way, I have to only appoint one senior centurion to command the Ninth, along with three junior centurions...instead of several commanding officers, not to mention finding them executive officers. Hard feelings aside, I don't see that we have a choice but to consolidate them. We're cut off from the empire, which means we're not getting reinforcement." Stiger paused for a long moment. "We are on our own and my mind is made up. We will roll them together and reform the Ninth."

"If I recall my history correctly, cohorts generally number about four hundred and eighty men, sir." Ikely leaned forward and picked up the tablet detailing the strength of Ninth Cohort from the neatly stacked pile. "The current strength totals for the legion show the Ninth with slightly under one hundred men. There are nearly five hundred between the garrison companies. Is the Ninth to be an over-strength cohort?"

"Might I suggest," Salt said, speaking up, "that we instead fill out First Cohort's numbers, bringing them back up to near full strength, and use the remainder to reform the Ninth?"

Stiger gave that some thought. He had been thinking the overflow would be spread about the legion. He picked up another tablet, showing First Cohort's strength totals. Sabinus's boys had been heavily involved in the recent fighting. They had taken over three hundred casualties. One hundred ninety-two had been terminal. The loss of so many good men, especially from First Cohort, the legion's best, was distressing. What Salt was suggesting made sense and would bring the First back up to not quite full strength as the legion's only double strength cohort, but close.

"We will bring the Ninth up to four hundred men," Stiger said, looking over at Salt. "The rest can go to the First."

"Sir," Salt said, "I am sure you know, customarily, the First gets the pick of veterans from the legion. This move will be unorthodox."

"Now," Stiger said, "I am thinking, is not the time to shake up the rest of the cohorts by pulling their best men and assigning them to the First."

"My thoughts exactly, sir," Salt said. "I believe Sabinus will understand too. Now, the big question…who shall command the Ninth? Who do you want as senior centurion, sir?"

"Since we're folding up the garrison companies, Lieutenant Brent will have that honor," Stiger said. "Salt, you don't know the lieutenant, do you?"

"I've not yet had the pleasure, sir," Salt said.

"He showed his mettle in fighting the Cyphan and then against the orcs," Stiger said. "He's a good man and solid under pressure."

"Yes, sir," Salt said. "Do you intend to give him the rank of captain or senior centurion?"

"For consistency with the legion's current rank structure, and to avoid confusion, he will be promoted to senior centurion," Stiger said. "Now, we'll need someone seasoned for his second. I'd prefer a candidate from the Thirteenth. Have anyone in mind that might be a good fit?"

"Trentonius," Salt said without hesitation. "He's an eighteen-year veteran, sir, knows his numbers, letters, and is as steady as they come."

"Trent?" Stiger said, thinking on what he knew of the man. Trentonius was a tall, burly man. Stiger remembered a rugged, weathered face, with a jagged scar on his chin. Beyond that, Stiger could not recall much more. "He's in Third Cohort, right?"

"Yes, sir," Salt said. "Fourth Century. A few years back, before I was appointed camp prefect, he served as my optio. He's hard as a nail and unflappable as they come. It will be a good opportunity for him to move up the ladder and prepare, ultimately, for a cohort of his own."

Stiger understood Salt's meaning. The centurionate were known for taking heavy casualties. It was a fact of life in the legions. Centurions and officers were expected to set the example, especially when it came to a fight. They led from the front. They were the toughest of the tough and promoted not only for their intelligence but also their aggressiveness. As such, they were feared by their own men, but also respected. The centurions were the glue that held the legion together, no matter how difficult things got. As long as they stood firm, the legion stood firm.

He eyed his camp prefect a moment more. Salt was an old veteran. Having risen from the ranks, he was a soldier's soldier, and yet he was also politically adept.

He'd led a distinguished career and achieved the coveted position of camp prefect, making him the third highest-ranking officer in the legion. That was, if the legion still had a senior tribune. Stiger realized Salt was gently reminding Stiger of the need to prepare for the loss of senior officers. The coming campaign might see multiple vacancies in short order.

"You are right," Stiger said, blowing out a breath. "Put together a list of men you think would make good cohort commanders. Start giving them extra jobs and responsibilities. Let's see how they do. If we need one in a pinch, I want to be ready."

"Yes, sir," Salt said. "Concerning the Ninth, what of the junior centurions? Do you want me to forward a list of men I deem fit? Or should I save you some time, sir? I can make the appointments and promote deserving optios up the ladder to centurion, if you wish."

"Promote men you feel as needed," Stiger said, for he trusted Salt's instincts implicitly. Besides, his camp prefect knew the men better than he did. "Run the list by me after you've done it, so I know who's been given the nod."

"I will have that for you in the morning, sir," Salt said.

Eli gave a shift of his feet and glanced over briefly to Taha'Leeth. Some unspoken communication passed between the two of them. Stiger supposed both elves had become bored with the proceedings.

"What of the garrison's cavalry company?" Ikely asked.

"I've already spoken with Lieutenant Cannol," Stiger said. "He will organize his cavalry under the legion's mounted wing, along with Lan's troop. Prefect Hux will command all of our mounted soldiers."

"Prefect Hux?" Ikely said. "I don't know him, sir."

"He came back with me. He's experienced and knows his business," Stiger said. "You won't find a man more suited to commanding horse soldiers than Hux."

"As an infantryman," Salt said to Ikely, "I have a ready disdain for the cavalry. Hux and his boys are the rare exception. At times, he can even be a little too aggressive, if that's possible."

Ikely gave a nod, then hesitated a moment, before asking, "What of Stiger's Tigers, sir?"

Stiger read the hope within his former executive officer's eyes. It was clear the lieutenant wanted a command of his own. He could not fault him for that. He regarded Ikely for a long moment, considering him. Stiger had different plans for him, something that was more important, demanding, and, he suspected, would prove incredibly challenging. The job he wanted Ikely to do would be vital to the coming campaign, and Stiger was unwilling to trust anyone else with it.

Stiger's thoughts shifted back to his old company. Though they were understrength, the Eighty-Fifth was seasoned and experienced. He'd personally trained and then led them through the fighting retreat to Castle Vrell. They had fought with distinction and honor. They were exceptional killers and he was proud of having had a hand in that.

"For the moment, I want to keep them together," Stiger said. "Should we have a need for special tasks, they will be it."

"And the commander?" Ikely pressed.

"Centurion Blake shall retain command," Stiger said, "with Ranl as his second."

Ikely gave an unhappy nod that was filled with clear disappointment. But he did not argue. The lieutenant knew his commander. The decision had been made.

"I have other plans for you, Ikely," Stiger said, struggling to suppress a grin of pleasure at what he was about to do.

"You do, sir?"

"I do," Stiger said and hesitated another long moment, intentionally dragging it out. Ikely shifted his stance from one foot to another as he waited. "I am promoting you to senior tribune of the legion."

"Tribune?" Ikely asked, blinking several times. "Senior tribune? That is the equivalent to a colonel. That's quite a jump. Can you do that, sir?"

"Yes," Stiger said. "Well, as a brevet promotion. It would need to be confirmed by the emperor or senate. The fact is, the legion's short on tribunes. I've only had Severus here to act as my aide. I am also missing a second in command. Tribune Arvus was killed before I took command of the legion, so you get the job."

"Tribune Arvus was a good man," Salt said to Ikely. "You have big sandals to fill, son."

Ikely gave a solemn nod.

"You've proved yourself in battle," Stiger said, "and as a leader of men. More important, like Salt, I value your judgment. You are now my second in command. End of the discussion."

"Yes, sir," Ikely said. The disappointment had vanished. In its place was barely contained excitement. "Thank you, sir."

"Congratulations, sir," Severus said and offered his hand. Ikely took it. Looking a little dazed, he shook.

"Moving up in this world, old boy," Eli said and clapped Ikely on the shoulder. "I am certain your new rank will come with all kinds of responsibilities and headaches."

"There is no doubt about that," Ikely said, "and knowing the captain, er…the legate, he will expect miracles out of me."

"I will," Stiger confirmed as he glanced over at Salt, whose face expressed no emotion whatsoever. An argument could have been made for the position of senior tribune going to Salt. The camp prefect had a lot of experience behind him. That was exactly why Stiger wanted Salt in a combat role, not a staff position.

Stiger had informed Salt of his decision to promote Ikely a short while earlier. To his credit, Salt had not objected in the slightest. He suspected the old veteran preferred to remain where he was, as a fighting soldier. Salt knew where he stood with Stiger, and it was time Ikely understood the camp prefect's importance as well.

"Thank you, sir," Ikely breathed.

"You're welcome." Stiger gestured toward Salt. "The camp prefect here has a great deal more experience in the field than you do. He has put in a lifetime of service. Should he deem, at any point, to offer you advice, I expect you to listen. Then make certain you heed what he has to say, particularly when it comes to fighting. He has my trust and he should have yours as well. Do we understand each other, Tribune?"

Ikely glanced over at Salt, who stood stone-faced. "I do, sir."

"Good." Stiger began gathering up the wax tablets. He handed one to Ikely. "When we are done here, see that the clerks issue the appropriate orders for the garrison companies and Ninth Cohort. I want their camps consolidated as soon as possible. Salt will handle the appointment of the junior centurions and I will personally speak with Brent prior to his assumption of command."

"Yes, sir," Ikely said. "Consider it done."

Stiger paused as he gathered his thoughts. "I will hold a meeting of the senior officers in the coming days to outline the initial steps of the campaign and how we will deal with the enemy on our doorstep."

Ikely rubbed the side of his jaw. "Can we handle the enemy by ourselves and without the dwarves? We will be heavily outnumbered, sir."

"Surprise will largely counter the enemy's numerical advantage," Stiger said. "Our move should catch them with their togas down around their ankles."

"Do you know how long it's been since I've seen a toga?" Salt said, a grin spreading across his craggy face. "Over three hundred years, sir."

Ikely's eyes snapped to Salt, as the realization once again seemed to smack home about the Thirteenth Legion and just where it had come from.

"I think that joke is beginning to age," Stiger said, "just like you, old boy."

"Very good, sir." Salt's grin became wider. "Now you're getting into the spirit of things."

"Sir," Ikely said, "you and I both know things never go to plan. Something always cocks them up."

"True," Stiger said. "Still, I feel good about our chances. We have the advantage of surprise, ground of our choosing, and quality of men. I received word just before this meeting that the thane's pioneers ambushed and overwhelmed a supply train along the Vrell road. They took two hundred wagons loaded with supply. The pioneers also captured prisoners and questioned them. It seems the bulk of the enemy's army is comprised of rebels."

"They should still have a core of Cyphan regulars," Taha'Leeth cautioned, "to give them backbone. But it is likely as you say. Most will be rebels. They are terrible soldiers, with little training and even less discipline. They were difficult to work with, prideful and overconfident. That overconfidence allowed you to slaughter them during your fighting retreat and likely will allow you to do it again."

Eli spoke up. "It is a bold plan. It has merit, and there is always the possibility with you that something will go wrong. Then we might get a little excitement."

"I could do without that, Eli," Stiger said.

Eli gave a half shrug of his shoulders.

"I am thinking it is the Cyphan that will pose the real threat." Eli looked over at Taha'Leeth. "Do you know how many are likely to be with the army?"

"Before I came over to your side," Taha'Leeth said, turning to face Stiger as she spoke, "there were more than six thousand Cyhpan slave soldiers with the army marching on Vrell. It is possible, once they reached the castle and it became clear a siege would be required, a goodly number marched away, leaving it to the rebels to keep us boxed in 'til spring. As I understood it, the focus of the campaign was to be against the empire, crushing the legions and striking out toward Mal'Zeel. Vrell was a side show, but they ultimately wanted the castle and the garrison removed."

Stiger sucked in a breath at that. Mal'Zeel was a long way off, even for the Cyphan. Still, he knew why the enemy wanted Mal'Zeel. The emperor had what they needed to fulfill the prophesy, and they would not rest until they had it.

"I had heard," Taha'Leeth said, "the marshal was able to put together a grand army, over four hundred thousand strong, for dealing with your empire."

"Four hundred thousand?" Ikely asked, in a near gasp of surprise. "Not counting our present army, I don't think the empire fields that many legionaries. Maybe, if you add all the auxiliary cohorts up together, we might come close. That is a very large number to put into the field, let alone support it. Are you certain?"

Stiger thought Ikely was on to something. Supply would be a real problem for a force that large.

"We were slaves," Taha'Leeth said. "The Cyphan did not confide in us. We went where we were told and did what we were told. You know what rumors are like in an army, yes?"

Stiger gave a nod.

"It could be an inflated number or not," Taha'Leeth continued. "Still, the need for trained soldiers was great, and the generals, when the time came, apparently argued as to how many to send to Vrell. I, myself, heard Lord General Kryven complain about the lack of regulars available. What you consider regulars, the slave soldiers, are the heart of the Cyphan military. I cannot be sure how many remain on Vrell's doorstep and how many are ill-trained rebels. Perhaps you will allow us to scout them and learn more?"

"It is something I had planned on asking of you," Stiger said to Taha'Leeth and Eli. "I need to know more of this army and their defenses."

Taha'Leeth gave a nod, as did Eli. "We are pleased to help in any way we can," she said.

Stiger shared a concerned glance with Salt. He certainly hoped the enemy's invasion force was not as large as Taha'Leeth suggested. If it was even half that size, the empire was in serious trouble. One problem at a time, he reminded himself. Just focus on one bloody problem at a time.

"Before I continue, are there any more questions on the plan so far?" Stiger asked.

There were none.

"Good." Stiger turned his gaze squarely to Ikely and then to Severus. He rubbed his hands together. Despite the fire that crackled in the hearth a few feet away, with Taha'Leeth's news, the room had lost much of its warm glow. Dog was still asleep and snoring softly by the fire, oblivious. Occasionally one of his legs would twitch as he dreamed of chasing something.

"We need to organize our supply," Stiger said, "build a train, and prepare for an extended movement. By extended, I mean all the way back to the empire." He gestured with a hand at his two tribunes. "You both will be working exclusively toward that effort. The army cannot march and fight on an empty belly. Braddock has brought up additional food stores from Old City, with more on the way. Those supplies are going to be moved to the new depot that is being built in the valley, at Bridgetown."

Stiger paused again and sucked in another breath.

"Bridgetown will become the main collection point for all supplies. I want our own supplies moved and added to that depot. We'll need to scrounge up any transport, mules, wagons, and carts you can lay your hands on. Supply will have to travel with us and after us as we march east along the Vrell road. Depots outside the valley will need to be established, with regular shipments following. As I see it, we must develop a supply system that will be able to continually replenish what we consume as we advance. That includes absorbing any supplies we capture or can manage to forage."

"That's a big job, sir," Ikely said.

"It is," Stiger said, "and why I want you both on it."

"Yes, sir," Ikely said. Severus shifted uncomfortably.

"Braddock," Stiger continued, "has assigned a dwarf by the name of Tegoth. I understand he is as old as the rocks and nearly an invalid, but he understands supply. He should be arriving at the valley depot with a staff in the morning. Go meet and coordinate with him." Stiger paused, looking between Ikely and Severus. "I want you both to keep me apprised of not only your thinking but your progress and… any problems that develop. As senior tribune, Ikely, you will lead this effort. Severus, you will assist."

"You can count on me, sir," Ikely said, after a very slight hesitation.

"Me too, sir," Severus said.

"I know I can," Stiger said. "Ikely, you are now in charge of all transport, wagons, carts, mules…whatever moves, it's yours. That does not include Hux's horses. Hux would likely skin you alive if you tried to take any of his beloved mounts."

"Yes, sir," Ikely said. "I won't touch his horses, unless I absolutely need to."

"Good," Stiger said. "Braddock and I decided you will spearhead this effort. Tegoth will assist you. He will remain behind in the valley, as he is too crippled by age to travel much."

"Yes, sir," Ikely said.

"Do either of you have any questions?"

"No, sir," Severus said.

"And you?" Stiger asked, when Ikely did not immediately answer. The newly promoted senior tribune had shifted his gaze down to the map and was rubbing his jaw thoughtfully.

Stiger had given Ikely a big job, and by his expression, he was fully coming to that realization. "Do you have any questions?"

"Plenty, sir," Ikely said, looking up. "Feeding an army of over eighty thousand is likely going to keep me a little busy. I will need a staff to help make it properly work and a good number of men and dwarves assigned to supply. Let me meet with Tegoth, see what he has to say, learn what resources the dwarves have available, and then get my thoughts in order before I begin throwing at you what I will need to make this work."

"That's agreeable." Stiger was pleased. It was the right answer and reinforced his decision to put Ikely in charge. "You both have a lot to do and time is short, as I intend to move just as soon as the road is ready."

"I understand, sir," Ikely said.

"Good," Stiger said. "I will not keep you any longer. Dismissed."

Ikely and Severus both snapped to attention, saluted, and stepped out of Stiger's office. He watched them go, then looked over at Salt, who appeared somewhat amused.

"I trust you will check in on them?" Stiger asked. "Get nosy and provide a little guidance now and again?"

"You know me better than that, sir," Salt said, with a wry smile. "I will hold their hands like they were my own children...well, at least until I'm confident they know what they're doing. I learned a long time back, over three hundred years ago to be precise, a full belly on campaign is preferable to an empty one, sir."

In many ways, Salt reminded Stiger of his old sergeant, Tiro. They were both cut from the same cloth, intelligent, practical, experienced, and unflappable. Salt was worth his weight in gold. He had also become a friend.

"That three hundred years joke is beginning to really wear thin," Stiger said. "So much so, it is almost threadbare."

"Is it, sir?" Salt asked. "I had not noticed."

Stiger gave an amused grunt.

"I do believe Salt and I will get along just fine," Eli said. "I approve of his humor."

"Great," Stiger said, looking between the two of them and rolling his eyes. "Just bloody great."

"If you will excuse me, sir," Salt said, "I have a lot to do, especially if the legion is to move within two weeks. I need to speak with each senior centurion, make sure the cohorts have what they need, gear- and equipment-wise. I will also let Ikely in on the little supply stash that Thoggle put into stasis with us. I just know he will be so thrilled to learn just how much needs to be moved out of the vault. The sooner I get started on all that, the better."

"I will catch up with you later," Stiger said. "There are some things we need to discuss in relation to the legion's auxiliary cohorts."

"Yes, sir." With that, Salt left the office, leaving Stiger alone with the elves.

Stiger looked over at the two of them. One was his closest friend in this world. The other was still a mystery to him. Whenever Stiger gazed upon Taha'Leeth, his pulse quickened, and he felt drawn to her. Elven females had that effect upon men. When it came to beauty, they were goddesses come to life.

But there was something more about Taha'Leeth that put her above the rest and called to him, almost primally. Stiger could not put his finger on what exactly that was. She was beautiful, for sure. There was no doubt about that. Taha'Leeth made other elven females he'd known look poor by comparison. But that wasn't quite it. He considered it might be how she carried herself. Like a light in the darkness, there was something about her bearing, a dignity despite her suffering that shone through. And Stiger understood suffering. Perhaps that was it?

"I like him," Eli said, drawing Stiger's attention back to the present. "He reminds me of Tiro."

"I've had similar thoughts," Stiger agreed. "I miss that old veteran."

"Me too," Eli said quietly.

There was a cough by the doorway. Venthus entered, with a jar that steamed and three mugs.

"I thought I left you down in the valley," Stiger said. "I expected you tomorrow at the earliest."

"And I thought"—Venthus set the jar and mugs down upon the table—"you might care for some refreshment, master. I have some heated wine."

Stiger shook his head. Venthus must have followed almost immediately after he'd left Old City. "Well, as usual, you thought right. I could use a drink."

Venthus gave a slight knowing smile and poured heated wine into the three mugs. He straightened, moved over to the desk. He gathered up Stiger's cold and half-eaten bowl of stew, along with the empty mug. "Do you need anything else, master?"

"No, not at the moment. That will be all. Thank you, Venthus."

"Very good, master," Venthus said. "Should you require anything further, your clerks will know where to find me."

Venthus bowed respectfully and left. Stiger considered his body slave for a moment. Calling the man a slave was misleading. Stiger had offered Venthus his freedom. Venthus had flatly refused his manumission, and yet Stiger knew, without a doubt, Venthus was no slave. He was more than that. Stiger wasn't quite sure what motivated Venthus to stay and play the part of a slave, but he had come to rely upon the man. Venthus made his life more bearable, and at times comfortable. They weren't friends, but each respected the other.

Taha'Leeth had followed Venthus out of the room with her eyes. Her face betrayed no emotion, but Stiger thought he read concern. Or was it wariness about his manservant? Stiger was not quite sure.

"I let you out of my sight for less than an hour," Eli said, "you manage to get yourself transported to the past and come back with not just a legion, but a slave to boot." The elf's gaze traveled over to the fire, where Dog slept. The big shaggy animal snored softly, his chest rising and falling contentedly. "And a mangy dog."

Stiger gave a chuckle then looked down at the wine.

"Since we have wine, shall we make a toast?" Stiger picked up a mug and handed it to Taha'Leeth. He gave one to Eli too.

"To friendships and new beginnings," Taha'Leeth said, before Stiger could propose a toast of his own.

"I will drink to that." Stiger held his own mug up and took a sip. He savored the taste of the valley-made wine. It was quite good, smooth even, and he'd grown fond of it. The warmth filled him.

"Now," Stiger said, setting the mug back down on the table, "let's talk about scouting the enemy's encampment when the time is right and what I want you to find out."

"Yes, let's." Eli looked briefly about the room. "I can't wait to get out of these stone walls and back into the action."

THREE

Stiger groaned as he lowered himself into the wooden chair. It had been a long and busy day, the second since arriving at the castle. Hooking a stool with his foot, he slid it over, then rested his feet upon it. The fire before him crackled pleasantly. He had just thrown on two fresh logs and the blaze was growing, crackling, and spitting sparks upward. The fire provided the only light in the darkened room, for he had not lit the lamp. Dog was curled up by the fire, sleeping. He had not even moved when Stiger had entered, other than wag his tail, before closing his eyes again.

"This feels good." Stiger leaned back, letting out a relieved sigh. "The only thing that could make this better is a warm bath. Gods, it has been years since I visited a proper bathhouse."

Dog opened an eye to look at him in a disinterested sort of way. When he saw that nothing of importance was going on, he closed it and promptly went back to sleep.

"You need a bath too," Stiger said to the animal.

Dog opened an eye again and gave a soft whine of protest.

"No complaining, you're overdue for a good bath." Stiger reflected longingly on taking a warm bath himself. Only there had not been one to be had. Castle Vrell was lacking when it came to bathing facilities. It was a fortress, with a single-minded purpose, not an imperial bathhouse. There were few creature comforts to be had, for the dwarves who had constructed the castle intended it that way.

This evening, Stiger had been forced to bathe out of a bucket. The water had been heated in the kitchen, but by the time it made its way up to him, it was lukewarm at best. Still, it was better than using cold water, and over the years he had bathed with frigid water more than he cared to admit.

He shifted slightly to get more comfortable in the chair. His body ached something fierce. He felt bruised and more than a little battered. He had sparred with Therik earlier, something that had become a regular occurrence.

They had both come to enjoy their matches. The orc was strong, fast, and very skilled. Therik held nothing back, whether it be with training weapons or just hands. The orc had seen Stiger bring down not only a dragon, but a mountain troll, the latter with nothing but a dagger.

Killing the troll seemed to have impressed Therik far more than the dragon. Why, Stiger was not quite sure. Perhaps it was because he'd used his sword on the dragon, which the king had seen suffused with magic, and only a plain dagger on the hulking troll.

Their sparring matches kept Stiger in shape and on his toes. Truth be told, he normally gave as good as he got. However, this time he had been somewhat distracted by the concerns of the coming campaign. Therik had come close to thrashing him, and badly. It was a blunt reminder that when one went into battle, one could not afford to become distracted by anything. Winning required a single-minded approach and focus.

He let out a breath and then touched his jaw lightly, which still throbbed painfully. He probed his lip with a hand and looked at his fingers. No blood. The cut had already stopped bleeding. Stiger was not surprised.

He ran his index finger along his lip, feeling for damaged skin. It was nearly mended. Ever since Father Thomas had given up his life to heal him, Stiger had found he mended more rapidly from minor wounds. He'd first discovered this a few months afterwards, when he'd been thrown from a horse and had skinned his forearm against a rock, amongst other minor injuries. The injury had bled a little, but within hours had healed completely, leaving no trace of a scar. Stiger figured it was one last parting gift from the paladin, or perhaps even his god. At least, he liked to think so.

Within the next hour, the swollen lip would look almost normal and the pain would be gone. He massaged at the soreness along his jawbone a moment, then turned his gaze to the fire. He stared at the flames for a time, thinking on the past and Father Thomas's sacrifice. Then his thoughts shifted to the future and what was to come, what might be required of him, perhaps even a sacrifice of his own.

He blew out a long breath and thought of taking a pipe. Stiger had always found something relaxing in the habit. The pipe and tobacco were across the room, in his travel chest. He did not feel the energy to pull himself to his feet and retrieve it. So, he did without and remained in his chair, enjoying the warmth from the blaze.

Stiger had taken a room in the keep that was a few doors down, a short walk from his headquarters. He had turned down Severus's selection for a larger room in favor of this one. Should he be needed, his clerks would not have far to go to fetch him.

His room was small and far from ostentatious. Besides a rope bed, there was an old, battered desk, a pair of wooden chairs, a small table, his travel trunk, and the stool he was resting his feet upon. It was one of the smaller rooms in the castle, but it had its own fireplace, which was another reason why he had chosen it. Due to its small size, the fire heated the room comfortably. It was almost to the point of it being too hot, for he felt beads of sweat begin to form on his forehead.

The shutters rattled as a strong gust of wind first pushed and then seemed to suck at them. The wind whistled, as if a ghost were crying out from the great beyond. Stiger glanced over at the thick shutters, then returned his gaze back to the fire, which guttered briefly and hissed.

Another winter storm had arrived. At ground level, the storm wasn't all that bad. It was simply delivering heavy amounts of snow, but the castle, high up in the pass, was continually buffeted by the mountain winds. When the wind gusted strongly, it sounded very much like a tempest raging at the world.

Despite his men camping in the open, Stiger wasn't concerned about them. They were well-equipped to withstand the storm. He himself had been through much worse in the north, with Third Legion. He was sure they would spend an uncomfortable night, but that would be all. Come morning, they would begin the laborious process of digging out.

The legions were accustomed to discomfort and would manage. He had no doubt about that. However, Stiger did feel a little guilty at being indoors, with a warm fire to keep him comfortable. He did not let that bother him much, for over the years, he had more than paid his dues.

Stiger's eyes tracked to the corner, where his sword in its ornate scabbard leaned against the wall. Where before he could sense the presence and mind of the crazed wizard within the sword, he now felt nothing, just emptiness. Rarokan had not spoken to him in years.

It had been that way ever since he'd almost died at the hands of Castor's minion. The sword had not come back to life when he had, nor even given him any hint the being within was still there. Rarokan remained just a simple sword, a piece of beautifully crafted steel. Stiger did not know whether to rejoice or be concerned.

When he touched the hilt, he no longer felt the comforting tingle, a sign of the bond forged between the two of them had broken. He'd reluctantly come to the conclusion that the life force that had once been Rarokan, High Master of the Blue, had died in that fateful battle with the minion. The wizard had given his all in a bid to keep Stiger alive. And so, the wizard's soul had finally passed from this world. All his plans and machinations had been for naught.

Stiger turned his gaze back to the growing blaze in the hearth. Had it not been for Father Thomas interceding, pulling him back from the abyss, Stiger would have died too. He had stood on the bank of the great river. He'd seen the ferryman and been more than prepared to cross over. Only, he had not had any coin to pay for the crossing. Father Thomas had seen to that.

Stiger blew out an unhappy breath, his eyes returning to the sword. He did not feel saddened by the wizard's passing. There was no true regret or sense of loss. Rarokan had planned on stealing his soul, taking over his body to escape his punishment and imprisonment. The wizard had nearly succeeded, too... Stiger's only real concern was the loss of the sword's power. The magic was gone. He would have to somehow manage without it, which, in a way, was both a blessing and a curse.

"Excuse me, master."

Stiger looked up. Venthus had entered with a jar and two mugs. The man wore a thick gray cloak over his tunic against the chill. He had pinned the front closed. The bottom of the cloak whispered across the stone as he moved into the room. Venthus placed both mugs down on the small table.

"I thought you might care for some refreshment, master." Venthus held up the wine jar.

"I would," Stiger said, with open weariness. Wine before turning in for the night sounded like a grand suggestion.

Venthus poured the steaming liquid into one of the two mugs and handed it to Stiger. His slave then returned to the table and poured a second mug.

Stiger's eyes narrowed.

"Who is the other mug for?" Stiger asked. He had spent most of the day with his headquarters staff or in meetings. Then had come the sparring session with Therik. All he desired was to enjoy his fire in peace and turn in for the night. It seemed Venthus had other ideas for him.

"Me," came a female voice through the door.

Stiger's gaze shifted to the open door and he scowled slightly.

"I hope you don't mind," Taha'Leeth said as she stepped into the room. She wore only a brown tunic that reached down to just above her knees, exposing her shapely legs. "We have unfinished business between us."

Dog opened his eyes and shifted his head to watch her.

"Unfinished?" Stiger wondered what she meant by that. Elves always seemed to go out of their way to make things complicated when they need not be. Why could they never get right to the point? It was almost maddening.

Venthus looked between them briefly before handing the mug to the elf. He turned to Stiger, clasping his hands before him. "If you don't require anything further, I will withdraw, master."

"No," Stiger said. "Thank you, Venthus. See that I am woken an hour before dawn, will you?"

"Very well, master." Venthus retreated, closing the door behind him.

"You will excuse me if I do not stand," Stiger said. "My sparring match with Therik became a little spirited." He gestured at the other chair by the desk. "Would you care to sit and join me by the fire?"

She appeared amused, her gaze flicking to his bruised jaw. Taha'Leeth slid the other chair across the stone floor to the fire. She angled it so that the chair faced the fire but also slightly toward Stiger. She sat down and pulled her legs up to sit cross-legged.

Dog turned his head away and closed his eyes, going back to sleep.

"It is warm in here," Taha'Leeth said, holding her hands out before her. "Unlike much of the keep."

"Rank has its privileges," Stiger said. "It's why I took this room over the larger ones, even though they, too, had fireplaces. A smaller room gets warmer quicker and tends to stay that way longer. The ceiling is also low, which helps too." He pointed toward a hole in the wall. "It would not have been an issue if the dwarven heating system was working. None of my boys can figure it out."

She looked over at him and raised a delicate eyebrow. "Have you asked Braddock to help?"

"There has been no time to ask the thane, as he's not in the castle, but directly overseeing the work on the roads. I did speak with Tyga. He sent over a team to look at it. They say a repair would take months. We won't be here that long, so I told them not to bother."

"I had heard you got him angry," Taha'Leeth said.

For a moment, Stiger was confused. He had not angered Tyga. Then he realized she was changing the subject.

"You mean Therik?"

She nodded. "I never thought to see an orc as an ally."

"Me neither," Stiger said, "let alone call one a friend."

"Wars occasionally make for strange bedfellows," Taha'Leeth said. "Like the dwarves and gnomes. Until I saw them working alongside one another here in Vrell, I never thought such a thing possible."

Stiger gave an absent nod.

"So, you made Therik angry?" Taha'Leeth said.

He looked back over at her and gave another nod. His sparring with the orc always seemed to attract a crowd. He was sure the men even wagered on the outcomes. They made bets on everything and anything. Such things were commonplace in the military. Therefore, it was no surprise to him she had heard about his latest match.

"We both gave as good as we got," Stiger said. He had gotten in a lucky blow to the stomach that had enraged the orc. In truth, Therik had more than made up for it, punishing Stiger with a shot to the jaw. It had been so powerfully delivered that the blow had laid him on his backside. Stiger had seen stars and been dazed for a few moments.

"It appears as if you got a little more than he did." Taha'Leeth reached over and ran a finger along his bruised jaw. Stiger winced at the touch, for it was still very sore. Her eyes sparkled with barely contained amusement.

Stiger gave a shrug of his shoulders and took a small sip of his heated wine. He could feel the warmth go right down to his belly. Feeling more than a little sleepy, he stifled a yawn.

Why was she here?

He glanced over at Taha'Leeth as the wind rattled the shutters again. Stiger was tired and weary. He had been looking forward to relaxing before turning in for the night. Now it did not seem like that would happen, at least until she got around to whatever she wished to discuss. What business was it that was unfinished between them? For the life of him, he could not think what it was.

She took a sip of her own wine and pulled her gaze away from his to the fire. Stiger continued to eye her for a long moment. Taha'Leeth appeared no older than her mid-twenties. She was truly a beautiful woman, made more so by her fiery red hair, which she had tied into a single braid down her back. A few strands had escaped and fallen around her face. He'd never known an elf who had red hair.

Taha'Leeth pulled the braid over her right shoulder and across her chest. Holding it with one hand, she slowly stroked the braid with the other as she gazed into the fire's depths. It seemed like an absent habit, something she'd long done. After a few moments, she glanced over at him, their eyes met briefly, and he realized he'd been staring.

A log in the fire popped loudly. Stiger gave a mental shrug and turned his own gaze back to the fire. He allowed the silence in the room to grow. It was broken only by the crackle of flames and the occasional rattling of the shutters as the wind gusted. He knew she would speak when she was ready, and Stiger was in no hurry.

On such a night, he could have had worse company or none at all to share the fire with, other than Dog. That was usually the worst part, because he was left to his memories and regrets. His annoyance at the interruption slipped away. He took another sip of his wine and settled in to wait. It did not take too long.

"My people are coming."

"I know," Stiger said, without looking over at her. "How long will it take them to get here?"

"Several months, at least, for most," Taha'Leeth said. "However, we should start seeing some of them sooner, perhaps within a few weeks."

"A few weeks?" Stiger was surprised to hear that. "How's that possible?"

"They were brought across the Narrow Sea, just like I was, when the Cyphan decided to challenge the empire. I sent word not only to my people back home but to those serving throughout the confederacy's armies. Word will spread. They will come."

"I see."

"They should bring with them intelligence as to what is going on outside Vrell. I know you seek to gain such information."

Stiger brightened at that prospect.

"How many of your people do you think we will see sooner rather than later?"

She was silent for several heartbeats. "Maybe two, possibly three hundred. It all depends on who feels the need to return home to help their families flee and who believes they can come without worry. I left it up to the individual."

"Three hundred?" Stiger exclaimed, sitting up, weariness gone. "All rangers?"

"Most." Taha'Leeth gave a nod. "Some are not rangers. They have other skills the confederacy deemed valuable."

Stiger had never seen that many elves together in one place, even when he'd lived in Eli's homeland. In the end, how many of her people would come? Thousands? Tens of thousands?

"I shall welcome your people," Stiger said and meant it.

"I thank you for that," Taha'Leeth said. "This is important for us, for me."

They fell into a silence. Stiger once again leaned back in the chair, which creaked, and returned his feet to the stool. He took another sip of his wine and considered that, between the dwarves, the legion, and now the elves, he was amassing a truly fearsome army.

Scratching at an itch on his arm, he shifted his feet slightly. The bottom of the stool scraped against the stone floor. Stiger knew he was moving toward his destiny, his fate. Where that was leading, he did not know. It could easily mean his death, for nothing in this world was certain. There was a time when such thoughts would have made him deeply uncomfortable. Now...he had come to accept who and what he was, the High Father's Champion, an instrument of a god.

"Tell me about the Cyphan," Stiger asked, breaking the silence.

"What would you like to know?"

"I've read about the confederacy," Stiger said, "but I've never traveled there. What I know is limited."

Taha'Leeth gave an absent nod and sipped at her wine, saying nothing.

"I have heard some claim the armies of the confederacy are almost as tough as the legions. I've fought against them. I know that part is true. They can be tough." Stiger took a pull on his wine and then slightly waved the half-empty mug at Taha'Leeth. "What I want to know is what kind of people are they? Who am I fighting? Would you tell me about them as a people?"

Taha'Leeth took a deep breath. She seemed almost to shudder as it came out. "The Cyphan are a cruel and depraved people, driven by a hard, unforgiving religion centered around Valoor."

"Valoor," Stiger said. He had never thought of that god as a cruel and dark deity, like Castor. There was even a temple honoring him in the capital. That said, he did not know much about him.

"Yes, Valoor, the so-called god of life and death and the in-between." Taha'Leeth took a pull on her wine. "Everything is built upon the backs of others and power is wielded by the few. As you know, for my actions…the destruction of the other World Gate…my people have suffered terribly at the Cyphan's hands. But we had a use and so they allowed us to prosper in a fashion, to live a little better than others so that we could serve."

She fell silent for several heartbeats as her gaze returned to the fire. She took another deep breath and let it out before continuing. "The confederacy is made up of individual states tied together through alliance, trade, and common interests. The ruling families of these states strengthen their ties through marriage. The priesthood also wields considerable influence and has a say in major decisions."

She took a sip of her wine.

"There is very little opportunity for anyone to advance within society, as everyone is born into their place. The ruling families hold most of the power and money. Think of them as simply the owners of everything, the masters."

"Is there a plebian class?" Stiger asked. "Equites?"

She scowled at him slightly, clearly not understanding what he was asking.

"In the empire we have the nobility," Stiger said. "The equites are called the equestrians, kind of like the middle class, then there are the masses, what we call the plebeians and the freed. After that, there are the slaves."

"You are of the nobility?" Taha'Leeth asked.

"I am," Stiger said. "Is there anything like the equites, plebeians, or the freed in the confederacy?"

"There is a middle class of sorts. They are the merchants, tradesmen, and skilled workers. They have it slightly better than the rest, but for the most part, the confederacy is filled with those who have very little. Suffering and misery abound. There are more slaves than citizens. Poverty is widespread. Most live like animals."

She paused, taking a pull from her mug and draining the last of the wine. Taha'Leeth stood and walked over to the table, where Venthus had left the wine jar. Refilling her mug, she returned to the chair. "Nearly all of the confederacy's professional soldiers are slaves. The rest are conscripts. There are a few professional military companies, what you would call mercenaries for hire."

Was she was telling him that power was controlled by a select few?

"Those soldiers fighting on behalf of the Cyphan are enslaved into the confederacy's armies? And the rest are forced to serve and fight when needed?"

"More correctly, they are born into it." She raised a finger and wagged it in the air as if to emphasize her point. "The confederacy's slave soldiers are raised and trained from birth to fight. Do not make the mistake of assuming they are not properly motivated. Yes, they are treated little better than animals. They have no say in whether they fight and die on behalf of their masters, but they do so willingly. It's all they know. So too with the conscripts."

It was Stiger's turn to scowl. Though the empire did not use slave soldiers, there had been more than a few slave revolts. What made the empire different from the Cyphan? Surely the slaves from the confederacy dreamed of freedom, a better life?

"I very much doubt you could ever get them to turn upon their masters," Taha'Leeth said.

"You switched sides," Stiger pointed out.

"We are different," Taha'Leeth said.

"How so?"

"The confederacy has a rigid caste system," Taha'Leeth said. "It is based on birth. As one would expect, they, like all slaves, dream of freedom. However, slaves cannot be granted, nor purchase, their freedom. So, they go about obtaining that which they greatly desire in a different manner, through dedicated service or by death on the battlefield, if their lot in life is to be a soldier."

"I don't understand," Stiger said as the fire popped loud enough to stir Dog slightly from his slumber. The big shaggy animal raised his head and looked toward the fire, yawned mightily, then laid his head upon his paws and promptly went back to sleep.

"Their devotion and motivation is tied directly to their faith. Valoor teaches servitude is the path to salvation. As such, you will find the confederacy's soldiers highly motivated. Simply, they believe in divine favor and reward for loyal service. They do not look for such in the mundane world. To serve or die well in battle is something they willingly seek."

Stiger was silent as he considered her troublesome words. He wondered what such a divine reward looked like.

"Those who are born malformed or deemed unable to serve due to age or disability are put to death. The Cyphan are truly a wretched people." Taha'Leeth paused, her gaze seeming to turn inward. She shuddered slightly. "Every year, there is the Sacred Culling. It is a day of festivity, celebration, games, but also murder. Those deemed worthless to society are ritually put to death, publicly...very publicly. You see, this way they are given a second chance."

"A second chance?"

"Yes," Taha'Leeth said. "They have the opportunity to be reborn and contribute."

"But you do not believe as they do." Stiger said this as a statement and not a question.

"No, I do not worship at Valoor's altar," Taha'Leeth said. "Tanithe is the god I honor, followed by the High Father."

"What about the rest of your people?"

"You do not have to worry about them. They will come and serve alongside the dwarves, your humans, and the gnomes. I promised. My people will fight with you and for the High Father's alignment. Tanithe is honored to sit on the High Father's left side."

Stiger gave a nod, recalling the small temple to Tanithe in the capital. His mother had taken him there as a child to offer devotion, like she had with many of the other gods. Tanithe was the god of cunning and mischief, amongst other things. He had always seemed a little mysterious to Stiger, but as he was part of the old order, he was honored. And so, the Stiger family had offered the god regular devotion.

"Do you know of the teachings of Valoor?" Taha'Leeth asked.

Stiger shook his head. Valoor was not part of the order and High Father's alignment. He'd never considered the god opposed to his until recently.

"Much of the confederacy follows the teachings of Valoor," Taha'Leeth said. "It is believed that service to one's god, no matter how menial, including enforced servitude, is a blessing. If you serve and work well, when you are reborn, your station in life will improve. The greater your service in life, the greater chance you have of being reborn to the middle class, as a priest, or even a higher station, as part of the nobility. Serve poorly and your station will decrease to that of a slave or...worse, say a beast of burden or maybe a rock, from which there is no return. I am simplifying a bit, but you get my point, yes?"

"Rebirth," Stiger said softly, suddenly feeling deeply unhappy. In the fight to come, he would truly be struggling against faith. Not that he had not faced that before, with Castor. But this meant the fight ahead would be quite difficult. "Rebirth in an improved station is what the soldiers of the confederacy seek as their reward?"

"It is all they yearn for and rightly expect," Taha'Leeth said, "and why they are such fearsome foes."

"What about the rebels?" Stiger asked. "Do they follow Valoor?"

"No," she replied. "They follow the High Father."

He rubbed his jaw and winced, as he had forgotten the soreness. In a few days' time, he would be fighting and killing followers of his own god. Stiger gave a slight scowl at that. It was not a satisfactory turn of events. But then again, he had a higher duty to consider.

"They made their choice," Stiger said, feeling his anger stir at what he would be required to do. "They are now the enemy and will be treated as such."

She said nothing to that, and once again they fell back into silence, both watching the fire. Dog slept on.

Taha'Leeth shifted in her chair abruptly and looked over at him. Their eyes met. She tilted her head slightly to the side while stroking her braid.

"You have changed, Ben Stiger. As I knew you would…as Tanithe revealed to me."

"Everyone changes," Stiger replied, becoming uncomfortable, though he was not quite sure why. For some strange reason, he felt like he could not look away. With the firelight flickering over her face, she appeared more alluring than ever. He knew she was not using a glamour on him. Menos, the noctalum, otherwise known as the dragon Sian Tane, had taught him how to block such simple tricks and guard his mind from intrusion. "Everyone changes."

"Not in the way you have," Taha'Leeth said as she released her braid. She was gazing very intently at him. She pointed. "You are unique."

"What do you mean by that?" Stiger wondered how much she knew about him being the High Father's Champion and what that entailed. The legion and dwarves knew the basics. Did she know more? How could she? No one, other than Menos, Ogg, Therik, Salt, and perhaps Eli, fully understood.

"I think perhaps you can sense it yourself," Taha'Leeth said in a near whisper. "The change that has come over you makes you more than you were." Her gaze flicked to his tunic around his neck. "I see by the blood on your tunic, your lip bled, yes?"

Stiger froze with the mug halfway to his lips. He slowly lowered it to his lap.

"Yet there is no sign of such a cut and orc blood is green, not red." She reached out a delicate finger toward his jaw, before pulling back. "Tell me the truth. You can feel it, the change, distancing you from your own kind, can't you?"

Stiger returned his gaze to the fire. He knew he had changed. It was as she said. He could feel it. When he'd fully embraced being the High Father's Champion, something inside him had opened, or perhaps he had unlocked whatever it was, a power he had not known he possessed or was capable of wielding. But now that he considered her words, he suspected that she was referring to something else.

"I know you know," Taha'Leeth said. "Deep down, inside...you've known for some time. Something happened to you, something extraordinary and profound, a rare event...something that only happens once an age and upsets the order of things."

She reached over and placed her hand on his forearm. He found her touch warm, hot even. The hairs on his arms stood on end. She ran her fingertips up his arm in a soft caress to his elbow and there stopped, staring into his eyes. Stiger found his heart suddenly hammering within his chest.

"You are most changed, Ben Stiger," Taha'Leeth said, removing her hand.

Stiger wanted nothing more than to reach out and hold her hand. There was something intoxicating about her touch. It was an intimacy that he'd lost and craved, yearned for. She seemed to sense what he was thinking. A knowing smile formed on her lovely face. Slowly, she pulled herself out of her chair and came over to his, standing before him. Leaning forward, she took his face in her hands and kissed him.

She tasted sweet, lips warm, inviting. Their tongues met and Stiger lost himself, no longer even feeling the soreness in his jaw. Then, after a long moment, she drew back, and once again, Stiger almost protested.

He sucked in a ragged breath. For a long while now, he'd thought he would never be able to care for anyone like he had for Sarai. Looking into Taha'Leeth's eyes, he was no longer sure about that. She glanced over at the bed and then returned her gaze to him. She bit her lip, a mischievous look to her gaze.

"Shall we?" she asked after a moment's more hesitation and jerked her head toward the bed.

Stiger was silent for a long moment. He wanted to take this exotic woman to bed. He needed it.

"That night in Old City…our conversation," Stiger said, hating himself for what needed to be said. It might ruin any chance he had of being with her.

"What of it?"

"You despise my kind for what they have done to you and your people," Stiger said. "I do not require this of you. You are no longer a slave, but a free woman. You do not owe me anything." Stiger paused. "If you wanted to leave tomorrow, I would regret it, but I would not stop you."

She laughed and it was a pleasant sound. She suddenly became serious, her eyes narrowing. "You loved and lost, didn't you? Tell me the truth. When you went back into the past."

"I did." Stiger found that his throat caught with the admission. "It was incredibly painful."

"So too have I loved and lost," Taha'Leeth said. "My mate was killed. You and I." She tapped him on the chest with a finger. "We have both suffered the worst agony. I lost my mate, you yours." She paused and her tone became firm. "I am giving myself to you, as you should give yourself to me."

Stiger felt himself frown, his scar pulling tight.

"I thought elves mate for life? I understood that they would never take another lover…that it was not in your nature to do so."

"You know much of my people," Taha'Leeth said. There was a question in her eyes. "How? Eli?"

"For a time," Stiger said, "I lived amongst Eli's people. I met a widow. She was one of the saddest beings I've ever known. I like to think I understand elves better than most, but in truth…you are as much a mystery to me as elves are to others."

She laughed again and it was a deep laugh, as if he had made a joke instead of a simple admission. The mischievous smile returned. She reached forward and grabbed his hand and pulled him out of the chair and up close against her. He found her body warm, almost radiating heat. She smelled faintly of some sort of flower. He could not identify it. Stiger had had enough. He grabbed her about the waist and pulled her tight against him and kissed her long and passionately. When they came up for air, she shoved him toward the bed, then stopped.

"I choose to be with you this night," Taha'Leeth said.

Looking into her eyes he found them deep, intense, and quite captivating…also at the same time alien. They were not human eyes. He thought he could lose himself within that gaze. It wasn't her beauty that called him. There was something else drawing them together and…it felt right.

There was a sudden growling from by the fire.

"Quiet you," Stiger snapped, looking over. Dog stopped his growling, but his eyes were fixed upon the two of them. He gave a soft whine.

Taha'Leeth extricated herself from Stiger's arms and climbed off the bed. She moved across the room and opened the door. The elf looked at Dog sternly.

"Out, naverum," she said in a firm tone. "I shall not ask again."

Dog gave another whine, stood, shook himself, and then padded across the room. At the door, he paused, glancing at Stiger, almost with a sheepish look. His tail gave a vigorous wag of what Stiger took to be approval and then he left. Taha'Leeth closed the door, throwing the bolt home.

The next thing Stiger knew, she was back on the bed straddling him and they were tearing at each other's clothes. The shutters rattled loudly as the wind pulled at them in outrage. Stiger did not care. She was all that mattered.

FOUR

Stiger found Eli waiting a few feet from the entrance to
the hall. It had been almost a week since he'd arrived
at the castle. The hall was the one where he and Father
Thomas had confronted the first minion, the one that had
corrupted Captain Aveeno. That encounter seemed like
such a long time ago. So much had transpired since then, it
was almost ancient history. Though for Eli and many others,
it had only been a matter of weeks.

Eli was leaning casually against the wall. Two guards
stood to either side of the entrance into the hall. Tail wagging, Dog left Stiger's side and padded up to the elf. He
received a scratch behind the ears for his troubles, though
Stiger could read the wariness in his friend's eyes as Eli
regarded the animal.

"Good day," Eli said, enthusiastically, as he came off the
wall and approached.

Stiger stopped before his friend and glanced past the
guards and into the hall. It was filled with his senior officers.
The drone of many voices could be heard out in the hallway. Standing together close to the door were Quintus and
Vargus, the senior centurions of the valley cohorts. Stiger
could also see Hux along with Lan by the cavalry prefect's
side. Though Lan was not a senior officer, he had been in

the castle, and so Hux must have brought him along. The four officers were conversing. Vargus said something that must have been funny, for the other three laughed.

Stiger turned his attention to the elf. He had known this moment was coming. There was no avoiding it, so he decided to hit the nail on the head.

"A good day?" Stiger said. "You tell me."

Eli arched an eyebrow and tilted his head slightly. The elf was silent for several heartbeats as he regarded Stiger.

"The snow stopped falling. You've assembled your officers and the legion is preparing for a fight. You've also made it plain you want me to scout the enemy's encampment. That means I will be getting out of these"—he held his arms out—"confining stone walls. Shortly, I will return to the freedom of the outdoors. And, Ben, you know how much I enjoy the trees, soooo," he said, dragging out the word, "I think yes. It is a good day."

Stiger gave a grunt and decided not to be put off.

"You know very well that's not what I mean," Stiger said. He was sure the elf had been avoiding him these last five days. Since arriving at the castle, he'd hardly seen Eli, and only when others were present. At first, Stiger had wondered and worried on it. But now as he looked into Eli's eyes, he was sure he read uncertainty within. It was why Eli had been waiting for him, instead of joining the others in the hall. Eli had also decided to put the matter plain between them, to discuss what was truly bothering him.

"Whatever are you on about, Ben?" Eli's face became a mask of pure innocence, and then his eyes lit up. He snapped his fingers. "Oh, I think I know."

"Do you?" Stiger crossed his arms. Eli loved his games, even when there were matters of importance to discuss. "Do you now?"

"Could it be your joining with Taha'Leeth?" Eli asked. "Yes, I think that's it. You know, now that I think on it...you are looking a little more tired than usual. Are those bags under your eyes? You can be honest with me. You've been staying up way too late with her." Eli paused a heartbeat. "Is that a smile I detect hiding behind your usual gruff exterior?"

"I'm not gonna bite."

"Taha'Leeth is quite a looker," Eli said with a grin, "even amongst my people. She's a nice catch."

Stiger bit his lip as he studied his friend. "You seem rather cavalier about us, don't you?"

"Ben." Eli placed a hand to his breast in an exaggerated manner. "You wound me, truly. It's as if you shot an arrow through my heart. Say, don't your people have a god that does that, and once a person is hit by the godly arrow, they fall in love? I seem to recall Tiro mentioning something about such a god."

"You don't have a problem with it, then?" Stiger asked, for he rather suspected it might become a problem with some elves. He had been worried Eli might be one of those who would disapprove and that was why his friend had been avoiding him. "You have no issue with any of it?"

"Personally, no," Eli said, becoming serious.

"But what?" Stiger asked, filling in for what his friend had not said.

"But," Eli said slowly, then glanced over at the guards, who, with their legate present, were locked into a position of attention and were looking fastidiously forward at invisible points in space.

Stiger drew back a few feet from the guards so they were just out of earshot. He lowered his voice a tad. "Well?"

"It does seem a little unnatural," Eli admitted, "you being a human and all."

"A little?" Stiger asked, knowing there was more to it than that. "Unnatural? Is that your only objection?"

"I did not say I objected," Eli said, then blew out a breath. "All right. You know who the Elantric Warden is, right?"

"I've never met her," Stiger said, "but as I recall, she is the spiritual leader of your people."

"That is a very simplistic way of looking at it," Eli said, with a slight scowl. "Ben, the Elantric Warden is not only the spiritual leader of my people, but effectively the leader. She is one of the oldest, most knowledgeable, and wisest of the High Born. Heck, she's so ancient, she knew your Emperor Karus, and well too. I have heard it said they were friends."

"Really?" Stiger asked, to which his friend gave a curt nod. Here was yet another link with the first emperor. "Karus?"

"To say the warden is well respected amongst us is an understatement," Eli said. "She embodies the spirit of our people. She guides our path, as a shepherd might a flock. Think of her as the steward."

"The steward of your people?"

Eli gave a nod. "We owe her much, for she looks after us."

"Why are you telling me this?" Stiger asked. "What has this got to do with Taha'Leeth and myself? Are you saying the warden will object?"

"I would not presume to know the mind of the warden," Eli said, seeming genuinely surprised by the suggestion. He hesitated, appearing to consider it. "I honestly don't know what she'd think about the two of you."

"Then what?" Stiger pressed, becoming impatient.

"The warden is a being of power," Eli said, lowering his voice, as if sharing a secret. "Taha'Leeth, for her people..." Eli hesitated, as if unsure what exactly to say, scowled slightly, and then pressed on. "You know she is a leader of her people, right? Well, think of her as the warden of her people, though from Aver'Mons, I've learned her role is not quite the same. But it's close enough. So, to simplify things...you are spending your nights with the equivalent of the warden, at least for her people. You know how my people view humans... Imagine how hers see yours...especially after all that they have suffered and been through. Do you see a slight problem with that?"

Stiger sucked in a startled breath, as he suddenly understood. He opened his mouth to say something then closed it, opened and closed it again.

"I personally don't object," Eli said, filling the sudden silence that had grown between them. "It's just that...I believe there are bigger things to consider..."

"Like her people?" Stiger asked.

"Yes," Eli said, "and yours."

"Mine?" Stiger glanced into the hall, where his officers waited. He had not considered them.

Eli shook his head. "It may cause trouble."

"May?" Stiger rubbed the bridge of his nose. He was feeling a headache coming on. This was just one more complication he did not need, especially now that he was almost ready to kick off the campaign. "I have a feeling you are understating matters."

"I am happy for you." Eli clapped Stiger on the upper arm. "I'm just glad you didn't pick my sister. It saves me the trouble of having to come up with an explanation for my father, one which sees him not prematurely ending your life."

"You don't have a sister," Stiger said, feeling himself frown. His scar pulled on his cheek.

"All the better," Eli said, then sobered. "I am truly happy for you. After Livia, Kehren, and then Hela, you deserve a little happiness, truly."

Stiger rubbed his jaw as unhappy memories bubbled up to the surface at the mention of those names. There were some days he thought unhappy memories and regrets were all he had left from the past. He glanced down at the stone floor and then back up at Eli. "When I went back in time, there was a woman by the name of Sarai. I was…happy, content. I did not want to come back."

"I know," Eli said, sadness creeping into his expression.

"You do?" Stiger was surprised by that, for he had not discussed Sarai's loss with him. He had intended to, but since returning, there had not been much time. Eli had also been avoiding him.

"Salt told me," Eli explained. "He spoke of what happened. I understand you were quite attached to her."

"I would have given up everything," Stiger said, "and I mean everything, to spend the rest of my days in such happiness." Stiger glanced down at his feet and ran a boot over the scuffed stone. He looked back up and met Eli's gaze. "But it was not meant to be. The gods, it seems, have other plans for me."

"I for one am pleased you did not give everything up," Eli said, a sudden smirk on his youthful face and a trace of amusement flickering in his eyes. "Let me be the first to thank you for coming back."

Stiger felt a tickle of grim amusement himself and a lightening of the mood. "You would have missed me?"

"Miss is a strong word. Let's just say things would have been a little less exciting without you," Eli said, a little grudgingly. "I would have had to find someone else to get me into trouble."

Stiger's thoughts drifted back to the warning his friend had just given. His sleeping with Taha'Leeth would cause problems. There was no doubt about that. Still, he was unwilling to give her up. Life was full of problems. This was just one more to deal with.

"We both agree there will be trouble," Stiger said, sobering. "When it rears its head with either the elves or my people...you will tell me?"

"We both know you attract trouble, like dead things do flies," Eli said. "But I will tell you should I notice anything that will become an imminent problem for you."

"You've given me a lot to think on," Stiger said.

"What are friends for, eh?" Eli gave a shrug as a burst of laughter from inside the hall reminded Stiger his officers were waiting.

"I would talk more with you later," Stiger said. "Would you stop by this evening and join me for a drink?"

"Of course," Eli said. "As long as it's wine and not dwarf spirits. I don't much like those."

"I am sure Venthus will have no trouble finding us some wine." Stiger gave a grateful nod. "Let's go."

With Eli at his side, he brushed past the two guards and entered the hall. Dog padded along behind them.

"Stand to attention," Salt shouted, cutting over the conversation. The prefect had been standing near the door.

He had a voice a drill sergeant could respect. Instantly, the drone of conversation dropped off and then ceased altogether. The officers turned toward the entrance and came to attention, all eyes on Stiger.

Most had been gathered around an oversized map that had been spread out on a long rectangular table, clearly speculating on the campaign that was to come. Stiger had had one of the legion's scribes draw it. The map was rough, but suitable for his needs this day.

On one end of the map, it began with Castle Vrell and covered the enemy's encampment. The map followed the Vrell road all the way out to where General Kromen's encampment had been. Points of interest were marked on the map, including the two dwarven roads, the Tol'Tabor and Tol'Ket. Stiger had even had the scribe add Delvaris's tomb and the Eighty-Fifth's initial campsite, the one they had constructed before he and his company had departed for Vrell on that fateful march.

"At ease," Stiger called as he made his way deeper into the hall. His officers moved aside as he walked up to the middle point of the map. Salt took a position to Stiger's right. Dog sat down on his other side. Eli chose a free spot a few feet away.

Stiger paused, glancing down at the map, then swung his gaze around his officers and motioned them closer about the table. Every single senior officer and cohort commander was present. There were a good number of junior officers present too.

"How are your horse soldiers, Hux?" Stiger asked as they gathered around the table. "Are you prepared for an extended movement?"

"As ordered, we're assembled, sir," Hux said and glanced down toward the map, then back up at Stiger. "My horses and boys are well-fed, rested, provisioned, and ready to go, sir. Just give the word."

"Very good," Stiger said, pleased. He had expected nothing less. His gaze moved on, then came to rest on Blake. He gave the centurion a nod. It was the first time since returning to the present that he'd seen his old sergeant-turned-centurion.

"Good to see you, Blake."

"You too, sir." Blake nodded in return.

Stiger's old company, the Eighty-Fifth, was camped in the valley, near the road that led up to Vrell. Next to Blake stood centurions Sabinus and Nantus.

"Brent," Stiger said, turning his attention to the man. "How's your new cohort coming?"

"Shaping up nicely, sir," Brent said. "I just wish we had more time together, sir."

"Understandable. Unfortunately, there's no helping that. I am sure you will do all that you can."

"Yes, sir. I will, sir."

Stiger gave a nod. Despite the inclement weather that had dropped several feet of snow over the last few days, the officers knew something was up. They would not have been called were it not so. Many looked tired and weary from their journey to the castle but no less eager to hear what was planned and in store.

Salt had also been busy meeting with each of those present to ensure they were ready for the coming campaign, though none of them knew what that would be. The anticipation that hung on the air was so thick, Stiger thought he could cut it with his sword.

Stiger saw Therik was present, standing against the back wall. The orc was playing with the nail of his right index finger, as if dislodging something that had become stuck underneath. He was acting as if this all bored him terribly. Stiger knew it to be an act, especially after he'd let the former king in on his intentions earlier that morning. Therik was more than ready for action, eager even.

Taha'Leeth and Aver'Mons were standing together. Stiger's eyes locked for a moment with hers. He almost smiled—almost. The last few nights had been not only exciting, but had left him feeling strangely whole for the first time in a long while.

Aver'Mons, on the other hand, appeared sullen, unhappy. The elf's eyes were not friendly. Eli's warning fresh to mind, Stiger resisted a frown.

"I appreciate you coming," Stiger said. "I know many of you traveled up from the valley floor and, what with the fresh snow, the going was difficult, with your travel taking most of the day. It was necessary. You have been called together to be briefed on the upcoming campaign, for the army will soon be stepping off. We will be moving from the defensive to the offensive, taking the initiative from the enemy and finally striking back."

"Surely not in this weather, sir?" Lieutenant Brent said. "I've spent two winters in Vrell, sir. There is a lot of snow out there, and I can assure you, more is on the way."

"That is exactly my intention," Stiger said and then held up his hands to forestall any additional comments, as several of his officers began to whisper amongst each other and some looked ready to speak. "Before I take any further questions, allow me a moment to review the situation and outline my plans. Despite there being challenges to overcome, I believe everything will rapidly become clear."

Stiger paused a moment, gathering his thoughts. He waited for the whispers to die down and then pointed toward Castle Vrell on the map.

"The enemy has an army of around thirty thousand blocking the entrance to the castle and pass. They believe going through the castle is the only way in or out of the valley, which means, in their mind, we are trapped. It is a reasonable assumption, as the mountains surrounding the valley are too rugged and steep to move a large force over."

Stiger paused again.

"There is, however, another way out of the valley and we're going to use it. We will not be going over the mountain, but under it."

That set off a few excited whispers. Stiger held up his hand for silence and got it.

"The dwarves have tunneled and mined out the surrounding mountains around the valley. These tunnels are old and have been abandoned for quite some time, with many that are far from safe. However, there are two underground roads that are suitable. One, the Tol'Tabor, will take us out of the valley, to this point here, just to the east of the enemy's camp." Stiger paused again, glancing up and looking at Brent. "Snow will not present a problem, at least until we exit the dwarven road. The enemy will not expect us to appear behind them. The dwarves are working on the road to reinforce it and make it safe for use. They are also working on the other road, the Tol'Ket, which lets out farther out into the forest. The repair work was originally expected to take two weeks. It is ahead of schedule. I am told that their work is almost complete and that within four days both roads will be ready for use."

Stiger allowed that to sink in for several heartbeats.

"So, let me tell you what I know of the situation outside the valley." Stiger pointed toward where General Kromen's encampment had been. "The legions, specifically the Fifteenth, Eighteenth, Twenty-Ninth, and Thirtieth, making up the heart of General Kromen's army, were forced into retreat by the Cyphan Confederacy and Southern rebels. Since that point, we do not know what has occurred. I have had no communication with the empire since before the legions pulled out and retreated. Whether or not there was a battle, I do not know. Riddled with sickness, those four legions were in poor condition to begin with. We can assume that since the enemy has an army encamped on our doorstep, General Kromen was unsuccessful in throwing the Cyphan back." Stiger privately suspected that all four legions had been brought to battle and defeated. But he did not say that. "It is likely, and please keep in mind this is all supposition, the battle lines have moved far to the north, perhaps even to the empire's border or beyond."

Stiger gave another pause. The officers about him were grim-faced. Several shared looks but they said nothing.

"What we do know is that the confederacy means to destroy the empire. All of you, at this point, understand why we are here. The Thirteenth Legion was sent to Vrell to reinforce the Compact, the alliance between the empire and the dwarves, aimed at protecting the World Gate. More importantly, the legion was also sent to help the empire in its time of greatest need, which is now." Stiger sucked in a breath. "Emperor Atticus had forewarning of what was to come and he dispatched his most experienced and finest formation."

There was some shifting of feet at that, especially from those not of the Thirteenth Legion. Atticus was long dead, an emperor those in Stiger's time knew only through history. For those original legionaries of the Thirteenth and her auxiliary cohorts, Atticus was their emperor, not the current one, Tioclesion.

"We've all seen hard fighting," Stiger said. "I can promise you we'll see more difficult times to come. That's a certainty, for the Cyphan mean to control the Gate. To do that, they need to first get the Key. The High Father entrusted the Key into the first emperor's keeping. Since then, it has been passed down from one emperor to the next. The Key has the power to unlock and unseal the World Gate. The emperor, as far as I know, still has it in his possession."

"I've never heard of it, sir," Blake said.

"That's not surprising," Stiger said. "As you can imagine, it is quite important. Steps were taken to conceal its true nature. It was intentionally hidden."

"Have you ever seen this Key, sir?" Sabinus asked.

"I have," Stiger said, "though at the time I did not know its importance. The thing to understand is that the Cyphan don't care about the empire. They don't want our lands, or our people enslaved, well at least not yet. Make no mistake, gentlemen, their objective is the World Gate. That is the purpose of their invasion. They will tear the empire apart to find the Key, and that is what they are likely attempting to do at this very moment."

There was more shifting of feet.

"The empire is in mortal danger. The Cyphan have assembled a vast army that, as impossible as it sounds, could see the crushing of the legions and the fall of the empire. If they are successful, once they've seized the Key, they will turn their attention to Vrell and us."

Stiger stopped once again, dragging his gaze around the room, looking at each officer in turn, meeting their gazes with his own steel. There was silence. No one moved. Everyone hung on his words, almost as if they feared breathing. It was clear to Stiger they understood what was at stake. That was good.

"I do not intend to wait for the enemy to come for us, or to allow them to destroy our beloved empire. We will take the fight to them. First, we won't just break the army before Castle Vrell, we will grind them under the heel of our boots and sandals. Then, we will go to the aid of the emperor and our comrades in the legions."

"Aye, sir," Centurion Nantus shouted, "we came to fight and fight we will." The centurion looked around at the gathered officers. "Isn't that right?"

The officers present gave a hearty cheer.

"Sir," Centurion Mectillius spoke up, once the cheer died down. "It seems to me that after we deal with this enemy army, and go looking for more, we will be behind the lines, operating in occupied territory. Is that not correct?"

"It is true," Stiger said, "that we are, and with the defeat of the army on the other side of the pass, we will still be behind the lines. Our enemy thinks that only a couple thousand men are trapped in Vrell. That's all. They have no idea there is an entire legion here, along with five auxiliary cohorts, not to mention a dwarven and a gnome army. Combined, we number close to one hundred thousand strong. We also have a wizard on our side and Sian Tane, a dragon. Gentlemen, we are far from helpless. We are quite dangerous, and soon I intend to give the enemy an education they are not likely to forget."

Stiger drew in a breath.

"We are right where we need to be." Stiger pointed at the map. He felt his anger stir at what was coming. "When we strike, it will catch the bastards completely by surprise. The hard part will not be destroying the rabble before the walls of the castle. Nor will it be working our way along a snow-packed road and down into the heart of the forest." Stiger pointed again downward, this time at the map. "The most difficult part, as I'm sure all of you can guess, will be after we march out of the forest. The tough bit will be fighting our way north to our comrades. We must help them completely and thoroughly defeat the confederacy. There should be no doubt. A hard path lies ahead. I have come to know you, fought alongside you. You have come to know me. I trust you, as you trust me." Stiger brought his hands together in a clap that echoed off the stone walls of the room. "We can do this." He paused a moment. "We cannot, under any circumstances, fail in this sacred duty. We must save the empire and, by doing so, the emperor. Once the Cyphan invasion is stopped and the threat over, only then will the Key and the World Gate be secure…as will the empire we love. Do you understand me?"

"Yes, sir," came the unified chorus.

"Now," Stiger said, "I will take a few questions before I continue."

"What is on the other side of the World Gate?" Centurion Vargus asked. "Do you know, sir?"

"Other than it being another world called Tanis, I do not know what waits should the Gate be opened," Stiger said. "The enemy has staked everything on getting the Key, so I can only assume that whatever is on the other side will not be friendly, or welcoming. It is more likely that allies of the confederacy stand ready to pour through the Gate into our world."

"Seems hard to believe, sir," Lan said, shaking his head in near disbelief.

"A few weeks ago," Stiger said, "you'd have thought orcs, dwarves, dragons, and gnomes were myths, creatures of fantasy. Am I right?"

"Yes, sir," Lan said, looking somewhat abashed.

"Why don't we wait for the weather to improve, sir?"

Stiger saw that it was Centurion Blake who had asked the question.

"You deserve honesty," Stiger said. "I've done my best to give it to you, as I see it. Blake, time is an issue. I am told by Ogg, the dwarven wizard, we have a little over twenty-four months to secure the Key. The World Gate has been sealed for many years. Apparently, something is about to happen, magically, that allows the Gate to be opened or, more correctly, unlocked. Once it is, the World Gate will remain open for a long time—or shut. So, we do not have the luxury of time. We must act. If we wait or delay, we may lose this opportunity before us. The empire may be defeated, and when the enemy comes, it will be in overwhelming numbers. No. We cannot wait. We must go now, while they remain ignorant of our presence. Surprise, initiative, and boldness will be our allies, at least in the beginning."

"I understand, sir," Blake said.

Stiger gestured with a hand over the map toward the Sentinel Forest. He pointed down at it. "The fighting season in the South is winter, except for here in Vrell, the surrounding mountains, and foothills. The elevation is such that winter is winter. However, at lower elevations to the east, beyond the foothills"—Stiger pointed toward the far side of the Sentinel Forest—"the ground hardens. The rest of the year sees a lot of rain and mud. So, whether we like it or not, now is the time to make our move, to strike. We must beat the enemy army besieging Vrell, then slog out of the mountains and foothills to the lower elevations, where the ground is firm. Any questions so far?"

There were none. That surprised Stiger. He had expected more questions. Very well, he thought. It was time to get into the operational and organizational aspects of what was to come.

"So, this is the plan of action," Stiger said. "Thane Braddock's army will march before us. The thane's pioneers have already cut the Vrell road. The enemy is being deprived of supply, and though likely not yet stretched for food...they will soon be." Stiger pointed at a line on the map. "Thane Braddock will take his army through the other underground road I mentioned, the Tol'Ket, farther out into the forest. At the point where he will emerge, the ground should be firm, at least the pioneers tell us so. Braddock will move his army onto the Vrell road about here and march down it toward where General Kromen's encampment was located, here. Our cavalry will go with him. Prefect Hux?"

"Sir?"

"After we're done, I want to see you and give you your orders personally. You will need to coordinate with the dwarves, and that, as you know, can be tricky. Braddock will be assigning you an officer as a liaison. With any luck, it will ease any problems that develop."

"Yes, sir," Hux said.

"The dwarves have some cavalry of their own," Stiger said. "Braddock and I have decided they will be under your command, and while attached to Braddock's army, you will be under his. You will also be spearheading the advance."

"Yes, sir," Hux said. "I understand, sir."

Stiger returned to addressing the officers in the hall. "While the dwarves, gnomes, and our cavalry forge ahead, it will be our responsibility to deal with the rabble blocking the castle gates and the pass. We will emerge from the dwarven road and set up a blocking position about here." Stiger pointed to an X that had been drawn on the map just to the east of the enemy encampment. "I wish we had the luxury of time to starve the bastards out, but for reasons already explained, we do not. We will fortify this line here, which cuts right across the road. I am told by the pioneers the terrain is quite good and lends itself easily to defense. It is inconceivable to me that the enemy will not notice our presence once we begin digging in. I think it very likely they will immediately move to attack, before we become too entrenched. It is either that or, in their minds, go hungry as their food stores run out and they slowly starve. Melting into the forests is not an option either. They are too far from civilization to support themselves. Make no mistake, gentlemen, they will attack our line, which is what I want them very much to do. They will throw their strength against our defenses and we will beat them like a rented mule. Then we will break them."

"Why not attack the enemy first and with everything we have?" Nantus asked. "Why bother to split our forces? It seems a risky move, sir."

"That's a good question," Stiger conceded. "We considered doing just that, but ultimately decided this was the better path."

"May I, sir?" Salt asked as Stiger was about to say more.

Stiger gave a nod.

"Once we deal with the enemy army," Salt said, "the problem becomes the Vrell road itself. It is the only road we have out of the Sentinel Forest. We know the enemy we face here at Vrell." Salt leaned forward and moved his hand eastward along the road. "What we don't know is what lies beyond the Sentinel Forest, essentially what has been going on in the war between the empire and the Cyphan Confederacy. With the numbers we have between the legion, dwarves, and gnomes, if we all march at once, the road will quickly become clogged with soldiers, supply, and artillery. Putting the entire army on the road at one time, narrow as it is, will see continual starting and stopping. All it will take is a broken wagon axle or a fallen tree and movement will slow to a complete crawl, not to mention any action from the enemy." Salt tapped the map with his index finger. "The road will become clogged. We won't even be able to move supply up to provide sufficient food for the advance units."

Nantus and others gave nods of understanding.

"To alleviate the road becoming a serious impediment," Stiger said, jumping in, "we decided to split the army in two. When we begin our march, Braddock's force should be well ahead of ours, giving the legion an open road."

Blake spoke up. "It's winter up in the hills and mountains. However, I imagine parts of the road beyond the hills and at a lower elevation could see mud. Under the weight of thousands of feet, hooves, and wagon wheels, the road could still become a problem. I've seen it happen before, sir, in the Wilds."

"If needed," Stiger said, thinking that he was quite right, "we will reinforce the road, corduroying it." Repairing the road would slow things down, but laying a log road over the muddy portions would ultimately speed up subsequent supply and any following units. Best to focus on one problem at a time, though. "We will handle that problem when it presents itself. Now, while we deal with the enemy before the castle, as I said, Braddock will get a head start on us. More importantly, he will secure the open ground at the edge of the forest, where the road terminates." Stiger tapped the area to the east, just beyond the Sentinel Forest's border. "The Cyphan, those outside the forest and to the east, may soon learn the road has been cut. If so, or when they do, they will most likely dispatch a force to investigate why they've lost contact with their army at Vrell. This is one of several unknowns, which reinforced our decision to split forces and have Braddock press forward with all possible haste to get ahead of such an eventuality."

"Once again, speed becomes our friend," Eli said quietly. "Especially for Braddock."

"Correct." Stiger gave a pleased nod. "We can't afford to give the Cyphan time to assemble a relief force strong enough to clear the road. And we don't want a meeting engagement somewhere out in the Sentinel Forest, where it will be difficult to maintain lines and keep reasonable control over our formations. There will be little room for maneuver. We may find ourselves boxed into a bloody and costly brawl before we can even break out into the open. That was another factor in our decision to have Braddock push forward on his own and anchor a position outside the forest."

Stiger glanced up. As expected, every eye was upon him.

"Now," Stiger said, "let's dive into the order of march and deployment upon the ground we will hold. Salt, do you have the dispositions?"

"I do, sir." Salt held a tablet in a hand. "First Cohort shall have the honor of marching at the legion's van, then Second…"

Stiger looked over at Sabinus as Salt continued outlining the order of march. The centurion stood straighter at the honor being bestowed. First Cohort represented the core of the legion, even with the recent addition of garrison legionaries. Stiger had made the decision to place them at the head of the line of march. If fighting broke out before the entirety of the legion could be deployed, it would fall to First to hold until reinforcement arrived. Stiger knew he could count on Sabinus for that. He was a very competent officer. From the look Sabinus gave him, he knew the centurion understood the same and what was being asked of him.

Turning his gaze back to the map, Stiger prayed he and Braddock had made the correct decision. For if the enemy did not attack his position, Stiger knew, he would be forced to attack theirs. And that would prove costly.

FIVE

The wind howled outside the shuttered window, rattling it occasionally. A fire crackled in the fireplace, once again the only light in his room. Stiger liked it that way, for he found it relaxing. Dog was stretched out on his side before the fire, soaking up the warmth, sleeping. It was late, sometime after midnight.

Stiger had spent the last few hours with his headquarters staff, making decisions and solving last-moment problems. He took a long pull on his pipe, enjoying the flavor of the tobacco and the warmth as he sucked it in. Taha'Leeth had departed with Eli a little over an hour before. Aver'Mons and Marcus had gone with them. They had a job to do, scouting the enemy's encampment.

Stiger had initially worried about Taha'Leeth's safety, then felt foolish. She was an elven ranger. The enemy would never know she was there, let alone Eli and the others. Deep down he knew he could not afford to burden himself with such concerns about her and the other rangers. He couldn't be so selfish. He was the legate of the Thirteenth Legion, and there were larger things at stake than the safety of one individual. Still, Stiger found himself worrying just the same.

Taha'Leeth had quickly come to fill a void in his life. Until he'd returned to his quarters, Stiger had not realized how much he missed her company. Despite the warmth of the fire, the room seemed somehow a little colder and less welcoming in her absence.

Taking another pull on the pipe, he shifted in the chair, making himself more comfortable. It had been a while since he had had any peace and quiet to enjoy a good pipe and with no company but his own thoughts. That was a rarity. He'd quickly discovered that Taha'Leeth frowned upon the habit, so he'd refrained from smoking in her presence.

He blew out a stream of smoke and glanced around the room. This would be his last comfortable evening for some time to come. Certainly, it would be weeks, if not months, before he slept in a bed again or, for that matter, enjoyed the comforts of a room with a fire. The best he could hope for was a tent with a cot. And even the cot would soon prove a luxury, for he had little doubt he would find times in the coming campaign where the best he could afford would be the ground and his arms for a pillow.

"It is what it is," Stiger said.

Dog opened an eye and looked his way. He closed it again and went back to sleep.

Braddock's army had already started marching, entering the dwarven underground that led to the Tol'Ket road. One unit after another, the dwarven and gnome army had started their movement over twenty hours before. The last of Braddock's army, like a great slithering snake, would march within the next few hours, opening the way for Stiger's legion and auxiliary cohorts to begin their movement.

With the majority of Braddock's army having moved, Stiger knew the advance cohorts of his own legion likely had already been woken and even now were preparing for their own movement. Undoubtedly, they were breaking down their camp, packing and checking gear. A hot meal would be served and precooked rations distributed. Then they would be off.

Stiger took a pull off his pipe and blew a long stream of smoke up into the air. Everything was in motion now. By sunset on the morrow, how many men would be dead or injured? How many maimed, crippled? He took another pull and then blew it out.

He was tired. The last few days had proven to be challenging. There had been so much to see to and do, the days had sped by in a blur. Despite his weariness and the early morning ahead, he was not ready for bed.

Ever since he had taken command of the Thirteenth, there had always been something that needed doing or some decision that had to be made, people waiting to see him. Only late at night, like this one, had Stiger come to appreciate the quiet, the silence, the uninterrupted peace.

There was a knock at the door.

Dog lifted his head and gave off a soft growl.

The knock came again, heavy and hard.

"Come," Stiger called, trying to keep the irritation he felt from his voice.

The door opened and one of his guards appeared. A draft of cold air flowed into the room like a strong breeze. Stiger suppressed a shiver.

"Sorry to bother you at such a late hour, sir," the guard said, sounding truly apologetic. "An elf is here to see you. He insisted, sir."

"I am no elf," came an irritated voice from the hallway.

Stiger well knew that voice. Dog's tail began wagging.

"It's all right," Stiger said, "send him in."

"Yes, sir." The guard stepped aside.

A moment later, Menos swept into the room. His black robe whispered across the floor. The noctalum glared at the guard as he passed, then paused as Dog gave a welcoming bark and bounded over to Menos, licking excitedly at the noctalum's hand.

Menos rubbed the top of dog's head. A trace of a smile appeared on his face as he gazed down on the animal. Dog's tail wagged even harder, shaking his entire body.

"You may leave us," Stiger said to the guard, who was standing in the doorway. "We're not to be disturbed."

"Yes, sir," the guard said. "I will see that no one bothers you, sir."

The guard closed the door.

"Don't you believe in more light?" Menos asked, glancing around the small room. "A lamp or candle perhaps? It's downright gloomy in here. I know elves can see in the dark pretty well, but you are human and your night vision is poor at best."

"The fire provides enough light for me," Stiger said. "Besides, I was just about to turn in for the night. I find it relaxing."

Without being invited, Menos sat down in the chair next to Stiger. Dog returned to his original position and laid down, stretching out before the fire.

"This seems rather humble for the legate of the Thirteenth and Champion of the High Father. Rather humble indeed."

"It suits my needs just fine." Stiger looked over at the noctalum, who had steepled his fingers over his chest and leaned back in his chair. The old chair creaked in protest.

Menos turned his gaze to the fire.

"Ogg lifted the memory block Thoggle put on you."

Stiger had figured that, at some point, the noctalum would seek him out, especially after his memory of the past had been restored. He had been looking forward to it and their reunion.

Menos pulled his gaze from the fire and gave Stiger a nod, which answered his question.

"It's about time," Stiger said and blew out another stream of smoke.

"Time," Menos said, "it's all about time, isn't it? That is the fire in which we burn."

Stiger gave a laugh and took another pull from his pipe. "That's a good one, really. It's only taken three hundred years, but your sense of humor is finally improving."

"It has been a long time." Menos paused. "My friend, a very long time."

"Not so long for me. It seems like I just left you and Thoggle a few days back."

"Well," Menos said, "thanks to Thoggle, I forgot to miss you. So, it really wasn't all that bad for me either."

Stiger gave a chuckle.

"Would you care for some wine? Venthus brought me a heated jar a short while ago. It should still be warm."

"That sounds good," Menos said. "Flying to the castle, though a short distance from the mountain, was not a comfortable experience. It is very cold out, and the winds up this high made it worse. I am not as young as I used to be. My bones feel the chill touch of winter more with each passing year."

"How old are you exactly?" Stiger stood and walked over to the desk, where the jar sat with an extra mug. "Older than that mountain, I'd hazard."

Menos spared Stiger an unhappy look before returning his gaze to the fire. "I'm not telling."

Stiger gave a grunt as he poured the noctalum a healthy portion of wine and handed it over. He returned to his seat. Menos sipped at the wine, seeming to savor the taste.

"You decided to keep Venthus, apparently," Menos said, not sounding too happy about that.

"In a manner of speaking. One could say it was the other way round," Stiger said. "I think he kept me."

"He's a slave," Menos said. "You are the master."

"Not much of a master. I think our relationship will remain the way it is as long as it suits him. I see no reason to rock that particular boat. Especially since we both know what he is. Do you disagree?"

Shaking his head once, Menos took another sip of wine. "I do not."

"How is Currose?"

"Gravely injured, but healing," Menos said. "It took much time, *Will*, and effort to help keep her from succumbing. Fighting both a minion of Castor and a wizard by yourself is not an easy undertaking, even for a noctalum. It is a wonder she survived the experience. I would be lost without her."

"I am pleased she will recover," Stiger said, wondering how long the two noctalum had been mated, how many thousands of years had passed.

Menos gave a simple nod. "Me as well. It will be some time before she is ready to rejoin the fight, many months, I think. Longer...maybe."

"I wish her a speedy recovery," Stiger said. He hoped she recovered sooner, for he was certain they would need all the help they could get in the weeks and months ahead.

"I will pass that along to her. She will appreciate your well wishes, even if they are from a human."

Stiger took another pull on his pipe and blew out a stream of smoke. "She never did take a shine to me."

"She believes you are a bad influence," Menos said. "Especially after Ka'Teg."

"All on account of what happened on that journey to see the elves?" Stiger asked. "She's still upset about that?"

Menos gave a shrug of his shoulders. "It was a close thing. We both almost died."

"You might have considered not telling her what happened, you know," Stiger said. "Did that thought ever occur to you?"

"I conceal nothing from my mate. Besides, it is hard to hide something like that…especially after a release of such energy and *Will*. She was able to sense that all the way back to the mountain." Menos waved a dismissive hand at Stiger. "That's ancient history now."

"Not so ancient for me," Stiger said, "or for Currose, apparently."

"My mate has a long memory," Menos said. "She does not easily forget. So, you are still a bad influence."

"Might I remind you it was your idea to stop to see that dormant volcano, not mine."

"I wanted to see the ruins of Ka'Teg, not the volcano."

"Same thing," Stiger said, "since those ruins were built on the slope of the volcano and you mentioned those hot springs. You wanted to take a—how did you put it? 'A relaxing dip,' I do think those were your very words."

It was Menos's turn to give a grunt.

"Those gnomes," Stiger said, "were plenty surprised when we dropped in on them and their religious ceremony."

"Yes, they were a little shaken." Menos looked suddenly uncomfortable.

"Shaken?" Stiger gave a laugh. "I think several fainted from shock alone."

"Who knew that bunch worshiped dragons," Menos said. "I have no idea on how that madness got started. I suppose gnomes just don't think like the other races."

"They wanted to keep you, oh great and magnificent God Dragon," Stiger said with amusement. "They almost succeeded too."

"It did not end well for them. Those gnomes were quite angry with us."

"In the making of our escape, we did kind of set off that volcano," Stiger said. "It destroyed their home and temple."

"Volcanoes will do that, you know," Menos said. "That was your idea, by the way, hence Currose seeing you as a bad influence. It's not everyone who goes around causing dormant volcanoes to blow their tops."

"I guess not," Stiger said and blew out a stream of smoke. "I could not have done it without your help."

"Of course not. The end result was certainly something to see."

"That is a bit of an understatement." Stiger paused a moment, looking over at the noctalum. "Think our gnomes know what happened and that it was us? The little bastards tend to hold grudges."

Menos was silent for a long moment. "I don't think our gnomes and those we encountered at Ka'Teg have contact. At least, I hope not. If they do, it could pose a problem, especially if they figure out it was us. Thank the gods this batch don't worship dragons."

Both fell into silence again.

"I hate to admit that the old wizard was right," Menos said, after a time. "Had I known what I know of our history together, there is a very good chance I might have acted differently when you first met me in the Gate room and inadvertently changed events to come."

"Likely true," Stiger said. "I know I would have."

"There are very few humans I've ever grown to like. Well, let's be honest…no one else really. You are the exception."

Stiger understood the truth of the statement. The two of them had been through a lot together. "I've missed our chats, my friend."

"Since I did not remember," Menos said, "it wasn't much of a problem. You cannot miss something you don't recall."

"I leave before dawn," Stiger said after another brief silence.

"I know," Menos said. "Braddock kept me informed of your plans. I could deal with that army out there, should you wish it. Make things a little easier for you."

"I had given it some serious thought," Stiger admitted, "but decided not to ask for your assistance in handling them."

"Why not?" Menos asked. "I would make short work of it and quickly scatter them to the winds."

"I have my reasons," Stiger said.

Menos turned his gaze from the fire. "You do not wish the enemy to know you have a pair of noctalum working with you, do you? You want to keep the Cyphan and Valoor's priests ignorant of that little fact, until you really need us."

"In truth, that was my main thinking on the matter. Braddock agrees too." Stiger was not at all surprised Menos had figured it out. "I fear the challenges ahead will be great. We will need every possible advantage just to succeed. Also, such an attack would surely scatter many thousands of the enemy out into the forest. One or two might make it back and report what they saw." Stiger paused. "I also don't want to have to worry about isolated bands of the enemy interdicting the road, preying upon my supply line to the point where I need to provide an armed escort, leaching my effective strength." Stiger shook his pipe at Menos. "I want to bag as many as I can. Besides, should you be agreeable, I have something far more important for you to do."

"More important?" Menos looked curious.

"I was going to ask you once I'd dealt with the enemy. It would mean leaving Currose for a period of time, if you can bear to do so. If she does not need you, that is."

"You want me to find out what's happening in the empire, where the legions are? Don't you?"

"That's right," Stiger said. "You can travel faster and farther than the elves can scout, and in a shorter time, too. I need to know where the fighting is, what the enemy is doing. I know nothing of what is going on out in the wider world, what other significant enemy forces are nearby. It might give us the edge in any fighting to come, and as it stands now, I am effectively blind. Would you do that for me, my friend?"

Menos was silent for several heartbeats. He took a sip of his wine before answering.

"It would mean leaving the World Gate undefended," Menos said. "Currose is not up to it. She is recovering in a deep thermal cavern."

"Ogg assures me that until the Gate is unlocked with the Key, it can't be operated again," Stiger said. "He says there are no other wizards with the required reserves of *Will* to even attempt opening it to a different time. I think the risk of leaving only the dwarven garrison in place more than worth it. So, will you do as I ask?"

Menos was silent for several heartbeats as he seemed to consider the request. "Though I do not like leaving Currose, I will."

"Thank you," Stiger said.

"Do not thank me yet." Menos's manner became grave. "There is something you need to know."

"What?"

"The sertalum," Menos said and took pull from his wine. The noctalum shook the mug slightly. "You know, this is really good wine."

"Sertalum? I don't know that word," Stiger said.

"The sertalum are the noctalum's sister race. There has long been one residing on this world. She is the enemy of my people."

"Of course she is." Stiger rubbed the back of his neck in frustration. "You did not think to mention this before now?"

"There was no need. She has been in hiding, waiting and watching," Menos said. "In truth, we, Currose and I, have an accommodation with her."

"You do?" Stiger was surprised by that. "What sort of an accommodation?"

"She does not bother us or interfere in what we do," Menos said, "and we don't hunt her down and kill her."

"And this sertalum is working with the Cyphan Confederacy?"

Menos shifted in his chair. "I am not sure."

"Then what is the problem?"

"Tixanu has left her lair," Menos said. "She is far to the west, well beyond the Great Steppe. She is on the move, traveling northward. Where she is going and why, I know not. I can sense her, just as she can sense us."

Stiger felt a cold sensation slither down his spine. "When you mean us, you mean you and Currose?"

"I mean all of us," Menos said. "Those with the *Will* to use it. You, me, Currose, Ogg to name a few. It was she whom your fool scout touched when he projected in the Gate room."

"Great," Stiger said. "Did Marcus wake her?"

"No, he did not. She's always been awake, watching, like us."

"In hindsight," Stiger said, "with all that's going on, don't you think it would have been better had you killed her when you had the chance?"

"Such an attempt would not have been so easy," Menos admitted. "The danger is truly great. In the process of taking her down, it could have seen the killing or maiming of me and my mate. It is why the sertalum and noctalum have historically avoided direct conflict. Such a thing might have been worse than blowing the top off that volcano. And you know how bad that was."

Stiger did not like that, not one bit.

"I take it you are telling me this for a reason?"

"Thoggle always thought you were limited," Menos said as he sipped at his wine. "I, on the other hand, thought you had some intelligence. It now seems that I was proven correct."

"Don't you think that's a little uncharitable?" Stiger said. "Unfair of you?"

"Unfair?" Menos shot Stiger a scowl. "Whatever do you mean? I was giving you a compliment."

"Thoggle is long dead," Stiger said. "You can no longer win arguments against him."

"Of course I can." Menos drained the last of his wine. He stood and barked out a harsh laugh. "I get the last word. I can win every argument now."

Stiger shook his head. "You will warn me if this Tixanu comes after us?"

"Now, sadly, I think I might have to reassess your intelligence level." Menos set the empty mug of wine on the table, next to the jar.

"Oh?"

"If I'm away scouting, how can I possibly tell you what she is up to or, more importantly, come to your aid? You can't have it both ways. Either I go or I stay. If I go, you may have to deal with her on your own, at least until I can return."

"That is just fantastic news, Menos," Stiger said, feeling intense frustration. "How do I deal with such a creature?"

"You do have a wizard available, and you are the High Father's Champion." Menos gave a shrug of his shoulders. "Figure it out."

"Figure it out?" Stiger asked.

"Then again, she might not be a bother," Menos said. "Tixanu is a powerful being in her own right. She may have her own purposes for leaving her lair."

"So, you are thinking it a coincidence? Are you seriously telling me that?"

"We don't know what her purpose is, yet," Menos said, "but no, I do not believe it a coincidence. She will involve herself in events, in some way or manner at some point. It might be she simply wants to get off this world herself or…"

"She might be working with the Cyphan," Stiger finished. "You always bring me the best news. You know that, right?"

Menos turned to leave, then stopped. He looked over at the sword, leaning against the wall next to the fireplace.

"It hasn't spoken to you?" Menos asked. "The sword…"

"It has not," Stiger confirmed. "I fear the wizard is now gone, the sword's power too. I sense nothing from it."

"Maybe, maybe not." Menos regarded the sword for another long moment before turning back. "Remember what I taught in the guarding of your mind. You must always be vigilant, prepared for another attempt by the wizard. Only time will tell if Rarokan is truly dead. We can both hope he is, but sometimes hope isn't enough. It is best to not underestimate any wizard, particularly a High Master."

Stiger gave a nod of agreement, then changed the subject. "I have a question for you. Perhaps you can help me with it?"

Menos raised delicate eyebrow. "If I am able, I will."

"Taha'Leeth told me I have changed," Stiger said. "She said I returned to this time more than I was… What exactly did she mean by that? I've felt a change…but…it could be just unlocking the potential within and accepting the mantle of Champion, my connection to the High Father."

Menos's gaze became piercing, and Stiger trailed off. The noctalum took a step closer and reached out a hand toward Stiger's face. Dog picked up his head and growled, a deep, menacing sound that made the small hairs on the back of Stiger's neck stand on end. Menos paused, looking over at Dog. He slowly withdrew his hand.

"Dog, down," Stiger said, surprised by both of their reactions. Dog immediately ceased his growling and lay back down, but the animal's gaze remained fixed upon the noctalum.

"I will not harm him," Menos assured Dog, then looked back to Stiger. "I had not considered the possibility of such a change. I will not attempt to probe your mind, for with the training I gave you, it would be difficult for me to do so. Perhaps even impossible, without destroying your mind in the process. I ask only that you permit me to touch your soul, your life force, the spark within. No harm or change will come of it. On that, you have my word."

"My soul?" Stiger asked suspiciously. "My spark? Why would you want that?"

Then, he suddenly became alarmed and stiffened, his eyes going toward the sword. Was that the reason the sword was no longer speaking to him? Had Rarokan's life force merged with his own? Oh, great gods, how he hoped not. Yet, in a way it all made sense. Had Rarokan inadvertently gotten what he had wanted, desired so badly? Was that long-dead wizard now a part Stiger's life force, his soul?

"Do you think I am Rarokan?" Stiger asked. "That...he is part of my soul, joined with me?"

"Why would you think that?" Menos asked, eyebrows drawing together. "Ah, I see...you drew that conclusion based off what happened when he attempted to seize control of your body. No, I do not believe a merging was ever possible. It was an all-or-nothing sort of thing. He would have taken your body and you would have been imprisoned within the sword."

Stiger let out a relieved breath and relaxed a little. "Then what is it?"

"I think, and it is only one possibility," Menos said, hesitantly, "that when you killed the wyrm with the sword, something of its essence, its spark, was absorbed by you." Menos shook a finger at him. "Perhaps even a part of the life force of all the beings Rarokan stole over the centuries, with the wyrm's portion being the mightiest. That may have been what passed on to you, merging with your soul, adding to your life force, your spark, if you will."

"How is that possible?" Stiger was concerned that he had some evil in him now, for wyrms were dark creatures that served vile gods. He was horrified by even the possibility. "Am I contaminated?"

"Of course not." Menos waved a hand, as if to dismiss the idea. "This is something very different. It has nothing to do with corruption."

"How so?"

"The aratalum, the wyrms, are ancient beings. They are almost as old as my race. Though no more intelligent than a horse and easily controlled, they are still powerful creatures. Their spark is quite strong. As such, they have very long lifespans, almost as long as their cousins, the taltalum."

"Taltalum? Another race of dragons?"

Menos scowled slightly. "A simple way of looking at it, but not an entirely incorrect one."

Stiger wondered how many different types of dragons were out there.

"Are there taltalum on this world?" Stiger had a feeling that there were.

"There are," Menos confirmed. "They live with the Vass."

"The Vass? You're just bringing me all kinds of fantastic news," Stiger said, wondering what or who the Vass were. "Will they want the Key and the Gate too? Do you save up all the bad news and then ration it out when you want to?"

"Not to fear," Menos said, holding up a hand. "The taltalum will not work with our enemies."

"Are you certain?" Stiger asked.

"Fairly certain." Menos gave a shrug of his shoulders. "They should not interfere with us. They live across the Eastern Ocean."

"There is land across the ocean?"

"Ignorant human," Menos scoffed. "How little you know of your own world. Did you think it was all ocean? There are lands almost as vast as those on this side of the world." Menos paused. "One day, when there is time and this business is all behind us, I might take you there, just to show you and help you expand your mind. Perhaps then you will understand how truly large a single world can be."

"So, they won't bother us, then," Stiger said, shaking his head slightly at the thought of unknown lands.

"I said they won't work with our enemies," Menos said. "The Vass and taltalum will do their own thing. Though I believe they will not interfere or, more correctly, should not. The Vass sought this world as a refuge from the Last War. But sometimes there is no telling with them, or reasoning. They do their own thing for reasons wholly their own. Sometimes it's not easy to figure out what those reasons are. When we fled Tanis, they worked with us. So, I think the likelihood of them working to counter our purposes small."

"They were allies at one time, then?"

"Of a sort," Menos said. "As I said, the Vass do their own thing."

"Do you think they might help us?"

"That," Menos said, "I do not know. To even reach them would require weeks of travel. The journey would be a long one, and dangerous too. I would not want to make it alone. And the Vass might not welcome me. They left…shall we say…unhappy with Currose and me…deeply unhappy."

Stiger shook his head in disbelief and then pushed his concerns about the Vass and more dragons aside. He had enough problems as it was. He turned his thinking to how he'd been changed. Stiger needed answers on that. He looked back at Menos after several heartbeats. "What about the wyrm's essence, the spark? Wouldn't it have left me, as I was dying? Before Father Thomas brought me back? Everything, it seemed, was being sucked out of me. Castor's pull was just too strong."

"When Father Thomas brought you back from the edge," Menos said, "he brought all of you back, not just some." Menos looked down at his hand and then back to Stiger. His eyes narrowed. "I will not hurt, nor harm, you. But I must be sure of my suspicions. May I proceed?"

Stiger glanced over at Dog, who was still staring intently at Menos. The animal had not relaxed and looked ready to jump to the attack.

"We are friends, yes?" Menos asked Stiger.

"We are friends."

"Then trust me in this," Menos said. "Noctalum have always been a curious race. Before the Last War, we sought only knowledge and the betterment of our people. That curiosity still burns through me like a raging fire. I have a suspicion that something profound is at work here, with you. Please, I ask you again to trust me in this. I must know."

The last sounded almost like pleading. Stiger hesitated a moment more, then gave a reluctant nod.

Menos looked over at Dog. "I also ask for your trust too, naverum. Do I have your permission to proceed?"

Dog gave a soft whine and then lowered his head to the floor, placing it between his paws. The tension seemed to go out of the animal.

Menos turned back to Stiger. "It will only take but a moment."

"Do it," Stiger said, wondering if there would be any pain.

Menos took a hesitant step forward and then another more resolved one, until he was standing directly in front of Stiger's chair. Oddly, Stiger noticed that the pipe had gone out.

Menos reached forward and touched Stiger's forehead with the palm of his hand. It wasn't painful, but he felt a funny tingling, like what he used to feel when he touched the sword. It raced through him and then was gone. A heartbeat later, Menos removed his hand. The noctalum took a stumbling half step backward, eyes almost impossibly wide and fixated directly upon Stiger.

"What is it?" Stiger asked.

Menos did not answer but continued to stare at Stiger with eyes that spoke of intense shock and perhaps even awe.

"What is it?" Stiger asked, becoming alarmed. "Tell me."

"This has not happened for an age," Menos said, in a near whisper. The noctalum started to speak, stopped, and started again. "I do not know if it was the gods or your encounter with the wyrm, but the elf is right. Who you were...are...has changed."

"Changed?" Stiger's alarm increased to new levels. "Changed how?"

"You are something...how do I put this? You are something new, essentially no longer completely human. New is the only way I can describe it. Your life force has been completely changed, altered. You may be the first of a new race, beings with power and the *Will* to use it."

"What?" Stiger almost yelled as he stood, feeling panicked. He could not believe what he was hearing. "I am no longer human? How can that be? I am just as human as the guards outside the door."

"Not anymore."

Stiger held both hands up before his face. Nothing about them had changed. He looked the same.

"You are more than you were," Menos said, shaking his head in disbelief. "I have only seen this once before, during the Age of Wonders. The gods directly intervened. I was honored to witness the creation of a new race, what all thought to be the last of us."

"I don't believe it," Stiger breathed.

"Though we were commanded to leave that world shortly after the deed had been done," Menos continued, as if he'd not heard Stiger, "it was a wondrous thing to see. To this day, I feel blessed." The noctalum fell silent a moment and then spoke the next in a whisper. "Now, I have witnessed such a miracle twice."

Stiger was rocked to his core by what Menos was telling him. He couldn't believe it. Sure, he felt a little different, but he was still human. Menos must be wrong. It was almost impossible to believe, and yet something deep inside told him it was all true. No matter how much he wanted to disbelieve, the noctalum was not lying. Something within him had changed and was still changing. He could not deny it. He sucked in a shuddering breath and then blew it out, feeling thoroughly ragged and worn.

"How did Taha'Leeth know of this?" Menos's eyes had narrowed suspiciously.

"I do not know," Stiger admitted.

Menos took another step back. His hand went to his mouth and he became ashen. He pointed a finger at Stiger. "She has taken you as her mate, hasn't she?"

It was not a question, but a statement.

"Lover would be more accurate," Stiger said.

"With elves," Menos said, "such distinctions are not always so simple. She is bonding with you. The gods must have had a hand in bringing you both together."

Stiger felt the color drain from his face. He remembered what she'd told him about Tanithe. The god had shown her a vision of him years before Stiger had even been born. Stiger's eyes went to the sword. Had the High Father and Tanithe been working together toward a common purpose? Had they intended this to happen? They must have.

"You both have been blessed," Menos said, "blessed beyond imagining."

Stiger did not know what to say. What could he say? He was already something different, something not quite human. And yet, he still felt human. What was different other than his connection with the High Father? The great god's power within him? The ability to heal quicker? What else was there?

"Of course, I could be wrong," Menos said.

"Oh really?" Stiger spat sarcastically. "Thoggle would roll over in his tomb were that to happen and you actually admit it."

"He might…but I do not think I am wrong," Menos said. "You are more than you were, and if I'm correct, then you have been greatly honored by the gods."

"It does not feel that way," Stiger said. "I feel like I was just hit by a runaway supply cart or perhaps gut-kicked by a mule."

Menos chuckled at that. "You are lucky, Champion of the High Father. Some are only blessed. Others are given nothing but their lives. You, on the other hand, have been endowed with so much more. Do not fret, do not worry about it, for there is no point. Feel honored and give thanks for your many blessings."

"Give thanks?" Stiger scoffed. "I never wanted this. I did not ask for it."

"No, you did not," Menos said and took two steps backward. "But your thanks are still in order."

Menos moved toward the door and gripped the handle. He looked back.

"I will do as you have asked. I will find you somewhere along your line of march. Until then, my friend…I bid you well."

Menos opened the door.

"Safe travels and thank you," Stiger said, feeling numb.

The noctalum gave a nod, hesitated a moment more, then stepped through and closed the door behind him. Stiger moved over to his desk and refilled his wine. He drained it in one swallow, wishing it were made of stronger stuff. He refilled the mug again and sat back down in the chair. He gazed into the flames of the fire, stunned almost beyond belief.

"I am something new," Stiger said after a time, still feeling like his world had been rocked, and terribly so. He knew there would be no sleep tonight, even if he tried. "What am I becoming? High Father…what have you done to me?"

There was no answer.

Dog stood, shook himself, ears flapping loudly. The animal padded up to Stiger and placed his head on Stiger's lap. Dog gave a soft whine. Stiger looked down on the animal. Dog looked back up at him with sad, watery eyes.

"Is that why you are here?" Stiger asked. "Is that the reason you were sent?"

Dog did not say anything.

"Because I have been so blessed?" Stiger pressed. "Because I am something new?"

Dog's tail wagged and he gave a clipped bark, as if in confirmation. He nudged Stiger's hand with his muzzle. Stiger reached out and began scratching the animal's head. Dog closed his eyes, in apparent bliss.

"Either way," Stiger said, "I'm glad you are here."

The animal's tail continued to wag and his eyes opened.

"I may have changed somehow," Stiger said, "but I am still me. My work is not complete. I have a job to do, and by the gods, I will do it."

Dog began wagging his tail more vigorously, as if he approved.

"You still need a bath," Stiger said, wrinkling his nose. "You stink."

Dog gave an unhappy whine and the tail ceased its wagging.

"Well," Stiger said, with a dark chuckle, "you have a reprieve on bathing, for tomorrow the legion marches and the campaign begins."

Six

With Dog padding along at his side, Stiger turned a corner in the hallway. Ahead, two guards standing before an open doorway at the end of the hallway snapped to attention. Stiger could see beyond them into his headquarters. As usual, it was a bustling hive of activity. A jumble of voices spilled out into the hallway, echoing off its stone walls.

A messenger, dispatch in hand, stepped out into the hallway, spotted Stiger, and immediately stood aside. He pulled himself to a position of attention and saluted.

Stiger stepped by him and the two guards to enter the legion's headquarters.

Headquarters was in a large room. Six oversized rectangular tables had been dragged in for the clerks. Stacks of tablets, parchment, and vellum rested on the tables in orderly rows before the clerks.

Hanging from the ceiling, oil lamps provided much of the light. There were also three big iron candelabras set against the walls, each with four fat tallow candles. A fireplace set into the far wall had a good-sized blaze going. With all the bodies and the fire, the room was hot, almost uncomfortably so. It stank strongly of smoke, oil, tallow, ink, and sweat.

There were more than two dozen present. Six of those were his clerks. Most of the others were messengers, who were standing to the sides of the room, waiting for dispatches or orders that needed delivering. Several, in a huddle, had been speaking amongst themselves. A pair of junior centurions were bent over a table, studying a map. Salt was there too, near the fireplace, speaking with one of the clerks.

The camp prefect looked tired and worn. Stiger suspected Salt had not managed any sleep either. Though unlike Stiger, he had likely worked through the night, overseeing the departure of the legion and ensuring everything went as smoothly as possible.

Stiger made his way deeper into the room, toward Salt. Dog padded over to Nepturus and promptly received a treat. Nepturus always kept something handy for the animal and Dog well knew it.

The clerk, Alanus, with whom Salt was speaking, excused himself and moved away as Stiger stepped up.

"Ready to depart, sir?" Salt asked.

"Almost," Stiger said. "I wanted to check in before I set out."

"Of course, sir," Salt said and gestured over to a jar sitting on the table next to him. A half-full mug sat next to the jar. A small map was spread out on the same table. "Would you care for some coffee, sir? It's cold, but I can find an extra mug."

"No thank you," Stiger said. "I won't be staying that long. I have to get on the road."

"To business then," Salt said. "I assume you would like an update on the progress of the legion?"

"I would," Stiger said, "very much so."

Salt picked up a wax tablet from the table, studied it a moment, and then set it back down. "The cavalry is obviously away, having marched with Braddock's army. First through Sixth Cohorts have also marched. Within the hour, the rest of the cohorts will begin stepping off. After that, the auxiliaries will start their movement."

"Any problems so far?"

"We've only had a handful of issues, which slowed the march of individual cohorts some. Nothing really worth mentioning." Salt blew out a weary breath. "Honestly, sir, I've never seen a legion march without something or other holding things up at some point. We're just a little behind schedule, is all." The camp prefect paused for a heartbeat. "Still, it's better than I'd hoped, sir."

"And the artillery?" Stiger asked, understanding the truth of the prefect's statement. No matter how well one planned, nothing ever went smoothly. It was a fact of life with the army.

"The artillery is ready to go, sir," Salt said. "I've taken the liberty of assigning extra men, stripping Tenth Cohort of about half her strength to help make certain their movement proceeds as well as can be expected. I also ordered the bolt throwers moved to the van of the artillery train. I hope you don't mind, sir, but you may find you have need of them on the defensive line, sooner rather than later. I think they might just come in handy."

Stiger gave it some thought and then decided Salt had made the correct decision. He had assumed that the enemy would strike him well before he could get his artillery up. Chances were, though, he'd need the bolt throwers, especially considering he wanted the enemy to assault his position and their numbers exceeded his.

Unlike the bolt throwers, the heavier stone throwers had been almost completely disassembled for their movement through the dwarven underground. They would require significant time to move, position, and then reassemble. Stiger very much doubted they would be ready for action when the fighting began, let alone in position. Then again, if his enemy hesitated, who knew how much time he would have to prepare. Salt's last-minute effort might end up paying off.

"Good thinking." Stiger glanced around, scanning the room. "Where's Ikely? I don't see Severus either. I had expected one of them to be present."

"Both are with the supply train, sir," Salt said and then cleared his throat. "The train, as you know, will move after the artillery. I strongly encouraged them both to be there, not only to make certain that someone senior was on hand to smooth out any difficulties with the teamsters, but also to get a sense of what it's like. I felt it might be good for them to see and direct a supply train personally, at least in the beginning, sir. That way, they will have a more realistic expectation of what can and can't be done. Hopefully, the experience will pay dividends in the weeks and months ahead."

"Such hands-on experience can only help," Stiger agreed, wishing he had thought of it himself. The farther they marched from Vrell, the longer their supply line would become and the more dependent upon Ikely the army would become. Stiger worried that, at some point, the enemy might cut the army's supply. What would happen then?

"And when will you be leaving, Salt?"

It was Salt's turn to glance around the room. "I had planned to leave with the last auxiliary cohort, sir. Headquarters will pack up after that. As you are aware, sir, your battlefield headquarters staff has already moved, marching with First Cohort. Sabinus will see they get set up in a good spot."

Stiger gave a nod. He expected no less from his senior centurion. "You seem to have everything well in hand here. Good work."

"Thank you, sir," Salt said, with no hint that he was pleased with the praise.

"Excuse me, sir." Stiger's lead clerk, Nepturus, stepped up to the two of them. He held out a dispatch. "This just came in for you, sir. It's from the dwarves."

Stiger took the dispatch and opened it. Nepturus retreated to the table where he worked by the fire. Stiger saw that the dispatch was from Braddock and it had been written in the common tongue, likely drafted by one of the thane's aides. He read through it.

"And how are our allies doing, sir?" Salt asked with mild interest.

"Well enough, it seems," Stiger said as he set the dispatch down on the table. "The dwarves are reporting no difficulty so far. The majority of Braddock's army is well on their way. Braddock expects to have his lead infantry units out of the underground and on the Vrell road in about a week and a half's time, the cavalry sooner, of course."

"That is good news, sir," Salt said simply and glanced over at the map that was laid out on the table to his right. He moved over to it and gave a low whistle. "The thane is pushing his boys hard, then. We had planned for that in maybe a fortnight, at best."

"Braddock's blood oath has motivated him and every other dwarf to get to the Cyphan," Stiger said. "Their Legend demands vengeance for what the Cyphan did to their kin. They may be a little overeager to settle that debt."

Privately, Stiger worried over the dwarves' eagerness to get at their sworn enemy. Though Braddock had assured him the affairs of the World Gate came first, he considered that at some point he might just have to intervene to check their bloodlust and keep them focused on what needed to be done. Revenge could be settled afterwards.

"Overeager or not, sir, it's a long road," Salt said, running his finger along the length, traveling eastward. "At some point he will need to slow his pace some, or his infantry won't be worth a damn when they emerge from the forest."

"No doubt," Stiger said. "You don't need to tell me. I about pushed my company to the limits on the Vrell road."

"Sorry to bother you, sir." Alanus had come up.

"Yes?" Stiger turned. "What is it?"

"Centurion Pansa Ruga is here to see you, sir," Alanus said. "He mentioned that you asked him to stop by headquarters, first thing."

"He showed up a couple of hours ago," Salt said meaningfully and gestured toward the door to what had come to be called the waiting room, a small antechamber by the entrance. It had likely once been a storeroom, at least until Nepturus had cleaned it out and placed several stools inside.

Stiger looked over and saw the centurion standing in the doorway to the waiting room, gazing his way. Ruga appeared just as Stiger remembered him, tough and confident, hard as chiseled stone. Stiger motioned the man over with a wave.

"Thank you," Stiger said to his clerk, and with that, Alanus stepped away.

"Reporting as ordered, sir," Ruga said, snapping to attention. He offered a crisp salute.

"Is your century assembled and waiting?" Stiger asked.

Ruga was from Vargus's valley cohort. Stiger liked the centurion. He'd personally seen him lead his century in the action in Forkham's Valley against the orcs. It had left Stiger impressed with his command and fighting abilities. He was a tough, unflappable bastard. Just how the legions liked their officers.

"They are, sir," Ruga said. "As ordered, I have them cooling their heels in the courtyard. Though, if I am to be honest, sir, I would have preferred to march with my cohort. It doesn't sit right, being left behind and all."

"I understand." Stiger appreciated Ruga's honesty. When he'd taken command of the legion, there had been several who had looked to curry favor through flattery and other means. Stiger intensely despised the sandal-lickers, like General Kromen's aide, Captain Handi. He always had. In Stiger's mind, such behavior was toxic to the efficient functioning of the legion. The sandal-lickers added nothing of value other than to soothe a commander's ego.

So, he had strongly discouraged the behavior, encouraging and supporting those who spoke honesty. It had taken some time and an example or two, but his officer corps rapidly got the message and conformed to his expectations.

Ruga, having come from this time, had likely not heard how Stiger preferred to be treated. That made such honesty from the centurion all the more refreshing.

"Centurion," Salt said, having clearly become irritated, "I don't like your tone."

Stiger held up a hand to restrain his camp prefect.

"Sorry, sir," Ruga said to Stiger, not sounding as if he truly meant it. "I've never been the tactful type. I think you know that. My boys and I just want in on the coming action, is all, sir." He paused and glanced around at the headquarters staff a bit sourly. "But it seems like you want us to sit this one out with some babysitting, or perhaps helping this bunch move...so manual labor, then. Do I have that right, sir?"

Despite the near insubordination, Stiger found himself terribly amused. It was a struggle to keep it from his face. He well understood the centurion's sentiment. Were their positions reversed, Stiger would not want to babysit either.

"I have a job that needs doing and I won't lie to you, Centurion," Stiger said, with a glance over at his camp prefect. "You will be babysitting. From this point onward, you and your century are officially detached from Second Cohort. At least, until I say otherwise. Is that understood?"

"Yes, sir," Ruga said, looking none too happy.

"Ruga," Stiger said, "you're in command of my personal bodyguard."

The centurion at first looked like he was going to protest, then his eyes widened slightly as realization hit home. He blinked several times. To be placed in command of a legate's personal guard was one of the highest honors within the legion. With it would come bragging rights, the best food, and other perks, including being exempted from regular duties like setting up the marching encampment.

"My century is to be your guard, sir?" Ruga asked to clarify, as if he'd not quite heard correctly.

"Yes, that's right," Stiger said.

"Yes, sir, very good, sir," Ruga said, recovering and straightening his back a little. The look of surprise faded, as if it had never been. It was hidden behind a carefully crafted mask that all professional soldiers learned to project to superiors. "On second thought, sir, babysitting doesn't sound all that bad, sir. Not that you need babysitting, sir. Thank you for thinking of us. You won't be disappointed, sir."

"Centurion," Salt said, with a hard edge to his tone, "we don't know each other."

"No, sir," Ruga said, "we do not."

"The legate here speaks highly of you," Salt said. "I would rather have assigned proven veterans from the Thirteenth, but Legate Stiger decided on you. Why? I don't know. I trust and I hope he has not misplaced his faith in your abilities or your men."

"He has not, sir," Ruga said and his face colored slightly as he took umbrage at the camp prefect's words, though his tone remained neutral. "My boys are the best, sir."

"We'll see," Salt said. "I expect you to do your utmost to keep the legate safe and out of trouble. I want your word on that, your personal guarantee you will keep him safe."

Ruga did not immediately reply. His eyes went from Salt to Stiger, shrewdly appraising his legate. The flush of heat drained from Ruga's cheeks.

"Well?" Salt demanded.

"I can't and won't promise, sir," Ruga said. "However, I will try, sir."

"Try?" Salt seemed surprised by the answer and his face hardened. "That doesn't exactly fill me with confidence, Centurion."

"It wasn't meant to, sir," Ruga said. "From what I understand of the legate, he tends to put himself in dangerous situations. Like any good officer, he prefers to set the example for others to follow. So, with that in mind, all I can promise is that me and my boys will do our best, sir, to keep him alive, sir. If that is unacceptable, there is an entire legion of centuries to pick from, sir, to replace us, that is."

Salt blinked, and his lips twitched with amusement at the suggestion. Stiger thought it was damn good answer. It was all he could do to keep from laughing.

"Seems he knows you quite well, sir," Salt said.

Stiger gave a grunt. He'd grown tired of the game. It was time to move things along. "Centurion, I will be down in the courtyard shortly. My manservant, Venthus, should have sent my pack and kit down to the stables. Would you see that my horse is brought out and saddled and my gear loaded?"

"I will, sir." Ruga saluted. "My century will be ready to march just as soon as you arrive, sir."

"Excellent," Stiger said.

"Thank you again for the honor of guarding your person, sir." Ruga saluted, spun on his heel, and marched out of headquarters, as if he were on parade.

"He's a cheeky bastard, that one," Salt said. "I like him, but I do not know him."

"I've seen him in action," Stiger said. "He will do. Besides, his century is badly understrength, but still with sufficient manpower to act as a personal bodyguard for me." Stiger blew out a breath. "I'd rather not strip more men from the fighting formations than needed. For soon we will need every sword."

"Agreed," Salt said.

"Excuse me, sir." Nepturus approached. "A Sergeant Arnold is here to see you, sir. If you are busy, I could send him away."

Stiger glanced over to the doorway to the hall and saw a nervous-looking Arnold standing there, gazing in their direction. He looked a bit unsure of himself. Stiger blew out an unhappy breath. He had planned to make some time for the sergeant, but with all that needed doing, it simply hadn't happened. He turned back to Salt.

"I have business to attend to with Arnold," Stiger said. "I will see you when we bring the legion back together in the forest."

"Yes, sir," Salt said. "Good luck, sir."

Stiger gave a nod and stepped away. He moved over toward Arnold. The grizzled old sergeant snapped to attention as Stiger approached. Arnold looked clean, was freshly shaved, and his armor had been meticulously detailed. He was almost presentable, but there was still a disagreeable or roguish look about him.

Stiger thought back to when he'd first met the rebellious and uncouth sergeant. Arnold had been placed in charge of the teamsters for the supply train to Vrell. He'd been quick to anger and ill-tempered. Arnold had also been difficult to work with. Since then, Stiger reflected, the man had come a long way.

Stiger could feel something was different about Arnold, and it wasn't simply his outward appearance. The feeling was strong, palpable. Stiger almost missed a step as he neared.

In the last few years, Stiger had become more sensitive to power, what Menos, Thoggle, and Ogg called *Will*. Under Menos's tutelage, he'd become more attuned to it. As a result, he could sense a power growing within Arnold that was eerily similar to his own.

That told Stiger the man's future did not belong with the legion. Arnold had a different path to walk, even if he had not yet come to fully realize that himself. But it was why he was here. Stiger was sure of it. The High Father had guided his steps to Stiger for a reason.

"Nepturus?" Stiger called, turning to look back.

"Sir?" Nepturus asked, standing from where he'd been seated before a table. He held a stylus in his ink-stained hands.

"I am departing," Stiger informed the clerk. "Nothing has changed since last night. You have your orders. Do you have any questions?"

"No, sir," Nepturus said. "The orders were plenty clear."

"Very good," Stiger said. "Carry on then."

"Yes, sir," Nepturus said. "Good luck, sir."

Stiger turned back to the sergeant and eyed him for a long moment.

"Walk with me, will you?" Stiger asked. It was not an outright command, but coming from the legate of the legion, a request always was an order. Stiger knew with utter certainty this would be the last order he would ever give Arnold.

"Yes, sir," Arnold said, rather nervously.

"Dog, come."

Stiger led the sergeant out into the hallway. Dog padded along behind them. The guards snapped to attention as they passed. Stiger continued down the hallway a ways before coming to a stop. He judged they were far enough from the prying ears of the guards to easily overhear what was about to be said. Stiger wanted this conversation private. He faced the sergeant. The hallway was cold, heavily shadowed, and drafty. Oil lamps had been set into mirrored recesses in the walls every ten feet, but they weren't enough to provide much light.

"Effective immediately," Stiger said, "you are released from service with the legion."

"What?" As plain as day, Stiger could read the horror in the other man's eyes. "I ain't no longer a legionary, sir?" Arnold put a hand to his mouth and rubbed his jaw. "Blessed gods…"

Arnold had surely spent his entire adult life with the legions. He knew nothing else. Until Father Thomas had seen something in him, Arnold had been just another disabled legionary. Years prior, he had taken a near-crippling wound to the knee.

Some officer had apparently taken pity upon him, likely for an act of bravery or the man's past service. Rather than being discharged to fend for himself on a partial pension, he had been assigned to supply. Stiger was sure Arnold had turned to drink and worse to drown his sorrows at his misfortune.

Father Thomas had brought Arnold back from that dark place. Seeing something in the man Stiger had not, the paladin had taken him under his wing. Father Thomas had even healed Arnold's bum knee. In response, the man had turned to the High Father like a duck to water and with a surprising vigor. Even now, Stiger noted, he held the High Father's holy book in one hand.

"You're no longer subject to my orders," Stiger said, softening his tone. "I think, perhaps, if you look within, you will know the why of it."

Arnold was silent a long moment. He continued absently rubbing his freshly shaven jaw. His gaze became distant. "This may sound strange, sir, but for some time I've...I dunno if I can explain..." Arnold fell silent, seemingly uncomfortable with continuing.

"Go on," Stiger urged.

"I've felt the High Father's touch, here in me chest, sir." Arnold placed the palm of his hand upon his armor, above his heart, and his voice became a near whisper. "I can feel it burning. Each day, it seems to grow a little stronger. If I close my eyes, I can all but see it."

Stiger understood exactly what Arnold was talking about. He felt the same himself. It was like a little white fire within, only it did not burn...but soothed. When Stiger mentally reached out to touch it, he felt a peaceful calm settle over him. He had come to understand it was his connection with the High Father. Though frustratingly, he did not fully understand how to use that connection or the power he'd been given. The few times he had used it had been sort of accidental. He'd been unable to reproduce it.

"That is why I am releasing you," Stiger said after a long moment. "I can sense the change within you. You've accepted the High Father and he has judged you worthy...more than worthy. I think it is safe to say you have been blessed."

"Me?" Arnold seemed surprised that anyone would consider him worthy, let alone the High Father. It was almost as if he'd never considered the possibility of it happening. "That cannot be, sir."

"You have devoted yourself to his teachings. Is that not correct?"

"I have, sir."

"I'm not an exactly an expert in these matters," Stiger said, "by any means. I am rather new to it myself. However, I suspect the High Father has plans of his own for you. It is quite possible...you will become a holy warrior in his service."

Even as he said it, even without Father Thomas present, Stiger understood he was speaking truth. How he knew, he could not say. He just did. The words felt right.

"A paladin? Me? Heck, sir, I'm a wretched sinner. I'd make a bloody poor paladin." Arnold scoffed and then remembered to whom he was speaking. "Sorry, sir."

Stiger recalled what Father Thomas had told him of his own youthful sins and how he'd changed as a person by accepting the High Father into his life.

"You may have to atone for your sins," Stiger said, "but it seems the High Father has plans for you just the same."

"That's kind of you to say, sir," Arnold said, sounding far from convinced. "However, I find that hard to believe."

"Regardless," Stiger said, "as the High Father's Champion, that is how I see it. I think you need to give this some thought, prayer even. Search for meaning from within and figure out what the High Father desires of you."

Arnold was staring at him now. The realization of what Stiger was saying began to sink in.

"I can't promise the path ahead will be an easy one, but it is yours to follow and yours alone. No one can walk that road but you, even as I walk my own, and mine has been plenty hard. Understand?"

Arnold was silent for several heartbeats, then he gave a slight nod. "It's something to think on, sir."

"Good," Stiger said and clapped the sergeant on the arm. "I would take it as a personal honor if you would stay with me, attaching yourself to my headquarters."

"Your headquarters, sir?" Arnold shifted uncomfortably. The former sergeant glanced back down the hall. "I'm not headquarters material, sir."

"No one is. That said, you are your own master, or really, the High Father is your master. Should you feel the call to go, you are free to do so."

That too also felt right to Stiger. Paladins came and went at the whim of the High Father's direction.

"Call, sir?" Arnold's brow furrowed.

"A pull or nudge," Stiger said. "You will know it, when it happens."

"If you say so, sir," Arnold said, sounding dubious, then hesitated. "About Father Thomas?"

Stiger had a sudden wash of sorrow overcome him. He cleared his throat. "He passed from this world. I...I owe him my life."

Grief spread across Arnold's face and his eyes watered slightly. "I was afraid it was true, sir, what I heard as rumor and such. Father Thomas was a good man, sir, a damn fine man. He saved me too. You see, I'd lost all respect for myself, sir. He gave it back."

"He was the best of men," Stiger agreed, then considered Arnold for a long moment. "It was always there within you…you just rediscovered your self-respect, is all. Honor his memory by serving others, just as he did. That would be a fine tribute, I think."

Arnold fell silent for several heartbeats. He glanced down at the stone floor. "I don't ever think I can do the man right, for what he done for me, sir."

"It's too early to tell," Stiger said, "and your journey is just beginning. That said, I can think of no greater role model for you than Father Thomas."

"Yes, sir," Arnold said. "Neither can I."

"Now," Stiger said, "go back to headquarters. Find Nepturus, my head clerk. You tell him to issue you a horse, kit, and some precooked rations, enough for a week. You can catch up with me later tonight, and if there is time, we will talk more."

"A horse, sir?" Arnold seemed confused by that. "I ain't no good with horses. Mules yes, but horses no."

"You're in the service of the High Father now," Stiger said. "Should he call you away, a horse might come in handy. Don't you think?"

Arnold seemed doubtful of that. "I'm not partial to horses, sir. I'd prefer a mule, sir."

"A horse," Stiger said. "The mules are needed for the supply trains. The messengers can do with one less mount."

"Well, they don't like me much, but I understand, sir. Thank you, sir."

With that, Stiger spared Arnold a final look, before he turned away, moving toward the stairs. It was time to put Castle Vrell behind him.

"Dog, come."

SEVEN

Marching a few yards to Stiger's front, in a column of two abreast, Seventh Cohort came to a shuffling halt. The sound of thousands of hobnailed sandals and voices reverberated off the walls of the underground road. Along with the constant starting and stopping, it was beginning to give him a headache.

Needing a break from riding, Stiger slid off Nomad. His hobnailed boots slapped onto the hard stone of the dwarven road. He took a moment to stretch out his back and then glanced around.

Dog was nowhere to be seen. He'd disappeared an hour before, racing ahead along the line of march. Apparently the repeated starting and stopping had bothered him as well. Where Dog was off to, Stiger had no idea. He was not worried though. When he was ready, Dog would return. He always did.

The Tol'Tabor was far from the largest dwarven road Stiger had ever seen. In fact, it was on the smaller side, and considerably so. Every few yards, numerous dark and forbidding shafts and side passages ran off its length. The dwarves had advised in the strongest terms possible that these ancient side passages not be explored, for they were very unsafe.

The ceiling of the road was also low, rounded at the top and lined with ancient brick that had been turned almost black with age and mold. By the thousands, small knife-sized stalactites hung from the ceiling, as if inching their way toward the ground. The road smelled unpleasantly of dampness, mold, and decay. It tickled at the nose.

To light the way, each cohort had been forced to bring torches and lanterns with them. Shadows flickered and played madly across the walls. There was none of the magical lighting he had seen on other more prominent dwarven roads.

A pair of wagon tracks had been worn into the stone that ran along the road's length. This led Stiger to believe the Tol'Tabor had not originally been intended for travel. Its purpose had clearly been for mining and hauling ore.

He had once been given a tour of an active dwarven mine. He'd seen similar tracks worn into the stone, along with the heavy wagons that hauled the ore. Their iron-rimmed wheels had, over countless years, made such tracks.

Ahead, in the distance, the glimmer of daylight beckoned. It seemed tantalizingly close. They were nearing the exit of this subterranean world of darkness and flickering shadow. The journey had taken a little over five hours. It should have been quicker, and that frustrated Stiger, but there was nothing to be done to speed things up.

The delay was primarily due to the stop-and-go nature of the legion's movement, as units farther along in the column of march, for whatever reason, came to a brief stop and then after a few moments started forward once again. Despite having allowed a half hour separation between cohorts, the legion still managed to stack up.

Stiger wanted nothing more than to ride ahead. He was itching to do it. And as legate, he had the option of doing just that, making his way forward. Instead, he restrained his frustration and waited behind the tail end of Seventh Cohort.

Sabinus had operational and tactical command of the legion, as First Cohort would be the first from the underground. The senior centurion was one of his most seasoned officers, and Stiger had long since learned to put his faith in such men.

Besides, Stiger understood nothing was likely to happen for several hours yet. Even if the enemy became aware of First Cohort's presence, it would take time for word to reach them and their general. Then, it would be hours before the enemy could assemble and march against the Thirteenth's position. Moving an army took not only time, but extensive planning and preparation. Stiger understood such things did not happen immediately.

Also, he had deployed the elves and the legion's scouts to the forest, hours before First Cohort marched out of the underground. To them had fallen the job of creating a protective screen around the Tol'Tabor's exit. Once First Cohort arrived, they would extend that screen out toward the Vrell road and ultimately beyond, in the direction of the enemy's encampment. Their mission was to blind the enemy, until it was too late and the majority of the legion was in place and deployed.

As a result, Stiger felt it was unlikely the enemy would discover the legion so soon. So, he remained patient as could be, at least outwardly...and waited for Seventh Cohort to painfully creep forward, a few steps at a time, before inevitably stopping again.

"Ah, sir," Ruga said, stepping over to him. The centurion cleared his throat loudly. "Might I be bold enough to make a suggestion to the legate? I hope you don't mind, sir."

Stiger felt himself frown slightly but nodded for Ruga to continue.

"Perhaps it might best to continue to ride, sir," Ruga said. "Then, at least one of us can keep his feet dry."

Stiger sucked in a cold breath of air through his nose and slowly let it out. The Tol'Tabor was in a serious state of disrepair. In places, parts of the ceiling had come down. The dwarves had had to move the debris out of the way and brace other portions of the tunnel with thick wood beams.

Much of the road was wet and slick, with flooded portions ranging from several inches deep to more than a foot. Water continually dripped from the ceiling, showering those below, making the march just that much more miserable.

Stiger glanced over at the centurion, then down at his feet. He was standing in a small pool of cold water. He looked over at the nearest of the men, who had only their sandals for protection. He was sure the march along the wet road was quite uncomfortable, just as it had been through the snow. However, the legionary sandal was more of a shoe or boot than true sandal that civilians tended to wear. It wrapped tightly around the foot. When it became wet, the leather dried quickly and helped to retain heat. It made marching in terrible conditions like this possible, at least for a time.

"It won't be the first time my feet have been wet," Stiger said as he cracked his neck. He would share the misery with his men. It was the least he could do. "I've been too long in the saddle anyway. I need to stretch my legs."

"Yes, sir," Ruga said, in a tone that conveyed he still thought it a bad idea. "If you think so, sir. I am sure the legate knows best."

"I do," Stiger said in a firm tone to end the matter.

Seventh Cohort to their front began moving again. Stiger started walking, tugging on Nomad's lead to get the horse going. The horse shook his head and pulled on the reins. Stiger gave a firmer tug and, with it, Nomad began clopping forward. Stiger's mount did not like the underground either. The animal had been skittish since they'd entered. Ruga's century started moving, and behind them, the lead elements of Eighth Cohort started forward too.

Fresh air from the exit ahead blew down the tunnel in a frigid breeze. Stiger shivered, as it reminded him of the freezing temperatures that waited aboveground. He drew his bearskin cloak closer about himself. The cloak had been a gift from Braddock's father, Brogan. Stiger treasured it, for it was quite warm and a princely present.

The cohort to their front, frustratingly, ground to a halt once again. Stiger resisted expelling a frustrated breath.

"This is a little maddening, sir," Ruga said.

"Hurry up and wait," Stiger replied. "In the army, it seems you're always waiting for something or other. The other is usually for someone else to do their job properly, so you can do yours. An old sergeant of mine, a fellow by the name of Tiro, told me once to 'best get accustomed to it, for it is the natural state of things in the army.'"

"That's good advice, sir," Ruga said. "What do you suppose the holdup is, sir? I don't much fancy the underground. Too dank and confining. I'd rather be waiting on the surface, sir."

"I don't like it either," Stiger said and then considered Ruga's question. "As each cohort leaves the road and marches out to the surface, likely the forest and snow are doing their best to conspire to slow things down." Stiger blew out a breath that was more sigh than anything else. "But in truth, were we marching under the open sky, along the Vrell road, there would likely still be delays and unexpected halts, just not as many as we're seeing today."

"It's a wonder the legion can move at all, sir," Ruga groused.

Stiger privately agreed with the centurion. The starting and stopping seemed rather excessive. He was beginning to worry that something serious had occurred or gone wrong. He pushed those concerns aside, for worry would only make his frustration worse. Besides, he figured, if it had, a messenger would have been rushed back to him with an update.

"I understand your niece married Lieutenant Lan," Stiger said, looking over at the centurion in hopes of passing the time with some idle conversation and keeping his mind from worrying.

"I am surprised you know about that, sir," Ruga said.

"All officers under my command must seek permission to marry," Stiger said, "not to mention the enlisted."

"I see, sir," Ruga said and then fell silent for several heartbeats before speaking. "The entire legion's not been together for over three hundred years. It's only been the two valley cohorts, sir. Until you came along, we didn't have a legate, sir, only the council for direction, and they didn't care who married who. So, much of this is new to me, sir." He dropped his voice in a conspiratorial manner. "Don't tell my children, but there are some things I do not know, sir."

Stiger chuckled.

"How many children do you have?" Stiger asked.

"Six, sir," Ruga said, "two boys and four girls. The oldest is serving in Third Cohort, the youngest is two. It's another reason why I continue to serve. While there is breath in my lungs, I will do my all to keep the valley safe, sir."

Stiger gave a nod to that. He'd heard similar sentiments from the other officers of the valley cohorts. He returned the conversation to its original course. "I spoke with Lan to make sure his mind was set on the matter before giving my permission. There were other things he needed to consider."

"You tried to talk him out of it?" Ruga asked curiously.

"No, I did not," Stiger said and thought for a moment on how he wanted to explain the complexity of the empire's nobility. "Centurion, you've spent your entire life in the valley. Do I understand that to be correct?"

"Born and raised in the valley," Ruga said. "I joined just as soon as I could, to do my part, sir."

"You don't know much about how things work in the empire, do you?"

"No, sir," Ruga admitted, "just what I've heard and what's been passed down through the years, sir."

"Lan is from a good family," Stiger said simply, "a family of means, part of the nobility."

"And Jenna is not," Ruga said in a flat tone.

"Good or not, she's doesn't hail from a noble household," Stiger said. "Undoubtedly, Lan's family sent him off to gain military experience. In the empire, such experience helps one secure a governmental position, say as a magistrate. It is the first step on the road to building a successful career in politics and strengthening the family's powerbase, essentially increasing prestige, even for a second and third son."

"I see, sir," Ruga said.

"I don't think so," Stiger said. "Lan's family will also be searching for a suitable match in a wife, someone to help increase his social and political standing, along with the family's. Though many such marriages are loveless, they serve to create and foster alliances between powerful houses or strengthen the weaker ones. Such alliances are critically important to gaining more prestige for the family, more power. It is how the empire works and has worked for centuries."

Ruga was silent for a long moment.

"Why, then, did you not deny him permission to marry?" Ruga asked, with a hard look. "Why allow him to go through with it, sir?"

Stiger thought about his answer for a moment, then decided to turn it around on Ruga.

"Why did Vargus approve of the union?"

"He didn't want to," Ruga said. "He asked them both to wait, to be sure…but in the end relented and gave his blessing."

"What changed his mind?"

"Let's just say Vargus took some convincing, sir," Ruga said with a shrug of his shoulders. "Let's leave it at that, shall we?"

The Seventh began moving again. Stiger gave Nomad a tug and they continued for another ten feet, before the cohort once again came to a halt.

"You approve, then?" Stiger asked, looking over at Ruga. "Of the marriage?"

"I didn't say that, sir," Ruga said. "She's my favorite niece and well, sir…she's been through a rough time of it. No one deserves what was done to her. So, I thought, with everything that's going on, you and the Thirteenth returning…who am I to begrudge her a little happiness? Get my meaning, sir?"

"Perfectly," Stiger said. "That was my reasoning as well, Centurion. In all this madness, there deserves to be some happiness."

Ruga eyed Stiger for a long moment and then gave a nod. The two of them fell silent. Seventh Cohort began once again to move. This time the cohort did not immediately stop. They went several yards before Ruga gave a low chuckle. Stiger glanced over at the centurion, wondering what he thought funny.

"If he survives," Ruga said, looking back at Stiger, "I bet his family's gonna be downright pissed." Ruga gave a bark of a laugh. "Those, I think, are the best kinds of marriages, sir. The ones you don't expect, sir."

"Ruga," Stiger said, "you may be on to something."

Ruga glanced over at Stiger. "Sir, may I ask a personal question?"

"Sure," Stiger said.

"You are from a powerful family, are you not?"

"I am," Stiger said, suddenly on guard.

"Then why, sir, are you not married?"

Stiger looked back front, staring into space for several steps. He looked back over at Ruga.

"My family is in disgrace," Stiger said, feeling sour. "None of the powerful families would ever consider tying theirs to mine, not now."

"I'd heard such, sir," Ruga said. "You get no choice on your family, sir. That's how the gods intended it. You do the best you can in this life. I think that is all any man can ask of you."

"It is what it is," Stiger said, after considering the centurion's words. They had likely been meant to help, but Stiger still felt sour at the mention of his family. His father's actions bothered him.

Ruga did not reply and the silence grew heavy between them as they continued following Seventh Cohort. A half hour later saw them reach the exit and emerge from the tunnel, out into the forest.

Blinking under the harsh light of the sun, which was almost directly overhead, Stiger watched his breath steam heavily in the air. It was much colder than the underground. Even with the sun he could feel no warmth. Still, he found it a relief to be back outside.

The road let out into a bowl-shaped depression. Snow covered the ground in a thick carpet around them, the top of which was a frozen crust and easily gave way, crunching underfoot. Where the legion had been marching, the snow had already been trampled down. But off to the sides, there was at least a foot of snow on the ground. The branches of the nearest trees above were bowed by the heavy snow.

"It's just grand being outside again, sir, just grand," Ruga said, sucking in a huge breath of fresh air. He set the bottom of his yoke on the ground and looked around. "Open sky and the sun, even in this bitter cold, is all that an old soldier could ask for."

Stiger found he could not disagree. Though he liked the dwarves and respected what they'd accomplished, he could never see himself spending most of his life living underground, like a mole.

As Eighth Cohort emerged behind them, Stiger led Nomad off to the side and out of the way. Ruga snapped an order and his century moved as well. A few moments later, Eighth Cohort ground to a halt as Seventh Cohort, which had started climbing out of the bowl-shaped depression ahead of them, stopped.

The snow beneath the men's feet had been ground down by the cohorts before them, then trampled into a slurry of mud, snow, and ice. Stiger blew out an unhappy breath, which steamed heavily in the wintery air. Now that they were out of the underground, he had no intention of following the cohorts as they struggled through the mud and inched their way forward toward the defensive position.

He looked back on the Tol'Tabor. The road's exit, a large stone door, stood wide open. It was almost impossibly thick, at least seven feet from front to back. It was also twelve feet high. The backside was reinforced steel. Where the dwarves had recently oiled them, massive black hinges glistened in the sunlight.

The door had been set into the side of a hill, with a steep cliff face that formed the back side of the bowl-shaped depression. The door had been made in such a way that, when sealed, it must have looked like a natural feature, a large slab of rock, where the vegetation and dirt had washed away from the hillside. Only a closer examination would have revealed the seams.

During his travels with the dwarves, Stiger had seen such things before. Not only were the dwarves skilled when it came to construction, but they were also very clever at being able to hide the entrances to their underground world, and in plain sight too. Even if you found one of the hidden doors, it was damn hard, if not impossible, to open. Some of the tunnels were even rigged with traps, where if the door was opened improperly, the tunnel beyond would collapse.

"Impressive," Ruga breathed, almost in awe.

Stiger turned and looked in the direction Ruga was gazing. He was watching Seventh Cohort as it started forward once again, marching up a small rise on a road that had been freshly cut through the forest. Somewhere out of view, the crack of axes could be heard in the distance as work continued. It never ceased to amaze Stiger on what could be accomplished in just a few short hours.

The felled trees had been stripped of their branches, dragged aside, and stacked neatly in piles. The stumps had been uprooted and manhandled out of the way, likely using teams of horses that had been sent ahead with the lead cohorts.

Along the sides of the road, teams of men labored at laying the beginnings of a corduroy road. They were placing one felled tree trunk after another on the ground, creating a makeshift wooden road for the artillery and supply train. Without such measures, the wagons and artillery would quickly become bogged down in the muddy mix.

"Damn impressive," Ruga said.

Stiger glanced over at the centurion again. His century was lined up behind them in a column of two. The men had set their yokes down on the snow and stood by, patiently waiting, while enjoying the unexpected break. Ruga still carried his on his shoulder.

"This is but one example of why the legions are so successful," Stiger said, with a wave toward the newly made road and the two cohorts. "Discipline and teamwork: you put those two together and it makes us strong. With common purpose, we can easily accomplish what others would consider the impossible or improbable."

"Yes, sir," Ruga said. "I am beginning to see that."

"Show the average legionary the improbable getting done on a regular basis and soon he begins to believe the legion can accomplish anything...expect the impossible to be overcome," Stiger said. "That's when the real miracles get done, stuff the historians chronicle."

"Like battles, sir?" Ruga asked.

"Like in battle," Stiger confirmed with a firm nod. "Life as a legionary is not easy. It is filled with unending toil, brutal training, discomfort, harsh discipline, terrible monotony, and moments of sheer terror. Yet despite all that, the men are intensely proud of who they are and what they are part of, the legion. We make the toughest, most resilient professional soldiers around, and for a reason, Centurion."

"Yes, sir," Ruga said, "to defend the empire, sir."

"That's right," Stiger said. "Even though you've never been to the empire, or the capital, you and your men, both of the valley cohorts, the entire Thirteenth, are the empire." Stiger placed a gloved hand upon his chest armor and patted it. "As long as our hearts beat, we all are the empire, no matter where we are or what we are doing. Understand my meaning?"

"Aye, sir," Ruga said. "It's why my ancestors gave up what they gave up, so me and my boys could defend what they loved, the empire."

Stiger gave a nod, pleased that Ruga understood, and then saw movement to his right. Centurion Mectillius was striding over. The centurion stopped before him and saluted. Stiger returned the salute.

"Centurion Sabinus sent me to guide you to headquarters, sir," Mectillius said.

"Detached you from your century, did he?" Stiger asked.

"My century is guarding headquarters, sir," Mectillius said. "I was at hand, was all, so the duty fell to me, rather than one of the messengers."

"Very well," Stiger said as both the Seventh and Eighth Cohorts began moving again, slogging through the muddy snow. He decided that Sabinus had chosen Mectillius on purpose, likely because he and Mectillius had history. "Lead on, Centurion."

"Yes, sir," Mectillius said, turning. "It's not far. If you would follow me, sir."

Stiger considered riding, but then disregarded the idea. He needed some exercise. He gave Nomad's reins a tug and started after Mectillius.

"Want me to have one of my boys take Nomad, sir?" Ruga asked.

"No," Stiger said, glancing back on his horse as he walked through the snow. Stuck in the past for the last five years, he'd missed his trusty mount. "I prefer to walk him, at least until we get to headquarters."

"Yes, sir," Ruga said, and fell back to his men.

Snow crunching under their feet, Mectillius led Stiger alongside the marching cohorts. Ruga and his century followed a few steps behind. The snow along the road had been packed down by the working details, who were laboring to lay the corduroy road. Thankfully, it wasn't muddy.

"Have we had any contact with the enemy yet?" Stiger asked.

"None that I know of, sir," Mectillius said. "The last few hours have been rather busy, sir, so I am afraid I don't know all that is going on. Centurion Sabinus should be able to fill you in, sir."

Stiger gave a nod of understanding.

"How are your boys?" Stiger asked.

"My century is good, sir. My boys are all doing well and eager for the coming fight, sir. I try to do as good a job as I can with them, sir, just as Pixus would have done."

Stiger felt a pang of loss at the centurion's name. Pixus had fallen in battle in the dwarven underground during a desperate fight against orcs. Stiger had promoted Mectillius to replace him.

"I am certain you are doing just fine," Stiger said, "otherwise I would have heard about it."

"Yes, sir," Mectillius said.

Stiger glanced over to his right, at the men slogging through the muddy mix. He knew from personal experience it was miserable, but at the same time it was something the men could handle and would endure. They were legionaries and accustomed to suffering through the worst conditions.

They passed several details laying the new wooden road. One of the details gave a cheer at the sight of Stiger. Then to their right, as if in response, Seventh Cohort gave up a massed cheer. Stiger raised a hand, and the men cheered more enthusiastically.

"Are the enemy up ahead, sir?" one of the legionaries in the Seventh called to Stiger when the cheering died down.

"They will be," Stiger called back, and held a fist up in the air, "and we're gonna show them why the legions are so feared."

The men roared in reply. He was heartened by their cheering, for it meant, despite the miserable conditions, morale was high. That boded well for what was to come.

It did not take long before Seventh Cohort gave over to the Sixth. Several officers alongside the road were conferring with Centurion Kiel, who commanded that formation. The officers stopped their conference, turned, and, as one, saluted. Stiger returned their salute.

"How's it going, Kiel?" Stiger asked, not stopping as he continued to follow Mectillius through the snow.

"Bloody muddy, sir," Kiel responded. The centurion's legs were slathered in mud. "Just bloody muddy and cold too, but what doesn't kill ya makes you stronger, sir."

"Too true," Stiger said. "Carry on, Centurion."

"Will do, sir," Kiel said.

Then they were by and overtaking the tail end of Fifth Cohort.

"Forty to fifty yards ahead is the Vrell road, sir," Mectillius said. "It's still little more than a dirt track. It seems the Cyphan did nothing to improve the road."

Stiger gave a nod but did not say anything. He continued to plod through the snow, which occasionally made his movements awkward. Then suddenly, almost before he knew it, they were on the snow-covered Vrell road. Stiger paused and glanced around. Fifth Cohort, like a snake, bent around and onto the road. Just ahead of the Fifth was the Fourth.

The last time his boots had touched this road, he had led a fighting retreat to the castle, just a few miles away. He'd done what had needed to be done and slowed the enemy, buying time for winter to arrive. But it had all come at a terrible cost in blood. It seemed like an eternity had passed and, in a way, one had.

"I'm back," Stiger said to himself, "and there will be no more retreating. I am here to stay."

Mectillius stopped, looked back, and caught Stiger's attention. He pointed in the direction of the castle, which wasn't visible from their current position. "Up that big beast of a hill is our defensive line, sir."

The road went straight up the hill about two hundred yards from their current position. Stiger could see teams of legionaries on the crest, toiling away. The work spread out of view, into the forest to the left and right of the road. More interesting to Stiger was the hill itself, for two larger hills seemed to spring up on either flank from the first hill's crest.

Stiger felt like smiling. The dwarves had not let him down. They had chosen this position well and he was heartened by the sight of it. When they came for him, the enemy would be fighting on his terms.

"It's good ground," Stiger said, "very good ground."

"Aye, sir," Ruga said, "it certainly looks that way, sir."

Stiger's gaze moved to Fourth Cohort. The cohort stopped. Fourth stretched up the road and hill to the crest. At the head of the column, Stiger could see a small detail of centurions gathered about an officer. That officer was pointing off to the right and was gesturing with his arms, clearly in the process of directing the cohort to their position in the line and outlining what was expected.

Mectillius started forward again, leading them up the hill. Stiger found his legs quickly burning with the climb. After the long ride through the chilly and damp underground, the exercise felt more than good. Stiger was an infantry officer at heart and had always made an effort to share the miles afoot with his men, at least, whenever it was practical to do so.

The meeting of officers broke up, with several slogging their way back to their centuries. Within moments, the Fourth began to move, working their way up the hill to the crest, before snaking to the right.

Within a short time, Stiger and party reached the top of the hill. In all directions, men were hard at work, laboring away. Axe parties were busy felling trees, laying the crest of the hill bare. While those men worked, others toiled at shoveling the snow aside. Where it had been removed, teams were using pickaxes to break the frozen ground open.

Stiger paused, looking to the left and then the right. The two hills that rose up on either side were very steep, more so than they had appeared from below. He turned his gaze ahead, following the Vrell road as it traveled downslope. The road disappeared into the forested hills about a half mile away as it turned a bend. Stiger's gaze moved to the horizon and the mountains. High up in the pass and nestled amidst the mountains, he could see the walls of Castle Vrell. From this long distance, the castle looked small and insignificant, a far cry from the stronghold it was.

Stiger tore his gaze from the castle and studied the work around him. His fortified line would eventually stretch out, up and over both hills, as more men arrived and were put to work. Holding the reins of his horse, he gave a clap of his gloved hands. The terrain was as described or, more correctly, was better than described. For lack of a better word, it was near perfect. Given enough time, perhaps just one full day, and the legion could construct a truly impregnable position.

Mectillius coughed. "This way, sir."

Stiger followed after the centurion, to the right, up the slope of the hill, and into the trees. Mectillius guided them to a natural clearing, where a series of tents had been raised. Two more were in the process of being laid out as support poles were set. Stiger recognized the large one as his headquarters tent.

A guard, some of Mectillius's men, stood around the legion's Eagle, which was planted by its entrance. Normally, the Eagle went with the legate, but Stiger had permitted it to travel with First Cohort as a reminder to the men of why they were here.

The sight of the Eagle never failed to stir Stiger's heart. It represented the honor of not only the legion, but the empire as well. He also felt some wonder that his Eagle was the fabled Thirteenth's, the Lost.

Several horses, likely for messengers, were picketed behind the tent. A fire, with an iron pot suspended over it, had been set a few yards away from the horses. Stiger smelled tea brewing as he made his way up to headquarters.

A legionary who had been busy helping another tie a train of mules together stepped away. The mules had likely been used to haul tents and the headquarters baggage. He strode forward.

"I can take your horse, sir," the legionary said and pointed. "I will picket him with the others."

"Thank you." Stiger handed over the reins, patted Nomad on the neck, and with that, the legionary led the horse off.

"Can I be of any further assistance, sir?" Mectillius asked. The guards, just a few feet away, stood at attention.

"No, I'm good. Thank you," Stiger said as a gentle, yet cold breeze rustled the snow-covered tree limbs about them. As the breeze let up, snow drifted lazily downward in a white cloud.

"Yes, sir," Mectillius saluted.

Stiger returned his salute, and with that, Mectillius left.

"Sir," Ruga said, drawing his attention.

"Yes?" Stiger asked, looking back. "What is it?"

"Since we're now your personal guard," Ruga said, with a glance to Mectillius's back as the other centurion walked off toward the fire, "do you want us to relieve the headquarters protection detail? Headquarters and your personal tent, I believe, should rightly be our responsibility now."

Stiger gave that a moment's thought.

"How many effectives do you have today?"

"Forty-two, sir," Ruga said. "Another four are in the sick tent. Bad food, sir. We think it was undercooked meat."

"Very well," Stiger said. "Speak with Mectillius and relieve the headquarters guard. He can return to his cohort. You are responsible for it all."

"Yes, sir," Ruga said. "At all times, I will have a detail of four standing by as a personal escort, sir. I would appreciate you taking the escort wherever you go, sir, even if it's for an after-dinner stroll about the camp."

"That's acceptable," Stiger said. "I will."

"Thank you, sir," Ruga said and saluted.

Stiger turned away and stepped into his headquarters tent. The heavy canvas tent was marginally warmer than the outside air, primarily because it was out of the wind. A small brazier smoked lazily in the back corner. Whatever heat it gave off was not enough to warm the tent much.

Sabinus was at the far end of the tent, bent over a camp table, examining a map. There were two other junior officers with him. Several clerks were scattered around the tent, working on portable camp tables. A handful of messengers waited off to the sides.

Sabinus looked up and spotted him as Stiger made his way over.

"Good to see you, sir," Sabinus said. "Welcome headquarters."

"Sabinus," Stiger said. He recognized Centurions Aguus and Graelix from First Cohort. "Gentlemen, I trust you both are doing well."

"Yes, sir," Aguus said.

"Tolerable, sir," Graelix said.

Stiger nodded to that. He'd always liked Graelix. The centurion was one tough bastard. Stiger had seen him take a serious wound and keep on fighting. He was the kind of officer you could not help but respect.

"Looks like things are off to a good start," Stiger said, turning his attention back to Sabinus.

"They are, sir," Sabinus affirmed. "We're only slightly behind schedule. I'm afraid all those feet made quick work of the snow and frozen dirt underneath. It's slowing the deployment of the legion a bit." Sabinus had a charcoal pencil in his hand. He pointed down at the map, which he had clearly drawn himself. "Let me fill you in on what's been done so far. This here is the road." He tapped it with the end of his pencil. "This is our position. These circles are those two hills that the road cuts through. Our line extends about two hundred yards in either direction of the road. In a few more hours, it will push over the tops of both hills and farther out into the forest." Sabinus looked up. "I've already done it, sir, but I suspect you will want to look the ground over, when you have a moment. The flanking terrain to either side of these two hills is rocky and hard to move over. Any turning movement by the enemy would be extremely difficult and take time to execute." Sabinus paused a moment. "The men are digging in, but they're having a difficult time of it, due to the frozen ground. The freeze goes about three to four inches down."

"Breaking open frozen ground can be a real bitch," Stiger said, recalling his time in the North. Winters there had proven extremely brutal, at times making it nearly impossible to dig in.

"No one said life in the legion would be easy, sir," Aguus said.

"Speak for yourself," Graelix said. "The recruiter told me I would get fed daily, all I could eat, and beef too, including a wine ration."

"Let me guess," Aguus said, "and the women would be lining up for miles around to bed you too, right?"

"Sounded like an easy life," Graelix said with a shrug of his shoulders. "He never mentioned I would have to pay for the women."

"You've always been a gullible sort," Aguus said. "It's a wonder you ever made centurion."

Sabinus cleared his throat and gestured down at the map, tapping it hard with the pencil. He looked meaningfully at both centurions. "Would you mind terribly if I continued to brief our legate?"

"Sorry, sir," Graelix said, looking from Sabinus to Stiger.

"My apologies, sir," Aguus said.

"By nightfall," Sabinus said, turning his gaze back to Stiger, "we should have the trench and defensive wall in place, sir. If we keep the men working through the night, we will have a defensive barricade along much of the line by morning. We should be more than ready to receive the enemy." He moved the pencil up the Vrell road, in the direction of the castle. "I have skirmishers out to our front at around a quarter mile. Scouts are beyond the skirmish line and free ranging. The enemy's camp lies just four miles away from our position."

Stiger absorbed that. "Tell me of the dispositions you've made so far."

"There has been no need to deviate from the plan, at least not yet. First Cohort is positioned on the ground between the two big hills, including on the road itself. I have Second and Third Cohorts on the right. Fourth is coming online now. You should have passed them on your climb up."

"I did," Stiger confirmed.

"Fourth will move farther to the right and anchor the far side of the hill, where it becomes rocky. Once they arrive, Fifth, Sixth, and Seventh will take the left flank. I have officers standing by to guide them into position. Eighth, Ninth, and Tenth are the reserve, that includes the auxiliaries too. They will be stacked behind the line as planned should the enemy make an appearance. Until that point, they will be put to work alongside the rest of the legion."

"Very good," Stiger said, pleased with all that he had heard so far. Everything was proceeding better than he had expected.

Ruga entered the tent and approached. "All set, sir. The guard has been relieved, and my boys are in place."

Stiger gave a nod and turned back to Sabinus. "Continue your report."

"I have ordered the hilltops and slopes to our front cut back by two hundred yards," Sabinus continued. "Once we have a decent trench and wall in place, we can begin work on a fortified camp. At the earliest, I figure that work will happen tomorrow morning sometime."

Stiger rubbed his jaw as he considered the report.

"That's fine," Stiger said, after several heartbeats. Without tents and shelter, it would be an uncomfortable night for the legion, but there was no helping that. His eyes went back to the map. "We will need to accommodate the artillery along the line, particularly the bolt throwers. Salt stripped Tenth of half her strength to speed up their movement."

"Yes, sir," Sabinus said. "The camp prefect sent word ahead. I have the engineers surveying and marking out positions now for the bolt throwers, with an eye toward covering the downward slope. It's another reason to cut the forest back, to give our light artillery open ground to shoot."

Sabinus paused a moment as he sucked in a breath. He tapped the map again. "As I'm sure you saw on your way up here, I've also ordered corduroying the new road we've cut into the forest. I have three hundred men working on that project. I did not want to allocate more, as our defensive position on these hills is the priority. We need something to fight behind. Once the auxiliaries arrive, I suggest we put more men on it, but not until then. The engineers tell me, with seven hundred men, the project can be completed by noon tomorrow. I personally think they are being too optimistic. It will likely be afternoon to evening before they are done."

Stiger thought Sabinus likely right. There was no point in worrying about it now though. Stiger agreed with Sabinus, the defensive line had priority. Later, when time permitted, he made a mental note to speak with the engineers and assign more resources to the project when they became available.

"Have you set aside space for the hospital and a depot for the supplies?"

"Yes, sir," Sabinus said. "I have a tent raised for the surgeons. We have three more large tents that should be up within the hour. It won't be very comfortable for any wounded when they come in, but at least they will be out of the elements to some degree."

"Tell me of the enemy," Stiger said. "What contact have we had with them?"

"Surprisingly, none, sir," Sabinus said.

"None?" Stiger said. "No skirmishes, no scouts?"

"No, sir," Aguus confirmed. "Not a peep from them, sir."

"We haven't even bumped into any patrols," Sabinus added. "As far as I can tell, the enemy has not even bothered to leave their encampment today. The scouts report that there is no activity from the enemy camp, at least none that indicates they intend to leave it anytime soon. Truth be told, sir, I don't even think they know we're here."

"You don't?" Stiger asked, hardly daring to believe it true.

"We may have to announce ourselves to get their attention," Sabinus said.

Stiger's mind raced. Was it possible the enemy felt completely secure in their camp? Or was it the dwarven pioneers? He wondered...had the enemy commander ceded the road to the dwarves or perhaps, with the fresh snow, was simply waiting until conditions improved before venturing to send patrols out? Still, no matter the conditions, regular patrols should have been put out. It was what he would have done. Perhaps they had missed something?

"Are you certain?" Stiger asked.

"Very," Sabinus said. "I'd say Fortuna has blessed us greatly this day. It's looking like we will have time to make our position truly formidable, something we'd not counted on, sir."

In his wildest imaginings, Stiger had not expected this. He had planned for the enemy to discover the legion's presence rather quickly.

"Are any of the elves about?" Stiger asked, thinking he needed more information.

"No, sir," Sabinus said. "They are forward, observing the enemy camp. Speaking of which, the early reports I have received indicate that their encampment is lacking in a basic defense."

"What?" Stiger asked, surprised at this latest bit of information. "Are you certain?"

"Certain, no," Sabinus said, "as I've not seen it myself. But I am fairly confident their information is correct."

Stiger thought about what he wanted to do.

"Right," Stiger said. "I think I will go forward to eyeball their encampment myself and speak with some of the scouts."

"Sir," Ruga said, speaking up from behind.

"I'm going, Centurion," Stiger said in a firm tone, turning to look squarely at Ruga. It was time the commander of his personal guard understood that at times the legate needed to take risks. "That's the end of the discussion on the matter."

"I'd not dream of arguing with you, sir," Ruga said with schooled innocence. "All I was just going to say was that I'm coming with you, sir. If you don't mind terribly, sir?"

"Fair enough," Stiger said. "We're not taking the entire century. Pick two reliable men, preferably ones that are good in the woods. The rest shall remain here on guard with your optio in command."

"Yes, sir," Ruga said, without hesitation.

Stiger turned back to Sabinus and raised an eyebrow, wondering if his senior centurion had any objection about the legate going forward personally.

"Very good, sir," Sabinus said, without any hesitation. "I have a scout standing by to guide you forward, sir. Eli and

Taha'Leeth are waiting for you out in the field. What with it quiet and all, I surmised you would want to see the enemy personally."

"While I am out," Stiger said to Sabinus, "you will retain command of the legion. At least until I return or when Salt arrives, whichever comes first. At that point, you can return to your cohort."

"Yes, sir," Sabinus said.

"Right," Stiger said, turning away and moving toward the exit. "Ruga, let's not keep the enemy waiting, shall we?"

"Wouldn't want to do that, sir," Ruga said as he followed Stiger out of the tent.

EIGHT

The trees around them were still, almost deathly so. Stiger thought it was as if the forest were holding its breath. Everything seemed to have been frozen into immobility by winter. After the previous day's storm, there wasn't even a breeze to stir the air or the snow-covered branches. A deep layer of fresh snow covered everything. It was also bitterly cold.

Stiger crunched his way through the snow. His own breathing had become labored from the effort of forcing his way forward, one step at a time. The snow was deep enough that it almost went up to the knees.

Despite the cold, he was perspiring. He felt hot and wanted to remove his cloak. But he knew better. The warmth, though welcome, was deceptive. From the snow, he was wet from the waist down. His boots had been soaked through too. If he wasn't careful, he would catch a cold, and that was when the real danger set in. So, he kept his cloak securely fastened for warmth.

Taha'Leeth was to his left and Eli to the right. There was about five feet of spacing between each of them and Stiger. Such was their skill that the elves hardly made any noise as they moved through the deep snow.

Silent or not, Eli and Taha'Leeth were having just as much difficulty as he was. Ruga trailed a few steps behind, and a glance backward told Stiger the centurion was walking in Stiger's footsteps.

Ruga was clearly no fool. He was using Stiger to blaze a trail for himself through the snow. In truth, Stiger did not mind too much. He viewed the effort as just more exercise, something, as legate, he was being denied more and more with each passing day. Too much of his time was being consumed by meetings, administrative work, or events that needed attending. Little time was left for exercise. Besides, the effort was warming him against the cold.

Stiger sucked air in through his nose and blew it out through his mouth in a steaming stream. He glanced around, studying his surroundings, as something occurred to him. He hadn't seen any tracks in the snow, which was odd, because he knew there was plenty of game in the forest. He was about to mention it to Eli, when he heard something.

Stiger stopped, becoming still. Eli and Taha'Leeth also came to a halt, looking over at him curiously, wondering what was wrong.

"I thought I heard something," Stiger whispered and then fell silent, ears straining, eyes searching the forest for movement.

Nothing.

Had he imagined it?

No. There it was again…a distant tapping.

"Hammering, from the enemy camp." Eli pointed toward a small rise to their front that led up the slope of the hill they were climbing. "We are very close. Come, let us show you the enemy."

They started forward again, continuing to climb the gentle slope of the hill. Stiger once again glanced back at

Ruga. The centurion's face was grim, hard, and red from the cold air and exertion. Stiger had left Ruga's two men twenty yards back. He had not wanted to bring too many forward. The risk of giving their presence away was just too great. As it was, four was almost too many.

Stiger's gaze strayed over to Taha'Leeth. She had pulled the hood of her cloak up halfway, concealing much of her braided hair. A few strands had come loose and fallen across her face. She looked proud, bold, and incredibly beautiful to his eyes.

Both elves were armed with bows and carried small packs strapped to their backs. Taha'Leeth held her bow loosely in one hand, along with an arrow. She moved with a lithe confidence that spoke of skill and ability. Stiger found himself enjoying the view, for even with her cloak about her, he found her figure very fetching.

She glanced over at him and caught him staring. He found he could not look away, for it was as if she had captured his gaze with some strange magic. Taha'Leeth smiled demurely before returning her full attention back to the trees around them and breaking the spell.

Though they had only been apart a few hours, it felt good to have her back by his side, to see her safe and sound.

Eli abruptly put a hand to Stiger's chest, forcefully arresting his movement. Startled, Stiger looked over at his friend in question. In answer, Eli pointed meaningfully to the ground. Stiger glanced down and saw a small branch, which, under the weight of the snow, had broken and fallen. He had been about to step on it.

"Best to pay attention to where one puts one's feet"—Eli leaned in close and then gestured at Taha'Leeth—"and not get distracted by a pair of pretty eyes and a shapely backside.

With the enemy just over that hill, I don't think we want to give ourselves away."

Eli's lip twitched with wry amusement, clearly savoring one of Stiger's rare lapses in attention. For his part, Stiger gave a nod. Despite his friend's apparent amusement and lighthearted tone, the rebuke had been well-earned.

Taha'Leeth paused, turned, and fixed Eli with an unhappy look that lasted several heartbeats before continuing. Clearly, she'd heard his words.

"It seems I am not the only one receiving a rebuke," Stiger said with an amused glance over at his friend.

"Indeed." Eli shook his head slightly and started after Taha'Leeth.

Stiger half turned back to Ruga and pointed at the branch so the centurion saw it. Ruga gave a nod of understanding.

Stiger made certain to pay better attention to where he placed his feet. As they neared the top of the hill, the trees began to thin considerably. This saw the beginnings of undergrowth that thickened the farther they went up the slope. Their pace slowed as they were forced to work their way around low-lying brush, bushes, and saplings.

Ahead, above the crest of the hill, Castle Vrell and the surrounding mountains loomed, almost seeming to hang over them. It made him feel tiny and insignificant, for they were very impressive.

Stiger could not yet see the enemy encampment, but he could certainly smell it. The stench of waste and smoke, at first faint, became more powerful and pervasive with every step forward.

Coming to the top of the hill, he followed Taha'Leeth around a large bush. On the other side, she squatted down in the snow and motioned for him to do the same. He went to a knee next to her, trying to ignore the cold bite of the snow against his skin.

Downslope and through a thin screen of bushes was the enemy's camp. The nearest campfire, with men clustered about it, was a mere fifty yards distant. He glanced over at Eli as he joined them, having gone around the other side of the bush. Eli also took a knee. Eli flashed a series of signs at him.

Stiger gave a nod of understanding. He turned back to Ruga. The centurion had stopped, just behind Stiger. He'd crouched down in the snow.

"This is as far as we go," Stiger whispered to Ruga, for he doubted the man knew the elven finger speak.

"I figured as much, sir," Ruga hissed back, his eyes on the enemy camp.

Stiger returned his attention to the enemy. Most of the trees on the downward slope had been chopped down, likely for firewood or building material. Their stumps were now no more than hundreds of mismatched lumps in the snow.

It took him a moment to make sense of what he was seeing of the enemy's encampment. There were tents by the thousands, huts, dugouts, animal pens, and more. Smoke from countless fires drifted up into the air, forming an ugly grayish-blue pall above.

The camp seemed very disordered to his professional eye, with no apparent effort at even attempting to organize—or perhaps the correct word was manage—the chaos. To the right, about one hundred yards away, part of the camp extended out into the forest and was lost from view. It looked to be more communal tents.

Much of the snow within the camp had been left where it had fallen. There were tracks and trails seemingly everywhere. They reminded Stiger of the paths the deer had made in the North, during the dead of winter, when the snow had piled up.

A legion would simply remove the snow, rather than permit it to remain. Snow removal was deemed a necessity for health reasons, as the men could only take being wet so long. Otherwise, sickness would set in, and if it did, that could prove disastrous. It also served as a way to maintain discipline and prevent the men from becoming overly idle during the long winter months.

Farther up the pass, the enemy's main wall that hemmed the castle in, with the barricade atop, appeared more impressive than it had from above. Stiger thought this especially true after studying the artillery that had been positioned on and behind the wall. The enemy's stone throwers were extremely large and impressive machines. He had no doubt that they would be capable, given time, of damaging the castle's walls.

Stiger noted the enemy's defenses were simply nonexistent when it came to the forest side of the camp. There seemed to have been the beginnings of an effort at digging a trench, but that looked to have been abandoned.

Despite having received the report from Sabinus, he'd still had some difficulty believing the enemy could be so confident they would neglect their own protection. But here it was before him, stark as could be. He had not dispatched scouts prior to the legion marching for fear that, with the fresh snow, their presence might be discovered, putting the enemy on guard.

"I'd say they have around twenty-five thousand men," Eli said quietly.

"It's about what we thought," Stiger said and then gestured toward the enemy with a hand.

"That's still a big camp, sir," Ruga said, "and twenty-five thousand is still a lot of men."

"It is," Stiger agreed, eyes studying the enemy critically.

"They have no defenses facing the forest, sir," Ruga said. "It's bold, sir, and arrogant too, like they expect no trouble."

Again, Stiger agreed with the centurion, but said nothing as he continued to study what was before him. He noted a handful of sentries along the edge of the camp. These had been posted near the forest, but none were within sixty yards of their position. It was likely why both elves had chosen this spot for observation.

"They certainly aren't expecting us," Eli said to Ruga.

Everything Stiger was seeing spoke of a complete lack of preparedness. None of the sentries were walking the perimeter of the camp. There was no one training. In fact, few were doing much of anything at all. It seemed as if the enemy, for the most part, was simply wasting away the day.

A handful of men were employed in construction work, but the vast majority were clustered around communal fires before tents or log shelters. There was movement inside the camp, but it appeared limited, almost as if nearly everyone desired the warmth of the fires and nothing else. There seemed to be no direction from any officer, no effort to improve the camp.

Most of the enemy appeared to be stood down. They wore no armor at all, instead wearing only what seemed to be mismatched civilian clothing instead of service tunics. Only the sentries were armed and armored.

"They certainly do not seem too active, sir," Ruga said.

"No, they don't," Stiger said, wondering what it all meant. He looked over at Eli. "You've seen no patrols?"

Eli shook his head.

"It is just as we've told you. There have been no patrols," Taha'Leeth said, "not since the last snowfall, at any rate. We've found no tracks, other than individuals who wandered a few yards out into the trees for whatever reason and the occasional hunter or trapper."

"How's the forest around here for game?" Stiger asked, looking between the two elves.

"Overhunted, at least for a few miles out," Eli said.

"Much of the large game is gone, deer, boar, bear, moose," Taha'Leeth added, "likely due to foraging parties when the army first got here. Only small animals are left. We did come across quite a few snares."

Stiger understood that. Hunting and trapping helped to supplement army rations, which tended to be bland at best. Over the years, he'd known quite a few legionaries who were very skilled at trapping, fishing, hunting, and thieving from other companies. The last bit had proven helpful on occasion.

"Some of the snares," Eli added, unhappily, "had not been checked in on for days on end. Those animals we could free, we did."

"They should have put patrols out," Stiger said as he rested a hand on his helmet. "I don't understand it. Are we missing something?"

"We're not." Eli cocked his head slightly to the side. "The enemy might believe they have nothing to fear. That could be why they have made no serious effort at fortifying their camp and bothering with patrols."

Stiger was not satisfied with that explanation.

"By my calculation," Stiger said, "they've had no communication with the outside world for at least three weeks, maybe a little more. They must know there is a problem with the road. So, why not come out and deal with it? It's not like they don't have the strength to do so. It is right there before us. Why sit in their camp and do nothing?"

Eli did not reply for several heartbeats and then gave a shrug. "They might think the lack of communication is weather-related."

"Perhaps," Ruga said, "they have enough supplies to last a few weeks."

"In that they don't feel the need to rush clearing the road?" Stiger looked over at Ruga. "That might be it, but it does not explain the lack of patrols out into the forest. Braddock's pioneers are operating well down the road, intentionally avoiding the enemy in and around this encampment." He shook his head. "They should have put patrols out. It's basic security and common sense. What is there to fear?"

"They could just be lazy, sir," Ruga suggested. "Lazy, ill-disciplined, and poorly led."

"Lazy?" Stiger asked, looking back on the centurion.

"Well, sir," Ruga said, "it's pretty damn cold out and they're building shelters with only a handful at it. We can all hear the hammering. Most of the bastards seem content to suffer through uncomfortable nights in cold tents, for I see a lot of men just sitting about down there, doing a big bunch of nothing." Ruga gestured about them. "And there is a whole forest full of building material readily at hand. Don't you think they should have teams out in the forest, bringing trees down, so they can build more shelters? Where are the teams gathering firewood? Seems fairly lazy to me, sir."

"He could be right," Eli said. "Remember General Kromen and what he did to the Southern legions?"

Stiger felt himself tense. The elf pointed a finger at him and wagged it.

"I don't care what you say about speaking against leadership," Eli said, "but that was incompetence of, how you say... command? Yes, I think that is the word. It was criminal what Kromen did. There is no denying it. So stop trying."

Stiger felt himself frown at the memory. Eli was right. Kromen had damaged those four legions likely beyond repair with his incompetence. What they'd both seen in the legionary encampment had horrified him, the rot, low morale, and disease. The thought of it still angered him. Was the same thing happening here? Or was it something else?

He turned his gaze back to the enemy. Ruga had a point and so too did Eli. It was just after midday. Why weren't the enemy more active? It just did not make sense to him. There had to be more to it.

"Those two large buildings, next to the animal pens." Taha'Leeth pointed at a couple of rough-looking log structures with arched roofs in the center of the camp. There was an extensive series of corrals besides the two buildings, where several hundred horses and mules were being kept. "There is a strong guard around those buildings. See them?"

"I do," Stiger said.

"I think that is where their supply is located," Taha'Leeth said. "If you look just to the left, there are a number of squat mounds covered in snow. Those, I am thinking, would likely be crates of supplies they were unable to fit inside."

Stiger rubbed his jaw as he studied the buildings. A third structure was in a partial state of construction, but no one seemed to be working on it. He suspected she was right.

The legion could use those supplies, mules, and horses. There were also hundreds of wagons and carts parked one next to another off to the side of the corrals. Stiger wanted those as well. Between the legion, dwarves and gnomes, the army was quite large. As he saw it, the more transport they had to move supply the better.

Still, it just did not make sense to him that the enemy would not send out patrols, nor seek to clear the road and open communications, especially given the strength they had on hand. This army had become just as isolated and cut off from the rest of the world as he was.

More telling was the complete lack of order and sanitation within the enemy's camp. With no defenses facing the forest, it smacked of a troubling lack of discipline and incompetence of command, just as Eli had said. Could the enemy general really be this incompetent?

"This army is mostly composed of Southern rebels," Taha'Leeth said. "As you can see, there is very little order below. The general in command was likely a civilian not too long ago, with no military experience. However, if you look off to the left, there are a number of tents lined up in neat rows." She pointed and Stiger followed her finger. "That tells me the vast majority of the Cyphan must have pulled out and left. Were there more regulars present, things would be very different."

"In that there would be defenses facing the forest?" Stiger asked.

She gave a nod. "Just as the legions do, the Cyphan fortify their marching encampments, and they would have placed a professional in command, but this is a rebel army, so the rebels elected their officers. It was likely a popularity contest rather than one based upon skill."

Stiger once again swept his gaze over the camp, critically looking, searching. He hoped she was right. After several moments, he returned to the small section of the camp where the tents were arranged in orderly rows.

"How many regulars would you think those tents amount to?" Stiger asked.

Taha'Leeth was silent as she studied the tent line. "I count enough tents for six such companies. Perhaps twelve hundred regulars, maybe more, maybe less. They might also be Cyphan conscripts. Whether slave soldier or conscript, they will be disciplined, well-trained, and motivated. You can expect them to be the biggest threat on a field of battle."

Stiger blew out a slow breath. He reached down and scooped up a handful of snow. With both hands, he formed it into a ball. As he did it, he had a brief recollection of having a snowball fight on the palace grounds when he was a mere child.

The memory brought up unwelcome feelings, for his best friend at the time and childhood playmate, Tioclesion, had ultimately gone on to become the current emperor. With the fires of a failed rebellion, that friendship had long since cooled and, for all intents and purposes, ended. The rebellion and his father's support of it had seen to that.

Feeling sour, he dropped the snowball back to the ground. Patting his hands clean, he returned his gaze to the enemy's camp, thoughts racing. Here before him was an opportunity. He was certain of it. By not fortifying their camp, Stiger's enemy had made a fatal mistake.

The question now became...should he alter the plan to take advantage of that mistake or stick with it and see his plan through? His eyes returned to the enemy's supply depot, wagons, and transport. Despite having plenty of supply, Stiger did not know how long the campaign would last. Seizing what the enemy had only made sense. More important was their transport. He knew he could not risk having it intentionally destroyed. In the coming days, it might prove invaluable to keeping the army fed.

"Seems like a wonderful opportunity, sir," Ruga said, as if he'd read Stiger's thoughts. "It would be a shame to pass it up, especially with the enemy being so obliging. It's almost as if they're inviting us over for dinner, sir."

Stiger rubbed his jaw as he considered the centurion's words. He was leaning toward striking, for he felt that to be the correct option. But...what if it wasn't?

"You are thinking of attacking, yes?" Eli asked plainly. It was more of a statement than question.

"I am," Stiger said, after a prolonged moment.

Eli shot a full-on grin, teeth and all, at Taha'Leeth. He seemed suddenly triumphant. "I win. I told you I'd win. The moment he saw their camp and its lack of defenses, didn't I tell you he'd change his mind?" He pointed a finger at Stiger. "I know you so well."

"There was no bet," Taha'Leeth said frostily. "It takes two to make a wager, or have you forgotten?"

"I still win," Eli said.

Stiger glanced at his friend and then over to the woman who had become his lover. She gave a shrug of her shoulders and rolled her eyes at the other elf.

"This," Stiger said, deciding to ignore them, "I think is too good an opportunity to waste. Without having put out any patrols, they are completely ignorant of our presence." Stiger pointed toward the enemy's camp. "More important, there are no defenses between them and us, only forest. Our enemy seems unprepared...quite unprepared." Stiger sucked in a breath, eyes going to one of the larger fires with men gathered around. "Yes, I am thinking that we strike them hard and as soon as possible, before they learn of the legion's presence."

As he said it, Stiger became more resolved. He felt his anger once again stir deep within his breast. It was directed toward his enemy and all who stood in his way. Though, at the same time, he wondered if such a move was a mistake. After all, he'd be giving up a perfectly good defensive position in favor of taking a risk against a numerically superior foe.

Stiger glanced up at the sky. It was late afternoon. In his head, he began estimating the time it would take to organize and then move the legion forward to a jump-off position for assault. That would require some serious planning and hasty work.

Could they do it before the sun set? He didn't think so and was unwilling to conduct a night assault with the entire legion. It was just too large a force to coordinate and maneuver through a forest by moonlight. There was also the serious potential and likelihood for everything to go balls up, with cohorts getting turned around, or worse, lost.

No. Any such attack must begin at dawn or just before it.

The men were ready for a fight. There was no doubt about that. After the march and work they were now toiling away at, they'd be tired. There would be precious little sleep tonight. But he knew that would not pose much of a problem. The men had endured worse and could endure much more. They were legionaries.

Stiger gave it a little more thought. He would order a cessation of work on the fortified line and instead focus on temporary shelters and fires to warm the men up. They carried seven days of precooked rations with them, so food would not be a problem. Yes…this could work.

Stiger had the element of surprise. Striking at dawn would require a night movement to jump-off positions. It would be tricky, but the legion's scouts and the elves could help guide the cohorts into position. Stiger sucked in a breath and then let it out slowly.

The decision was made.

He would not sit behind a defensive line and wait for the enemy to come to him. Stiger made a fist with his hand. He would instead strike and crush this army completely. He would take what they had and then march away, leaving ruin and destruction in his wake.

"I am resolved." He smacked the fist into his open palm. "We will attack."

Stiger turned and, keeping himself crouched, patted Ruga on the shoulder as he stepped by the centurion. It was time to return to headquarters. He had a lot to do in the coming hours and not much time.

NINE

The sky was just beginning to brighten. The first hint of color had appeared, a slight shade of purple. Stiger stood atop the same hill he had been on just a few hours ago, when Eli and Taha'Leeth had led him forward. As earlier, he gazed down upon the enemy's camp.

The hill was a natural vantage point for the battle to come. It wasn't perfect, as he could not see everything, but after consulting Eli and Taha'Leeth, he'd become convinced it was the best spot on what would shortly become a field of battle. So, he'd chosen it for his command post.

The forest behind, like the enemy's camp, was dark and heavily shadowed. A slight, wispy fog hugged the ground. Downhill, the fog seemed to thicken a tad and had partially obscured the enemy's camp. That served his purposes just fine, as it would help to conceal the legion as it moved into jump-off positions for the assault.

Besides it being bitterly cold, he thought there was an ominous feel to the air. It was as if something was not quite right, a wrongness. Stiger scanned the encampment, searching for any hint that there was a problem or that the enemy knew they were coming. He saw nothing out of the ordinary.

He chided himself and chalked it up to nerves. He always got anxious before a battle, running through the what-ifs. This time was no different. His scouts had been observing the enemy all night. If there had been any activity, they would have reported it to him. Still, the feeling would not go away, and that troubled him a little.

The risk that came with his attack upon the enemy was greater than what he'd initially planned with Salt. In the coming fight, there were no fortifications for the legion to fight behind. He was throwing the dice, gambling that surprise and sheer audacity would win the day against a numerically superior foe. Well, that and the legion's iron discipline, training, and organization. It was a gamble to be sure, and one Stiger hoped would pay off.

In the darkness around him, the cohorts were moving into the position, readying themselves as quietly as they could. Despite taking efforts to minimize noise, with so many men being deployed, Stiger could hear the faint jingle and chink of armor. He understood that some sound would carry. There was simply no helping it, and he hoped the noise did not carry to the enemy. Even if the enemy discovered the legion and sounded the alarm, Stiger was committed. The die had already been cast. What happened now was in Fortuna's hands.

Like unsuspecting prey being closed in upon by a pack of hungry wolves, the enemy slept, unaware of what was about to descend upon them. In truth, Stiger was amazed he'd been able to move the legion up so close without detection, nearly to the edge of the encampment itself. It was hard to fathom the enemy commander's incompetence.

"Never become complacent," Stiger said, barely above a whisper, thinking that here before him was a powerful lesson to take to heart. It was a prime example of what not to do.

"That's good advice, sir." Salt stood at his side, observing the enemy's camp. "Very good advice, sir. It's a good thing the enemy did not think of it first."

Stiger glanced over at his camp prefect. Despite the ironic tone, Salt was grim, for he, like Stiger, knew what was at hand. Both of them were worried about how the next few hours were going to play out. Stiger could read it plainly in the other's eyes, just as Salt likely could in his too. But to others, both senior officers would appear calm and collected, as if they were merely prepared to watch a regular training.

Next to Salt stood Arnold. The man was wearing his legionary armor. Stiger sensed that Arnold felt uncomfortable in their presence, almost as if he did not belong amongst the senior officers of the legion. Stiger did not care. The man would get used to it soon enough, for Stiger did not intend to let the budding paladin far from his sight, unless, of course, he was called away by the High Father.

"In all my years, sir," Arnold said, in a hushed tone that was full of awe, "I've never seen an entire legion sidle up to an enemy army without being found out. The High Father surely has blessed us this day."

"The High Father loves his legionaries," Salt said and held out both hands, gesturing about them out into the darkness. "Our god watches over us. This is but one more example of that truth."

There was a muffled curse from behind, followed by a solid-sounding thud as something was dropped. Stiger looked back. He could not see what had happened or who had made the noise.

Under the supervision of Tribune Severus, his clerks were busy setting up his command post. Several tables had already been assembled and the snow was being shoveled aside. The canvas of the headquarters tent had been unpacked and laid out, along with the poles. Once the attack went forward, the tent would be raised.

A handful of Ruga's men were assisting the clerks with setting up the command post. Legionary Beck, holding the Eagle, stood off and out of the way. The Eagle had been wrapped in a black cloth to keep it from being seen by the enemy. In the darkness, the standard was only a dark, indistinct shape.

The Eagle guard, an entire century, stood around Beck and the empire's honor. They would guard it with their lives, for to lose the Eagle was to lose their honor.

Javelins and shields in hand, the rest of Stiger's guard, Ruga's men all, had been deployed protectively around the hill. An auxiliary with a bow and horn stood just a few feet away. He waited upon Stiger's command. A small shielded fire smoked at his feet.

Several runners and messengers were huddled a few yards back, talking quietly amongst themselves. Beyond them and on the back side of the hill was a team of mules. The mules had brought forward the essential baggage that headquarters would require. Men were moving back and forth from the train, carrying stools, tables, and small crates.

"It appears we caught them without their sandals on," Salt said in a hard but low tone.

"What?" Stiger asked. "No more toga jokes?"

"I thought you said I wore that one thin, sir?" Salt asked. "Thought I'd try another approach."

Stiger chuckled and felt a slight lightening of his mood. "You did wear that fairly thin."

"They're about to learn a very painful lesson," Salt said, growing serious once again.

"Agreed," Stiger said, his gaze returning to the enemy, who were sleeping blissfully away. With each passing heartbeat, the sky lightened. Stiger felt it was light enough to send his men forward without too much of a problem. "We're about to give them an education."

"That we will, sir," Salt said.

A messenger jogged in. He was red-faced and out of breath from his exertions through the snow. Stiger turned to watch briefly as the messenger saluted and then reported his news to the tribune. Severus replied. The messenger gave another salute and then started back the way he'd come, at a slower pace.

Somewhere out in the darkness, a dog began barking, drawing Stiger's attention back to the enemy's camp. He sucked in an unhappy breath, for the dog surely sensed something was out in the forest. A shout followed and the dog ceased its barking.

It did not surprise Stiger that the enemy had a dog. There were also likely camp followers down there too. That would include women, children, whores, and more. It saddened him slightly, for in a short while there would be terror below, along with a great effusion of blood. Lives would be forever altered by his command.

But there was no helping that. He could not worry about the enemy, and that included the innocent, the children. He had a job to do and fully intended to do it, as ruthlessly as possible. For in war, a commander who was not ruthless ran the risk of defeat and failure. Compassion was something he simply could not afford.

Boots crunching the snow, Tribune Severus came up behind him. He cleared his throat. "Excuse me, sir."

Stiger looked over as Severus stepped up to his side. When Stiger had first met him, the tribune had been a mere boy, barely into his teens. Since that time, five long years had passed. Severus had turned into a young man, growing taller and fit. He was becoming more capable by the day and was developing into a fine officer, one Stiger was proud to lead.

Stiger gave a nod for Severus to speak.

"We have confirmation that all legionary cohorts are in position, sir," Severus reported and then hesitated a heartbeat. "All except the Sixth, sir. Both auxiliary cohorts are also in position and ready, sir. Their archers and slingers are also deployed and ready, sir."

Stiger wondered what had happened to Katurus's cohort. That they were not in position was troubling and irritating.

"What's happened to the Sixth, son?" Salt asked. "What's keeping them?"

"No idea, sir," Severus said. "We've had no word from them. I've sent a runner to locate the Sixth, but he's not reported back yet."

"They may have gotten lost in the darkness, sir," Salt said, turning to Stiger. "I expect they will turn up soon. At least, I hope they do, sir."

Stiger felt a stab of intense frustration. The Sixth was responsible for covering his extreme left flank. Guides had been provided to each and every cohort. Taha'Leeth, Eli, and Aver'Mons were also out there somewhere in the trees, helping to lead the legion forward. Had he more elven rangers, he doubted this would have happened.

In a perfect world, there would have been no problems, no issues. However, Stiger was a realist, or perhaps it was just that he was the ultimate pessimist, for he expected things to go wrong. In his experience, when it came to battle, something or someone always managed to cock up the best of plans. Nothing ever went completely right, and if it did, you needed to worry…for something was about to go terribly wrong.

Stiger rubbed his hands together for warmth as he considered the situation. Even with his gloves on, his fingers were cold and ached. He glanced up at the sky again. The color had increased, and the sky had lightened considerably. Within an hour, the sun would be up and daylight would be upon them.

With most of the legion in position to jump off into the attack, it was bound to be only a matter of time before a bright-eyed sentry spotted them. That was, if they weren't all asleep. The enemy seemed lax when it came to basic precautions for their security.

His thoughts returning to the Sixth, Stiger sucked in a breath of the cool air and expelled it. He shook his head, feeling the frustration keenly. In the coming fight he needed every single sword and shield.

"Send a team to find them," Stiger said. "I want the Sixth in position, as rapidly as possible."

"Yes, sir." Severus saluted and stepped away.

"It was bound to happen, sir," Salt said, once Severus was out of earshot.

"I know," Stiger replied. "We're lucky it's just one cohort that's gone missing and not more. I would hate to have to delay the attack. Such a thing would give the bastards down there a chance to become organized. And we can't have that, now, can we?"

"I don't think we can afford to wait on Sixth Cohort," Salt said. "Everyone else is in position and ready. We have the element of surprise on our side. If we lose it…well, that will translate into greater casualties for us. We can't have that either, sir."

"No we can't." Stiger turned his gaze back to the sleeping encampment below. He rubbed his jaw. Upon his command waited the entire legion, thousands of men poised and ready to be released upon the enemy. He had no reserves. He'd considered designating one of the auxiliary cohorts as a fire brigade, a unit to be thrown at a problem point. But after some reflection, he had, in the end, rejected the idea.

The enemy camp was very large. Stiger figured the legion's assault force, without Sixth Cohort, was outnumbered by a factor of more than three to one. For the attack to succeed, he needed to stretch out his entire line and bring as much of the encampment on his side under assault as possible. The legion had to be seen as an oncoming armored wall that was rolling over the entire camp.

By doing that, the bastards would not know the size disparity between the two forces. At least, he hoped so. Stiger was counting on that and the resulting confusion that an attack without warning would cause. The more men he panicked, the fewer that would stand against the legion, and the easier it would be to break the enemy. That was how he saw it. He hoped he was correct.

Stiger sucked in another breath and let it out slowly. Somewhere out in the fog, Death patiently waited. By day's end, there would be a line waiting for the ferryman's services, for thousands would surely perish before the sun, which had yet to rise, would set.

It was something he thought worthy of a moment's hesitation and reflection. Stiger glanced up at the sky and his thoughts went to his god. Normally, he would have taken a moment to say a silent prayer before action, but given the circumstances, he felt that would not have been appropriate. He glanced over at Salt and Arnold.

"Gentlemen, shall we take a moment to pray?" Stiger asked.

Without hesitation, Salt bowed his head, as did Arnold.

"High Father," Stiger said softly, bowing his head and closing his eyes, "lead us to victory this day. Spare as many of our men as possible from death, dismemberment, and injury. Give us the strength to see through what must be done, to carry forth your will, your holy standard, and break this army before us. Harden the men's arms and hearts to their duty." Stiger paused a heartbeat. He'd never been one for praying aloud but felt he'd said enough. The High Father would get his meaning. "Through this legion, may your will in this world be done."

With those last words, Stiger felt his connection to the High Father grow heated, warming him against the cold. Startled, he opened his eyes, blinking rapidly. The sensation faded, and then passed altogether. Had he imagined it?

No. He hadn't.

The High Father had answered his prayer. The great god was with them. Stiger was heartened by that.

"Amen," Arnold said.

"I believe it time, sir," Salt said. "What are your orders?"

Behind him, almost hidden in the darkness, sat Dog. The animal had returned an hour ago as the legion was moving into position. Dog let loose a low whine. Stiger spared the animal a brief glance and then looked over at Salt.

Salt was right. It was time.

There was no sense in delaying things further. Doing so would increase the chance of discovery.

"Would you kindly give the order for the attack to go forward?" Stiger asked, though both of them knew it was an order.

"I would be honored, sir." The prefect turned toward the auxiliary with the bow. The man held an unlit fire arrow in his other hand. Snow had been shoveled and built up around the fire, to hide the light from the enemy.

"Give the signal," Salt ordered, his voice almost as harsh as it was hard. "Shoot the bloody arrow."

The auxiliary immediately stuck the tip of the arrow into the fire. He waited a moment for it to catch. Then, he quickly nocked it, raised the bow skyward toward the enemy's camp, and loosed.

The arrow was a brilliant dart of light as it streaked across the ever-brightening sky. It left a thin stream of smoke to mark its passage. Stiger tracked the missile with his eyes as it arced upward and then began to fall, until it hit the ground, right next to one of the sentry fires. The sentry had been sitting on a felled log, with his back to the forest. He jumped up, clearly startled.

At first, nothing happened, then Stiger heard a shout of alarm from the sentry. It was picked up by others. A heartbeat later, an indistinct shout rang out from Stiger's right. It was clearly an order. Several heartbeats later, the sound of hundreds of bows twanged. A wave of arrows, making a hissing sound, arced up into the air.

The arrows slammed down into the enemy's encampment, a deadly hail of iron-tipped rain. There were more shouts of alarm, exclamations, oaths, and agonized screams of pain as the arrows undoubtedly tore through tent fabric to strike the men within.

Another hissing volley followed the first, followed rapidly by a third.

Stiger stood there with Salt and Arnold. The three of them silently watched the drama unfold. Stiger knew he should be feeling elation, for it was clear the enemy had been caught completely by surprise.

Instead, he felt somewhat helpless and more than a little useless. There was not much more that he could do. When he gave the order to advance, the rest would be up to his cohort commanders, men like Sabinus, whom he had complete faith in. But that still did not change how he felt. He had planned and done all he could. The rest was now in the hands of others, and Stiger found that feeling...unsatisfactory.

Two more volleys arced out into the darkness. The enemy's camp was a riot of confusion. Men emerged from tents and ran about in a muddled cacophony of shouting and screaming. Officers were undoubtedly attempting to establish some sort of order, but the confusion was just too great. It was more than Stiger had expected, could have hoped for.

His orders had called for several more volleys before his heavy infantry started forward and stormed the camp. Stiger had wanted to instill as much chaos as possible before launching the main attack. However, the enemy's camp was already in a state of extreme chaos. He did not think it could get much more confused. Additional volleys would not change that. If anything, he considered, the enemy might become more organized as officers managed to exert control and rally their men to the defense.

"I think that's enough softening up," Stiger said to Salt. "Time to send the infantry forward."

"Are you certain, sir?" Salt asked with a glance over at him. "Our archers are doing plenty of damage. We could keep it up a little longer, inflict more casualties on them."

"I do not believe it will change matters much, other than to give the enemy a chance to rally a defense," Stiger said. "Sound the advance."

"Yes, sir," Salt said and then turned to look back at the same auxiliary who had fired the arrow. The man had slung his bow and held a horn poised near his lips. He stood ready and waiting. "Sound the call to advance."

The auxiliary raised the horn to his lips and blew one short blast, followed by two long ones. He paused to take a deep breath and repeated the call a second time. The horn cut over the noise, and for a single brief moment, there was near silence.

Then, all along Stiger's line, harsh orders were shouted. This was followed by a series of massed shouts as the cohorts in individual block-like formations began emerging from the cover of the trees. One cohort in the gloom began hammering their swords upon the insides of their shields in a steady beat. It was rapidly picked up by the entire legion. The sound of it seemed to vibrate the very air.

A solid block of men, at least six ranks deep, came into view from the trees on the right side of the hill. Standard-bearers marched to the front, with the cohort commander in the lead. He drew his sword, waved it above his head for his men to see, and shouted something Stiger could not make out.

A moment later, on Stiger's left, a second block of men appeared. This was First Cohort. Second Cohort was the formation on the right. Stiger watched, feeling pride as his legion fully emerged from the tree line and began making their way toward the enemy.

There was no heedless charge toward the enemy's camp, no headlong rush, just a measured pace no greater than a leisurely walk, with the archers following close behind. To have charged forward through the fresh snow in a headlong rush would have quickly exhausted the men. Worse, each cohort would have lost its cohesion and organization, which would lead to each and every man fighting on his own, as an individual. So, the advance was slow, steady, and measured, just as it should have been. The legion would strike the enemy as a unified force.

"Steady, boys," Sabinus shouted. He had not yet drawn his sword. "Slow and steady. Watch your footing and keep ranks. There's no sense in rushing. We will get there when we get there and not before."

Off to Stiger's right, where the encampment disappeared into the trees, the clash of arms rang out, as did screams and cries. The right flank was Third Cohort's responsibility, along with elements of the auxiliary cohorts' light infantry and Stiger's old company, the Eighty-Fifth. Quintus commanded the forces assigned to the right.

The sound of the fighting seemed to increase the panic and confusion to Stiger's front. It was what Stiger wanted to see. A panicked enemy was one who would not fight as effectively. The officers would have a very difficult time organizing a solid defense.

That said, some of the enemy had begun to form a line along the edge of camp, facing outward toward the legion. It was a pathetically thin line, but with every passing heartbeat more of the enemy joined the growing defense. Officers and sergeants moved amongst them, shouting and calling out orders, working frantically to pull the line together in time to meet the legion, which was just yards away. Many of the men joining the defensive line appeared to be armed only with sword or spear. They were wearing tunics and, for the most part, had not had time to don their armor.

The battering of sword and shield by legionaries was an ominous *thunk, thunk, thunk* as they closed on the enemy. Stiger was sure the sound of it was incredibly intimidating, as was the sight of the legion closing in.

As planned, the cohorts paused almost at the boundary of the enemy's camp, just ten yards short. They came together, dressed themselves so that the legion's battle formation was one unbroken line, straight, organized, and six ranks deep. Behind them, the archers had moved forward. They loosed another deadly volley that arced up over the heads of the legionaries before crashing down in the enemy's midst. More screams rang out as the iron-tipped missiles took their toll.

Dozens of skirmishers carrying slings were spread out just in advance of the legion. As rapidly as they could, they were using them to deadly effect, firing the lead bullets into the line the enemy was forming. From the hilltop, Stiger could hear the distinct whirring and cracking of the slingers, who were doing their best to sow confusion amongst the enemy ranks, even as another volley of arrows rained down.

"Excuse me, sir," Severus said.

Stiger looked over at his tribune.

"A runner just came in from Third Cohort," Severus said. "They have pushed their way into the camp on the right, with limited resistance so far. Centurion Quintus states the enemy are falling back before his line."

Stiger turned his gaze to the right, where the enemy's camp disappeared into the trees. As he did, a wall of infantry from Third Cohort came into view, emerging from the trees. It seemed the enemy were fleeing before them. More important, Stiger noted that Quintus had kept the integrity of his line as he advanced through that portion of the camp.

"Very good," Stiger said. "My compliments to Centurion Quintus. Advise him the enemy's center is forming a line. He is to continue to push forward and break any resistance that coalesces to his front."

"Yes, sir," Severus said and saluted, then stepped away toward the messengers.

Sabinus, standing to the front of First Cohort, gave an order, which, over the din of chaos, was impossible for Stiger to hear. However, the legionaries heard, and the junior centurions passed along the order.

The legion's front rank took a step forward. Javelins were readied. There was a pause before another order was called out and the javelins were released. Like a wave, they arced up into the air. The missiles seemed to hang suspended for a heartbeat. Then, they crashed down with a clatter, slamming into the enemy's line. Those few with shields held them up for protection. The enemy seemed to shiver under the impact of the volley, for it had been exceptionally well thrown. Soldiers fell by the score.

"Draw swords," Sabinus hollered in a parade-ground voice only a veteran centurion could manage.

The order was repeated up and down the line. Swords were pulled out and shields raised. Sabinus lifted his sword above his head and then brought it down in a slashing motion, ending with it pointing toward the enemy.

"Advance!"

The entire line stepped off toward the enemy. One measured step after another brought them closer as the heartbeats ticked away. Additional orders were shouted and the shields came up, locking together in an unbroken wall. Swords were held at the ready. The last few yards between the two lines seemed almost painfully slow as Stiger watched the armored wall of men move forward toward the enemy.

Several arrows were fired from the camp. Stiger saw one of his men fall out of the line, clearly injured. He staggered several steps, attempting to keep up with his comrades. After a moment, he dropped both his sword and shield. He held his thigh, which an arrow had gone clean through. Then he fell to the ground. The legionary writhed in agony on the trampled snow as his comrades in the ranks behind stepped over and around him, then left him behind, his blood darkening the snow.

Stiger found he'd balled his fists. He forced himself to open his hands and relax. While he stood back and watched from a safe distance, it was an incredibly painful experience to send men into battle. He wanted to be with them, on the line, helping them go forward. It was unfair he could not share in the danger, the risk, but someone needed to command.

"This is always the most difficult part," Salt said, with a glance over at Stiger. "When I was promoted from senior centurion to camp prefect, I found it difficult to stand by and watch as other men went into battle. My job was to command, to fight only when it became desperate or an example needed to be made. Even now, after all these years, I am still not fully accustomed to it."

"I find it no less maddening," Stiger admitted.

"As you should, sir," Salt said. "I'd be worried were it not so."

A moment later, the two lines came together. There was a loud clash as the first rank of the legion met the enemy.

Thin or not, the enemy's defensive line clearly numbered several thousand men. The clash of arms beat on the air, as did shouts, screams, cries, and orders being called. The enemy's line was not a long one, which meant along the flanks of it, unobstructed, Stiger's line continued to advance deeper into the enemy's camp, which was full of confusion.

One of the cohorts on the right, without any organized enemy to their front, came to an orderly halt. The officer in front—Stiger could not make out who it was in the early morning gloom—stepped out before his men. He turned, faced his men, and shouted something. The officer pointed his sword toward the enemy's line. The cohort began moving again, but instead of continuing to advance forward, as it had been moments before, it began a wheeling movement, swinging around like a door closing upon the enemy's flank.

Stiger applauded the initiative. It was why the legion was broken into cohorts and why there were senior centurions. This allowed portions of the legion, upon the cohort commander's own initiative, to react to battlefield conditions and make adjustments they felt needed.

The movement took time and to Stiger seemed almost painfully slow. But it was well executed, and when the cohort's movement was brought home, it began to push back the enemy's line, curving it backward at that point. The enemy's defensive line was now being pressured not only from the front, but also from the flank. Exerting immense pressure, the cohort began the process of rolling up the right flank.

"Sir," Salt said and pointed off to the right. "Look there. Some of the enemy are making a break for it."

Stiger saw a stream of disorganized people running off to the right, on the far side of the encampment and farther back than where Third Cohort was. The intention was clear.

They were fleeing, trying to make it around the legion's flank and to the safety of the forest.

"Severus," Stiger called back.

The tribune stepped over.

"See that bunch fleeing off to the right?" Stiger pointed.

"Yes, sir," Severus said.

"Send a runner to the right flank," Stiger said, and used his hand to show what he wanted. He understood that by the time the runner got there, and Third Cohort could react, it might be too late to catch a good number of them, but perhaps he could block more from escaping. "Tell Quintus I want him to pick up the pace, double-time it, and swing around to block the enemy from fleeing, basically put his cohort in their way. They are to execute that maneuver with all possible haste and cut those bastards off. I want to bag as many as we can. Got it?"

"Understood, sir," Severus said and jogged off, calling to a messenger.

"I would say," Salt said, with a nod toward the fleeing enemy, "that's a very encouraging sign."

"Agreed. However, there are plenty still resisting," Stiger said, watching the struggle of the line to his front. The legionary cohorts had continued their advance, even after they had come into direct contact with the enemy's hastily organized line. The enemy was equipped with whatever weapon was close at hand. Very few wore any armor at all, though a good number carried shields. The fighting was hard and bitter. And yet, against Stiger's heavy infantry, who were fully equipped and better trained, the enemy stood no real chance of success.

Stiger sensed victory was at hand. The enemy would not stand long. As poorly equipped as they were, how could they? He knew it, could feel it, could taste it. Victory was his!

"Severus?" Stiger called.

"Sir?" Severus stepped back over.

"Dispatch messengers to all cohort commanders," Stiger said. "Remind them that the enemy's supplies are to be taken intact. That includes all wagons, carts, tents, mules… there is to be no fire, no destruction, no looting. Reinforce my standing orders, will you?"

"Yes, sir," Severus said. "I will get right on that."

"Thank you."

Severus stepped away toward the messengers.

Stiger turned his attention back to the battle. The legion had pushed and shoved their way forward. Behind them, bodies littered the ground. Stiger was pleased to see that most of the wounded and dead did not appear to be from the legion. His boys were slaughtering the enemy, and badly too.

The sound of the fight increased in tempo and seemed to abruptly become more intense. Stiger studied the line. The enemy was attempting to hold firm. For a moment, they seemed to hold their ground and push back against the legion. Then, the center of his line made a massive, unified push, shoving the enemy roughly back.

It was an incredible effort and had been well made. The enemy began to surrender ground, yards at a time now, instead of just feet, fighting their way backward into their camp. The number of men attempting to flee on the right side had grown to a virtual flood as more sought escape.

Quintus had yet to move to plug the hole. Stiger was irritated that so many of the enemy were getting away. But at the same time, he knew there had not been time for the messenger to reach the flank and pass on his orders, let alone give Quintus time to react.

His gaze went to the left side of the enemy camp. It was interesting that none of the enemy were attempting to flee off to that side, where he was weakest. He searched for his missing cohort. The Sixth was still not in position. Then his eyes returned to the fleeing mass of men heading out into the forest on the right. It seemed almost as if it was a sort of herd mentality that drove them to the right and not the left.

"Are those our men?" Salt asked abruptly. He was pointing farther to their left. Stiger looked, peering through the gloom. There was a small group of men, company-sized, perhaps two hundred in total, moving away from the battle and toward the trees far to the left. They had gone well around the fighting of the line and were moving as if organized and under command of officers. They had flanked the fighting and turned toward the forest. A thin line of archers stood in their path.

"No," Stiger said, eyeing them. "I don't think they are."

He watched as one of the enemy cut down an archer who had become distracted as he was searching a body for loot. The other archers scattered and gave the enemy company distance, allowing them to pass. A couple fired arrows, but for the most part they did nothing to slow the enemy company. Watching it, Stiger felt incredible frustration.

The enemy company continued, drawing closer to the trees, which were about three hundred yards away. They had a team of mules with them. The mules appeared to be heavily loaded, which meant they likely carried food stores. Whoever their company commander was, the man had kept his head when most others had panicked.

They were escaping right where Sixth Cohort was supposed to be. Stiger could see what appeared to be an officer directing them in their flight. He knew they could not be allowed to escape. Organized men would be trouble, especially if they had enough supply to last them several weeks, enough to make their way potentially out of the forest and spread word of what had happened here.

Stiger glanced around and saw Ruga a few yards off, silently watching the battle play out with his optio, a man named Extus.

"Ruga," Stiger shouted.

"Sir?"

"Get your men together," Stiger said. "We're leaving."

"You can't mean to go after them," Salt said, appalled. "If you must send men, allow me to go in your stead."

Stiger's frustration was almost boiling over. By the Sixth not being in position, they were allowing an entire enemy company to escape.

"No," Stiger said. "I am going. You stay here and manage the battle." Stiger paused, studying the battle. If he was any judge, the enemy's will to resist would shortly snap. "Send word to Nantus. I want Fifth Cohort to pull half of his strength to go after that enemy company. Ruga and I will try to block them until help arrives from the Fifth. That is, if we can reach them in time."

Salt stepped closer to Stiger and leaned in. "Sir, you cannot go down there. It is an unnecessary risk and one, as legate, you should not be taking."

Stiger looked into his camp prefect's eyes, suddenly enraged by the prefect attempting to check his desire to stop the enemy. He was about to speak when Salt beat him to it.

"Sir, you are too important to the legion," Salt said. "I would like to remind the legate of his duty. Your post is here, sir. Besides, one understrength century is not going to slow down two hundred of the enemy, especially with them being organized." Salt pointed. "They're armed and armored. It is likely they are Cyphan regulars, which means they are well trained too. Take Ruga and his century to block their escape and all it will do is get some good boys dead, along with the legion's legate. And I don't think Ikely is prepared to step into your boots, sir. For that matter, neither am I."

Stiger ground his teeth at the thought of the enemy getting away, particularly regulars. However, no matter how much he disliked it, he understood Salt was right. His place was here, not rashly chasing after a group of the enemy, who were in effect fleeing a lost cause. He could send scouts and some men after them later. He forced himself to calm down. The elves would easily be able to track them.

"Very well," Stiger said, letting it go. "You win."

"Thank you, sir," Salt said, looking immensely relieved.

"Ruga," Stiger called. "Disregard. We're staying."

"Yes, sir," Ruga said, also appearing relieved.

At that moment, to the left, there was a massed shout. Both Salt and Stiger looked over. Sixth Cohort had finally arrived. They were emerging from the trees in a line of battle six deep, right in the path of the enemy who were seeking to escape. Stiger could not have planned it better had he tried.

The fleeing enemy company stopped abruptly. There were thirty yards separating the Sixth from the enemy company. After a moment's hesitation, the enemy began forming a line of their own. Since escape was no longer an option, Stiger suspected they intended to sell their lives dearly.

Sixth Cohort advanced and met the enemy company. From the hilltop, Stiger could clearly hear the sharp clash of arms from this encounter. The fighting appeared quite intense. And yet, despite the quality of the enemy, it was still a one-sided affair. The Sixth outnumbered the enemy company by more than two to one, and Centurion Katurus was using that advantage to put pressure on their flanks, nearly enveloping the enemy to his front.

The fighting, from what Stiger could tell, was hard and brutal. When it was over, not one of the enemy from that company was left standing, nor had any attempted flight. Stiger suspected Salt was right. These were the Cyphan's slave soldiers. It told Stiger that hard fighting lay ahead. Still, a sense of intense relief and satisfaction washed over him at the checking of their escape.

He returned his attention back to the main battle. His men had pushed more than halfway into the enemy's camp. The defensive line had broken up into several small groups. The enemy fought with desperation, for should they survive, slavery, at best, was their reward for rebellion against the empire. Those of the enemy that were fighting likely knew they were fighting a losing battle, but still they fought on. Stiger could respect that.

Then one of the defensive formations broke, with the surviving enemy running for their lives. A great shout rose up from amongst the cohorts as they sensed the will of the enemy snap. Another group of the enemy dissolved. The organized resistance ended a handful of heartbeats later and so too did the organization of many of his cohorts as they pounded after the fleeing enemy.

Stiger closed his eyes, knowing that the real slaughter had just begun. It had taken less than an hour, but he had broken an entire army. For a moment, it did not seem quite real. He had done it. The legion would be victorious this day.

"Might I be the first to congratulate you, sir," Salt said, turning to him.

Stiger opened his eyes and looked over at his camp prefect. Salt was a good man and had become an even better friend. The camp prefect extended his hand. Stiger took it and shook.

"This is only the beginning," Stiger said and turned his gaze back out to the utter chaos in the enemy's encampment, where his legionaries were doing their very best to slaughter any enemy soldier they could get their hands on. On the right flank, Quintus was finally reacting and positioning his cohort to stem the tide of flight.

Stiger's thoughts shifted from victory to what was to come. His gaze swept across the encampment. How long would it take him to sort this mess out? How long until he could begin marching after Braddock?

He would need to deal with the prisoners, captured supplies, equipment, and of course the wounded. The legion also required rest, for the men had not gotten much sleep over the last day. After the battle, they would need a day or two to recover…at worst three days. He looked up at the sky, which was clear. The sun was almost up. Would the weather cooperate?

"As you say, sir," Salt said, "it is only the beginning."

"The real challenge lies ahead," Stiger said and, despite his elation at winning, felt a dampening of his spirits. He still had that ominous feeling and could not shake it. He'd won, so what was the matter? He felt almost sick to his stomach, mildly nauseated. Had he eaten bad food? Undercooked meat?

"Yes, sir," Salt said.

"Severus?" Stiger turned and looked back on his tribune.

"Sir?"

"Send messengers to all senior centurions," Stiger said. "They are to reform their cohorts and take prisoners, whenever practical. Any enemy who resist are to be put to the sword. I want the slaughter and any looting to end as soon as possible. I also want the enemy's senior officers taken alive. They might have intelligence we could use. Understand?"

"Yes, sir," Severus said.

"Ruga," Stiger called.

"Sir?" Ruga said.

"Organize an escort. We're going down there," Stiger said. "I wish to see my enemy and their camp."

"Yes, sir," Ruga said.

"Right," Stiger said and made to step away. He stopped and looked over at Arnold, who was still staring at the chaos that had overrun the entirety of the enemy's camp. Arnold looked like a troubled man.

"Arnold," Stiger said, feeling a sudden urge to take the man with him. "Would you care to join me?"

Arnold looked over. He hesitated and then gave a nod. "Aye, sir, I would."

"Right," Stiger said, "let's get moving then. Dog, come."

TEN

The snow crunched softly under Stiger's boots as he picked his way through the field of bodies that lay just before what had been the enemy's camp. He glanced over at the nearest tents. Now it was his camp, along with everything that was within it that could be taken or salvaged.

There were bodies everywhere. Some were lying face-down in the snow where they'd fallen. Others were on their backs or sides. One a few feet away was even sitting up, leaning against the stump of a tree. It was as if he were just resting, only he wasn't. He was stone-dead. Blood from a vicious chest wound had darkened his tunic and stained the snow around him.

The sun was up, but it shed very little warmth. Stiger's cheeks burned with the cold. His lips had become dry and cracked from it. He glanced up at the brilliant blue sky and thought it near perfect in its magnificence. The blue was quite a contrast to the ugliness about him. He rubbed his hands together for warmth and let out a long breath that steamed heavily in the frigid air.

A raven gave a frustrated cry, squawking loudly. He looked over and saw one of the dread birds, not ten feet away. It was picking at the eyeball of one of the recently deceased. The sight of the bird made him feel ill.

It never ceased to amaze Stiger at how quickly the carrion eaters arrived. In a few hours' time, there would be thousands of the birds, eager for a feast before everything froze solid.

The battle had seen a great effusion of blood. The proof of it was in the snow, which had been stained an ugly reddish color, almost as if someone had sprinkled dye everywhere. In places, so much blood had spilt, it melted holes straight to the ground below. Some of those who had recently succumbed to their wounds were still warm. Their open wounds steamed in the cold air. It was a disturbing sight and one he'd never quite grown accustomed to. Instead of shying away, he made sure to look, to take it all in…for all of this had been done upon his orders.

Wherever heavy fighting had taken place, there were tightly packed clusters of bodies. Large groups of the dead lay in straight lines, as if they'd gone to sleep next to one another or someone had intentionally arranged them that way. Stiger knew different. Such lines were an indicator of where a line of the enemy had stood firm and paid a steep price for it.

Stiger blew out an unhappy breath as he stepped over the body of an enemy soldier. He was a boy of no more than fourteen, but he'd fought like a man. An unblooded sword lay tightly clutched in his left hand. The face was pale, lips blue. The first hints of acne were on his stubble-free cheeks.

The boy's throat had been ripped open to the spine, the result of a short sword's jab. The subsequent gush of blood had melted the snow underneath the boy's back and neck. The top half of his body was angled downward, with the legs pointing upward at an awkward angle.

This was not the first time he had seen such things. Stiger supposed it would not be the last. Yet, he found it no less disagreeable. The boy should have been on a farm or learning a trade as an apprentice, not just another body amongst thousands that would soon be buried in a mass grave and then forgotten.

An unhappy breath was expelled just to Stiger's left. Sword drawn, Ruga walked on Stiger's left side and close at hand. Clearly the centurion thought it disagreeable too. Arnold followed a few steps behind. One of Ruga's men was on Stiger's right. Two more were a few yards to the front and another two trailed behind Arnold.

Stiger's escort was alert and vigilant. They had their weapons drawn and their shields held at the ready, for not all those lying in the snow were dead. A good number of the enemy were merely wounded and hoping to escape detection.

As they walked through the aftermath of the battle and came across bodies in their path, Stiger's escort poked at them with their swords to make sure they were dead. If they weren't, despite any protests or begging, an efficient jab rapidly sent them on their way to the afterlife.

Stiger paused, stopping to look around. His escort stopped as well and faced outward. Teams of legionaries had been sent out to look for wounded to be helped and carried back to the surgeons.

The dead would be dealt with later. The priority was the legion's injured. From experience, Stiger understood that many would succumb to their wounds or the cold, long before help could arrive. Only after they had been tended to would a thought be given for the enemy's wounded. For most, that would simply be too late. Very few would survive, for the legion would not be staying long. Stiger would be taking his surgeons and doctors with him. Both the legion's wounded and the enemy would be left in the care of the valley's residents and the dwarves. Not for the first time did he consider that it was a harsh world. That was the one he lived in, and he did not make the rules.

Stiger's gaze fell upon three legionaries tending to a fallen comrade. The man had been wounded in the hip. Two of the men were feverishly fashioning a makeshift litter using a shield and two javelins. The third was doing his best to bandage the wound, which bled freely. His arms were slathered up to his elbows with the wounded man's blood. While he worked, the man lay there and moaned softly for his mother.

The sight tore at his heart, as did the bodies of his men that they'd passed. They suffered because he'd ordered them forward. Here on the edge of nowhere, they'd met their fate. Their own personal stories had come to an end. The responsibility rested solely with him, as it always did, which was why he felt required to tour the battlefield. Stiger rubbed at his tired eyes. It never got any easier.

He ran his gaze once more around the field of battle. The temperature was below freezing. Within hours, the recently deceased would be frozen solid. That would make disposing of the bodies a much more difficult process. Still, the work would get done. He had no doubt about that. They now had prisoners and lots of them, a large pool of labor, to see that it was finished properly.

Stiger began moving again. Ruga and his escort stayed with him as he continued his exploration of the battlefield. Dog padded along a few yards away, occasionally stopping to sniff or nose a body. The animal almost seemed depressed. His tail and head hung low.

The small groups of legionaries and auxiliaries they passed ceased their searching, came to attention, and saluted.

Stiger made a point of returning their salutes. After a time, he stopped again and returned the gaze to the morning sky. He held an arm up to shield his eyes against the sun. He had been walking the battlefield for over an hour, and his mood had gone from a feeling of triumph at this victory to sullen, almost resentful anger over its cost in blood. It was good that he saw the cost, for he never wanted to forget it.

Ruga and Arnold, clearly having sensed Stiger's mood, had refrained from speech. They'd left him to his own thoughts, which he appreciated. Stiger turned and made his way over to where the Sixth had encountered and successfully blocked the enemy company attempting to flee the battle.

Katurus's cohort had long since moved on, leaving only the dead behind and one of the enemy's mules. Where the other mules had gone, Stiger had no idea. Perhaps they had just wandered off? The animal's bridle was still gripped in the hand of one of the fallen.

Stiger looked over at the mule. Sacks and casks had been secured to her back. He reached out a hand and felt one of the sacks. It gave slightly and he felt powder inside, most likely flour. It was as he had thought. The mules had carried supply.

Stiger turned his attention to the dead. The men of this company had been armed with a sword that was a little longer than a legionary short sword. The blade was thinner and had been intended for not only stabbing but slashing attacks as well. He saw no sign they'd carried spears.

Interestingly, each soldier wore a small bronze collar about the neck. Stiger took this to be a sign that this company had been composed of slave soldiers. The collars were similar to the steel ones that imperial slavers used to keep slaves from running off while shipping them to market. They did this by simply chaining them together. However, the collar these soldiers wore was more elegantly made than the ones he'd seen in the empire. The collars had also been polished, as if it were one of the soldiers' few prized possessions. They gleamed under the morning sunlight.

The enemy wore chainmail armor that draped down to just above their knees. Their helmets were conical in shape and had long nose guards that came down to the chin. There were no cheek guards, like those used by the legion.

Stiger noted that the enemy's equipment was exceptionally well maintained. He bent down and picked up a shield. It was smaller than a legionary's and rounded. It too looked well cared for. There was writing on the inside. Stiger could not read the script, but he supposed it had been the soldier's name and unit, for legionaries did the same with their own equipment. He tossed the shield back down onto the snow, suddenly feeling disgust.

These were the enemy, but from what he'd observed during the fighting, they'd been good soldiers. Stiger rubbed the back of his neck, feeling a mounting frustration. These boys lying dead in the snow at his feet had just followed the wrong side, was all, an accident of birth. The bodies before him represented a waste of good infantry.

Stiger looked around and searched for their officer. He spotted the man a few yards off. Two dead legionaries lay still by the officer's side. The three were almost touching. Their swords and shields lay discarded in the snow where they'd been dropped. Stiger moved over.

Blood stained the snow all around the three. The officer had taken several wounds, a bad slash to his arm, a cut to his cheek, a serious cut to his right hand, and what looked like the finishing blow, his leg ripped open to the bone.

The officer's face was incredibly pale, almost matching the snow, a clear sign he'd bled almost completely out. His black mustache stood in contrast to the paleness of the skin.

Interestingly, he too wore a bronze collar. Was the officer a slave as well? Stiger suspected he was.

"These bastards died hard, sir," Ruga said, breaking the silence.

"They did," Stiger agreed.

"Faith," Arnold said, stepping up to Stiger. He had a book in his hand that had snow on it. He handed it over to Stiger. As he took it, Stiger felt slightly repulsed, as if the book were a vile thing. It made his skin crawl, just touching it.

Stiger shook off the snow and ice, then flipped through the pages. The book was thick, battered, and appeared to be well-used. It looked as if the pages were made of deer, or perhaps cow, skin. A scrawl he was unfamiliar with was written within. The book was also illustrated, with hand-drawn images of impressive quality.

"I can't read this," Stiger said, looking back to Arnold.

"I can't read the bloody thing either, sir," Arnold said. "But if you look on the cover, the mark of Valoor is stamped there."

Stiger closed the book and studied its cover. Sure enough, there was a small black palm print etched onto the cover, near the bottom, under the same ornate script that had been written inside. It was Valoor's mark.

"I think that is Valoor's scripture or holy book or whatever you want to call it," Arnold said. "I found it clutched to the breast of one of the enemy, sir. I suspect it gave him some comfort as he passed from this world to the next. Though it makes me ill just looking upon it."

"You too, huh?" Stiger asked.

Arnold gave a nod as Stiger handed the book back to him. Immediately, the feeling of revulsion passed. Over the last few years, Stiger had become more sensitive to such things. Thoggle and Menos had told him it was the High Father's disapproval made plain for him. Stiger turned away to gaze down on the dead officer, feeling very dissatisfied with what he'd seen and learned.

"Sir?" Arnold asked.

"Yes?" Stiger looked back over.

"Would you mind if I kept this?" Arnold held up the book.

"Whatever for?" Just the thought of doing so made Stiger slightly queasy. The desire to burn the book or bury it was strong. "You can't read it. You said so yourself."

"Well," Arnold said, glancing down at the book in his hands, "there's bound to be some poor bastard amongst the prisoners who can translate for me. I want to learn more of our enemy's beliefs. If you don't mind, sir. I want to hang onto it. I feel the need to, sir."

Stiger gave it some thought. "Very well. If you want to study that vile thing, do it."

"Thank you, sir," Arnold said.

Stiger was about to turn away again, when he hesitated.

"Now, it is my turn to ask a favor," Stiger said. "I too would learn more on our enemy's beliefs. Would you pass on what you glean from that thing?"

"Of course, sir," Arnold said.

Stiger gave a nod, turned away, and began walking back toward the enemy's camp. As he walked, he wondered how many had gone to sleep the night before, not realizing that they were living out the last hours of their lives.

Even though they were the enemy, he regretted that so many had died. Yet, he would not take it back. The breaking of this army and the slaughter of the enemy had been necessary. The carnage around him represented a good day's work.

Stiger felt his anger stir with such thoughts. He would bring the death and destruction to the enemy, just as they intended to do to the empire. That was his sacred duty. The enemy would feel his wrath before this was all over. He would see to that.

At the boundary of the camp, he came across a file of resting legionaries. They looked weary and exhausted, thoroughly played out. Some were sitting in the snow. One legionary even sat upon the chest of a dead enemy and held his face in his hands. None were talking.

"On yer feet, ya savages," the optio in charge of the file said, making to stand himself. The optio was older and had a hard look about him. A thin scar ran across his right cheek.

"As you were." Stiger held up a hand, not wishing to disturb them. The men returned to their positions, their eyes on him.

"Which cohort?" Stiger asked the optio.

"First, sar," the optio said.

"You saw some difficult fighting," Stiger said. "How are your boys doing?"

"A little tired, is all, sar," the optio responded with a glance at his men. "Always that way after a fight, sar. The exhaustion sets in, if you know what I mean, sar."

"I do," Stiger said.

"With a little rest, sar," the optio said, "we will be right as rain."

"We sure gave it to them something fierce, sir," one of the men said, an older man. "Didn't we?"

"Yes, you did." Stiger ran his gaze around the file. "You all did good. You made me proud of what you did here this day."

More than a few weary smiles broke out at the rare praise. It was what he intended, and in truth, he was proud of them. They had gone into battle cold, wet, tired, and come out victorious. He could not have asked more from them, but he knew in the days and weeks ahead he most assuredly would. There too would be a cost for that.

Stiger studied the men of the file. He could read not only the exhaustion in their weary gazes, but the shock at having survived. After battle, every soldier went through a period of self-reflection. It was at moments like these, when the danger had passed, that one realized how tenuous life could be, especially if one lost a mate or had killed a man. Praise was more than welcome. It was necessary and needed to help reinforce that everything would be all right, would eventually return to normal. If there was a normal. Stiger wasn't sure anymore.

"Did you take any casualties?" Stiger asked the optio.

"Just one man, sar," the optio said. "We got lucky, sar. Menorus took a blow to the helmet from a spear. Put a good-sized dent right in it. Knocked him a bit silly, it did, sar. I sent a man with him to make sure he got to see the surgeon, just to be sure, sar. Ya never can tell with blows to the head. I'm a-guessin' he will just have a bad headache when he gets his senses back, sar. Perhaps an ugly lump too for his troubles. Maybe it will teach the fool to bloody duck next time when someone swings a spear shaft at him."

Stiger gave an absent nod. A shout drew his attention. He looked in the direction of the shouting to see a centurion over a hundred yards away hollering to another. Stiger could not tell what was being said, but neither man seemed alarmed, so he disregarded it. He returned his attention to the file of men.

"We've got a long road ahead of us," Stiger said to them, choosing his words carefully. What was said here would likely be passed along. Within a few short hours, much of the legion would hear of it, and there was the very real chance it would be embellished in the telling. "Hard days are coming. Harder than this one. But have no doubt, we will break the Cyphan just like we did these bastards here." Stiger paused, meeting each of their gazes in turn. "Years from now, you will have one heck of a tale to tell your children and grand-children. It will be something to hold your head up above other men and proudly state you were there, with me, when it all happened."

There was a long moment of silence as they absorbed that.

"I am already damn proud of being in the Thirteenth, sir," one of the legionaries said, coming to his feet. He was missing several front teeth and, like a boxer, his nose appeared to have been broken repeatedly. "We will do what needs doing, sir. Just ask and we will get it done for you. You can count on us, sir. Right, boys?"

There was a round of agreement at that as the rest of the men got to their feet. Their sentiment warmed his heart. These were good boys and they were his. He loved them for that.

"I know I can." Stiger paused and glanced around. "We have to clean up this mess, so we won't be marching for a couple of days. Rest and recover."

"Yes, sar," the optio said.

"And make sure you get your boys something to eat," Stiger said.

"I will, sar," the optio said.

Stiger left them and walked into the camp itself. The file watched him go. Stiger could feel their gazes upon his back. The farther he went into the camp, the more bodies he came across. The smell of smoke, mixed with the stench of blood, urine, and human waste, was strong on the air. It was awful, but again, nothing he'd not experienced before.

A file of men moved by, carrying a wounded comrade on a stretcher. The man had been injured in the right leg. The wound had been bandaged and a tourniquet tied around the leg. Blood was seeping through the bandage.

The injured legionary was extremely pale. His hands trembled. It bothered Stiger to see men maimed and injured in such a way. Worse, Stiger knew he could not afford to replace those he lost, whether to injury or death. In the weeks ahead, he had to be careful with how he used the legion…very careful. Much depended upon that.

The sound of hasty footsteps in the snow behind him caused him to stop and turn. A legionary jogged up. The man was red in the face from his exertions. His breath steamed heavily in the air.

"Excuse me, sir," the legionary said and saluted. He held forth a dispatch.

As he took it, Stiger wondered what bad news it contained. He opened the dispatch and scanning the contents, saw that it was from Salt. Stiger's camp prefect reported that another small group of organized soldiers had escaped on the right. He estimated the group's size to be no more than one hundred. Salt believed them to be Cyphan regulars and had dispatched three centuries to chase them down.

Aver'Mons and Marcus were tracking the enemy. Salt was hopeful that they would be hunted down within the next few hours.

Stiger looked up at the messenger and handed back the dispatch.

"Tell the camp prefect to keep me updated on this matter," Stiger said. "I want to hear as soon as he gets any news."

"I will see that he gets the message, sir," the legionary said and saluted. He left the way he'd come, working his way back to headquarters.

Stiger glanced around the enemy's camp. Even before his legionaries had torn their way through it, the camp had been a jumbled mess. Sanitation had clearly not been a concern. Stiger saw frozen human waste had been dumped just to the sides of tents, with no thought of proper disposal. The enemy had been literally living in their own filth. There was no excuse for it.

Not only were bodies strewn all over, but kit lay scattered haphazardly about. Shields, helmets, swords, packs, sacks, boots, sandals, pots, pans, and hundreds other items lay where they'd been discarded in the enemy's panic. Some of the tents had collapsed, likely the result of the fighting as the legion pushed its way into the camp.

Dotting the ground, arrows were everywhere, even seeming to sprout from several bodies. Stiger stepped over to a communal tent. Holding back the flap, he saw the devastating effect the arrow barrage had had. He held his breath, for the tent stank terribly of unwashed bodies and filth.

Inside, three men had died where they slept. One man had taken an arrow square in the forehead. From the wound, a small trickle of frozen blood had run down the side of his head. He'd died instantly, never knowing what had killed him. The other two had multiple arrows protruding from their chests.

He let the tent flap fall back into place and looked around. Stiger spotted Sabinus conferring with several of his officers a short distance off. With them was Therik. Stiger started over. Just behind Sabinus were a dozen or more prisoners, under guard. The officers turned at Stiger's approach. All of them snapped to attention, and Sabinus offered a crisp salute.

"How goes it here?" Stiger asked his primus pilus.

Ruga stepped past Stiger and over to the prisoners, clearly intent upon examining them. Stiger ignored the centurion and focused his attention squarely on Sabinus.

"Very well, sir," Sabinus said, though he looked and sounded tired, "very well indeed."

Stiger's gaze went to Therik. The orc's armor was covered in dried and frozen blood, as was Sabinus's.

"Where have you been?" Stiger asked the orc. He'd not seen Therik for several hours.

"I thought it would be fun fight," Therik said, sounding disappointed. The orc gestured toward the prisoners with a large hand. "These did not offer much of a challenge. It was not much of a fight."

Sabinus gave a grunt. "I will take a battle like this one over a more challenging one any day."

Stiger glanced over at the prisoners. Beyond them, he could see larger groups of the enemy. Some were sitting down, huddled together in groups. Others were being marched out of the camp. All were under a heavy guard.

"Any idea on how many we bagged?" Stiger asked as Dog padded up to his side. The animal sat down, his gaze on Sabinus, almost as if he too was interested in the information.

"We don't have an accurate count yet, but my guess, based on the number I have here…at least six thousand prisoners. It is possible there are more, as I'm not sure how many were taken on the other side of the camp. Once we have a proper count, I will forward that number onto head-quarters, sir."

"Any idea on casualties?" Stiger asked, almost fearing to ask the question. Though he had not seen very many legion-ary dead, he'd not walked the entire camp itself. There was no telling how many had fallen once the fighting had reached its most bitter point.

"I don't know about the other cohorts, sir," Sabinus said. "However, I suspect the legion's terminal casualties will likely prove to be rather light. My cohort lost just ten men, sir, with another twenty-eight wounded. Of those, only three have serious wounds, sir, and have been sent to the surgeons. The rest will be placed on light duty and should recover in a few weeks' time and be fully able to return to service."

"Are you certain?" Stiger asked, for First Cohort had seen some of the heaviest fighting on the field. He hardly dared believe his ears. "Just thirty-eight?"

"Yes, sir," Sabinus said. "To be fair, I had expected the butcher's toll to be higher, sir."

Stiger had as well, though he did not voice that within hearing of the other officers and men. He felt incredible relief at the possibility that casualties across the legion would be light. The High Father had blessed the entire legion this day…surely. Still, even having taken light casualties, good men had died under his command. It bothered him no less.

He glanced around the camp at the bodies of the enemy scattered all over. Some had fallen so close together that his legionaries combing through the bodies were forced to walk over the dead. He shook his head in near dismay. He had completely and thoroughly crushed this enemy army. There was no other way to describe it.

Had he been in contact with the empire, it would have been a major feat, an accomplishment to be recorded in the histories. The victory would have been celebrated back home with games, dinners, and grand banquets. His family would have gained prestige, something it had been severely lacking of late. He might have even been honored with an ovation by the senate and emperor. However, no one knew he still lived, let alone that he'd just crushed an army more than double the size of his own.

"Send a messenger back to headquarters," Stiger said to Sabinus. "Tell Nepturus I want a full accounting of all cohorts, effectives, dead, and injured. I also want the prisoners tallied, both the living and deceased. Find their headquarters and see if they kept any records. I want to know how many of the enemy are missing."

That got Stiger thinking on the prisoners. They would need guarding and, with so many taken, that guard would drain his strength. Stiger knew he could not bring them with him back to the empire. There was too much risk in that, for some would escape with vital intelligence. They might even rise up at the first opportunity. It put him in a difficult position, for he wasn't inclined to kill them…but perhaps they could be put to work, beyond simply disposing of the dead, helping to advance his effort somehow. He needed to think on it.

"Any questions?" Stiger asked, when Sabinus had not responded. The centurion had been looking past Stiger toward the prisoners, as if distracted by something.

"No, sir," Sabinus said, turning back to him. "I will see that it is done."

"Good." Stiger looked over Sabinus's officers, who were standing there, respectfully waiting and watching.

"I am extremely pleased with the work you've done this day," Stiger said to the gathered officers. "We have crushed our enemy here and we will do the same to any other force we come across. Good job. Pass that on to your men."

"Of course, sir," Sabinus said, glancing at his officers. "We will, sir."

Stiger's gaze shifted to the prisoners. "Did we capture any senior officers?"

"We did, sir," Sabinus said and turned, leading Stiger over to a separate group of prisoners that he had not seen. These were being held behind a communal tent. There were three men in total. Swords drawn, five legionaries stood around the prisoners, who sat in the muddy and dirty snow, looking quite miserable.

The prisoners stood when they saw Sabinus approaching. Stiger could read the concern upon their faces. All three were disheveled and only wore tunics, which were dirty and stained with blood, that appeared to be not their own.

Sabinus pointed to an overweight man, who looked more like a merchant than a soldier. "He is the most senior one we could identify so far, a general. He's not the army commander, but apparently the second in command. The other two were responsible for parts of the army. I am not sure their rank translates to anything we have, but I believe you might have called them colonels in this time."

Stiger studied the general. The man was tall, bearded, and had a belly that bulged from under a dirty gray tunic. His hands and arms were a little pudgy and showed no telltale marks of arms training. He reminded Stiger more of a baker he'd once known back in the capital.

Stiger thought for a moment, trying to recall the baker's name. He snapped his fingers. Thetas, yes…that was his name. He'd baked bread and pastries for Stiger's family. Thetas had been a client of his family's—at the time, one of thousands.

When Stiger had left to join the legions in the North, his family's number of clients had dwindled to only a few loyal dozen, Thetas included. The rest had abandoned the Stigers for other powerful families. In truth, Stiger could not blame them, for who wanted to align themselves with a house in disgrace and under imperial disfavor.

Where Thetas had appeared kindly, this man appeared spoiled and privileged. There was something in his eyes that Stiger just did not like.

"Do you speak Common?" Stiger asked the man.

"I will tell you nothing," the man said in fluent Common. His voice, however, trembled.

Stiger stepped closer, with Dog following a few paces behind. Ruga had returned from looking over the other group of prisoners. The centurion moved around to Stiger's side, with the clear intention of intervening, should the prisoner become aggressive.

"What is your name?" Stiger asked.

"General Zoc," Sabinus said, when the general refused to respond. "His own bodyguard pointed him out to us. That bunch over there." Sabinus pointed to the first group Stiger had seen.

Zoc shot the other group an unhappy scowl.

"I would recommend you cooperate," Sabinus said to Zoc. "Your army is shattered. There is no one coming to save you. Our legate holds your fate in his hands."

Zoc's eyes narrowed slightly and shifted from Sabinus to Stiger. At first, he looked uncertain, then his gaze hardened. He drew himself up, chin jutting.

"I have sworn myself to Valoor. Do your worst to me. I shall be rewarded in death with life and rebirth." Zoc's features twisted with hate. He spat on Stiger's boots. "Imperial scum…the Cyphan will defeat you and crush the empire. You will get nothing from me but disappointment."

Without hesitation, Ruga slammed the hilt of his sword into the side of the general's face. Zoc had not seen the blow coming and went down like a bag of potatoes tossed from the back of the wagon.

"When you speak to Legate Stiger"—Ruga stood over him—"you will show more respect or that is the least you will receive from me, you traitorous bastard. You'll be lucky if he doesn't crucify the lot of you rebels."

Ruga kicked Zoc powerfully in the side. The general's breath whuffed out and he rolled in the snow. The other two prisoners took a step back.

"That's enough," Stiger said, when Ruga looked about to deliver another kick.

"Legate Stiger?" one of the other prisoners gasped. "You are a Stiger?"

"I am," Stiger said and it came out more as a growl.

"I will tell you whatever you want to know," the man said. "Please don't kill me. As long as you spare my life. I will tell you everything."

"What is your name?" Stiger asked the man, who looked to be in his mid-forties. He had the look of a farmer about him. His hands were calloused and his skin had a weathered appearance.

"Tacus," the man said, his voice trembling with fear.

Stiger looked back on Zoc, who had rolled onto his back. The general was staring in horror at Stiger. His cheek bled from where Ruga had struck him.

"All three of you will tell us everything we want to know," Stiger said quietly. "Of that, there will be no doubt. The longer you hold your tongues, the more difficult it will be for you, the more you will suffer."

Stiger met each of their gazes before taking several steps away. He beckoned Sabinus over.

"Question them," Stiger said. "Use whatever means you feel needed. I want to know what they know of the strategic situation in the outside world."

"I will see to it, sir," Sabinus said with a glance back at the three. "I will put a good man on it. They won't hold out on us."

"I know they won't," Stiger said. He looked back at the three prisoners. Zoc was still on the ground, his fearful eyes upon Stiger.

"There is something not right with that man over there," Arnold said, drawing their attention.

Stiger had forgotten about the former sergeant. He had not initially followed Stiger over to see the senior officers. Arnold was now around three yards away and had turned back toward the other group. He was pointing.

Stiger turned his gaze to the prisoners. There were ten of them. Five wore armor. Stiger figured they had been on guard duty when the attack had gone forward. The rest had on only tunics. Most did not even have footwear. One had a bad cut on his right arm. He cradled it with his left, but the wound still bled freely.

At first, he wondered what Arnold was on about. Then Stiger went cold and his hand dropped to the hilt of his sword. His gaze locked onto the man Arnold was pointing to. He wore armor and looked just like the other guards, only he wasn't like them.

Dog growled. It was deep and menacing. The animal's hair stood on end.

Stiger felt an intense dislike for the man, worse than he'd felt when he'd held Valoor's holy book. It was mixed with a feeling of disgust, almost strong enough to turn his stomach and make him gag.

Gaze fixed upon Stiger, the man stood. Stiger knew this man was no guard for the general. He was something else.

"He is General Zoc's personal priest," Tacus said, "a devotee of Valoor."

The priest must have tried to conceal himself by donning the armor of one of the guard. Stiger felt the cold sensation settle in his stomach. This priest could use *Will*. He could sense it, the dark, malevolent power roiling within the man. That made him dangerous.

"Seize that man," Sabinus said and pointed.

Swords held at the ready, two of the legionaries guarding the prisoners moved forward. The priest remained perfectly still as they closed in. Then, a knife seemed to materialize into his hand. From where it had come, Stiger did not know, but suspected the prisoners had not been searched as thoroughly as they should have been.

The priest lunged, taking the first legionary by surprise. Almost inhumanly fast, the knife flashed and ripped open the legionary's throat. The second legionary thrust with his sword. It was a hasty, ill prepared strike. The priest dodged and brought the dagger around and down, plunging it into the man's thigh. Screaming in agony, the legionary staggered back and fell to the ground.

It had all happened in a flash. There was a stunned moment of silence. Sabinus, his officers, the other guards, and prisoners stood there in mute shock. Then, the other prisoners scrambled to their feet and drew back, fear on their faces, not of retribution, but of the priest.

The priest turned his gaze to Stiger. The eyes were hard and cold.

"Take him," Sabinus ordered to the other guards, who had surrounded the priest. They started forward, along with Ruga, only Stiger could not let that happen. The priest could use *Will*.

"Hold," Stiger ordered in a hard tone.

They stopped.

"Drop the dagger," Stiger ordered. "I will see that your death is clean and quick."

"My master sent me," the priest said to Stiger in perfect Common.

"Yeah?" Stiger asked, taking a step forward.

"Valoor showed me a vision of you, Champion," the priest said.

That stopped Stiger. The priest knew he was the High Father's Champion.

"I hope he showed you your death, too," Stiger said, hand upon his sword hilt.

"My god sent me as a messenger," the priest said. "In his infinite mercy, he understands that you have been misled by the High Father. Valoor gives you the opportunity to renounce the High Father. Do so and you may live. Refuse him and you will die, as will all who you care about."

"Not happening," Stiger said.

"You disappoint me," the priest said.

"I am happy to disappoint then," Stiger said.

Stiger's eyes went to the man the priest had killed and then the other, who was injured. His anger flared. The priest caught his gaze, reversed his grip on the dagger, and in a flash threw it, not at Stiger but at the injured legionary, who had fallen to the ground.

The shaft of the dagger embedded itself in the man's neck. He went rigid, in stunned shock, then fell back to the snow, bleeding out and choking on his own blood. The priest looked up and smiled at Stiger, as if pleased with himself.

Rage filled Stiger's heart. Suddenly, without realizing he had done it, his sword was in his hand and he was advancing, with murder in his heart. Ruga was at his side as they closed. The priest casually held up a hand, palm outward, toward the centurion. Stiger saw the tips of the priest's fingers begin to glow.

He shoved Ruga roughly aside, just as a spidery web with a reddish brown color shot out toward them. Instinctively, Stiger held up his sword to block the priestly magic, but then at the last moment remembered that Rarokan, the wizard inside the blade, was no more. He should have dodged, only it was too late. The web contacted the blade with an audible crack that assailed the ears painfully.

The force of the attack staggered Stiger, almost driving him to his knees. He felt his connection within glow brilliantly as the High Father came to his aid. The hilt of the sword grew scaldingly hot in his hands. There was a humming in the air and another loud crack.

The attack was over, almost as quickly as it had begun. Incredibly, the web was gone. Stiger blinked in astonishment and glanced at his sword. Blue flame licked along the length of the steel blade. He felt the power throb within, but no Rarokan. There was no hint of the wizard's presence.

He had survived. His body tingled from head to toe and the snow around him had melted. But he'd lived.

The priest blinked in astonishment. He had clearly expected the attack to kill Stiger outright. Doubt filled his eyes. That and exhaustion. Stiger figured the priest had expended much of his energy with the attack.

The rage within his breast returned, igniting a fury. This priest had killed two of his men and was why earlier he'd felt the sense of wrongness in the enemy's camp. Stiger was sure of it. He took a breath and gripped the sword hilt tightly. The blue fire along the length of the blade grew in intensity.

He advanced, intent on removing this menace from the world, like he had the minions. In response, the priest raised his hand, the fingertips beginning to once again glow. Stiger braced himself for the coming attack.

Something shot by him, a blur of gray fur. Dog literally flew through the air. Growling fearsomely, the animal latched onto the priest's arm, knocking and spinning the man around and causing him to cry out in pain.

There was a sudden brilliant white flash and the sound of a bell tolling. Momentarily blinded, Stiger closed his eyes. The light faded, and with it, Stiger opened his eyes. Arnold was before him, wielding a large war hammer that seemed to throb with holy light.

As the priest grappled with Dog, Arnold slammed the hammer into the priest's chest. There was another flash and a deep, sickening thud. The snow all around the two exploded up into the air, as if a great wind had kicked it up, to the point where there was a complete whiteout, blinding Stiger and everyone else.

When the snow settled back to the ground in a slow misty spray, Stiger saw Arnold, his chest heaving, standing above the priest's body. Dog was there too, sniffing at the corpse as Arnold gazed down on the priest. He held the glowing war hammer lightly in one hand, as if it weighed nothing. The priest had been driven down into the snow. His body smoked, looking shriveled, a cruel mockery of the man.

There was silence all around. Sabinus and his officers stared at Arnold in astonishment, as did the prisoners. Stiger sheathed his sword, for he sensed the danger had passed. The wrongness was gone, the taint wiped from the world as if it had never been. So too had gone his rage and fury. It left him feeling drained and exhausted.

He glanced over at Ruga, who was lying in the snow, propped up on his elbows and staring like the others with shocked eyes at Arnold. Stiger held out a hand. After a brief hesitation, Ruga took the proffered hand. Stiger pulled him to his feet.

"You all right?" Stiger asked the centurion.

"I ache all over," Ruga said. "Whatever that priest threw at us would have killed me, had you not shoved me aside."

"You can return the favor one day," Stiger said.

"Yes, sir," Ruga said, "and thank you, sir."

Stiger surveyed the scene. All eyes were on Arnold. He knew, by nightfall, the entire legion would be treating Arnold differently. Word of what had occurred would spread like wildfire. It had begun in Castle Vrell and had finished on this battlefield. If there had been any doubt, now there was none. Arnold was in service to the High Father.

"Your elf friend is right," Therik said, stepping up to the two of them. "It is much more exciting around you. Next battle, I stay with you and wait for something to happen."

"Right," Stiger said, his gaze shifting from the orc to Arnold.

"He has strong medicine," Therik said, pointing at Arnold, "like that warrior priest you kept around, Father Thomas."

Stiger gave a nod and with that left Therik and Ruga for Arnold.

"See," Stiger said. He gestured at the hammer. "I told you the High Father had plans for you."

"It seems that way, sir," Arnold said, gazing down in wonder at the holy weapon he held in his hand. "I called it. The idea sort of popped into my head and it just came."

In less than a handful of heartbeats, the weapon in Arnold's hand lost its glow and faded to nothingness. Arnold opened his hand and looked at it, for he no longer held anything but air. He looked at Stiger, questions written all over his face.

"Better get used to it," Stiger said and clapped him on the shoulder, "Paladin Arnold."

Eleven

Stiger plodded along, holding Nomad's reins loosely in one hand as he led the animal forward. His legs were tired, his back ached, and his feet hurt. Heck, there wasn't one part of his body that did not feel aggrieved to some degree or another. He'd not marched this much in several years, and though he wasn't carrying a shield or his gear, he felt every mile.

It had been almost two weeks since the battle before Castle Vrell. After two days of rest, he'd given the order for much of the legion to march. They'd left the hills and mountains, along with the deep snow, far behind and were now in the heart of the Sentinel Forest.

With each passing day, the temperature had warmed slightly. The road had mostly dried, almost becoming firm. But that did not mean that the roadbed was in good shape. It was torn up, and badly. This was the product of Braddock's army marching before them. Thousands of feet, hooves from the cavalry, and Braddock's baggage train had damaged the road long before the legion had reached it. Stiger's legionaries had only made it worse.

The road had become pitted, scarred, holed, or badly rutted where wagons had struggled through mud that had since dried. Stiger well knew it might've been worse. They could have been fighting their way through mud up to their knees or trudging through snow. He was thankful for that mercy, for despite the deteriorated road, the legion was making good time.

Ten yards to his front marched Fifth Cohort, who had just finished singing a marching song. It had been a bawdry tune of a lovely girl pining after her lover, a legionary who'd given his life in battle against barbarians assailing the empire. Apparently, as the tune went, no other man could satisfy her like the legionary, and so *she pined her days away and pined and pined and pined away until another legionary had come to save the day*. It was a catchy tune and one of many that helped keep up morale, as the miles passed slowly by, one after another.

A cloud of dust had been kicked up into the air by the cohort and the formations farther ahead on the line of march. The dust settled on those behind. It wasn't as bad as it could have been, because the ground was somewhat moist. However, the dust was no less an irritant. It got into the eyes, tickled at the nose, and caused coughing fits.

Just behind Stiger marched his guard and then, a quarter mile back, was Eighth Cohort. Dog trotted happily along at Stiger's side, occasionally breaking away to examine something that caught his interest. The animal seemed to be the only one really enjoying himself. Everyone else was more than weary of the march and ready for it to end.

"I'd have thought you'd want to rest those legs, sir," Ruga said. The centurion had been speaking with one of his men farther back in the line of march. He fell in at Stiger's side as Dog stopped by the roadside to investigate an interesting smell.

Stiger glanced over at Ruga, who was fairly coated in dust. It had become a running joke between the two of them, for Ruga had become accustomed to Stiger sharing the miles afoot with the men.

"I tell you, sir, if I had a horse, sir, I'd be riding the miles away. A fine day for riding, don't you think?"

Stiger had heard it all by this point, from Ruga and various others over the years. He held out the reins to Ruga. "You can borrow my mount if you'd like." He'd made similar offers before. Not once had the wily centurion taken him up on the offer.

Ruga shook his head in a vehement fashion. "It wouldn't be proper for me to take your horse, now, would it, sir?"

"I think, as legate of the legion, I'm the one who decides what's proper and what's not," Stiger said and then turned it around on the centurion. "Don't you agree?"

"It's not that I disagree with you, sir," Ruga said. "You are the legate and of course you decide what is proper. You see, were I to ride, it might give me airs of importance, sir. And me, just a lowly centurion." Ruga made a show of glancing back at his men. His look became sheepish. "And then there is the men, sir."

"What of them?"

"What would they think of me riding, sir?" Ruga sounded scandalized.

Stiger had to laugh at that one, for it was terribly well contrived. Ruga was a tough old centurion, with a fine sense of humor. It was something Stiger could well appreciate, especially on a long march. Banter and humor helped to pass the time, along with the monotonous miles that seemed to crawl painfully by.

Not for the first time did Ruga remind him of Sergeant Tiro. It was one of the reasons he'd chosen the man to command his guard. There was something about Ruga that Stiger liked.

"Well," Ruga said, glancing up at the sky, "at least the rain's held off."

"And the snow," Stiger added.

"Don't remind me, sir," Ruga said.

It had snowed on them a week back. The storm had not been terribly bad. But the snow had accumulated, dropping several inches, which made the march more difficult. The roadbed had been quickly churned up into a soupy mixture of half-frozen mud that made every step a miserable and trying experience.

"Aye, sir," Ruga said. "Now we just need to rid ourselves of this cold."

Stiger couldn't help but agree. The temperature was cold, hovering just above freezing.

"At least the march for the day is almost over." It was Stiger's turn to glance up at the sky. In four hours' time, it would be dark. He looked around at Ruga's men. They appeared worn and tired. The legion as a whole needed rest, perhaps a day or more to recover. Stiger just did not know if he could spare a day, for who knew what was waiting at the end of the road for Braddock.

His gaze shifted to the area they were marching through. The desperate fighting retreat along this road had been like a bad nightmare. A mile back, they'd passed a spot where he'd led his men in an ambush against the enemy. Though he'd been victorious and had mauled an enemy company, Stiger had lost more than a few in that fight. He let out an unhappy breath at the memories of that desperate time. It was as if a dark cloud had scudded its way across the sun, dampening his spirits. Even when one did everything right, good men still managed to die.

Ruga seemed to sense his mood change and grew silent. The road ahead snaked around a bend. As they followed the tail end of the Fifth around the bend, a dispatch rider was coming the other way, walking his horse. He saluted as he made his way past. Stiger returned the salute and then they were by, still following the turn in the road.

As the road straightened out again, they found Therik waiting by the roadside. The orc was sitting on a tree trunk that had been dragged off to the side. He was playing with a dagger, repeatedly tossing it up into the air and catching it by the hilt.

Therik spotted them and pulled himself to his feet. He reached down and grabbed his pack from where it had been sitting and slung it over a shoulder. Exchanging a nod with Ruga, the orc fell in with Stiger.

"He's gone moody again," Therik said to Ruga, "hasn't he?"

Stiger glanced over at the centurion and raised an eyebrow, wondering how the wily old bastard would respond. Ruga did not miss the look.

"I'm too smart to fall for that one," Ruga said.

Stiger felt a mild stab of amusement. It served to lighten his mood a tad.

"You worry too much." Therik sheathed his dagger and pointed a finger at Stiger. "That is your problem, too much worry."

"Someone has to worry," Stiger said.

"I think I meant brood," Therik said and looked over at Ruga in question. "Brood is the right word?"

"I may be a dumb grunt," Ruga said, "but I am not that dumb."

"You mean to tell me," Stiger said to Therik, "in all those years you were king, you never once worried about anything? Brooded on something?"

"Of course I worry," Therik said. "What fool wouldn't? As king, you do not worry, you end up dead."

"And you're telling me not to worry?" Stiger asked. "That's rich, old boy."

"No," Therik said. "I did not say that."

"I believe," Ruga said, in an exceptionally helpful tone, "he's saying it's okay to brood, but he thinks you spend too much time doing it, sir. Do I have that right, Therik? He broods too much?"

"Right," Therik said. "I could not have said better."

"Thank you, Centurion." Stiger looked over at Ruga, who appeared suddenly to be the soul of innocence. "Thank you for that insightful interpretation of Therik's intent. I found it just exceptionally helpful."

"You're welcome, sir," Ruga said, fairly beaming. "I'm happy to help."

"It's been an entire day," Stiger said, having grown abruptly tired of the game. "Where have you been?"

"Hunting."

"People or food?" Ruga asked, somewhat warily.

Stiger did not have to ask. He already knew. After the battle, at least five thousand of the enemy were unaccounted for. The only organized force that had managed to escape had been rapidly hunted down and dealt with. Back in the hills, with winter full on, food, not to mention shelter, would be scarce. Most of those who'd escaped had likely already perished from exposure or were in the process of doing so.

Still, Therik had taken it upon himself to go looking anyway and had done so almost daily since the legion had marched. Stiger knew, from the reports of the scouts and elves, there had been no sign of any enemy working their way through the forest alongside the road, at least in their general area. The enemy seemed to have fled out into the forest itself.

"Therik, we've come a long way," Ruga said. "I doubt any of those that escaped managed to make it this far, especially with the legion hogging the only road. It ain't exactly gonna be easy to travel cross-country through that forest." Ruga jabbed a thumb at the trees lining the road.

Therik gave a half shrug of his shoulders and offered a noncommittal grunt.

"Did you find anything?" Ruga asked, curiously.

"Just a boar and a moose." Therik sounded disappointed. "No Cyphan, no rebels."

"A pity," Ruga said.

"I think so too," Therik said in agreement. "As you say, a pity."

Stiger shook his head. The orc was bored, and when Therik got that way, he tended to cause problems. Stiger was surprised he'd not noticed Therik's boredom himself. But with the responsibility that was weighing his shoulders down, there had been little time for his friend or, for that matter, anyone else, including Taha'Leeth. Stiger regretted that.

He eyed the orc for a long moment. Therik wasn't a half-bad scout. He knew his way about the forest and was a competent hunter. It was now apparent he needed a job, something to keep him busy. Perhaps Salt could arrange for him to go out with a team of scouts.

It would have to be handled carefully, for if Therik thought he was being given busywork or being manipulated, he'd likely refuse and become irate. The more Stiger thought on it, the more he liked that idea. He would speak to Salt and see that it got done.

"Moose would sure taste good tonight," Ruga said, eyeing Therik's pack suspiciously. "You didn't eat the whole thing, did you?" Ruga looked over at Stiger. "I've seen him eat, sir. You don't think he ate it all, do you?"

"I did not kill the moose." Therik sounded almost shocked by the suggestion.

"Why not?" Ruga asked.

"I had no need to take its life." Therik patted his pack. "I had food with me. It was a magnificent creature worthy of"—Therik paused, seeming to struggle to find the right word in Common—"enjoyment."

"Enjoyment?" Ruga spat on the road. "That's a pile of mule shit and you know it."

Stiger had to struggle to not laugh. After marching with the orc, day after day, Ruga had become comfortable with Therik. He'd lost whatever wariness he'd had. That was, if he'd had any to begin with. Ruga and Therik frequently got into heated debates that at times had almost become full-on arguments. Stiger had only had to intercede twice to keep them from blows. Despite that, he knew each respected the other, possibly almost to the point of friendship.

"Mule shit?" Therik looked over at the centurion, eyes widening slightly.

"That's right, I said mule shit, you big bugger. I bet you didn't stop once to think of Uncle Ruga?" the centurion asked and then jerked a thumb behind. "Or my boys? Did ya?"

Therik grunted at that and looked over at Stiger. "What is this word, uncle?"

Stiger knew that Therik had gotten Ruga's meaning. Then suspicion stole over him. It wasn't like Therik to pass up a good meal in favor of army food. "This moose of yours was big?"

Therik held out his arms wide. "Very. Why?"

Stiger snapped his fingers. "You didn't want to have to haul it back, did you? Too much effort, eh?"

Therik was silent for a long moment as he regarded Stiger. The orc's eyes narrowed.

"Now that is one big pile of mule shit." Ruga blew out a disgusted breath. "Isn't it?"

"It was a long way from the road," Therik admitted with a shrug of his shoulders. "A very long way. I would have had to leave much of the meat for scavengers. So, I let it go. I settled for a hare."

"A hare? A hare? Next time you go hunting, you green bastard," Ruga said, "take some of my boys with you. They'll help you haul whatever you take down." The centurion patted his yoke, just below where his haversack hung. "The army's rations are already getting old and you bloody well passed up on a moose. Those things are damn good eating."

Therik looked back on Ruga's men. "Can they hunt?"

"Of course they can bloody well hunt," Ruga said, "and carry too."

"They probably won't be able to keep up, but...next time I will take a few with me," Therik conceded after a long moment's thought. "The food you legionaries eat is awful. Fresh meat is worth me having to put up with your men."

That seemed to satisfy Ruga. "They will keep up and I agree that the food the legion provides is plain awful."

"We would not feed that salt pork you eat to our dogs," Therik said.

"Tell me about it," Stiger said.

"Sir," Ruga said, turning his attention to Stiger, "since you are the legate and all, may I make a humble request?"

Stiger looked over at the centurion. He gave a nod for him to continue, half expecting what was coming.

"Since you decide what is proper and all," Ruga said, "perhaps you can get us some better rations? Salt beef, instead of pork, would be more than welcome...even fish is preferable."

"Right," Stiger said. "I am gonna make sure all you get issued is salt pork, and only the stuff from the bottom of the barrel too."

"Now that's just unkind, sir," Ruga said, "very unkind to old Uncle Ruga."

"Whoever said the army was fair?" Stiger said.

"You have me there, sir," Ruga said. "You have me there."

Another thirty minutes of marching saw them arriving at the spot the engineers had selected for the legion's nightly encampment. Several cohorts had already arrived before them. The campsite bordered the right side of the road. Stiger remembered the spot, for the road crossed a good-sized stream just ahead. It was likely why his engineers had chosen this spot for the legion's camp, for the fresh water.

The forest along the right side of the road had been significantly cut back. Hundreds of axes could be heard cracking away in the trees to either side. A few yards from the road, a wide trench was being dug.

By Stiger's calculation, based upon how much work had already been accomplished, he figured the lead cohort had arrived perhaps four hours earlier. In that short time, they had achieved a lot.

With thousands of men hard at work, the legion's nightly encampment was shaping up nicely. There were entire cohorts toiling away at digging the trench that, when complete, would extend completely around the encampment, while others built up a berm from the dirt that was being freshly excavated. Teams of men were hauling logs and stacking them inside the camp. These would be emplaced as a barricade atop the berm. Once the trench, wall, and barricade were complete, only then would the cohort's tents be raised and the latrines dug.

As standard practice, an advance team from headquarters had traveled with the lead cohort. Salt had marched with them, so Stiger had known things were well in hand. That was the value in having competent subordinates and letting them do their thing. The evidence of that was before him, plain as could be.

Ahead, Fifth Cohort was called to a halt. The men lowered their yokes and set them down on the ground. Stiger could almost sense their relief that the day's march was done, even though hours of backbreaking work lay ahead. This would be followed up by cleaning their kit free of dust and grime from the road.

Centurion Nantus called his officers to him. As the officers hustled toward their senior centurion, Stiger and his escorts moved around the side of the cohort. Dog caught back up and then immediately broke off. The animal moved along the line of tired and dusty legionaries, of which more than a few gave the animal a friendly pat upon the head or a scratch behind the ears. One even offered Dog a treat of bacon, which was quickly devoured.

Stiger and his escort continued by the Fifth. As they passed Nantus, the gathered officers turned, facing Stiger. They came to attention, with the senior centurion saluting. Stiger returned Nantus's salute.

"Carry on, Centurion," Stiger said.

"Yes, sir," Nantus replied.

Stiger looked around.

"Dog," Stiger called, "come."

The animal broke away and sprinted over to his side.

Stiger made his way across the rough planked bridge over the trench and into the encampment. With Ruga and his men following, he weaved his way through the work parties toward where headquarters was located.

Each afternoon, the encampment was constructed exactly in the same way. The chaos and frenetic pace of the work posed no problem. Stiger knew the way and he found his headquarters compound with ease.

Three of the six tents had already been raised. He did not see his own personal tent, but the one used as his office was up. As usual, it had been pitched adjacent to the administrative tent, where his clerks would have easy access to him and he to them.

Two wagons were parked beside the administrative tent. The wagons were in the process of being unloaded by a file of men. Under the tent, of which the sides had been left rolled up, were several tables and his clerks, already hard at work. A guard had been posted around the compound.

"Century," Ruga called, "halt. Stand easy."

One of the guards broke away from the others and stepped forward to take Nomad as Ruga's men began setting their yokes on the ground. Stiger imagined the men were relieved the day's march had come to an end. He knew he was.

"May I take your horse, sir?" the legionary asked Stiger.

"See that he gets brushed down, fed, and watered," Stiger said as he handed the reins over.

"I will, sir," the legionary said and began leading the animal away toward a picket line, where several other horses were tethered.

"Sir," Ruga said, "with your permission, I will relieve the current guard. It looks like Aguus's century again. I'd like to post half my men on guard duty and have the rest help get the headquarters compound squared away."

"Very well," Stiger said and then hesitated. When most of the rest of the legion turned in for the night, a quarter of Ruga's century would remain on duty. They would be guarding Stiger and headquarters. "It was a long day's march. Might as well see that your century's tents are raised while you are at it and there's still light."

"I will, sir," Ruga said.

"Those standing duty tonight," Stiger said, "can get a few hours of sleep."

"Very well, sir." Ruga offered a crisp salute.

Stiger returned the salute, and with that, Ruga left him to attend to his men. Stiger glanced around at the camp being constructed. He gave a satisfied nod, then turned to Therik.

"Care to join me?" Stiger asked his friend.

"Why not?" Therik said, in a bored tone. "There's not much else to do."

Stiger turned away, thinking Therik definitely needed a job. Dog brushed by them as they entered the tent and rushed up to Nepturus's table. The clerk had been writing on a wax tablet with a stylus. He'd been absorbed in his work and looked up, surprised as Dog began licking at his face. He pushed the animal back and stood, laughing.

"Sorry, the treats are still in the wagon," Nepturus said, scratching behind Dog's ears with both hands. "You will just have to wait."

Dog gave a low whine.

The clerk abruptly looked up and around as realization sank home. He spotted Stiger.

"Sir," Nepturus said, coming to a position of attention. The rest of those in the tent continued working. Stiger had long-since excused his staff from having to rise and come to attention every time he entered headquarters. There was just too much work to be done to have it routinely interrupted. "Welcome to headquarters."

"Nepturus," Stiger greeted, feeling weary from the march. All he wanted to do was sit down, have a mug of mulled wine, and rest. Then bathe to get all the dust and grime off. Yet he well knew work waited. Likely, people already wanted to see him. As the camp neared completion, a line would undoubtedly form. Each issue they brought would take time to deal with. Then there were reports and dispatches that would require his personal attention. No, there would be no resting for him, at least not until late into the night. Such were the burdens of command, and Stiger could not pass that responsibility onto another. Even if he could, he was unwilling to do so.

Dog broke away and went to pester one of the other clerks.

"Things are well in hand, I trust?"

"They are, sir," the clerk said. "We're just waiting on a few more items, including the braziers. Once we have those and a few lamps, I will drop the walls of the tent. With any luck, we'll get a little heat in here. The same goes for your office, sir."

"Sounds good," Stiger said, rubbing his hands together for warmth. "We could all do with a little warmth, I think."

"Your personal tent should be up within the next half hour, sir," the senior clerk reported. "There was a problem with the wagon, a broken axle, sir. Apparently, it took some time to replace. The road has been murder on the transport. The wagon arrived a short while ago. It will be the next one unloaded."

"That's quite all right," Stiger said, thinking, with his concerns and worries, a broken axle was a very minor issue. He could do without a tent for a few hours. Besides, he would not be able to retire until later tonight. There was just too much to do. There always was.

"I received a report from the chief engineer a short while ago, sir," Nepturus reported. "He feels the camp's trench and wall will be completed before sunset."

"So, they are on schedule then," Stiger said. He had expected no less.

"Yes, sir. Oh, I have a few people waiting to see you, sir," Nepturus said. "Nothing terribly pressing. I have them cooling their heels outside. When you're ready for them, just let me know."

Stiger gave a nod.

"This, ah…" Nepturus glanced down at the table, which was covered over with tablets and dispatches. He sorted through the dispatches and picked one up, handing it over. "This came in about an hour ago, sir. It's from the dwarves, a message directly from Braddock. I did not open it, as it was addressed specifically to you."

Stiger opened the dispatch and quickly scanned through its contents.

"Anything interesting, sir?"

Stiger glanced up to see Salt striding into the tent. The prefect was just as dusty as the rest of them. However, he looked like he could march another dozen miles and then some. Despite his age, Salt seemed to have more energy than anyone else.

"I'd heard you'd arrived, sir," Salt said. "Thought I'd stop by and answer any questions you might have before returning to oversee the construction efforts." Salt's gaze went to the orc. "Therik, staying out of trouble, I presume?"

Therik bared his tusks at Salt, in what was a grin for the orc. Dog padded up to Salt and brushed against the prefect's leg. Salt absently reached down and rubbed the top of Dog's head. A moment later, he came away with a wet hand from the animal's lightning-fast tongue. He shot the animal a slight scowl.

"It seems," Stiger said, tapping the dispatch with a finger, "Braddock's army has encountered the enemy. They ambushed a supply column along the road that was moving toward Vrell. The column had a significant infantry escort, numbering several hundred infantry and light cavalry. The dwarves captured the train nearly intact, two hundred fifty wagons, all told. Hux had a hand in it as well."

"That's a good catch, sir," Salt said. "I assume Braddock is adding that supply to his own train?"

"He is," Stiger confirmed, "and Braddock is delighted about that."

Stiger rubbed his jaw, feeling a stab of frustration. The letter had been written two days earlier. He reread the letter. There was no mention of prisoners having been taken.

"Braddock has sent forward our cavalry," Stiger said, "along with his mounted soldiers to the north-south road."

"The thane," Salt said, "is moving to cut communications between the confederacy's forces that advanced to the North. Braddock wasn't supposed to make that move until his army was closer to the boundary of the forest. The cavalry will essentially be unsupported should they run into trouble."

"It's worse than that," Stiger said, blowing out a long breath. "Though he doesn't come right out and say so, Braddock apparently believes he might have been discovered."

"Some of the enemy must have escaped the ambush," Therik said. "At some point, the Cyphan were bound to discover the army's presence."

"I'd just hoped it would take a few more days," Stiger said.

"You can hope all you want," Therik said. "Assume the enemy has always known we are coming."

Stiger did not like that possibility, but the fact that they'd sent a large supply train argued against that. The question now was what local forces could the enemy pull together to oppose them? Were there any other enemy armies within easy marching distance from the end of the road?

"Nepturus," Stiger asked, looking over to the clerk. "Do you have a map of the South handy?"

"I do, sir," Nepturus said. "Give me a moment please."

The clerk went to a good-sized chest and opened it. He rooted around inside for a moment before pulling out a large folded parchment. It had yellowed and looked quite old, which meant the map was not a copy that one of the camp scribes had made. The clerk moved around the table he was working at and over to one that had nothing on it. Stiger, Salt, and Therik followed him over. Nepturus carefully unfolded the map on the table and then backed away, returning to his work.

Stiger handed over the dispatch to Salt, who began reading. Placing his palms on the edge of the rough planked wood of the table, Stiger stared down at the map and studied it for several long moments, then looked up. He waited until Salt was finished with the dispatch. The prefect set it down onto the table.

"I believe you are right, sir," Salt said. "Some of the enemy must have escaped the ambush. Otherwise, there was no reason to push the cavalry out so far, so soon."

"If I had to guess, I think Braddock's column is about here." Stiger tapped the map. "I'd say about a week's march to the edge of the forest, maybe a day, more or less."

"That sounds about right, sir," Salt said and blew out a long breath. "The thane may push his boys harder and shave a day or two off if he can."

"He might," Stiger said and then decided the thane would.

"Knowing Hux," Salt said, with an abrupt chuckle, "now that he's been freed, he is probably already on the north-south road causing all kinds of havoc."

"Just the thought of it makes me wish horses and I got along," Therik said. "I could be with him. It sounds like fun."

"I can get you a horse," Stiger said. "You can catch up with Hux, if you like?"

Therik bared his tusks at Stiger and barked out a laugh. After a moment, he sobered, gaze locking with Stiger's. "I will stay with you. I can't let anyone else kill you. Never forget, your life belongs to me. I alone have that honor."

"That you do"—Stiger grinned at the orc—"that is, if you can take me in a fight."

Therik's hand went to the hilt of his sword. "Care to spar and find out?"

Salt looked between the two of them and then shook his head. He gazed back down at the map and ran a finger along the north-south road. He stopped at the city of Aeda, around two hundred miles to the north. The prefect cleared his throat, drawing their attention.

"Aeda," Salt said. "This was a little town in my time. Is it still there?"

"It's a city now," Stiger said.

"A city, really?" Salt asked. "Of how many?"

"About fifty thousand," Stiger said.

Salt whistled. "You don't think Hux will go that far, do you?"

"No," Stiger said. "Braddock likely gave him orders to remain close to the Vrell road, at least until he arrives with his army."

"You know Hux, sir," Salt said. "He will push those orders a bit."

"Yes," Stiger said, "but even he knows what's at stake. He won't go that far and leave Braddock blind. Hux knows his duty to the army."

Freed from the leash, Stiger's cavalry commander was likely very active along the north-south road. To say Hux was enthusiastic about his work was an understatement. Any isolated enemy within at least a thirty-mile range of the end of the Vrell road was likely not safe, perhaps even as far out as fifty miles. Still, he hoped Hux did not bite off more than he could chew before Braddock arrived. They could not afford to lose the cavalry. Hux and his mounted soldiers were the eyes and ears of the army. Without them, they were blind.

"What is the name of this road?" Salt asked, pointing at the north-south road. "It did not exist in my time."

Stiger felt himself frown as he tried to recall the name of the road. It had been so long. He snapped his fingers. "It's called King's Highway."

"I assume there was a kingdom in this area at some point?" Salt asked.

Stiger gave a nod of confirmation. "No more. The empire annexed it about a century ago, though politics and greed in the senate have kept this area being fully absorbed into the empire. Hence our troubles now with the rebellion."

Salt nodded and went back to studying the map, then chuckled lightly again. "Hux and his boys are likely having the time of their lives."

"I would agree with that." Stiger felt his frustration mount. It was maddening. He had no idea what was going on outside of the Sentinel Forest. There had been no word from Menos either, which was even more frustrating. Stiger took a calming breath. He understood that it was likely too soon to hear from the noctalum. He rubbed his tired eyes and decided there was no helping it. He shouldn't worry about what he could not influence, but it gnawed at him no less.

"Any word on how the artillery train is faring?" Stiger asked. The reports he'd received over the last two days had been discouraging. Due to the state of the ground to the west, the train was moving at a snail's pace. He'd hoped the farther east they moved, and the more the ground improved, the fewer problems the artillery would have. So far, it had not played out that way. The road had been seriously torn up by Braddock's army, and now his legion and supply train were distressing it further. The artillery wagons and transport were heavy and slow, which made their movement much more difficult.

"We received a report from them an hour ago, sir," Salt said. "As you know, the engineers are having to repair parts of the road before they can move forward. The process is taking significant time. It is possible that when we exit the forest, the artillery train could be a week or more behind us, perhaps even two weeks. It's a shame the enemy did nothing to improve the road."

"A little thoughtless of them," Stiger said.

"Yes, sir," Salt said. "If we have to fight a proper battle, we may have to do it without any artillery."

"That's far from ideal," Stiger said, rapping his knuckles on the table lightly, "not ideal at all. We're going to need the artillery before this is all over. Do you think there is anything that can be done to speed things up?"

Salt shook his head. "They're doing all that they can, sir. The problem is the road. It was never meant for such traffic, not in my time and certainly not in this time, where it has degraded and seen little maintenance."

Stiger gave a nod.

"At least the supply train is making good time," Salt said, "and keeping up."

"There is that," Stiger said. "It means we won't be starving, at least."

"Yes, sir," Salt said, "too true."

"More salt pork," Therik said in an unenthusiastic tone.

"You're the one who passed up on a moose," Stiger said.

"Who needs moose when you have pork, and plenty of it too?" Salt said. "I'll take that any day. Pork builds the constitution, sir. The legion marches on it."

Stiger regarded his prefect for a long moment. "I guess it beats hardtack."

"That it does, sir," Salt said.

Stiger blew out a long breath. With the news from Braddock, it made his next decision even more difficult.

"I am thinking of resting the legion a day," Stiger said. "I am not happy about it, but the legion needs at least a day's break before pushing on. Do you disagree?"

"No, sir. The boys could use a rest," Salt said. "Even a day will do wonders."

"It's settled then," Stiger said. "We will remain here for a day."

"Very good, sir," Salt said and then looked over at Stiger's head clerk. "Nepturus, we could use some good news. Do you have the tally of the haul from the battle? Not the estimate, but the detailed one from Ikely you showed me earlier."

"The one that arrived this morning, sir?" Nepturus asked.

"That's the one I want," Salt said.

Stiger's clerk stepped over with several tablets in hand. He set them down on the table and backed away.

"This should brighten your mood, sir," Salt said, sorting through the wax tablets, searching for the one he wanted. "It took some time to tally it all, but we scored quite a haul. Ah…here we go. We captured three hundred wagons, of which at least one hundred are in excellent condition. The rest need some work or refurbishment. Twenty-four have been deemed of no value, other than spare parts, wheels, axles, and such. Five hundred and two mules were captured, along with seventy-three horses. Of the horses, twenty-one were marked with imperial brands from the legion."

Stiger felt sour about that. Had the enemy captured them in battle or had some enterprising supply officer sold them for personal gain? It had been known to happen, and from the state of General Kromen's Southern legions, he would not have put it past the supply officers to be corrupt.

"We seized a herd of two hundred head of cattle, seventy goats, and another fifty-odd sheep." Salt put the tablet down on the table and picked up another. "The enemy was kind enough to provide us with two hundred and eighty tons of flour, over three hundred barrels and large casks of salt pork, about fifty barrels of salted beef, another couple hundred tons of potatoes...the list of food stores goes on." Salt set the tablet down and picked up another. "Moving on to armaments seized, we have secured twenty-one thousand swords of various types and quality, ten thousand spears, forty-six thousand daggers, one thousand bows that are considered useful, two thousand slings of various sizes, fifteen thousand entrenching tools, ten thousand breastplates, another seventeen thousand assorted pieces of armor, such as grieves, bucklers, shields... You name it...it's here. We've also seized twenty-three hundred and four communal tents, and another two hundred individual tents of varying sizes and quality."

"We could equip an entire army from that," Stiger said, thinking it indeed an impressive haul.

"No doubt," Salt said, picking up a tablet and studying it. "I also received a thorough report from Tribune Ikely on what we've learned from questioning the rebel officers. Would you like to hear a summary now? Or would you prefer to review the report yourself?"

"Give me the summary now," Stiger said. "I will study the report itself later tonight."

Salt glanced down at the tablet a moment.

"Zoc was, as we thought, the highest ranking officer to survive. The commanding general, a man named Pintak, died in the fighting. Ikely was able to locate and identify his body. The prisoners we've questioned, mostly officers... including Zoc, know little of what is going on beyond the Sentinel Forest. What information they did have was weeks old and is now likely useless. To make matters worse, the Cyphan did not see fit to confide in Pintak and his officers on their overall plans. They apparently didn't trust the bastards and kept them, for the most, part in the dark."

"I see," Stiger said. This was not good news.

"In addition," Salt said, "despite promises to the contrary, the confederacy has treated the rebels poorly. They've occupied the cities supporting the rebellion, from which Pintak's army was drawn. Apparently, the Cyphan have been very hard. There is a detailed list in the report itself of things they've done to the rebel civilians, including the public execution of all teachers, tutors, philosophers, and anyone who spoke out against either Valoor or the confederacy. They also went out of their way to kill priests of the High Father and raze any temples not dedicated to Valoor. Belief in any other god has been banned. Food and stores of all kinds, along with draft animals and transport were confiscated. As you can imagine, this has led to mass hunger in the rebel held areas."

Salt paused and glanced back down at the tablet.

"It should come as no surprise that morale amongst the men of Pintak's army was in the sewer. Had the rebel army not marched to Vrell and been so isolated, I expect they would have suffered terribly from desertion. There was simply nowhere for disaffected men to go since no ready sources of food were available in the event they wanted to leave. That said, two days before we attacked, Pintak put down a partial mutiny of his men, killing several hundred. It seems he was fond of making examples and publicly tortured several of the mutineers to death. Zoc felt it was only a matter of time before the entire army revolted against its leadership and the Cyphan."

Stiger gave a nod and let out a long breath, feeling thoroughly dissatisfied by what he was hearing. He had already received preliminary reports on the questioning of the enemy. Beyond providing a little more color on the conditions in the rebel-held lands and their army, the report was also nothing he did not already know or suspect.

"Concerning intelligence of the goings-on beyond the Sentinel Forest, about all they knew after turning toward Vrell was that the confederacy's main army marched after General Kromen's legions." Salt stopped for a heartbeat. "There were rumors of a battle and victory for the confederacy, but no solid confirmation could be corroborated. Unfortunately, none of the Cyphan survived the battle to be captured. They were either killed in the fighting or ended their own lives before we could get our hands on them."

Feeling keenly disappointed, Stiger wished they had known more. Stiger rubbed his jaw.

"Heck," Salt said, sounding frustrated himself, "even the prisoners from the supply trains Braddock's boys captured knew nothing of what was going on to the north. It's as if there is no real communication between the forces that went after General Kromen's army and those that remained behind in rebel-held lands to the south."

"Yes," Stiger said, "I agree. It is very strange."

"That's basically it, sir." Salt set the tablet down and picked up another, which he handed to Stiger. He pointed to a figure at the bottom. "On the bright side, we've also secured large amounts of coin and other valuables."

"That is a lot of money," Stiger said as he studied the tablet, surprised the enemy had brought so much with them. "It's virtually a king's ransom. We could bribe more than one senator with that much money."

Salt laughed. "Do you think we might need to?"

"Who knows? Well, at least the men will be pleased when their portion is allotted to their pensions and pay at the next disbursement."

"They should be, sir," Salt said and then hesitated. "At twenty-percent share, it also makes the senior officers rich men, sir."

Stiger had not thought of that. His portion, as legate, would be a considerable fortune. For so long, he had been forced to watch his money like a hawk, spending to the point of frugality and only when necessary.

"Unless the share has been reduced in this time period?" Salt asked. "Has it?"

"No," Stiger said, "it hasn't. The senior officers are entitled to a twenty-percent cut of any plunder. You, me, and Ikely are rich men. Severus too."

"That makes me very happy, sir," Salt said. "And my father said I'd never amount to much."

"Now we just need to save the empire," Therik said, "so you can spend it."

Salt gave a grunt. "The truth is I'm not sure what I'd do with so much coin."

"I am sure you will find something to do with it," Stiger said, then recalled the note he'd received from Braddock the night before. "What of the prisoners?"

"Ikely has put two thousand of the bastards to work hauling the loot back to Old City, where it will be stored," Salt said. "Another thousand have been employed with supply, general labor and such. As discussed, the rest are being marched back to the dwarven nations, where they will be broken up, put to work and guarded by Braddock's militia."

"Braddock is still not happy about that," Stiger said. "I received a stern note last night on the subject."

"I would assume he wants them all put to death?" Salt said.

"Your assumption is correct." Stiger rubbed the back of his neck. He looked around and spotted his chief clerk. The clerk was waiting patiently for Stiger to finish with Salt. It was a sign there was a lot to be done.

"Nepturus," Stiger said, "you can bring over the dispatches."

"Yes, sir." Nepturus hurried over and set a stack of dispatches down on the table before Stiger. "Nothing terribly important, but you will want to see them regardless. I have already taken the liberty of responding to most. My replies are attached to each dispatch. Should you wish changes, sir, please let me know."

"What would I do without you?" Stiger asked the clerk as he picked up the first of the dispatches. There were twelve of them. Though at times a little cantankerous, Nepturus had become part of his headquarters family and over the last few years had proven invaluable to the legion's operation. The man was incredibly efficient, almost in a scary way.

He was also a rock, in that he would not allow the legion's centurions to bully him.

"Most probably promote one of the others to this thankless job, sir," the clerk said and then returned to his table.

"I probably would," Stiger called after him.

"I know, sir," Nepturus said.

"Sir," Salt said, clearly sensing Stiger wanted to get to work, "will there be anything else? I would like to get back to overseeing the construction of the encampment."

"Nothing pressing," Stiger said. "How much time do you need?"

"Before the legion can settle in for the night?" Salt considered his answer for a long moment. "At least three, maybe four hours, sir. I'd like to clean up too and wash off all this dust."

"Right then," Stiger said. "I will see you for dinner. We will talk additional business then."

"Yes, sir," Salt said. He gave Stiger a salute, then eyed the orc for a prolonged moment. "Therik, would you join me for a tour of the defensive works? I am sure the legate has a great deal of work that needs attending to."

"I would," Therik said, with an unhappy glance around the administrative tent. His eyes settled on the dispatches, then Stiger. "I will leave you to your work. Enjoy."

Stiger nodded absently as he began reading the first of the dispatches. When he looked up, several moments later, both Salt and Therik were gone. Dog had disappeared too.

Stiger set the dispatch down on the table, untied the straps to his helmet, and then lifted the heavy thing off his head. He set the helmet down with a solid-sounding thunk. He rubbed the back of his neck, which was stiff and sore.

He scooped up the dispatches and started for his office. Looking in, he saw only his desk had been set up.

"Nepturus, do you have a stool so I can sit?"

"I will find one for you, sir," Nepturus said.

"That would be just grand," Stiger said as he made his way to his desk, for his legs and feet ached something fierce. He opened the next dispatch and began reading, then called back out, "Some wine to wash the dust from my mouth would be good too."

TWELVE

Stiger lay down on his cot, resisting the temptation to groan. Two thick blankets had been neatly folded at the end by Venthus. He rested his legs upon them. That felt good, more than good. It was great.

He'd just finished the end-of-day business and had retired for a brief respite of quiet. The sun had set. His tent was lit by a single lantern, which hung from the central support pole. A brazier smoked in the corner, providing more smoke than heat. The smoke swirled about the ceiling of the tent and around the lantern.

Dog was curled up next to the cot. His legs twitched, and he gave a growl as he was caught up in a dream. Stiger idly wondered what animal he was chasing.

Outside the tent, he could hear the usual noises of the legion, men calling to one another, the harsh bark of laughter, coughing, the chink of armor, the sound of a hammer. It was something that he had long become accustomed to. Only in the middle of the night would most of the noise cease. Still, there would be the occasional order snapped from an officer, or challenge given by a sentry. Legionary camps were by nature never completely quiet. It was just how it was and Stiger would not have it any other way. The legion was his true home.

From his cot, Stiger gazed up at the top of his tent, study-ing the canvas. It was superbly made, using only the finest of materials. Venthus had told him Delvaris had purchased the tent in Mal'Zeel, before the legion had marched south. He had acquired it from a tentmaker named Teltanic. Teltanic, like everyone else left behind in that time, was now long dead. Stiger wondered if his family was still in the business of tent making. It was an interesting thought. If he ever made it back to the capital and needed a new tent, it might bear looking into.

Dog stirred slightly and opened an eye. Seeing nothing interesting was going on, he yawned powerfully, then rolled onto his side and promptly went back to sleep.

Stiger rubbed at tired eyes. The legion would wake early, and the march would once again resume. It had been almost three weeks since the battle. They were averaging ten to twelve miles a day. Stiger had done better with his old company, but this was an entire army. He was pleased with their progress, for there were always delays of some kind, especially when confined to a single road that was quite narrow.

There was also the fact that the legion stopped each afternoon and built a fortified encampment. That took time away from the miles marched. With so much at stake, Stiger was unwilling to sacrifice safety for speed. While at its most vulnerable, defensive works ensured the legion's safety at night. The proof of that was the enemy army he'd so handily crushed before Vrell.

In a few days, they would come to the forest's bound-ary and join up with Braddock's army. Stiger had no idea where fate would take them, other than a likely march north toward the empire in pursuit of the enemy.

"Excuse me, sir," Venthus said from the entrance flap. He held a mug. "I have some heated wine. Would you care for some?"

Stiger propped himself up on his elbows and then sat up, swinging his legs over the side of the cot to the rug. "I would."

Venthus stepped up. The contents steamed in the cold air. Stiger took the mug and felt its welcome warmth through his fingers. He sat there for a moment, enjoying the warming sensation.

"I have a jar simmering over a low fire, master," Venthus said. "Should you require more, just call."

Venthus's tent was pitched next to Stiger's. The slave turned to go.

"Venthus?"

"Sir?"

"How are you holding up?" Stiger asked, for the march had been a difficult one and Venthus was older. Delvaris had asked Stiger to look after Venthus, and he intended to. Only there were complications in doing so, for the man was no ordinary slave.

"Well enough," Venthus said. "I believe you have more pressing matters to concern yourself with than me, master."

"That would be an incorrect assumption," Stiger said. "How are you really holding up?"

Venthus was silent for a long moment, his gray eyes studying Stiger.

"Like everyone else," Venthus said with a sort of sigh, "I am sore and tired. I fear I'm getting too old for campaigning. This"—the slave paused and glanced about the tent—"will likely be my last campaign."

"Then," Stiger said, "we have something in common."

"We've always had something in common, master." Venthus's eyes narrowed ever so slightly. "We both know that, now, don't we?"

Stiger took a sip of the heated wine and savored it as the warmth traveled down to his belly. Stiger knew Venthus's secret, and yet there was much he did not understand. Many simply overlooked him and considered the legate's slave, like so many others, simply irrelevant. That was a mistake. Calling Venthus dangerous was something of an understatement.

"And what is that exactly?" Stiger asked.

Venthus did not immediately reply. He took a step closer to Stiger and brought his hands together before him, interlacing his fingers.

"Why, a devotion to duty," Venthus answered in a near whisper, "and service to our respective gods. That is what we have in common, master."

The last word, master, had been said almost sarcastically. Stiger had thought he'd come to understand Venthus, but now...in this moment, he wasn't quite so sure.

"Is that all?" Stiger asked.

"Of course not," Venthus said, in the same hushed tone. "We both will do whatever we deem necessary, no matter how distasteful, to achieve our goals. That is what we have in common. Do you disagree?"

Stiger sucked in a breath. There was a lot of truth in what Venthus said.

"No," Stiger said after a brief hesitation. "I do not disagree."

"Then we agree," Venthus said, "and we understand one another."

"Yes, I believe we do," Stiger said.

A silence settled between them. Stiger chose to break it.

"Make sure you take some time for yourself," Stiger said. "If that entails turning in early, do so. The legion marches again in the morning."

"As you wish, master. I believe I will take advantage of your kind offer."

Venthus bowed respectfully and turned away.

"Venthus?"

The slave swung back again, arching an eyebrow.

"I could arrange for a horse or even a spot on one of the wagons," Stiger suggested. "That might make it a bit easier on you."

"That is very kind of you, master," Venthus said.

"You won't take me up on it, will you?" Stiger asked.

"No," Venthus said.

"Why not?"

"For my sins," Venthus said simply.

"Don't you think you've suffered enough?" Stiger asked. They had had this conversation before.

"No," Venthus said. "I atone daily…in my own way, you might say, through service and suffering."

Stiger rubbed his jaw as he considered his slave. He felt a wave of sadness and pity wash over him. Venthus sucked in a breath and stiffened, clearly sensing Stiger's thoughts.

"If there will be nothing else, master, I shall retire for the evening."

"Thank you for the wine," Stiger said.

With that Venthus bowed, then retreated from the tent.

Stiger glanced over at Dog. The animal was staring at the tent flap, from which Venthus had just left. Dog looked over at Stiger and gave a soft whine.

"I know," Stiger said to the animal. "It is not an ideal arrangement, but I trust him. You should too."

Dog regarded Stiger for several heartbeats, then laid his head back down upon his paws and closed his eyes.

"Right," Stiger said and took another sip of his wine before setting it down on the table at the head of his cot. He lay back and resumed staring at the canvas ceiling. No matter how much he desired sleep, it wasn't time to turn in for the evening. He still had a working dinner with Salt. There was yet business to discuss.

He also wanted to walk through the camp and spend some time visiting the campfires. It had become part of his nightly routine and something he'd come to value, for it reinforced his connection with the men. It also told him how they were holding up. So far, the legion had responded nicely to the extended march. Morale was high.

He blew a steaming breath up into the air. There had still been no word from Menos. He was becoming worried about that.

What was keeping him?

Had something happened to the dragon? Stiger certainly hoped not, but the silence was troubling. It nagged at him.

His thoughts shifted to the latest dispatches that had come in from Braddock. Three days earlier, the thane had pushed out from the forest and fought a minor battle on the King's Highway. According to Braddock, the dwarves had slaughtered at least a brigade of the enemy and broken another. They had even taken prisoners, which had come as a surprise to Stiger, for he'd expected the dwarves to slaughter all of the enemy that fell into their hands.

Hux had patrols out to the north, south, and east. The cavalry prefect had destroyed a number of smaller enemy detachments and unsuspecting garrisons. He had also seized an astonishing quantity of supplies. That was the welcome news, at least.

Braddock had sent along some bad news as well. Apparently, the Southern legions had been brought to battle south of Aeda and been soundly defeated. Cavalry scouts had discovered the battle site a few miles off the road. The slaughter was reputed to have been great.

Stiger had suspected as much, so that did not come as a total surprise. The conditions of those four legions had been dreadful. Had they been asked to put down a small riot, he suspected General Kromen would've been unable to do so. Still, the thought of such a defeat bothered him no less. It was a stain upon the empire, one Stiger fully intended to erase.

In addition to all of that, some of the prisoners taken had reported that the might of the empire had been brought to battle and defeated farther to the north. Worse, they said the emperor had fallen in the fighting.

Braddock had included his own personal assessment that this was rumor and not established fact. He could not, as yet, corroborate it, for they had not captured an enemy who'd been there when it had happened. Stiger certainly hoped it was not true, for if the information was correct, he was already too late. That made the absence of Menos even more troubling.

What was the noctalum doing?

Stiger blew out a long breath. He felt incredibly tired and weary. The burden of the world rested upon his shoulders and of late it weighed heavily. He yawned, eyes watering with tears.

"Perhaps just a little nap before dinner," Stiger said and closed his eyes. He knew, when it was time, Salt would come for him.

"Perhaps not."

Stiger opened his eyes and looked over. Taha'Leeth had pushed the tent flap aside. Her eyes were on him as she entered. He sat up and grinned at the sight of her, his mood instantly lightening. His weariness fled with her arrival.

"It has been a few days," Taha'Leeth said in Elven as she set her pack and bow down on the rug.

"It's been too long," Stiger replied in Elven.

Since the legion had marched, he'd only seen her a few times, and of those, during the march, they had spent four incredible nights together and a couple days in each other's company. However, for the most part, she'd been out in the field. As the legion moved through the forest, on the Vrell road, the elves, along with the legion's scouts, were his eyes and ears. They probed the surrounding forest, searching and hunting for threats.

He had found himself missing her company more with each passing day, his thoughts continually straying to her. Taha'Leeth's presence had become one of his true pleasures, nearly a dangerous vice.

Standing before him, she looked incredible to his eyes. Stiger sucked in a breath that shuddered slightly. Taha'Leeth was an exotic creature of stunning beauty and he wanted... needed her in his life.

Taha'Leeth undid her braid and shook out her fiery red hair. She removed her boots next, flexing her toes upon the rich pattered rug that covered the ground. She bit her lip a moment as she gazed upon him, then her eyes tracked to Dog.

"Naverum"—Taha'Leeth pointed toward the tent flap—"kindly leave. I require private time with him."

Stiger felt his heart quicken.

Dog gave a soft whine, looking from Taha'Leeth to Stiger.

"Out, old boy," Stiger said and gestured with his chin toward the exit. "We need some alone time."

The animal stood and shook himself vigorously, ears flapping loudly. With one more almost forlorn look to Stiger, he padded out of the tent, leaving the two of them alone.

Taha'Leeth slowly moved toward his cot, until she stood above him. Eyes sparkling with mischief, she removed her tunic, revealing her naked breasts underneath, along with a firm, muscular body. She tossed the tunic aside, where it landed on a stool. All that remained were her brown leather pants. Like a man dying of thirst, he drank in the sight of her.

"Is there room on that cot for two?"

She leaned forward and kissed him. Her lips were soft, intoxicating. Stiger pulled her to him, the cot creaking in protest.

"I missed you," Stiger admitted, "badly."

Taha'Leeth looked into his eyes for several heartbeats. "Did you?"

"I did," Stiger said. "I worry about you, when you're out in the field."

She smiled as her eyes searched his face.

"I choose you, Bennulius Stiger. You must understand this. With all my heart and soul, I am giving you all that I am. There will be none other than you, ever. On this I swear. Do you understand me in this?"

He realized that something profound was happening, almost as life changing as when he'd accepted the mantle of

Champion. It hit him like one of the High Father's thunderbolts. Gazing into her eyes, he found them deep, intense, and quite captivating...also at the same time alien. They were not human eyes, and there was an intriguing depth to them. He thought he could lose himself within that mesmerizing gaze. It wasn't her beauty that called him. There was something else drawing them together and...it felt right, as if it were meant to be.

"I understand," Stiger said after a brief hesitation. "I will give myself to you, freely, my heart and everything else that I am..." He suddenly thought of Sarai and a wave of sadness crashed over him. "But I truly cannot bear to lose another."

"And I could not bear to lose you," Taha'Leeth said.

"Then let's not do this," Stiger said.

Confusion clouded her face and she pulled away.

"I do not understand. I'm giving myself to you and you to me, freely. We will bond, share ourselves, our lives, and mate for life."

"That's just it," Stiger said. "If this is for life, then you will see me grow old and die. I have loved and lost. I have left friends I held dear on the battlefield and in the past. You will suffer all over again and in just a few short years, too, when I pass from this world. I cannot ask that of you. It is not fair. I will not have another suffer...as I have. How can I ask that of you?"

She laughed. And it wasn't an amused laugh. It was heartfelt. Her eyes brimmed with unshed tears.

"Why are you laughing? I am serious."

"Because you still do not understand," Taha'Leeth said. "As I have said, you have changed. It is not simply that you are now the High Father's Champion. You have truly changed."

"Then what is it?"

"You have been given a tremendous gift." She laid a hand upon his chest and closed her eyes. "I can feel the transformation within you. Your longevity is no longer an issue. Like elvenkind, you will watch others, mortals, age before your eyes. They will pass on from this world, and all that shall remain will be your memory of them. You shall go on, witnessing the world change, while others pass on to the next plane of existence and their remains molder and turn to dust."

She opened her eyes, blinking. A tear ran down her cheek. "I am sorry for that, truly. You must now bear our burden, and at times it can be terrible watching those you care for pass from this world."

Stiger was stunned.

"How can this be?"

"You took something, I suspect," Taha'Leeth said, "while in the past."

"You must be wrong. Menos said I'd changed, but this cannot be."

"I am not wrong," Taha'Leeth said firmly. "Even Eli can sense the change within you. Though he fears what it means and dreads mentioning it."

"But while I was stuck in the past, those five years," Stiger said, "I aged. I can see it when I look in a mirror."

"I suspect the change within you took time to complete. The aging process has now slowed, perhaps even stopped altogether. Proof of this is your ability to heal, like elves. You should never know another cold, nor disease. Yes, you took something into your being. Your soul spark is more than what it was and has begun to change you in ways I suspect you cannot yet begin to imagine."

Stiger did not like the sound of that. He recalled his conversation with Menos back in the keep and found his eyes straying toward the sword in the tent's corner. Was it like Menos had said? Had Rarokan transferred something to him from the souls it had taken? Perhaps from the minion? Or was it from the dragon he'd killed? Had something passed through the sword to him? Or was it a gift from his god? There was so much that he did not know…but in truth, he knew deep down what she and Menos said was true. He was changed, no longer altogether human. That frightened him.

Taha'Leeth followed his gaze to the sword and gave a nod. "You mastered it, didn't you?"

"I fought the wizard," Stiger said, "and with Father Thomas's help, I was able to defeat him. That said, I do not think I ever truly mastered Rarokan. The wizard within the sword has essentially been dead…since I almost crossed over the great river myself. I can no longer sense his presence within." Stiger paused and turned his gaze back to her.

"I think," Taha'Leeth said slowly, "the sword helped make you more than you were, as was always intended."

"What am I?" The words came out as barely more than a whisper.

"Something new." Taha'Leeth's eyes flicked toward the bed. "And together we will make a new beginning, you and I. We shall share our lives."

"Then why—?"

She cut him off by placing a finger to his lips.

"No more whys. You are still you…but now more than you were. You are you, just changed, is all."

"You're not helping," Stiger said.

"I can help ease your mind in other ways." Straddling him, she pushed him back onto the cot, which creaked alarmingly. She looked down, her eyes searching his face, just bare inches from his. There was an animal-like ferocity in her gaze. "Accept me, for I have chosen you." She leaned down and gave him a light kiss, then whispered, more insistently, "Accept me."

Stiger swallowed. All thoughts and concerns for the sword and what he was becoming were suddenly gone. Looking up into Taha'Leeth's eyes, he understood he wanted her, and badly. It felt right, deep down, more than right. For a long while, he had been missing something. A hole had been ripped from his soul when Sarai died. He suspected that Taha'Leeth had the same feeling, as she'd suffered from the loss of her mate. He had thought he was meant for Sarai, but that was not to be. Looking into her eyes, Stiger suddenly understood, his destiny lay with Taha'Leeth, and for the first time in a long while, the tight fist that had gripped his heart loosened. The hard shell around it cracked and then broke.

"I choose you." The words were out of his mouth before his brain even registered what he'd said. Taha'Leeth kissed him hard, smashing her lips against his. Stiger felt that his life had suddenly changed beyond recognition. But he didn't care. All he wanted, all he needed, was here in this woman. The fact that she was of a different race mattered little. She was his and he was hers. He pulled her closer and kissed her back.

She was all that mattered.

THIRTEEN

"Excuse me, sir," a voice called from just outside the tent. Stiger's eyes snapped open. It felt like he'd just gone to sleep. He pulled the thick blanket off and sat up, swinging his feet to the rug. The cot creaked, as if unhappy at being disturbed in the middle of the night. Stiger shivered at the cold bite of the air. It was times like this when he missed the comfort of the fire he'd had back in the castle.

Taha'Leeth had slipped away. The cot he'd moved into the tent for her was empty. He wondered where she'd gone.

"May I enter, sir?"

"Come," Stiger called.

Lantern in hand, Tribune Severus pulled aside the tent flap. He held the lantern up, shining light into the tent.

"I'm sorry to wake you, sir."

"That's quite all right." Stiger rubbed at his tired eyes. "When did you arrive?"

"A few hours ago, sir, with the latest supply train." Severus stepped fully into the tent and let the flap fall back into place. He went to Stiger's desk, where an oil lamp sat. The tribune took a taper from a holder next to the lamp and used his own lantern to light it. Within moments, he had Stiger's lamp burning and, with it, the light inside the tent grew.

"It's good seeing you, Severus," Stiger said.

"You too, sir," Severus said.

"I am very pleased with the supply situation. You and Ikely have done a fine job."

"Thank you, sir. It hasn't been easy," Severus said, "but I seem to recall you telling me, 'nothing done right is ever easy.'"

"Did I say that?" Stiger asked, knowing he had.

"You did, sir," Severus confirmed.

Stiger knew that Severus looked upon him as almost a father figure. In a way, the tribune had become like a son to Stiger. He was proud of the man Severus was becoming and his own hand in helping to shape the lad.

"What time is it?" Stiger asked.

"A little after three bells, sir," Severus said.

"Early then," Stiger said and rubbed at his eyes again. He'd only managed two hours of sleep.

"Just a tad early, sir."

"Given the hour, I assume this visit," Stiger said as he stifled a yawn, "is not social in nature?"

"No, sir," Severus said, becoming all business. "Camp Prefect Oney asked me to get you. You're needed at head-quarters, sir."

"Very well," Stiger said, wondering what crisis or bad news required his attention at such an early hour. He decided not to press Severus for information. Were it a true emergency, Salt would have begun rousting the legion. There would have been no missing that. "Kindly inform the prefect I will be there shortly."

"Yes, sir," Severus said and left the tent.

Stiger stood, feeling incredibly stiff and worn out. He was clearly going to pay a price for staying up late with

Taha'Leeth. With all his responsibilities, the only private time the two of them had together was when he retired to his tent, usually late at night, and then only when she was in camp and not in the field.

He slipped his boots on and gave another great yawn before picking up his sword by the hilt from where he'd left it on a table. There was no tingling sensation as he would have felt in the past. Stiger almost missed that feeling…almost, for it had been a sign of the mad wizard locked within.

Before turning in for the night, he'd cleaned the blade while he and Taha'Leeth had talked. Under the dim light of the lamp, he examined the steel. Satisfied with his work, he slid the sword into its lacquered sheath, then settled the straps comfortably over his shoulder.

"Gods," Stiger said quietly, resisting another yawn, "I'm tired."

At some point, he knew he'd have to catch up on sleep. When that would be, he simply did not know. He looked around the tent once more. Over the last few weeks it had become home.

Stiger shivered in the cold air. He retrieved his bearskin cloak from where Venthus had carefully laid it over one of his trunks. Like he did every night, Venthus had cleaned and brushed it. Stiger wrapped the cloak about himself and almost immediately began to feel warmed by it.

On his desk, Venthus had left him a jar of wine. Stiger grabbed one of the mugs and filled it. He drank it all, swishing the last swallow around his mouth before downing it, to rid himself from the sour taste of sleep.

Setting the mug back down on the table, he glanced once more around the tent. Dog was nowhere to be seen.

He and Taha'Leeth had given the animal the boot from the tent so that they could have some privacy. He'd not returned. If anyone was suffering from their relationship, it was Dog. Stiger regretted that a bit, but not too much.

As he stepped out into the night, he found the encampment for the most part still, nearly quiet. The two sentries on duty, standing to either side of the tent flap, snapped to attention. Stiger paused and glanced around. There were about a dozen guards in view. These had been placed strategically around the headquarters compound, which included the administrative tents and his office, along with his personal tent and Salt's. Just out of view, Stiger knew there were more men on duty. Ruga took his job at protecting Stiger seriously.

A fire had been set a few feet from the sentries and the entrance to his tent. The light from the fire pushed back on the darkness to some degree. He went up to it and held out his hands to warm them.

In truth, Stiger was bothered by the need to be guarded. He no longer had any semblance of privacy. Someone was always at hand, watching, shadowing him, and undoubtedly listening. He should have become accustomed to it. But he wasn't.

It made him especially uncomfortable now that he spent nights with Taha'Leeth. He understood there was no helping it. He had been the target of assassinations before and had no doubt the enemy, should they get the chance, would strike directly at him. The stakes of the game he was playing were just too high. He needed the protection and it was as simple as that. So, he put up with his guard, but he resented it no less.

The sky above was crystal clear and quite beautiful. The stars twinkled brightly in their infinite multitude. The moon, a half crescent, hung low on the horizon, just above the tree line, and provided very little light.

Ten feet away, he spotted Dog. Sitting on his haunches, the animal wagged his tail in the dirt enthusiastically as he stared in Stiger's direction.

"Has he been there long?" Stiger asked one of the sentries and nodded toward Dog.

"No, sir," the sentry replied. "He showed up just before you came out."

Stiger resisted a scowl at that. He glanced in the direction of the administrative tent just a few yards away, wondering what was so important that Salt had seen fit to wake him. The sides of the tent had been lowered against the cold. The tent was illuminated from the inside by lantern light, which shone through the canvas sides. That Dog had showed up at this moment was telling and, Stiger thought, a little worrying.

"Dog, come," Stiger said, as he started for the tent.

Dog dutifully followed him. As he approached, the guards snapped to attention and one of the two standing by the entrance held the flap aside for him.

Stiger ducked his way inside and found the interior of the tent was brightly lit. There were several lanterns hanging from support poles overhead. The tent was also warmer, likely due to iron braziers that smoked in the corners. Three clerks were busily at work, drafting orders for the coming day, when the legion would resume its march. Two messengers were waiting. One of the messengers was dusty, looked weary, and appeared to have recently arrived.

Nepturus looked a little disheveled, as if he, too, had been just awoken. He moved around the table he'd been sitting at and approached.

"They're in your office, sir," the senior clerk said and gestured toward the tent flap that led to Stiger's office.

"They?" Stiger asked. He had only been expecting Salt. "Who exactly are they?"

"Eli'Far, Taha'Leeth, the camp prefect, Tribune Severus, and two other elves," Nepturus said. "I am afraid I do not know the newcomers. They arrived a short while ago and in Eli's company. I sent for the camp prefect, who thought it prudent to have you woken, sir."

"Other elves?" Stiger glanced toward his office.

"Yes, sir," Nepturus said. "And they aren't dressed like any ranger I've ever seen. They're wearing armor, sir, like heavy infantry."

"Armor?" Stiger asked, surprised. "Elves wearing armor?"

"Yes, sir," Nepturus said, "more ceremonial in nature… like something the emperor's Praetorian Guard might wear on parade to impress civilians."

Stiger considered the tent flap to his office for a long moment. Were these new elves the first of Taha'Leeth's people to arrive? Dog gave a low, almost menacing growl. Both he and the clerk glanced down at the animal. It was then Stiger realized Dog had not rushed up to Nepturus in search of a treat. Stiger found that an ominous sign.

"Thank you," Stiger said. "Return to your duty."

"Yes, sir."

Stiger moved forward and, holding aside the flap, entered his office. Those inside had been in discussion. They turned to face him. Stiger stopped cold and allowed the flap to fall back into place after Dog padded through.

Two elves wearing elegant armor that looked more for show than practicality stood with Eli, Taha'Leeth, and Salt. Severus was off to the side and appeared to have been

simply observing. Stiger knew that though the highly polished chainmail armor seemed ceremonial, it was anything
but. These two elves were clearly warriors and, knowing
elvenkind, they were likely more than good at soldiering.

One of the elves stepped forward toward him. His sandy
brown hair fell down his back, as if freshly brushed. Under
his arm he held a helmet with a red crest. At his side, he carried a long sword with a well-worn grip. He had the bearing
of one long accustomed to command.

Stiger blinked, not quite sure he believed his eyes. This
elf was the spitting image of Eli, and Stiger realized that he
knew him. He was sure of it, though he did not know the
second elf, whose grim face was disfigured by a patchwork
of rough scars.

The silence in the tent stretched. Then Eli stepped
forward.

"Ben," Eli said, in a neutral tone, "you recall my father,
do you not?"

"Of course," Stiger said, recovering. He cleared his
throat. "Tenya'Far, it is an honor to welcome you to the
Thirteenth Legion's camp."

Eli's father had never approved of Stiger, which begged
the question, why was he here? In fact, why had he even left
elven lands in the first place? Elders simply did not travel,
ever. It was a fact. Eli had even told Stiger as much. Only
youths were ever known to venture out into the wider world.
Stiger's eyes went to Eli, who himself was aged over a thousand years. By his people's standards, Eli was still considered
young, a mere child just into his teens.

"Legate." Tenya'Far inclined his head slightly in a sign of
respect, which was something Eli's father had never before
offered him. When he'd lived amongst the elves, Stiger had

gotten the distinct impression Tenya'Far had resented his presence and friendship with Eli. "I am pleased that you are well, very pleased."

Stiger was at first unsure how to respond. His eyes flicked from Tenya'Far to Taha'Leeth. She shot him a wink, and despite his shock, he almost smiled back at her.

Salt cleared his throat.

"Tenya'Far was just saying," Salt said, "that he has brought a group of elven warriors with him, to aid us, sir, to fight at our side."

"Warriors?" Stiger asked. He had only ever seen elven warriors on guard before the warden's palace, which he'd never been permitted to enter.

What was going on here?

"You've come to help?" Stiger asked, hardly daring to believe it was true. "To fight with us?"

"We have," Tenya'Far said, "with your emperor's blessing and support."

"The emperor?" Stiger asked, wondering how the emperor knew that he'd needed help.

"Emperor Tioclesion received the messenger you dispatched," Tenya'Far said. "Your scouts won through to the emperor's army and reported the events that occurred in Vrell, with Castor's minion and Captain Aveeno. The emperor was very pleased to learn you lived and had overcome such evil. So too was General Treim."

"General Treim?" Stiger had forgotten he'd sent two of Eli's scouts back from Vrell, before the enemy had completely sealed and closed the road. It was good to know the emperor knew that, unlike the Southern legions, he had done his duty. In fact, Stiger found it quite a relief.

"I had the honor of meeting your General Treim," Tenya'Far explained. "He too was pleased you live. Though it certainly appears," Tenya'Far said, with a glance to Salt and then to Taha'Leeth, "more has occurred that we did not know of or, for that matter, could anticipate."

"That is an understatement," Stiger said, thinking this a fantastical turn of events.

"Legate, your emperor gave me this letter for you." Tenya'Far withdrew a letter from behind his armor and handed it over. Stiger saw the emperor's mark was plain on the wax seal, which was unbroken. "He asked that you read it in private."

Stiger glanced down at it and then back up at Eli's father. It occurred to him that more was going on than simply help being dispatched. Delvaris's own letter, delivered by the late Garrack, had said that the current emperor would support Atticus's order, promoting Stiger to legate. He'd not understood how that would happen and had worried about it more than a little. He had been concerned that Tioclesion would not endorse what he'd done. However, Tenya'Far's presence said otherwise, and so too did the letter.

The gravity of what was occurring suddenly slammed home. The emperor had sent elves to his aid. Since the campaign in the Wilds, Eli's people had stood apart from the empire. And yet, now it seemed they had come to help. They had rejoined the empire and it appeared were now willingly fighting alongside her legions. Tenya'Far had also referred to Stiger by his current rank. Stiger glanced down at the letter again, flipping it over. On the other side, it was addressed to Bennulius Stiger, Legate of the Thirteenth Legion.

"In truth," Tenya'Far said, "we had thought you only had a few men, perhaps at most a thousand. We did not guess you had an entire legion at your back and then some."

"I've been busy," Stiger said, the answer sounding somewhat inadequate to his ears, as his excitement suddenly grew at the news.

"It certainly seems so," Tenya'Far said. "From what my son tells me, you also restored the Second Compact and the dwarves marched ahead of you."

"The Second Compact?" Stiger asked, confused, then understanding dawned on the second part of what Eli's father had said. "Wait a moment, you did not pass by Braddock and his army?"

"No," Tenya'Far said, "we did not come by way of the Vrell road."

"We traveled a more direct route," the scarred elf said. "So much so that we had to chase after you. We went straight to Vrell. However, you were no longer there."

"Elves don't need roads," Stiger said, thinking that Tenya'Far and his warriors had gone directly through the forest to get to Vrell.

Tenya'Far inclined his head slightly, then turned to the other elf with him. "May I introduce Teden'Thor, my second in command."

"It is an honor to meet you, Teden'Thor," Stiger said, studying the elf and thinking he had the look of a fighter about him. The terrible scars were a testament to past fights, perhaps hundreds, if not thousands of years ago. Stiger then turned back to Eli's father. "How many did you bring with you?"

"Sixteen hundred warriors," Tenya'Far said. "We come to fight alongside you, for we would not have the Cyphan

triumph over the empire"—the elf paused a long moment—
"if you will have us."

"Sixteen hundred?" Stiger was astonished. "All warriors?"

"Warriors all," Tenya'Far confirmed. "Ten thousand
of our best warriors marched out of our homeland a few
months back. I would have brought more, but the warden
thought it prudent the rest of our army would be better
served helping to defend the empire. Sixteen hundred is
all she and your emperor would allow me to bring this far
south."

Stiger sucked in a breath. He shook his head slightly in
dismay.

"Your warriors are very welcome," Salt said. "We need all
the help we can get."

"Yes, I am grateful you have come," Stiger said, after a
long moment. "Truly grateful. How far away is your main
body?"

"About two miles from this spot," Teden'Thor said. "We
did not want to alarm you by bringing them any closer."

Stiger glanced over to Salt, who shot him a grin in reply.

Dog moved forward toward Eli's father. For the first
time, the elf's gaze went to the animal. Stiger thought he
read shock, for Tenya'Far stiffened ever so slightly. The elf
recovered quickly. He held out a tentative hand for Dog to
sniff. After a moment of doing so, Dog gave a single lick
to Tenya'Far's hand, then returned to Stiger's side, sitting
down.

"I think he approves of you, Father," Eli said. "One of
the few dogs to do so."

"This is no normal dog," Tenya'Far said to his son.

"No, he's not," Taha'Leeth said and then gestured to
Stiger, "and then my mate is no average human either."

Tenya'Far's gaze snapped to Taha'Leeth in clear surprise, if not shock. After a heartbeat or two, his expression hardened like cold granite, before shifting over to Stiger. There was an intensity in the elf's eyes that Stiger did not like.

"Mate?" Tenya'Far asked in Elven, returning his gaze to Taha'Leeth. "You two have mated? This cannot be true. Tell me it is not so."

Stiger knew Tenya'Far was using Elven to exclude Salt and Severus. More concerning to Stiger was that Eli's father had directly questioned the word of another elf, which he understood to be a terrible insult. Taha'Leeth became still. Stiger felt a bubble of anger pulse within his breast.

"It is," Stiger answered in Common, before Taha'Leeth could respond. "Taha'Leeth and I are lovers, mates if you will. We fully intend to spend the rest of our lives together… for however long that is."

Salt's expression hardened a tad as understanding sank in about what Tenya'Far had questioned. Eli shifted uncomfortably, looking between them. Tenya'Far's gaze shifted over to Stiger, before he shared a look with Teden'Thor.

"Do you have a problem with that?" Stiger asked, fully recalling Eli's warning, back at Castle Vrell. "Best say so now and get it out in the open."

"I do," Tenya'Far said, this time in Common. The elf's voice was cold, harsh even. "However, that will not stop me from performing my duty. At the behest of the warden, I am here to support you. Distaste aside, that is what I shall do."

"Very good," Stiger said. "I am pleased we understand one another."

"Do we?" Tenya'Far asked. "I doubt that very much. It will be for the warden to decide how we, as a people, respond to this...this abomination of a union." He made the word union sound dirty.

Stiger's anger surged.

"No," Taha'Leeth said, "it is not your warden's decision and never will be. It is ours alone. You may be kin, but you have no say over me or my people. Understand that now. If I need to explain it to your warden, then I shall do so."

Tenya'Far's gaze rested unhappily on Taha'Leeth. "Eli tells me your people are coming. I doubt very many of them will be pleased by your actions, Rasensa, when they learn of what you have done."

Stiger did not know the Elven word Tenya'Far had used. He scowled, suspecting Taha'Leeth had just been terribly insulted. He made a mental note to ask her about it later.

"That is none of your concern," Taha'Leeth said. "I suggest you not seek to interfere, if you know what is good for you."

Tenya'Far looked about to reply, when Teden'Thor laid a hand upon his forearm. Eli's father glanced over at his second in command. A sort of silent communication passed between them. Then Tenya'Far gave a nod and returned his attention to Stiger. There was no hint of emotion on the elf's face, no sign of the outrage.

That just pissed off Stiger even more. Why couldn't things ever be easy? Then, Dog growled. It was filled with terrible menace and directed at Tenya'Far.

"Perhaps, Father," Eli said in a tone that was almost mocking, "Dog has changed his opinion of you. That or he doesn't approve of your position concerning their union."

Tenya'Far's gaze snapped to his son, anger returning and plain for all to see. Stiger rubbed the back of his neck, acutely feeling his frustration at the situation.

Dog's growl intensified and the animal stood, baring his teeth at the elf.

"Dog," Stiger said, before things escalated further, "down."

Dog sat back down. The growling stopped, but the animal's entire attention was focused on Tenya'Far.

"Father, I don't think it wise to get on the wrong side of a naverum," Eli added, with the trace of a smile, "especially when the creature is Ben's guardian. Such behavior might just prove unhealthy. It would be a shame to have to tell Mother that you died prematurely due to rudeness. Then again"—Eli gave a shrug of his shoulders—"she might welcome the news of your passing. Who knows? Mother is like that."

Feeling a headache coming on, Stiger closed his eyes and pinched the bridge of his nose. Nothing was ever easy, and his allies, elves now included, were the proof of that. He did not need this, not now when they were just days from leaving the forest behind.

"Legate," Tenya'Far said, with barely suppressed rage, "with your permission, I will bring my warriors into your encampment."

"Your warriors are more than welcome to join us," Stiger said.

Tenya'Far put his helmet on and then, with Teden'Thor following, swept from the tent.

"Do you always have to poke the bear?" Stiger asked Eli, after they'd gone.

"That could have gone worse," Eli said.

"Eli, I believe you meant the word better," Salt said, correcting the elf.

"No, I meant worse," Eli said and jerked a thumb at Stiger. "He could be marrying my sister."

Taha'Leeth threw an unhappy scowl at Eli.

"You don't have a sister," Stiger said, running a hand through his hair.

"Oh right," Eli said. "Thank you for reminding me."

Stiger turned his gaze in the direction Tenya'Far had gone. His anger drained away and the excitement abruptly returned. His army was growing. Dwarves, gnomes, and now the elves had come. The enemy, when he found them, would be in for a shock.

FOURTEEN

Stiger ducked into his personal tent, with Taha'Leeth following close behind. He tossed the emperor's unopened letter onto his desk and sat down on a stool. He still couldn't believe that Eli's father had brought sixteen hundred elven warriors with him. It seemed so unreal, such an impossible thing to have happened, and Taha'Leeth's people had not even begun to arrive yet. He blew out a long breath and felt a wave of weariness wash over him.

"Great gods, I'm tired," Stiger said, rubbing at his eyes. "I mean truly tired, and not just from the continual marching."

Outside, the morning horn sounded in one long, continuous blast that lasted a ten count. The legion's day had begun and so too would Stiger's when Nepturus brought the morning reports by.

It had been much easier when he'd only commanded a company. He almost groaned at the thought of all that would soon be awaiting him at headquarters, and he'd just left it, getting only a partial night's sleep. Marching was always a welcome relief from the administrative work, but as the miles wore on, that brought its own physical trials. Everything combined to wear him out.

"You need sleep," Taha'Leeth said, eying him, "more than you are getting now."

"There is too much that needs doing," Stiger said.

"That sounds like an excuse." Taha'Leeth poured herself a mug of wine. She set the wine jar back down on the table by his cot and turned back to face him. "I thought you weren't one who tolerated excuses?"

Stifling a yawn, Stiger did not bother to respond. Instead he attempted to change the subject. "A coffee would be nice about now."

"Is that your way of asking me to get you some coffee? Like a good little wife? I think not." Taha'Leeth crossed her arms. "I believe you have a servant for fetching you what you want. Venthus is his name."

"It was just a comment, not a request." Stiger held up both hands, feeling very weary. Before he joined the march this day, he needed some sleep. That was for certain. Maybe he could sneak in an hour or two? There were advantages to being in command.

"I know," Taha'Leeth said, with a sly smile, "I am teasing you, my lover."

Stiger chuckled. "Don't tell me you are going to do your best to drive me insane? Just like Eli? You know, he views it as his mission in life to push me over the edge. I don't think I could handle that, not with you."

"No," Taha'Leeth said. "My intent is to make you happy."

"Happy?" Stiger asked himself and marveled at the thought of being happy, content even, with no worries. The last time he had experienced such feelings had been with Sarai. Still, as he gazed upon Taha'Leeth, he realized that she had begun making him happy.

"I like Eli," Taha'Leeth said, approaching the desk. "He reminds me of my brother."

"You have a brother?" Stiger asked. He wondered if she had any other siblings.

"I did," Taha'Leeth said, her face clouding. "He passed many years ago."

"I am sorry for that," Stiger said and truly he was. She, like him, had suffered terribly. Perhaps when all this madness was behind them, they could find peace, contentment, and happiness in each other's company. Somewhere quiet and without too many responsibilities, he thought. Was that too much to ask?

Taha'Leeth brightened. "He lived life to its most and had a fine sense of humor, very much like your Eli."

"What was his name?" Stiger asked.

"Aren'Leeth," she said. "He too pushed his father to the edge of madness, and sometimes me also." She paused, her gaze becoming briefly unfocused, as if she were reliving the past. "I think you would have liked him and he you."

"Would he have accepted us," Stiger asked, "being together?"

Taha'Leeth was silent for several heartbeats. When she spoke, her voice was a near whisper. "I like to think he would, after he understood the why of it. Still, he died on another world, long before my people became enslaved. Things... now are different than they once were. At that time in my life, being with you would have been worse than repugnant." She gave a shrug of her shoulders. "I would have killed you first rather than share your bed."

"It's good things change, then," Stiger said.

"They do. All it takes is time."

"Rasensa?" Stiger asked. "What does that word mean? I have never heard of it before today."

Taha'Leeth took a sip of her wine as she regarded him. "It represents my responsibility, my burden to bear. Eli's warden's title is Elantric. That has its own meaning. Amongst my people, I am the Rasensa, opposite of the Elantric."

"The Rasensa Warden?" Stiger asked. "Eli did tell me your role is somewhat different than the warden's and yet you have the same title?"

"No, I am not a warden." Taha'Leeth took another sip of the wine and appeared to savor it for several heartbeats. "The gods never saw fit to grant me *Will* over the occult. What they gifted was very different in nature and being. I am, instead, the Rasensa Sovereign."

Stiger leaned back on his stool, studying her. "So, you are like a queen?"

"Not quite," Taha'Leeth said. "However, it is a close approximation. My people call me the sovereign. I am considered by the Cyphan to be the ruler of my people, but it is not the same as being a queen. My authority is not nearly so absolute, nor would I wish it to be. Think of me as a respected and wise leader, one who guides our council and settles disputes amongst the elders."

"So," Stiger said, suddenly amused, "I would be your consort or something like that?"

"Something like that," Taha'Leeth said.

Stiger was silent for a prolonged moment as he thought. He recalled Eli's words back at Castle Vrell, specifically his warning.

"Was he right?" Stiger asked. "Was Tenya'Far correct about how his people and yours will see us? As an abomination?"

Taha'Leeth stepped back over to the wine jar and poured herself some more. When she turned back to face him, her face was grave. "It will be difficult for many. Some will accept my choice, and some will not. As we just discussed, all things, given time…change. I hope many will come to understand and live with our union."

"What if they don't?"

"Then there will be a new sovereign," Taha'Leeth said.

"I don't think I like the sound of that," Stiger said.

"In a manner of speaking, it would be a relief. Long have I been sovereign. It might be time for me to pass that responsibility to another."

"You would give up everything for me?"

"What matters is the two of us," Taha'Leeth said. "When Tanithe showed me the vision, I resisted, rejected it, railed against my destiny. I did so knowing that it meant hope, freedom, and a new path for my people…and yet, the gods, in their wisdom, give us free will. I never conceived I would or could love a human, stand to be with one even, and share his bed." She fell silent as a single tear ran down her cheek. "Then, I got to know you, see you in action, and touch your spirit. Ben, I have made my choice and am happy for doing so. Would I could, I would not take any of it back, even the worst of my mistakes. You and I are meant to be together."

Stiger took a few moments to absorb that. "We could tear your people apart."

"That is one possibility. Change is another," Taha'Leeth said. "Tanithe and the High Father saw fit to bring us together for a purpose. You and I are fulfilling that purpose. My people have been through a lot. I believe in time they will come to understanding and acceptance."

"I hope you are right," Stiger said, for he had enough problems. Then something occurred to him. "How has Aver'Mons taken the news?"

"Not well," Taha'Leeth said, "but I believe he is coming around. It is a little more complicated with him. I was mated to his brother."

"And you're telling me this now?" Stiger was aghast.

"Would it have mattered?" Taha'Leeth asked him. "He will despise you just the same if he desires."

"No," Stiger said, after thinking about it for a moment. "You are right. It would not have mattered."

He turned his gaze back to his desk and leaned forward, reaching out a hand toward the emperor's letter. He hesitated. It was almost as if he feared the letter would burn him. He prodded it with a finger, then picked it up.

"We are meant to be together," Taha'Leeth said insistently. "That is the end of it. Do you understand? No others have a say in the matter but us."

Stiger gave a nod and returned his attention to the unopened letter.

"Well?" she asked, stepping nearer.

"Well what?" Stiger looked up at her.

"Aren't you going to open it?" Taha'Leeth asked, gesturing at the letter with her mug. "What are you waiting for?"

That was a very good question. For a long while he had been out of contact with the empire. There had been no direction to follow, no orders constraining him. It had allowed Stiger tremendous freedom to take the path he thought right. The emperor's letter represented a return to imperial control and authority, which was why he hesitated and was procrastinating even now. What orders or instructions would the letter contain? How would it affect actions he felt compelled to take?

"Enough," Stiger said under his breath and broke the wax seal with his thumbnail. He tore it open and pulled out the letter from within. Unfolding the parchment, he read. It was brief, more so than he had expected. He read it a second time and then expelled a breath, realizing it had been written in the emperor's own hand, which was unusual. He recognized the writing. It meant either the emperor had been rushed or he had not wanted anyone else to know the contents. He set the letter down on the desk, leaned back on his stool, and closed his eyes with a feeling of utter relief.

"What did it say?"

Stiger motioned for her to take the letter, which she did.

"Ben," she read aloud, "old friend, I am confirming your appointment as legate of the Thirteenth Imperial Legion. This will ultimately prove unpopular with the senate, not to mention many other powerful families. I have no doubt about that. However, I must consider and weigh the survival of the empire. In this, I am serving the empire's needs. The days ahead will be dark and trying...so says the master wizard who counsels us. As was foretold, during Atticus's reign, you are in the right place at the right time. The hand of destiny guides you as Champion. I am assembling the legions north of Lorium. By the time this letter reaches you, this information will be weeks, if not months, old. Do what you will and what must be done. In the name of the empire and the High Father, you have my full support. With any luck, we shall once again meet as friends. Tioclesion."

It was not at all what he had expected. He wished it had been more informative and helpful. And yet, it left him with more questions. Who was this wizard? Would Ogg know him?

Was he a threat? Was the advice the emperor was receiving sound? Tioclesion's full support and a free hand to do what he thought best? He had not expected that, not in the least.

She set the letter back down on the table. "You are friends with the emperor, this Tioclesion? Eli told me your family was in disgrace, yes? Your father led a rebellion against the empire. And yet both you and the emperor are friends? How?"

Stiger looked up into her captivating eyes. She was the most beautiful woman he had ever seen, so much so, at times just gazing upon her was an almost physical hurt. He felt he could easily lose himself within her gaze. Heck, he wanted to.

"Boyhood friends only. We played together in the palace." Stiger sucked in a breath and let it out slowly. "There was a fight over succession to the throne. It escalated into an all-out civil war. My father was one of the most respected generals of the empire. He chose to back the eldest son, the one he considered the rightful heir, and led his legions against Tioclesion. Unfortunately, it would end up proving to be the wrong side to back. My family paid a steep price. It almost undid us."

"Was your father defeated in battle?" Taha'Leeth asked.

"No," Stiger said. "I don't think he ever lost a battle he fought. Though I hate to admit it, he was that good."

"What happened to the heir your father supported?"

"He was assassinated," Stiger said, "and then there was nothing to fight for, no other claimants to the curule chair. Well, none the senate would consider supporting. The rebellion swiftly collapsed and then it was over."

"Because of your friendship with the current emperor, your family survived?" Taha'Leeth surmised.

"Partly," Stiger said. "Many others were put to death or enslaved as punishment. We were lucky, if you could call it that. My father and I escaped with our lives and not much more than that. You see, he agreed to surrender his legions without a fight. That was really the main reason we were spared."

Taha'Leeth took a long pull from her wine. She eyed him for several heartbeats.

"You blame him," Taha'Leeth said, "for all that happened to you, including the surrender?"

"I do," Stiger said.

"Some of my people blame me for my actions," Taha'Leeth admitted. "They will never forgive." She looked down into her mug and swirled the contents around. "Have you considered that your father's choices and your own have made you into the man you are today, the High Father's Champion, a great leader of men, and my mate?"

Stiger felt the scar on his cheek pull tight as he frowned at the thought. For so long, he had blamed his father for all his ills and everything that had happened to the family. It seemed strange suddenly to consider without him... he would not be where he was today, sitting in this tent with the most beautiful and exotic woman he'd ever met, not to mention leading a legion to help save the empire and spearhead the High Father's cause. Stiger rubbed his jaw as he contemplated her point.

"You have been greatly blessed," Taha'Leeth said. "There is no denying that."

"I've always judged him harshly," Stiger admitted. "Perhaps there is truth in what you say."

"There is no perhaps about it. Our choices, and those made before us, make us who we are." She touched her chest with the palm of her hand. "They shape and mold us. You may rightly blame your father for the mistakes he made on his own personal journey through life and the adversity you faced, but without that...you would not be you. Understand my meaning?"

"I would be different," Stiger breathed as he followed her reasoning home, "almost in a way someone else completely. Things might be better or worse."

"Exactly," Taha'Leeth said. "I have lived a very long life, many of your lifetimes. I've made mistakes, terrible ones too, that led to the suffering of my people. I shall never be able to atone for all the wrong I've done... And yet, knowing what I know now, if I could go back and change my past, I would not. Without making missteps or failing, there is no experience to be gained, nothing to learn from, no regrets to make us try harder the next time...do better."

Stiger glanced down at the letter, seeing it with new eyes. "It is something to think on."

"Yes, it is. And now, your friend, the emperor is putting his faith in you," Taha'Leeth said.

"It would seem so," Stiger said.

She picked up the letter again, scanning it. "There doesn't appear to be any seeming to do with it. It is very clear to me. He has faith in you." She looked up. "I too have put my faith in you. You will not fail me, just as you won't fail the emperor or your empire. You will do what you think right, just as you've always done. You are the High Father's Champion."

Stiger gave her a simple nod. The burden he bore at times seemed very heavy. After reading Tioclesion's letter, it weighed more heavily upon him. There had been no real instruction, and that, in a way, made the burden heavier to bear. Everyone had faith in him to do the correct thing, even the gods.

Stiger was exhausted. He felt it to his core. His return to the present, the clearing out of Old City, the battle before Vrell and then the long march…all of it had taken a toll. He stifled another yawn. His eye began to twitch in the most annoying manner. He rubbed at it, trying to get it to stop.

"You are tired," Taha'Leeth said.

"I am," Stiger agreed, "very."

"You need more sleep."

"You can say that again," Stiger said and stifled yet another yawn.

"I am serious, Ben," Taha'Leeth said. "You need to be rested for what is to come."

"I cannot disagree with you," Stiger said. "Even though I delegate, there is just too much to do and not enough time to do it all. There are days I wonder how General Treim managed to command an army twice the size of my own. He had four legions under his command and more than twenty auxiliary cohorts. That did not even include the camp followers…heck, ours we left behind in Vrell." Stiger paused as he thought back to his time in the North. "It was an awesome force he commanded. The general was so tireless and in complete control. He focused on what mattered and never took his eye off his objective. At times, I feel I am only just managing things and that my efforts pale in comparison."

She suddenly gave a light laugh. He found it a pleasant sound and wondered what was so amusing. He liked when she laughed.

"You are still new to commanding a large force, an army, yes?"

"I am," Stiger admitted. "But that is no excuse. I must try harder, work harder."

She laughed again.

"You may not realize it," Taha'Leeth said, "but your men see you as tireless, in control, and focused...just like you see your General Treim."

For a moment, Stiger thought she might be jesting. From her look, he decided she wasn't. It got him thinking. When General Treim was fighting the Rivan in the North...had he been just as bone-tired? Had he concealed his weariness from the men, his worries, his doubts and concerns? Now that she had gotten him thinking on it, Stiger suspected Treim had. It was an intriguing thought and one that, if ever he was reunited with the general, might be worth asking.

"Your men have told me so," Taha'Leeth continued, "and I've heard your legionaries speak amongst themselves when they thought no one listening. They think highly of you. Did the men of General Treim's army love him?"

"They did," Stiger said, with dawning comprehension and a feeling of discomfort, "just as my men love me."

Stiger's mind raced. Why had he not seen it before? Probably because he'd never considered himself an equal to the general, his mentor and patron. Even though Stiger had led thousands of men in desperate battles, somehow, it just did not seem right to compare himself to General Treim. Taha'Leeth had given him a lot to think on.

He yawned mightily.

"Before I leave, I will speak with Salt and Venthus," Taha'Leeth said firmly. "Between the two of them, they will see that you get more sleep."

Stiger almost laughed at her earnest look.

"Don't you dare laugh at me." She tapped her foot on the rug for emphasis, and in that moment, he felt incredibly drawn to her.

"When are you leaving?"

"Before dawn," she said. "I am meeting up with a team of scouts. Eli, Aver'Mons, and I have been working hard at the training of them...Marcus too. Many show real promise."

He had heard the same from Eli. Stiger eyed her for a long moment, his thoughts shifting away from the scouts and to something altogether different. His exhaustion retreated a little.

"Dawn's a little over an hour away." Outside, the legion was beginning the day. Stiger could hear the shouts of the officers as they got their men moving, fed, and organized, readying them for the day's march. He ignored it all, instead struggling to hide his smile as he drank in her beauty like a fine wine. "You and I...we have some time before you must depart."

"I know what's on your mind." Taha'Leeth smiled demurely. "You should go to bed while there is time."

"I want to," Stiger said, "with you."

Her eyes went to his cot. She turned her gaze back to him and bit her lip, clearly thinking about it.

"If I say yes...will you promise to get some sleep after?" Taha'Leeth asked. "Sleep for a few hours at least, before you march?"

"Consider it motivation to do so."

"I want your word of honor," she said.

"You doubt me?" Stiger teased.

"In this," Taha'Leeth said, "yes. You push yourself harder than the rest. So, what will it be? Some time in my arms or not?"

"You drive a hard bargain," Stiger said. "Barring an emergency, I will leave orders that I am not to be disturbed until the auxiliaries begin preparing to march. That will give me about four hours of sleep after the first cohort starts out. Will that do?"

"It will, as a start."

Taha'Leeth set her mug down on his desk and held out her hand to him. Stiger took her hand, feeling the warmth. She seemed to radiate heat. It was something he loved about her, especially when they shared a bed on a cold night. The thought of her naked body pressed against his started his heart beating a little quicker. She hauled him to his feet and drew him in close, kissing him.

Stiger heard the tent flap being pulled aside. He broke away and looked over to see Nepturus standing there, with a stack of tablets in hand. The clerk's eyes were wide with alarm.

Stiger found himself intensely irritated. "What is it?"

"Excuse me, sir," Nepturus stammered, clearly embarrassed. "I did not mean to interrupt. I have the morning reports, sir."

"He will see those later," Taha'Leeth informed the clerk in a firm tone. "Your legate needs sleep and I intend to put him to bed. Barring an emergency, he is not to be woken until the first of the auxiliary cohorts march. Is that understood?"

Nepturus glanced from Taha'Leeth to Stiger and then back again, as if unsure who to take orders from.

"It's as she says," Stiger said. "In this, she is the boss."

"Understood, my lady," Nepturus said, recovering. "I will see that appropriate orders are issued. The legate will not be disturbed."

"Thank you, Nepturus," Taha'Leeth said, flashing the clerk a pleased smile. "When I next return, I will bring you a pheasant or a quail for your cook pot."

"In that case," Nepturus said, "I will get those orders passed along right away. If you will excuse me, sir?"

Stiger gave a nod. The senior clerk stepped back and allowed the tent flap to fall back into place.

Taha'Leeth turned back to Stiger. "You had better sleep."

"I wish we had more time than just an hour together," Stiger said, "and I don't mean spending it all in bed. Though to be honest, that wouldn't be so bad."

"Oh really? You think I am bad in bed? Keep at it and you won't see any action 'til you next encounter the enemy."

Stiger grinned at her. She leaned forward and kissed him passionately.

"When this is all over," Taha'Leeth said, "there will be plenty of time."

"I pray you are right," Stiger said.

"I am," Taha'Leeth said firmly. "Now, enough talk or you will waste the little time we have."

Taha'Leeth took his hand again and drew him toward the cot.

FIFTEEN

Stiger stood off to the side of the road with Eli and Dog. The boundary of the Sentinel Forest was several miles back. For the past hour, they had been watching the legion march by, one cohort after another. Then had come the elves. A few yards behind and off the road waited Ruga's century. The centurion had detailed a man to hold both Nomad and Wind Runner's reins.

The sky overhead was clear and blue as could be. The air was almost deceptively warm. Stiger felt like taking off his bearskin cloak, almost. He knew it only felt warm because the temperature over the last few weeks had been well below freezing. And though it felt like a heat wave, it was still cold and so he kept the cloak on.

Having finally left the forest behind—it had taken nearly four weeks to travel from Vrell—they were now marching through abandoned and overgrown farm fields. It was a land almost completely empty of people, the result of the rebellion, which had burned its way through the South long before he and Eli had arrived from the North.

Braddock's army was camped less than a dozen miles away. Much of the legion had already made its way past the spot where Stiger now stood, moving toward the fortified dwarven encampment. After the elves would come the auxiliaries and then the rearguard.

As if on parade, formed up into four ranks, one of Tenya'Far's elven companies was passing before them. With flashes of sunlight glinting brightly under the midday sun, the elves looked quite splendid in their polished chainmail armor and helms. They carried oval-shaped shields that had been painted with intricate patterns and runes. The elves wore heavy packs and were all armed with swords and short spears. This was the second of the eight elven infantry companies to make their way by.

"Eyes right," the captain of the company shouted in Elven. The warriors' heads snapped to the right, toward Stiger. The officer offered Stiger a crisp salute. Surprisingly, it was a legionary salute, fist to chest.

"Lokeen'Han," Eli said quietly to Stiger, "captain of the Radiant Aternat Company. They are a very old formation and were around during the time of your first emperor, Karus. They fought alongside his legionaries. This is one of the warden's finest fighting formations, you could say almost the pride of my people, if we felt such for warriors."

Stiger gave a mental nod to that information and returned Lokeen's salute. Then the captain was past them.

"They show you great honor," Eli said.

Stiger rubbed his jaw as he considered the elves, their boots crunching in unison on the dry roadbed.

"When I lived amongst your people"—Stiger gestured toward the company as he glanced over at Eli—"they were either outright hostile to the point of offense or pretended I did not exist."

"Not all of them," Eli said.

"Enough so that it was uncomfortable," Stiger said. "I was left with the impression I was not a welcome visitor."

"We don't allow very many humans into our lands," Eli said with a pained look. "Such a thing is an incredibly rare event. I am saddened to admit there were some who resented your presence."

"That is a bit of an understatement," Stiger said. "Don't you think?"

Eli did not respond, so Stiger decided to continue.

"Being resentful is fine, but that did not make it right. I wonder how I'd be received now?"

"Time changes all things," Eli said.

"You sound like Taha'Leeth," Stiger replied.

"Do I?" Eli asked. "I could see how I might. Consider it a High Born thing."

"Oh really?"

Eli gave a shrug of his shoulders. "We elves see time passing differently than others."

Stiger scratched at an itch on his arm as he regarded his friend for a long moment. From the day's march Stiger was coated with a film of road dust. It was even in his mouth, and no matter how much he tried to wash it out, he could still feel the grit on his teeth. Dust was one of a legionary's worst enemies.

"Taha'Leeth says I will begin seeing things like you," Stiger said, "as the years ahead pass one after another."

Eli glanced over at him, eyes narrowing ever so slightly, before quickly looking away. They had not spoken on his newfound longevity. When they'd seen each other over the past few weeks, Eli had appeared uncomfortable whenever Stiger had hinted at it or been on the verge of bringing it up. Instead, he'd danced around the issue, actively working to change the subject.

Seeing his friend's reaction, Stiger figured it was time they got the matter out in the open and before them.

"How do you feel about that?" Stiger pressed, switching to Elven, so those nearest men could not understand what was said between them. "The change in me, the added years, all of it. I want to hear your thoughts."

"Are you sure you wish to discuss this now?" Eli asked, replying in Elven. "Here?"

"You know I do," Stiger said. "I do not like anything to get in the way of our friendship."

"Neither do I," Eli said quietly. "Our friendship is secure. You need not worry yourself."

"Well then?" Stiger asked. "I would have your thoughts."

Eli did not immediately reply, instead turning his gaze to watch elven warriors march by. And so, Stiger settled in to wait the elf out.

Lokeen's company gave way to another, this one marching in two ranks. At the van, a standard-bearer marched directly behind two officers. A green hawk was emblazoned on the banner.

The senior officer, wearing armor that seemed almost too ornate to be practical, marched to the front of his company. The officer's shield, oval like the others, was painted and etched with what looked like golden runes. At his right hand and a step behind was his lieutenant. Both had their swords drawn.

"Eyes right," the officer shouted. Obediently, the warriors' heads snapped to the right. The officer and his lieutenant both saluted by looking to the right also and bringing the blades up before their faces.

"Captain Ensil'Ket," Eli said, "First Company of the Anasadoom. Their history is even more ancient than the

Radiant Aternat. Each member is an elder, what you would consider a head of household in the empire. They have not seen any action for quite some time, but that does not mean they can't fight. I would consider each the equivalent of one of your battle-hardened veterans. Though, with their proficiency with weapons, I would think they would be superior fighters."

The name of the company meant nothing to Stiger, as he was unfamiliar with elven formations, but Eli's background information helped him learn what he needed to know about the elves. It also reminded him of who his allies were. He'd never imagined that the elves had so many warriors, for when he'd lived amongst them, he'd been left with the impression Eli's people were far from numerous. It seemed that might not have been true.

Stiger returned the officer's salute and wondered how many of those paying him respect now inwardly despised and resented him for his relationship with Taha'Leeth. He looked over at Eli once the officers had passed, feeling inpatient.

"Are you going to let me die of old age or will you answer me?"

Eli eyed him for a long moment before speaking. "You're going to live a lot longer than the average human."

"Is that all you have to say on the matter?" Stiger asked. "I already knew that."

"The added years do give me more time to, shall we say, push you over the edge." Eli shot him a closed-mouth grin. "As you know, it is my mission in life."

Stiger had to chuckle.

"It is good that you think I jest," Eli said, "for I am very serious."

Stiger felt a sudden fondness for his friend. Over the last few weeks of marching, they had hardly seen one another. He'd seen Taha'Leeth more than Eli. They had both been busy, and yet Stiger knew that Eli had been avoiding him and this very conversation. Why, he did not know, though behind Eli's amusement he detected a certain grimness.

"If you haven't been able to do it yet," Stiger said gamely, "I doubt you ever will."

"Ben, remember we're talking about time," Eli said. "With your newfound longevity, I have all the time that I will need to turn you into a gibbering wreck of the man you are today."

Stiger gave a grunt and turned his attention back to the elven company. A team of six heavily laden ponies trailed behind the warriors. Unlike the legions, the elves seemed to prefer ponies over mules for their supply trains.

"The ponies even offer you their respect," Eli said.

"Do they speak to you like the trees do?" Stiger asked and cupped a hand to his ear. "Is that a pony song I hear?"

"No." Eli's grin became a tad wider. "They don't speak to me. I can just tell. You have most definitely earned their respect."

"Have I now?" Stiger asked. "If this is your idea of trying to drive me nuts, it's a pretty feeble attempt, even for you. I know you can do better."

"Consider it a start. I am beginning small....think baby steps, Ben."

"Right," Stiger said, "baby steps. Seriously though...back to my question."

"They do offer you great respect," Eli said, after Stiger had exchanged a salute with the next captain.

"The ponies or your fellow elves?" Stiger asked.

"As the High Father's Champion," Eli said, ignoring the comment, "you have great standing amongst my people."

"All it took was a god's favor, eh?" Stiger asked. "And as Taha'Leeth's mate?"

Eli hesitated a heartbeat. "Ah...it was not welcome news for most."

Stiger could imagine.

"Some see it as the gods' will, divine intervention. Others...well, let's just say they don't like it...not at all."

"Nothing is ever easy," Stiger said with a small shake of his head.

"With you, it is always the hard path," Eli said. "You never take the easier one, like settling down with Miranda."

"Miranda? The emperor's sister?" Stiger asked, looking over. With his trip to the past, he'd not thought of her in years. "You can't be serious?"

"She was rather fond of you."

"Right," Stiger said. "She was looking for someone to settle down with."

"Miranda is the perfect example of what I am talking about. By not entertaining the possibility of marriage, you chose the hard way... Let me add to that, with you...there is no easy way. I think it is perhaps one of the reasons I enjoy tagging along with you."

"I am beginning to suspect you are on to something there, my friend," Stiger said and glanced briefly back at his escort. Ruga had allowed most of the century to down yokes and relax. The men were sitting on the ground, digging through haversacks or reclining about, enjoying the unexpected break. Two were even engaged in a game of dice.

The centurion, however, stood a few feet back from Stiger and Eli, with two men. They were close enough to be at hand, should the need arise. The centurion's eyes were on the elves marching by. They were wary, suspicious.

"And your father?" Stiger asked, turning back to Eli. "What does he think?"

"Bah," Eli said, expelling a frustrated breath. The elf waved a dismissive hand. "As if he'd ever consider confiding in me."

It was rare for his friend to show exasperation. Eli caught the look and scowled slightly.

"He's not talking to you?" Stiger surmised.

"No," Eli admitted after a moment. "He refuses to see me. I think he still blames me for bringing you home, like some stray I found."

"Perhaps it's the father who's intentionally driving the son crazy." Stiger grinned at Eli. "Wouldn't that be a twist? The boot would be on the other foot for a change."

"You know he and I never really got along," Eli said. "It's one of the reasons I felt drawn to you, Ben."

"Oh?"

"You, like me"—Eli placed a hand to his chest—"have your own daddy issues."

"We both know why you attached yourself to me and Seventh Company all those years ago," Stiger said, "now, don't we?"

"You have me there," Eli said and hesitated a moment. "You must have wondered on it for so long…"

"As in, why me?" Stiger asked. "And why Seventh Company?"

Eli gave a nod.

"I did wonder," Stiger said. "At first I thought it might be due to your history with Tiro. But then, as the years passed...I began to wonder, to question. Now I know the truth and why you could say nothing."

"Finally." Eli clapped his hands softly together. "Everything is out in the open between us."

"Almost," Stiger replied. "You still have not answered my original question."

"I did not?" Eli shot him an innocent look.

"No. You told me about how others feel, instead."

"You know me only too well," Eli said, growing grave. "Are you certain you wish me to give you my thoughts?"

"I am."

Eli hesitated. "As a true friend, I am saddened for you. The world in which we live is one of change. Nothing at all is permanent, not the trees, the rocks...everything you see lacks permanence. All things, given time, change, some more slowly than others..."

He sucked in a breath and let it out as a heavy sigh. "I feel wretched, for you will suffer, like we do. That is the curse with which we elves must live." Eli pointed at him. "And now you will share the deep sadness with us. It is one of the reasons why we lock ourselves in our forests and away from others...those with shorter lifespans. And why some would pretend you did not exist or wish you gone from our domain." Eli gestured at the elves marching by. "It is why our elders rarely leave the confines of our lands. We elves, the High Born, named so by the gods, are lovers of life. We despise death with a passion. Even when we have to take life...we hate it. Death is change. You see, Ben, it is not that my people dislike you. They simply do not want to know you, to grow to care for you, just to have to watch you age and then die. Loss for us is incredibly painful."

Eli fell silent. Stiger looked over at his friend and felt himself scowl. What Eli had revealed gave him serious pause. He turned his gaze back to the elves marching by, seeing them with new eyes, a dawning understanding.

"The torment of watching the world change," Stiger said, "without being able to fully stop it from doing so. That is the curse."

"Partly," Eli said. "The worst part is watching those you care about die and over time your memory of them fades. Yes, it is memory...which is the most painful. For as the years pass...memory fails to the point where you can't remember the faces of the ones you loved. I myself have already experienced this with..." Eli cleared his throat. "With a friend by the name of Kyven."

Stiger said nothing as Eli seemed to look inward.

"He was a man like yourself," Eli continued after a long moment. "Someone I tagged along with, sharing the dangers he encountered. He was kind of like you, actually, attracted all bunches of trouble and kept me terribly entertained." Eli let out a shuddering breath. His eyes watered and he looked away. "Only now, four hundred odd years later..." Eli cleared his throat again and turned back to face him, grief-stricken. "Ben, I can't remember what he looked like. You have no idea how painful that is to me. As a friend, I owe him more than to simply forget him. It is so unfair, but that is how it is. That is the true suffering of my people. Do you understand my pain? Our pain?"

"I do," Stiger said in barely a whisper. He clapped a hand to the elf's shoulder. "I do, Eli. I really do."

Stiger already knew what Eli spoke of. Over the years, he'd lost a good number of men. Some he remembered; others he could not recall what they looked like or even their names. All had served under his command. It troubled him greatly when he thought on it.

They both fell silent, each lost in his own thoughts. Stiger turned his attention back up the road in the direction of the forest and Vrell, which was no longer in view. From the morning's reports, the artillery and supply train lagged as much as fifty miles behind. In the last few days, the artillery had begun making better progress as the road hardened, but they were still well behind the main body. He found it incredibly frustrating, but there was nothing to be done to speed them up.

"What do you think Miranda will make of Taha'Leeth?" Eli asked, wiping at his eyes with the back of a hand.

Stiger felt himself scowl at the change of subject. "What?"

"I assume once we link up with the dwarves," Eli said, "we will begin moving north. Have you given her any thought? You might see her again if we make it all the way back to Mal'Zeel. Perhaps the real question is...what do you think Taha'Leeth will think of your former lover?"

Stiger chuckled as the mood between them lightened. Miranda had never been his lover and Eli well knew that.

"You know...I don't really care," Stiger said and then laughed at the absurdity of the suggestion. His gaze returned to the elves marching by. "Emperor's sister or no, she and I were never meant to be. Besides, a life at court is not one I find inviting, let alone appealing. Too much intrigue, backbiting. There are too many ass kissers. You well know that, especially after what we went through in Thresh."

"Thresh," Eli said. "Now that was an exciting time."

"We almost both died," Stiger said. "It was perhaps a little too exciting."

"Almost doesn't quite count. We survived to tell that tale. That's what matters."

They fell silent again. Three more companies marched by, with Eli giving their names, backgrounds, and pointing out the officers. After exchanging salutes, Stiger found his thoughts shifting away from the elves. It had taken weeks of travel, but tonight, he and his men would be reunited with Braddock's army. Stiger was looking forward to seeing the thane again.

Three days prior, Braddock had fought a small battle with the enemy. A garrison in a town had marched against him, coming out from behind the protection of the town's walls. The enemy commander had brought four thousand rebel soldiers against the thane. He'd clearly not known Braddock's strength. If he had, he would have sat back behind the town's stone walls and waited, likely quaking in fear. Had he done so, they would have been forced to deal with the garrison before moving on. But he hadn't.

Hux's cavalry had blinded the enemy to the thane's presence. The enemy had assumed they were only facing a small cavalry raid, designed to distract from the real fighting to the north. They had marched to chase the raiders off and reopen the King's Highway, restoring their communications with the Cyphan. By the time they figured out their mistake, it was too late. The dwarves made short work of the garrison, taking over five hundred prisoners. They'd slaughtered the rest.

Braddock had not included his casualties in the report. Stiger supposed they had been light, for what he'd seen of the rebels, they were poor soldiers. He felt a bubble of frustration. Despite seizing and questioning prisoners, he and Braddock still only had limited information as to what was happening to the north and Tenya'Far had not been able to supply much more information. Eli's father's knowledge of events was weeks old.

On Braddock's orders, Hux had sent scouts riding north to gather additional intelligence. Those that had returned hadn't found out much more than wild rumors. Having fallen in battle, the emperor was dead. That and the empire had collapsed. The list went on, each rumor and tale more fantastical than the last.

Stiger did not believe any of it, would not and could not...for the empire was vast. He could not conceive in so short a time the Cyphan could have crushed the empire. It was impossible. And if the emperor fell in battle, another would surely rise.

In the past, the empire had taken hard hits, seen emperors slain in battle, and suffered terrible defeats that would have been mortal blows to other nations...only Stiger's people never gave up. They kept on fighting, and if the empire was pushed out of an area...it might take months, years, or decades, but the legions always returned, pushing back when they came.

However, one thing they did know for certain. Hux had discovered the battle site where the confederacy had defeated General Kromen's Southern legions. After stripping them of armor and equipment and looting what they could, the enemy had left the dead where they had fallen.

They'd not even bothered to bury them, instead leaving a feast for the carrion eaters. The men of the Southern legions had deserved better. It was a message to the imperials, likely designed to instill fear. The thought of what the Cyphan had done instead irritated Stiger immensely, stoking his wrath.

Hux had also discovered that Aeda had been thoroughly sacked. The population had been put to the sword. Beyond that, the best Stiger and Braddock could figure, the fighting had moved north to the empire's border, perhaps even beyond.

There seemed to be no serious enemy presence within a fifty-mile radius, which Stiger thought was an encouraging sign. It meant they would be able to begin marching northward without immediate concern.

Stiger felt sour. The senate had annexed the occupied lands to the south, but they had never gotten around to conferring citizenship on the people residing there. Had they done so, they might have stopped the rebellion long before it could have begun. Instead, the senate had settled for simply exploiting the occupied lands for all they were worth, making life miserable for those who lived there. By doing so, they'd inadvertently left the door open for the Cyphan.

Stiger slapped his thigh and expelled an unhappy breath. There was so much he did not know about what was going on to the north.

"Where is Menos?"

Eli looked over at him.

"You are concerned about the dragon?" Eli asked.

"I am," Stiger said. "That and what's waiting for us to the north. There is so much I am ignorant of. Menos should have returned by now and reported what he learned."

"He's a dragon," Eli said.

"What does that mean?" Stiger asked.

"Maybe he saw a herd of cattle and stopped for a snack?" Eli said. "Who knows with such ancient creatures? They do their own thing, have their own agendas. I imagine he will turn up soon, when he's ready."

Stiger knew Eli had meant to make light of the situation and to ease his mind a little, but it had not helped. Menos was a friend too, and Stiger was becoming worried. What could have delayed a noctalum?

"Something must have happened to him." Stiger felt the keen bite of frustration. He turned around and looked beyond Ruga and his men, at the remains of the small camp a few dozen yards off the road.

Eli followed his gaze.

"It all started here," Stiger said as his eyes took in the camp the Eighty-Fifth had built, before starting out for Vrell. Someone had gone to the trouble of tearing down the outer wall and filling in the trench. Why they bothered, Stiger had no idea. The interior of the camp was slightly overgrown. Weeds had popped up and the grass had grown tall. The old, rundown farmhouse had also been pulled down. Now it was no more than a heap of debris.

"No, it most certainly did not begin here," Eli said. "Yes, we started out for Vrell from here, but this all began with the gods. Without them and the Last War, we would not be here today, nor doing what we are doing."

"I suppose so." Stiger felt uncomfortable, for he detected a note of censure in his friend's tone. Eli was blaming the gods for all that had and would happen. And in a manner of speaking, he was right.

Stiger's gaze returned to the ruined campsite. He considered going in and poking around. Then, he disregarded the idea. It was time to stop looking back to the past. No matter how difficult, he had set his sight on the path ahead. He would look back no more. He had a job to do and he meant to do it.

"Ruga," Stiger said, switching back to Common, "get your men on their feet. We're leaving."

"Will you be riding, sir?" the centurion asked and gestured to the man holding the reins of both horses.

Stiger looked to Nomad for a long moment. The frustration was still there, just bubbling under the surface. A little marching would help work that out.

"No, I believe I will stay afoot," Stiger said.

"Yes, sir, very good, sir." Ruga turned to his men. "All right, you lazy bastards, you heard the legate, on your feet."

SIXTEEN

Stiger, along with Taha'Leeth, Tenya'Far, Salt, and Therik, were being led through the dwarven encampment. Ruga and another legionary followed them. Dog, tail wagging, trotted behind the two legionaries. Their escort included an entire company of Braddock's personal guard. Stiger understood it had not been necessary to send so many. The thane was simply honoring him and doing it in a way no one could misunderstand.

Braddock's army had encamped on a large hilltop that could almost be described as a small-to-medium-sized mountain. The spot was about five miles from where General Kromen's legionary encampment had been located and it dominated the surrounding terrain.

The army had been here for several days and had not been idle. The dwarves and gnomes had fortified their position with multiple trenches and a high wall topped by a stout barricade. It was an impressive defensive position and would be a difficult nut to crack.

Captain Jethga, captain of the escort, had explained the position had been carefully scouted and chosen by an advance team of Braddock's engineers. Stiger's legion, along with the elves, was encamping on an adjacent hill, a quarter of a mile distant. The dwarves had selected that as well. It, too, despite being smaller, was good defensive ground.

The sun had fallen, and despite it being dark and moonless, Stiger was impressed with what he had seen. The interior of the encampment was a veritable sea of life. Marching in a loose formation, half of Jethga's company preceded them, forcing dwarves and gnomes alike aside to make room, sometimes not so gently when those in the way did not move fast enough.

Once they realized it was Stiger who was being escorted, Braddock's dwarves and gnomes quickly moved to the side. They became quite still, lining both sides of the street. Some even saluted or came to attention, gnomes included, which Stiger found somewhat unsettling.

He knew from personal experience the vicious little bastards showed little respect to anyone, even for their own leaders. It was clear to Stiger he had become more than just a man or venerated leader. He'd become a symbol of faith. Once, that would have made him terribly uncomfortable. No more. He was who he was and that was the end of it.

Jethga, walking at his side, led them onward through a confusing maze of streets that were lined with communal tents, past company messes, armorers with portable forges, supply depots, artillery parks, and animal pens. There were thousands of communal fires with large numbers of dwarves and gnomes gathered around each for warmth. There were dwarves talking, laughing, eating, gaming, maintaining kit, and doing hundreds of other things. They passed training fields where entire companies drilled under torch and firelight.

Though he'd spent time with the dwarves, Stiger still found himself looking at all the strange sights and sounds, thoroughly fascinated. And had he been forced to navigate the encampment alone, Stiger knew he would have quickly become turned around and lost. It was that confusing, even though Jethga had assured him there was an order to everything.

"Is that a spider?" Salt asked in a horrified tone and pointed to a row of cook fires. Its legs dangling, a large spider was being roasted on a spit over one of the fires. Stiger suppressed a shudder of revulsion. He'd never much liked spiders.

"Krata," Therik said, "it's good eating, but they are dangerous critters. They live in the mountains around Vrell. In my youth, I used to hunt them. It was good fun and kept you on your toes, because they are highly venomous."

"They're very good eating," Jethga said in agreement, stressing the word very. "Earlier today, one of our foraging companies came across a den. This land has been empty for so long, it seems the more dangerous creatures are moving in. If you'd like, sir, I could arrange for you to get some when it's cooked. I believe you might like it. Krata is considered a delicacy amongst my people."

"Thank you," Stiger said, "but no."

"Are you certain, sir?" the officer asked. "I assure you, krata meat is quite tasty."

"I am very sure," Stiger said and shared a glance with Eli. They both well recalled Hans, a servant of Avaya, and his pets. His so-called pets had been krata. The memory of that experience still occasionally haunted his dreams. "I think I'd rather have salt pork."

Jethga appeared amused and clearly understood Stiger's reluctance.

"I can arrange that too, sir," Jethga said, "that is, if you are hungry."

"No thank you, Captain," Stiger said, amused by the suggestion, as they put the cook fires behind them. "I had my dinner before making the trek over."

"Yes, sir."

Eventually, they came to what was obviously Braddock's headquarters compound. This consisted of a cluster of medium to large tents. A small defensive wall had been constructed around the compound, along with a trench. After Hrove's betrayal before Old City, Braddock was clearly not taking any chances. What appeared to be an overstrength guard company was posted about the tents and bridge. The warriors wore the purple of Braddock's own clan.

Messengers came and went from what looked to be an administrative tent on the left side of the compound. There were also several officers standing to the side of the entrance, apparently waiting for admittance. It reminded him of the legion's headquarters. He imagined that Braddock had his own version of Nepturus. It was an amusing thought.

It was then, Stiger realized, he was in a good mood. Not only was the entire army back together, but they had been reinforced by Tenya'Far's elves and made it out of the Sentinel Forest without the enemy moving to stop them. In a day or so, the entire army would undoubtedly begin moving north. Then there was Taha'Leeth. She was back with him and would be for the next few days.

As if sensing his attention, she looked over and caught his gaze. She shot him a knowing wink. Then Jethga ordered his dwarves to halt, breaking the moment. He personally led them up to the bridge with the gate, which was open. The gate guard stood aside, coming to positions of attention.

"This is where I will leave you, sir," Jethga said. He offered a salute.

Stiger returned the salute. "Thank you for the escort, Captain."

Stiger saw that Naggock was waiting for them just past the gate on the other side of the bridge over the trench. As usual, the commander of Braddock's guard had a grave, hard look to him. Naggock took his duty of protecting the thane very seriously.

"Legate Stiger," Naggock said, in Dwarven, as Stiger moved over the bridge with the others following. "Welcome to our army's encampment. I hope you did not have too much trouble finding it."

"Was that a joke?" Stiger asked, suddenly amused by the cheeky comment. "How could we miss an army this size? Especially with our lead cohort being guided by Braddock's pioneers? Why, Naggock...I did not think you were capable of jesting. "

"I'm not," Naggock said, his beard twitching slightly as he came as close to a grin as Stiger had ever seen. "It just took you awhile to get here."

"We did have to fight an army first," Stiger said.

"I think that might have been a poor attempt at a joke," Eli said in Dwarven. "Though our friend Naggock here has always been a little too serious, dour might be a better description...a lightening of his mood suits him, don't you think?"

"It does," Stiger said.

"Humor aside," Naggock said, "the thane is very pleased you have arrived."

"It is good to finally have made it," Stiger said. "The march from Vrell was a long one."

"That it was," Naggock said, looking beyond Stiger at Therik. The dwarf eyed the orc with open suspicion. Stiger almost feared he would deny Therik entry, forcing the orc to wait. Naggock turned to Stiger and pointed at the orc. "You will take personal responsibility for him?"

"I speak Dwarven," Therik said acidly.

"I think he feels you need a keeper, Therik," Eli said.

Stiger struggled to suppress a grin.

Therik bared his tusks at Naggock, in what was most definitely not a grin. "I will teach him the meaning of respect."

Stiger held up a hand to Therik as the orc took a step forward.

"Naggock," Stiger said in a firm tone, "Therik is a trusted friend. Either he goes with us or the thane can come see me in my encampment." Stiger spared a glance over at the orc to make sure he was not about to assault Naggock. "In truth, Therik is his own keeper. My terms are non-negotiable."

Naggock shot Stiger an unhappy look, then seemed to reach some internal decision. He gave a shrug. "If you will follow me, sir, the thane has been waiting for you"—he shot an unhappy glance at Therik—"all of you."

"Lead on," Stiger said.

Therik muttered something under his breath about snooty dwarves. Luckily Naggock seemed not to hear it or, if he did, he purposely ignored the comment. He turned and led them up to the thane's command tent. It was large and ostentatious, with four long purple pennants flying above from the support poles, which emerged from the top of the canvas covering. Braddock's personal colors and standard also flew before the tent. The two guards by the entrance flap, standing next to a hissing torch, came to attention.

Naggock held aside the tent flap for Stiger. "He is expecting you."

"Ruga," Stiger said, turning to the centurion. "You and your man stay here."

"Yes, sir," Ruga said.

Stiger hesitated. He pointed to a fire that had been set nearby. "We'll likely be a good bit. Might as well warm up, while you have the chance."

"Thank you, sir," Ruga said. "I will avail myself of dwarven hospitality."

"I might have some spirits for them," Naggock said. "If you don't mind?"

"Now that sounds like a grand suggestion," Ruga replied in heavily accented Dwarven, almost to the point of being broken. Then the centurion remembered himself, switching to Common and addressing Stiger, "Moderation, sir. That will be my watchword tonight. You have my word on that, sir."

Stiger had not known the valley-raised centurion spoke Dwarven. It seemed Ruga had a few surprises of his own.

"I served as one of the valley's representatives," Ruga said, having guessed Stiger's thoughts. "It required me to learn their language, sir. I speak it passably."

"If Naggock wants to share spirits with you, that's his business," Stiger said. "Yours is making sure you can do your duty when I am done here. I don't want to have to deal with the embarrassment of having a party of gnomes drag you back."

"Yes, sir," Ruga said with a look to Naggock. "That sounds like a challenge, sir."

Stiger gave a grunt and stepped past Naggock, entering the tent. Braddock, wearing a richly cut purple tunic, was standing at a large table in the center of the tent, as was another dwarf he did not know. The tent itself was clearly the thane's office.

Lanterns hanging from the ceiling provided the light. A thick rug covered the ground. There was a desk, with several stools and a number of trunks that had been pushed up against the left wall. Two braziers by the back wall smoked heavily, creating a slight haze under the yellowed light. The tent smelled strongly of coal.

Eli, Taha'Leeth, Tenya'Far, Salt and Therik followed Stiger into the tent. Dog came last. The guards looked as if they might object to the animal entering, but when Dog gave a low, menacing growl, they changed their minds and stood back. The animal was, after all, very large, especially to a dwarf.

"Ah, Legate, we meet again," Braddock said, turning to face them. He stepped forward and held out his arm, which Stiger clasped. "It has been too long. I find it is good to see you, my ally and friend."

Dog padded up to them and sat down at Stiger's side, tongue hanging out of his mouth as he gazed upon the thane. Stiger almost frowned, for the animal was exhibiting incredible self-control, which in and of itself was unusual.

"I would have come over sooner, but I wanted to see the legion settled first," Stiger said, then half turned. "Thane Braddock, you know Taha'Leeth, Salt, Eli, and Therik."

Braddock gave a nod. "I do. I welcome you as well."

"I would like to introduce you to Tenya'Far," Stiger said, "commander of the elven contingent the Elantric Warden sent us."

Braddock eyed Tenya'Far for a long moment. The thane's gaze became almost frosty. He took a half step toward the elf. Stiger knew that Braddock harbored an intense dislike for elves, as did most other dwarves he'd met. The thane's jaw flexed.

"We are pleased you are with us, Tenya'Far," Braddock said in Common. "I understand from the legate you brought a small army with you."

"I did and I am most gratified to be here, your majesty." Tenya'Far gave a short bow. The elf spoke in Common.

"You may call me Braddock," the thane said, though his tone was icy cold.

"You show me great honor," Tenya'Far said. "Perhaps... this will be the first step toward restoring faith and friendship between our two peoples."

Braddock did not immediately respond. He ran a hand through the tight braids of his beard and seemed to consider Tenya'Far for several heartbeats. Stiger thought about interceding, to help smooth things out, for they all needed to work together. But he understood it was not his place to do so. Braddock and Tenya'Far needed to sort out their own differences, no matter how painful that might be. Only then would their little coalition work. And for it to work, each needed to trust the other.

"Time will tell," Braddock finally said, "and we both know it all boils down to time with your people."

Tenya'Far inclined his head slightly, as if acknowledging Braddock's assertion, and then glanced to Stiger. "I had thought I was coming to the rescue of Legate Stiger and his men. You cannot imagine how surprised I was to find out he needed no such rescuing."

"It was no less a shock," Braddock said, "when he showed up with an entire legion from the time of my father. The legate is remarkable for a human."

"It seems he's just full of surprises," Tenya'Far said.

Taha'Leeth shifted slightly, as if suddenly uncomfortable. Had that been a dig intended for her?

"Your reinforcement, Tenya'Far," Stiger said, deciding to ignore the comment, "is no less welcome. I fear, before this is over, we will need the warriors you brought with you. Tough days lie ahead for all of us. That is a certainty."

"No doubt," Tenya'Far said.

Braddock looked between the two of them, then turned and gestured toward the other dwarf. "May I introduce Kiello, Chieftain of the Bloody Axe. He is my advisor. His great-grandfather fought alongside Karus and, I believe, you as well, Tenya'Far. If I understand my history, that would have been under the First Compact."

Tenya'Far turned his gaze to Kiello and was silent for several heartbeats. When he spoke, his voice was firm. "I knew your great-grandfather, Kenso, well. He was one I named a friend. Kenso was a warrior with great Legend. You should feel honored to be his descendent."

"I know him only by name and through the stories told by my father and mother," Kiello said, in a voice that was raspy, almost harsh, as if he did a lot of shouting. "I thank you for your kind words, Tenya'Far, even if in the end, you and the rest of your kind abandoned him, along with the rest of my people, during our greatest need."

Eli stiffened as the tent went still. Stiger closed his eyes. His good mood evaporated in an instant.

"What you say is true," Tenya'Far said. "I will not deny it. We did walk away from the First Compact and for our own reasons." He held up both hands. "I will not go into it nor debate our actions. What I will say is that, given hindsight and reflection, our decision might not have been the wisest."

Kiello said nothing to that.

"I trust you will not walk away a second time?" Braddock asked. "Because if there is a chance you will, I would ask that you and your warriors leave us now. If we cannot rely upon you, I don't want you."

Stiger felt his scar pull tight as he gave a scowl. This was not at all going how he'd thought. Why couldn't things ever go smoothly?

"You dwarves have always been a direct people," Tenya'Far said. Eli's father had not lost his composure. Tenya'Far seemed as if he were having a simple conversation about the weather. There was no hint whatsoever that he had taken offense to anything Braddock or Kiello had said.

"I would not have it any other way," Braddock said. "Unlike you elves, we wear our passions openly. So, tell us, Tenya'Far...will you fight at our side and remain there no matter how difficult things become? Or will you cut and run like the last time?"

The tension in the tent increased.

"We will fight at your side," Tenya'Far said, "as if the First Compact was still in effect. The warden asked that I pass along her promise to fight to the bitter end. You have my personal and most solemn vow on that, as well. I will be there with you...until this is over, or the life has left my body."

"Those are certainly fine words," Braddock said.

"Words I will back up by deed," Tenya'Far replied.

Braddock paused. "Perhaps this will truly become the start at mending what was sundered."

"Indeed," Kiello said with a look to his thane. "I pray it is such a beginning."

"As do I," Tenya'Far said.

"And you, my lady," Braddock said, looking to Taha'Leeth, "I understand your people are on their way.

Though they had nothing to do with sundering of the First Compact, will you and they fight at our side?"

"I have pledged it so," Taha'Leeth said. "My people will come. We will fight with you against the Cyphan Confederacy, our enslavers."

"How can we be certain?" Kiello rasped. "We have been betrayed by elves before. You were their slaves. How can we know your coming is not a ploy to get us to lower our guard?"

Tenya'Far stiffened ever so slightly.

"Do you dispute that account?" Kiello asked Tenya'Far, having noticed the break in composure. "Do you dispute your people broke the Compact and betrayed us? For that is what you did."

"No," Eli's father said, locking gazes with the dwarf. "I do not dispute we left the alliance."

"Well?" Kiello asked, swinging his heated gaze back to Taha'Leeth. "How can we trust you?"

Stiger was growing angry. All sense of good humor and feeling was gone. He did not like the tone this meeting had taken, especially with the hostility Kiello was now directing at Taha'Leeth. He was about to put this upstart of a chieftain in his place, when he felt a touch on his forearm. It startled him. Stiger saw it was Eli. His friend simply shook his head slightly and flashed a sign with his fingers. *No.* Then Eli looked meaningfully at Taha'Leeth. Stiger followed his gaze.

Taha'Leeth's eyes flashed as she looked first at Kiello and then Braddock. "You both dare insult me? I come willingly to your side and yet you throw bile upon my doorstep. My mate fights with you. Yet you do not question his integrity. So, why am I different? Because I hail from elfkind?"

"Your mate?" Braddock asked, confused, and looked to Eli in question. "Him?"

"No," Taha'Leeth said, heat plain in her tone, "Ben."

"What?" Braddock exclaimed. Shock was written across his face, turning to Stiger. "Elf and human? Surely you are not serious?"

"She is thoroughly sincere." Tenya'Far's tone was hard. "She has taken him as mate."

"You have?" Kiello asked.

"And I have taken her," Stiger confirmed.

"I've never heard of such a thing happening," Braddock said. "Of course, other than those present, we have not had much contact with the elves of late."

"This is a first," Eli said, "for us as well."

Braddock's gaze shifted shrewdly from Taha'Leeth to Stiger. He snapped his fingers. "You have sealed your alliance by marriage? Is that it?"

"I guess," Stiger said, looking over at Taha'Leeth. Their eyes met and he found himself captured by her gaze. In them he saw love, caring, and comfort. It almost took effort to break away and turn back to Braddock. "I guess in a way we have. Though there was no formal ceremony."

"Well then," Braddock said, having recovered from his shock, "I congratulate the both of you and wish you well."

"Thank you, Thane Braddock," Taha'Leeth said, her tone softening as the heat left it.

"I apologize for questioning your commitment," Kiello said. "It was unwarranted, my lady."

"Think nothing of it," Taha'Leeth said, as if the chieftain's challenge had never happened. Then she added more, her tone hardening again. "But never challenge me again, for next time, I will not tolerate such disrespect."

Kiello stiffened, then forcibly relaxed and gave a curt nod.

Stiger felt a lessening of the tension in the tent. Their challenging Taha'Leeth still bothered him. He could understand being suspicious of Tenya'Far and Eli's people, but not hers. They had done nothing to violate trust. But she'd handled herself, and well. Stiger suddenly felt foolish. He was being overprotective, and he knew it. She, like he, had her own battles to fight. He had to keep that in mind.

"Elves, humans, and dwarves," Braddock said, clapping his hands together, "fighting again as allies, just like the last days on Tanis. This calls for a toast. Kiello, pour the wine, will you?" The thane turned back to look on the elves. "I would rather drink spirits, but I know elves prefer wine."

"I thank you for your consideration," Taha'Leeth said. "Wine is most preferable and welcome. I too would share drink with you."

Eli simply inclined his head.

"Wine is quite acceptable," Tenya'Far said.

"Legate," Braddock said, as if suddenly remembering Stiger. "You and Salt do not mind wine, do you?"

"I would welcome wine," Stiger said, "though Brogan did share his love for spirits with me. Some of his favorites could strip leather if given the chance."

"Hah," Braddock said and clapped Stiger powerfully on the shoulder. The unexpected blow almost knocked him to the ground. "The fact that you drank with my father as a dear friend just warms my heart. I hope, one day, when time permits, you will share a few stories of your time with him. Sadly, all I have now are my memories."

"When we have a spare moment or two, I would be pleased to do so," Stiger said and shared a brief look with

Eli. Their recent conversation struck home, for to Stiger Brogan was also now but a memory.

"I like spirits," Therik said, clearly not content to be left out. "You dwarves make strong drink and Brogan had some of the best."

"Therik was named a friend by Brogan," Stiger said. "The two of them could down a small barrel of spirits by themselves and on occasion did."

"Is true," Therik said with a huge grin. "Brogan was a good drinker, but I could put him under the table."

Stiger did not remember it that way but wasn't about to contradict his friend. Braddock eyed the orc for a long moment and gave a nod. Stiger knew it would take time for Braddock to become comfortable with the former king. He hoped he warmed up to him like Brogan had.

"I will take wine," Therik said, "since that is what you offer."

"Good," Braddock said. "I will have a sampling of some of my best spirits sent over to your camp later tonight. You let me know what you think, eh?"

"I will," Therik promised, sounding eager.

Kiello had stepped over to a table upon which sat several jars of wine, along with more than a dozen large stone mugs. He poured wine into the mugs and then handed everyone a drink.

"Allow me the honor of making the first toast," Braddock said, holding up his mug. "To allies."

"To allies," everyone repeated and drank.

Stiger found the wine good and smooth. After the day's march, it tasted wonderful, much better than canteen water. He saw Braddock looking to him expectantly.

"To new friends and old...working together," Stiger said. They took another drink.

"To new beginnings," Taha'Leeth said.

They drank again.

"To killing our enemies," Therik said, "and grinding their bones to dust beneath our boots."

"I will most certainly drink to that," Braddock said, and he drank deeply from his mug. He wiped his lips with the back of his arm. "I intend to piss on their graves too, if I can."

"You remind me of your father," Therik said. "I am thinking, Thane, we will get along well... I wonder if you can drink as well as he could?"

Braddock gave a hearty laugh and shook his mug at the orc, spilling some of the contents on the rug. "One night you and I shall drink together, yes? We will see if you can back up that big talk, my green friend."

Therik held up his mug in a mock salute. "Oh, I will, little Dvergr."

Braddock stilled for a heartbeat, clearly deciding whether to take offense. Then he barked out a laugh.

"To winning it all," Tenya'Far said, "and being the only ones in control of the World Gate, when it all matters."

There was a long moment of silence.

"I will drink to that," Stiger said.

"As will I," Braddock said.

Everyone drank.

"Now that that is done," Braddock said, returning his empty mug to the table with the jars, "we have a war to plan. Let's get to business and then afterwards we can eat and drink some more. I have ordered a meal prepared." The thane gestured toward a large table on the other side of the tent. "Join me, if you will."

Braddock stepped over to the table, upon which lay a map. Stiger set his mug down on the table with the jars and made his way over to the table. He took the opposite side from Braddock as everyone else gathered around. The map was of the South and covered not only the occupied lands but the southern end of the empire. Stiger recognized the map as a scribe copy, one of his own. Nepturus had likely provided it to the thane.

"Your cavalry commander, Prefect Hux, has been invaluable," Braddock said, looking to Stiger. "He has worked very well with my own horse soldiers. I understand he will be arriving tonight."

"He sent me word as well," Stiger said. "I am looking forward to speaking with him and getting a personal report of his activities."

Braddock looked around those gathered. "Kiello, if you would...bring them up to date on what we know."

"Yes, My Thane," Kiello said. "Legate, you may already know some of this from the letters you exchanged with the thane."

"I understand," Stiger said.

"This is our position here," Kiello said. "This line running north and south is the King's Highway. This mark here is our encampment." He ran a wide circular motion around the encampment's position with his finger. "Our combined cavalry has pushed out a screen of patrols a little more than fifty miles to the north and east. The screen has been extended at least seventy miles to the south. The Sentinel Forest lies to the west and...well, there was no need to patrol more than a dozen miles in that direction, as you destroyed the only viable force located there."

Kiello paused.

"There are no significant enemy forces within the cavalry screen, only isolated garrisons, the largest of which we destroyed in battle three days ago. Those remaining garrisons hold rebel held cities to the south. The nearest is forty miles distant. We do not think them a serious threat." He ran his finger on the map, moving it northward. "We have sent mounted scouts in small groups farther afield. What we know for certain is that this city here, to the north, Aeda, was sacked and the population put to the sword."

Even though he already had that information, Stiger still felt a stab of anger. Though Aeda had been an occupied city, a good number of imperials had settled there. The city, for the most part, had not supported the rebellion. That was likely the cause for its sacking.

"I can confirm that as well," Tenya'Far said. "We passed Aeda on our way south. What was done to the population was quite heinous, barbaric even. You humans can be quite cruel to one another."

Stiger did not respond to that, for he knew elves could be just as cruel. He'd seen it with his own eyes and been personally on the receiving end.

"Any towns and villages in the surrounding area around Aeda saw similar treatment," Kiello continued. "The enemy has done a fine job of stripping the countryside bare, taking anything with them that wasn't nailed down and burning the rest. This includes the destruction of bridges over major rivers to the north."

Stiger rubbed his jaw and wondered why they would do that. He could understand the foraging, but why destroy the towns, villages, and infrastructure? That would hinder their resupply effort, especially the destruction of the bridges.

"We received a report less than an hour ago," Kiello said, "that there is an imperial legion or the remnants of several legions—we're unsure just how many—under siege and holding the city of Lorium to the north of Aeda, here."

"Lorium?" Stiger asked, recalling the emperor's letter and looking closer at the map.

Kiello tapped the map with a thick index finger where Lorium was located. Stiger had passed through the city with Eli on their way south. It was around one hundred miles from Aeda.

"How credible is that report?" Stiger asked. "Do we know if the city is still in imperial hands?"

"The report came from people who had fled that area and run into a team of our scouts," Braddock said. "The scouts looking to investigate were unable to get close to the city to eyeball the siege directly. The area was thick with enemy cavalry patrols. Their standing orders were to avoid a general engagement, so they fell back. However, they did manage to capture prisoners and interrogate them. The prisoners included a low-ranking officer who confirmed the report. From everything we could gather, it seems the city is besieged. The enemy do not hold it or, more correctly, did not a week and a half ago when the dispatch rider was sent back to us."

"So, it is a credible report then?" Salt said.

"We believe it is," Kiello said. "The report mentioned that a number of legions were defeated, and the survivors withdrew to Lorium, including the emperor."

Stiger wondered what legion or legions were there, holding the city.

"The emperor was massing his legions just north of that city," Tenya'Far said. "When I left him, he was expecting a battle somewhere south of Lorium...in a matter of weeks, if not days. Should such an action have gone poorly, the survivors could have fallen back upon Lorium like he said. The city walls are impressive and, given sufficient supply, could easily withstand a protracted siege."

Stiger sucked in a breath at that. Was he already too late?

"I met with the emperor personally," Tenya'Far said. "General Treim was to command the combined imperial forces."

Stiger shared a glance with Eli.

"Unfortunately," Tenya'Far said, "the rest of the warden's army was several weeks away. We were the advance force."

"And still the emperor sent you to us?" Stiger asked, thinking such a move would have depleted the army's strength when the emperor would have likely needed every sword.

"He and I were under the impression you needed relief," Tenya'Far said. "With the Sentinel Forest as a barrier and the Vrell road in enemy hands, we were the logical choice to send."

"Do we have an idea on the size of the enemy army besieging Lorium?" Taha'Leeth asked.

"No," Kiello said, "other than it is quite a large force, numbering in the tens of thousands."

Stiger wondered on the size of this army and its quality. Were they composed of rebels or mainly Cyphan or a mix of the two?

"We also have information," Kiello continued, "from the same source, that the main enemy body has taken Ivera to the east and is marching toward the coastal roads that run from Asti to Venney and then ultimately to Mal'Zeel. We feel confident this is reliable information, as our scouts were able to see evidence of a large army having moved recently in the direction of Asti."

"Why move that way?" Stiger asked. "There are better routes that travel north, an entire network of roads that are paved. Those coastal roads are not the most reliable nor direct, and certainly not the kind of roads I would want to march an army over. What kind of prisoner was he? Infantry, cavalry?"

"Supply," Kiello said. "He was captured with a foraging team and was questioned by our scouts. So were two of his men that survived the ambush. They all sang the same tune. Apparently, the confederacy intends to resupply their armies from the port of Asti. Since they are a seafaring power, this makes sense."

"Until then," Stiger surmised, "they are living off the land. That is why they are stripping what they can and heading for the coast. As they advance up the coast to the capital, they can keep themselves supplied from the sea."

"It also explains," Braddock said, "why we've only seized a small amount of supply moving along the King's Highway, destined for rebel-held garrisons in the area. And why there are no Cyphan garrisons of any consequence nearby. They seem to have taken most of their soldiers with them north."

"You said armies," Stiger said.

"The enemy apparently has three armies," Braddock said. "Well, *had* three, if you take into account the one that was at Vrell...the rebel army you destroyed."

"I would think someone from supply might know the strengths of those armies," Salt said. "Did your interrogators ask the prisoner?"

Kiello cleared his throat. "He was a low-ranking officer and unfortunately expired before we could obtain that information. The other two knew even less than he did and were fairly illiterate."

"Our interrogators were a little too aggressive," Braddock said. "My people feel a keen hatred toward the Cyphan."

"They must put that hatred aside," Stiger said. "We can't afford to pass up vital intelligence in favor of revenge."

Braddock gave a nod. "It has already been addressed. This will not happen again."

"Well," Stiger said, "there's nothing we can do about that now. I am sure, as we move north, we will take additional prisoners and get a better idea on what we face."

"So, the question is," Braddock said, "with the information we have, what do we do? The three of us"—the thane looked from Tenya'Far to Stiger—"should be in agreement on our next steps."

"The four of us," Taha'Leeth said. There was steel in her voice. "Though my people have yet to arrive, they will come."

"The four of us," Braddock corrected. "My apologies, my lady."

"A pursuit seems predetermined," Eli said.

"It does," Taha'Leeth agreed. "We must stop them from taking Mal'Zeel and obtaining the Key."

"I am not completely sold on a pursuit." Stiger pointed down at the map. "The enemy to the north may not yet know we are here. Though if they are destroying the bridges over the rivers, they know some sort of threat is down here in the South."

"Or, sir," Salt said, "they could be destroying what they can't take with them so that the empire can't use what's left behind. By razing Aeda and putting the population to the sword, they've denied us manpower. Given time, we could have raised an auxiliary cohort or two from that city."

"Good point," Stiger said, then leaned forward and tapped the map where Asti was located. "If they'd taken Asti, they've likely advanced too far to have gotten word yet of our presence."

"I feel fairly confident they will receive word soon enough," Braddock said. "Eventually, they will send cavalry in strength to scout us out and then they will know we have an army to their rear."

"Agreed," Stiger said. "Lorium seems like the next logical move while we have the element of surprise."

"It is," Therik agreed. "Deal with what's close at hand and easy to reach first. Then worry about the rest later."

Stiger studied the map for a long moment.

"We can't bypass Lorium," Stiger said, "especially with an enemy army there. If we go and pursue the enemy's main drive to the coast"—he touched the map—"this army at Lorium could break the siege of the city and come after us. We might find ourselves caught on two sides and badly outnumbered. It makes sense to deal with Lorium first and eliminate what's there."

"I agree," Kiello said.

"If the enemy did go to the coast," Stiger continued, "after we deal with the force at Lorium, we can still beat them to Mal'Zeel by taking the direct route over main imperial roads... paved roads. And, more importantly, there are potential allies in Lorium, a legion or more." Stiger paused and looked up at the thane. "What do you think, Braddock?"

"I was going to suggest the same thing," Braddock said. "I am told the terrain between Lorium and here is fairly open, with only a scattering of small forests and wooded areas. Some of the rivers will require bridging, but we can plan for that and should have no problem moving north."

"We have bridging equipment," Salt said. "And we can easily make more if needed."

Salt leaned forward and tapped the city of Lorium with a finger.

"Lorium's, what, two hundred fifty miles," Salt said, "maybe three hundred from here?"

"More like three hundred," Kiello said. "It's at least two hundred to Aeda and then another one hundred or more to Lorium."

"We could be at the city in twenty days," Braddock said, "maybe less if we push our march a bit."

"They won't have a good picture of our strength for some time," Stiger said. "Especially with our cavalry screen in place. To make the screen more difficult to penetrate, we will need to pull them in and closer to the line of march. There is a risk with that, as it will limit our own scouting. But with fewer miles to cover, the thicker our protective screen will become, making it more difficult for enemy scouts to win through and eyeball our army." Stiger rubbed his jaw. "Though when they do discover our strength, and they will, the army at Lorium will likely turn and face us head on. That will mean a battle somewhere on the road south of the city."

"I like it," Braddock said. "We could be all the way to Lorium, knocking on the enemy's door, before the army that went east can react and backtrack."

"Of course," a voice wizened by age said, from the tent flap, "that all depends on what the enemy's wyrms are doing. They could spot you pretty quick and get that intelligence back to the enemy in just a day or two if the enemy sends them our way."

Stiger turned, as did everyone else. It was Ogg. The wizard stumped over to them, leaning heavily upon his staff. Stiger found his appearance quite shocking. He looked seriously aged, almost ancient. The effort to hold open the Gate had clearly taken a severe toll upon him.

"They have wyrms?" Stiger asked and closed his eyes in exasperation. "Of course they do. Why not? Castor's force had wyrms. Why not Valoor's boys too?"

"They brought a wyrm with them when they crossed the Narrow Sea," Taha'Leeth said. "The Cyphan have a breeding pair."

"You knew?" Stiger asked, surprised she'd not told him. He wondered why she'd withheld that information.

"I thought you knew," Taha'Leeth said.

"Why would you think that?" Stiger asked.

"You have a friend who is noctalum," Taha'Leeth said. "He surely would have told you, for they can sense wyrms."

Ogg turned to Taha'Leeth. "Very few know this... but wyrms cannot be sensed from a great distance, which means Menos would not have known the Cyphan had any. The creatures have *Will*, yes...but unlike a noctalum's...it is almost insignificant, which means he would have had to have been fairly close to sense them."

Taha'Leeth seemed horrified by that news. She looked to Stiger, seemingly at a loss for words.

"Do you know how many wyrms the confederacy has?" Ogg asked, drawing her attention back to him.

"I know of twelve wyrms," Taha'Leeth said. "But as I said, there was only one that I was aware of that came north. The lords of the Cyphan are very careful with their wyrms. The creatures help guarantee their control and power. Without them, they are vulnerable. I was led to believe they would be keeping most of them at home."

"Well," Ogg said, "they've got more than one with them now. How many? I don't know."

"How can you sense them," Stiger asked, "if Menos could not? Are they close?"

"I have other means," Ogg said. "And as to close...let's just say they are close enough. I'd much prefer them to be far to the south."

"This just keeps getting better and better," Stiger said.

"It does." Ogg stepped over to Stiger and tapped him on the chest. "I have an important question for you. Tell me...what did you do with our noctalum? Where did you send him? For I cannot sense his presence anywhere on this continent and, given his strength of *Will*, that should be impossible."

"You can't?" Stiger asked in dismay, a cold feeling settling over him.

"No," Ogg said. "And I am sure you know that is not good."

"Oh shit," Stiger said as another part of the puzzle fell into place. If Ogg could not sense Menos, then it meant the noctalum was likely dead. And now, he knew the enemy had dragons of their own.

SEVENTEEN

Stiger sat on a stool in his personal tent, thoroughly depressed. Across from him was Ogg, who looked unhappy, almost beyond measure. The wizard shifted slightly on his own stool as if uncomfortable. The meeting in Braddock's tent had ended several hours before, as had the feast that had followed. Stiger had not eaten much. After hearing the wizard's news, he'd not felt like it.

"You cannot sense him?" Stiger asked, again. "Are you absolutely certain?"

Appearing somewhat resentful, Ogg took a deep breath and closed his eyes. Stiger could feel the wizard's power surge slightly as he used his *Will*. It made the small hairs on Stiger's arms stand on end. Ogg opened his eyes and shook his head.

"I am certain." The wizard's tone was cantankerous. "As I've already told you multiple times, I cannot sense Menos. You should never have sent him off without checking with me first. It was a fool thing to do."

"You weren't around," Stiger said.

"That's right," Ogg snapped back. "I was traveling with Braddock."

"What about Currose?" Stiger asked. "Can you sense her?"

"Now she," Ogg said, "I can. Currose is where we left her, at the mountain."

"Well," Stiger said, "at least that is something."

"Yes," Ogg said sarcastically, "I can sense an injured dragon who can do us absolutely no good in aiding our cause further."

"Is it possible that Menos might be concealing himself from you?"

"I doubt it," Ogg said.

"Perhaps he has a reason for doing so," Stiger said. "In that he's concealing himself from something else."

"Like what?" Ogg asked.

"The enemy has wyrms. He could be hiding himself from them."

"Wyrms cannot detect him in that way," Ogg said. "They are relatively stupid creatures, no smarter than your average horse. I am telling you he's not concealing himself."

Stiger rubbed his jaw, feeling his frustration mount. "You are certain?"

Ogg gave a nod.

"Then he's dead," Stiger said.

"Perhaps," Ogg said.

"What do you mean perhaps?" Stiger was becoming irritated, the depression giving way to anger. "Why can't you wizards ever just say what you mean?"

"Very well, then," Ogg said. "I shall make myself clear. He might be dead. He might not be. Noctalum have powers that wizards do not. Some of those powers I simply do not know about or understand. Remember, the noctalum are of the First Race, the creators of the World Gate network. They think very differently than the rest of us. Yes, it is not unheard of for them to conceal themselves from prying eyes, but that requires a tremendous amount of *Will.* So much so, I very much doubt Menos would be willing to part with it. So, to answer your question...yes, he could be shielding himself from me, but it is unlikely he is doing so."

Stiger felt ill.

"As such, there are a few possibilities to explain what might have occurred," Ogg said. "Do you want to hear them?"

"I do."

"He may no longer be on this world."

"Dead, then."

"Since the World Gate is sealed," Ogg said, "then yes, dead is one distinct possibility."

"What is another?"

"He may have gone somewhere else," Ogg said and then hesitated, as if trying to think of a way to explain. "He may have gone somewhere that is shielded from my vision but still remains in this world."

"How is that possible?" Stiger asked.

"It shouldn't be"—Ogg's expression became one of distaste—"but unfortunately, it is."

"Explain yourself," Stiger said, feeling his anger increase.

Ogg's eyes narrowed as he studied Stiger. "Your anger has been growing again. I can feel it roiling beneath the surface, radiating from you like a warm fire."

Stiger followed the wizard's gaze as it shifted over to his sword, which he'd left lying against his desk.

"Are you sure the sword is not feeding your anger?" Ogg asked, returning his attention to Stiger. "Like it was before?"

Stiger did not immediately respond. The question was a valid one, only the sword was dead and it was feeding him nothing.

"I would very much appreciate you answering my question," Ogg insisted quietly, all anger from the wizard seeming to have fled. It was replaced with intense curiosity.

"The sword is dead," Stiger said, gesturing vaguely at Rarokan with a hand. "I can't feel anything from it. Not even the tingle."

"Tingle?"

"What do you mean it shouldn't be possible?" Stiger asked, not wanting to speak on his connection with the sword nor be diverted from the subject at hand. The thing was dead, so the line of questioning did not matter. What did, was Menos.

"There are places in this world," Ogg said, "where the world of the dead meets the world of the living."

"Are you serious?" Stiger sat back on the stool, horrified by the prospect.

"Yes, I am," Ogg said. "I am always serious."

"It did not seem like that before," Stiger shot back. "You were always quite mad. Or was that an act?"

"It was no act," Ogg snapped. "That was the near insanity caused by holding onto nearly enough power to fry my brain. I almost lost who I was…" The wizard calmed himself by taking a deep breath and letting it out. "Tingle? What did you mean by that?"

Stiger blew out a breath of his own, knowing Ogg would not stop until he got his answer. "I was recently able to summon the sword's magic. Yet, in the past, every time I touched the sword, a tingle ran up my arm. Now…there is nothing, no sensation, no connection. The wizard within is gone. He has been for some time."

"The magic may have come from within…your power." Ogg scratched at his shaved chin. "The tingle could be a sign of the bond…or something else. Then again, the lack of it might be just as important. I will have to think on it."

"What of this…world of the dead?" Stiger asked, the thought of it filling him with intense distaste. It was as if the High Father disapproved.

"The fabric of what you might call reality," Ogg said, "was long ago torn. How does not matter, but if Menos went there…I would be unable to sense him."

Stiger was silent for a long moment.

"Why would he go there?" Stiger asked.

"Before I answer," Ogg said, "tell me…this anger of yours…has it been getting worse?"

"These days, I am almost always angry, bitter really… I think I have cause. Now, why would he go there? To this world of the dead?"

"I don't know," Ogg said. "These places are called Gray Fields. To my knowledge there are several on every world. Traveling to one would be incredibly dangerous, even for a noctalum. Once he entered the field, he would not be able to survive very long."

"What is the other possibility?" Stiger asked.

"When you are with Taha'Leeth," Ogg said, "do you still feel angered?"

"No," Stiger said. "I feel happy, content, mostly."

"Good," Ogg said, "you have access to vast power…you need a calming influence."

"Power?"

"Of course, the power of your god. Still, I am concerned about the anger, the rage. You have to control it, master it. What about with Dog?" Ogg asked, before Stiger could say anything. He seemed very intent and interested. "Do you feel your anger increase when he is around?"

Stiger was at a loss for words for a moment. "I do not know. I've not given it any thought."

"Do so," Ogg said. "You need to discover if the anger grows while he is around. It may be important."

"I will. Now, let's get back to Menos," Stiger said. "What is another possibility for his disappearance?"

"He might have traveled farther than I can reach out with my senses," Ogg said, "which would have to have been very far...perhaps halfway around the world. I do not know why he would do that."

That did not make sense to Stiger either. Menos knew just what was at stake. He would not have left them. Stiger had a sinking feeling in the pit of his stomach. He glanced down at the rug that covered the ground in his tent, thinking.

"Could you hop back to Currose?" Stiger asked hopefully, looking back up. "Perhaps she knows what happened? Or where he went?"

"Hop?" Ogg asked in an almost incredulous tone. "Is that what you think I do?"

"What would you call it?" Stiger asked. "You brought Braddock and Garrack to my camp in the forest and then transported me and Braddock to the Gate room. It seems like you just hop magically around whenever you want to."

"Hop?" Ogg's tone became disgusted. "Let me try to explain this for your feeble mind. When I move, it is through what you might call space and is a sophisticated version of teleportation, a warping of reality. There is no hopping around to it. Have I ever told you you are an ignorant savage? I can't imagine what the High Father sees in you."

"Whatever you call it," Stiger said, "why don't you check with Currose? She might have the answers you seek."

"No doubt she might," Ogg said. "But...I can't do that."

"Why not?"

"After what occurred at the World Gate," Ogg said, "my reserves are low. I cannot afford to waste what power I have left and have managed to accumulate. Besides...with the noctalum gone, it would be foolish for me to leave the army. I am nearly the only protection you have against the enemy's wyrms. And believe me, I won't be much help. You need to begin thinking of ways to protect yourself from those dragons."

Stiger did not like the sound of that.

"How do we do that?"

"Large bolt throwers have been used in the past," Ogg said. "The gnomes have them. They..." Ogg fell silent. He sat up straight, as if something had just occurred to him.

"What?" Stiger asked.

"There is another possibility," Ogg said. "You know there were once two Gates on this world?"

Stiger gave a nod. "Now there is only one."

"Your girlfriend's people destroyed the second Gate, while it was open," Ogg said, "which should not have been possible. It has long troubled me on how exactly they managed to do it, for the release of so much energy would have surely wiped out all life on this world. Somehow they managed to contain the blast, and without a wizard too."

"Which means...?" Stiger pressed, not quite sure where Ogg was going.

"Well...the remains of the Gate are below the Narrow Sea." The wizard paused, as if thinking. "Though the elves thought they were successful, they might not have actually destroyed the World Gate. It may still be functioning fully or in some reduced manner."

Stiger once again leaned back on his stool. "You mean the World Gate could be open, just under a lot of water?"

"That is exactly what I am saying."

"Being underneath an ocean still achieves the same effect, right?" Stiger said. "No one can come through it?"

"Maybe," Ogg said.

Stiger did not like that answer. "Would the elves know their attempt to destroy the Gate failed?"

"I don't know…but I think it unlikely. Once it was moved to the bottom of the ocean, there would be no way for them to verify."

Stiger thought for a moment. "And the noctalum might know the Gate was not destroyed? Is that what you are saying?"

"Yes," Ogg said.

"And Currose would likely know, too?"

"If I were able to travel back to Old City, I feel certain Currose would surely know the truth of the matter…though there is the strong possibility she might lie to me rather than reveal that truth, whatever it is. There would be no way for me to prove whatever she decides to tell me."

"Why would she lie?" Stiger asked.

"Why indeed?" Ogg said. "But she might."

"If it is below the Narrow Sea," Stiger said, "how can anyone reach it?"

"The noctalum would have the ability to get to it. They are shape-changers beyond compare."

Stiger had not thought of that.

"The World Gate to Tanis," Stiger said after a moment, "was moved, right? It wasn't always in the Gate room under the keep?"

Ogg gave a nod.

"Who moved it?" Stiger asked.

"The noctalum," Ogg said. "Ah...I see where your thoughts are going. Was the other World Gate moved too? That is an interesting line of thinking."

"Even if the Gate was still functioning and they moved it, the question remains...why would Menos leave this world?" Stiger asked. "Why would he leave his mate behind, who's been gravely injured?"

"Why indeed?" Ogg said. "Figuring out how noctalum think is difficult in the best of times. But I believe you are right... He would not leave, especially with Currose here. Besides, there would be nothing of value on the other side of the Gate...only an old enemy of the noctalum. One... which I doubt Menos would want to see again."

None of the possibilities Ogg described made any sense.

"He's my friend," Stiger said. "He would not abandon us. Something must have happened to him."

"You need to understand," Ogg said and his gaze became intense as he leaned forward on his stool, "noctalum have no friends."

The wizard pulled himself slowly to his feet, as if to go. He picked up his staff, which he'd leaned against the support pole.

"Ogg," Stiger said, "what do you think happened to Menos?"

Ogg was silent for several heartbeats as he looked down at the ground. Then he just shook his head sadly. "I just don't know." Ogg turned for the entrance flap. "I really don't and I fear we need him now more than ever."

"What about the sertalum?" Stiger asked, turning back.

"What about her?"

"Can you still sense her?"

"Yes," Ogg said.

"Where is she?"

"Somewhere in the mountains to the west," Ogg said and gestured. "And before you ask, no…I have no idea what she is up to. Nor do I wish to know. All I want is for her to leave us be…to stay out of things."

"Do you think that likely?"

Ogg did not answer, but instead walked to the tent flap. "I must speak with Braddock before it gets too late. He will need to help you prepare to fight the enemy's wyrms, and that means getting the gnomes' help. I bid you a good night."

With that, the wizard stepped out of the tent, leaving Stiger alone.

"Things are never easy."

He sat there for a time, wondering what had happened to Menos. To say he was worried was an understatement.

"Excuse me, sir." One of the guards pulled aside the tent flap and ducked in. "Sergeant Arnold to see you, sir."

"Send him in."

Arnold entered. He was wearing his service tunic and looked slightly different. There was a growing confidence within. Stiger could feel it, just as he could sense the budding power.

"Sir," Arnold said, "I am sorry to bother you. Your guards said you were still up. I hope you don't mind."

"Not at all," Stiger said. "How can I help you?"

Arnold suddenly looked uncomfortable, glancing at his feet and then back up at Stiger. "When we spoke back at the castle, in Vrell, sir, I…ah…"

Stiger immediately knew where this was going.

"You feel the call to leave, don't you?"

"I do, sir," Arnold said. "The tug is quite strong. The High Father is calling me away..."

Stiger gave an absent nod. Though he hated to see Arnold go...there were other considerations. He had foreseen that, and it felt like the right thing to do, to let him go.

"Though I wish you would stay, I suspected the call would come. You are in the service of the High Father now. You go where he wills."

"Thank you, sir."

Stiger thought Arnold still looked uncomfortable and unsure of exactly what he wanted to say.

"Do you know where you are off to?" Stiger asked.

"No, sir. Just that I need to go." Arnold paused. "I feel like I am abandoning you."

"Don't," Stiger said. "The High Father has a job for you. Do it well, and with any luck, we will see each other again."

"Yes, sir."

"Whatever you require, Nepturus will see you are well provisioned." Stiger stood and offered his hand, which Arnold took. "He will also see that you get a pass for travel out of the camp."

"Thank you, sir," Arnold said and then stepped toward the exit. He looked back. "Good luck, sir."

"You too," Stiger said.

Arnold stepped out of the tent and was gone.

Stiger moved over to his table, where his pipe lay. Next to it was a small bag of tobacco Venthus had found for him. He filled the pipe and then, using a taper, lit it from the lamp's flame. He took several puffs to get up a good burn before returning to the stool.

He smoked for a time, feeling extremely wretched about Menos. He suspected his friend was dead. It was really the only thing that made sense. Menos would not have abandoned them. And no matter what Ogg said, Menos was a friend.

Stiger blew out a long stream of smoke. The noctalum's shade would be yet one more to haunt his nights.

"Excuse me, sir," the guard said, poking his head back into the tent. "Camp Prefect Oney is here to see you."

"Send him in," Stiger said.

"Sir," Salt said, coming in.

"Salt," Stiger said and motioned to a table with a pitcher and mugs. "Wine?"

"Ah…no thank you, sir. There was too much of that during Braddock's feast. If I have any more, it will put me to sleep and I have a few hours of work ahead of me yet."

"Business then." Stiger knew Salt would not have stopped by had he not had something important to bring to Stiger's attention.

"Yes, sir," Salt said. "I understand the need for haste in getting to Lorium, but the legion is worn down. We've marched hard since leaving Vrell, with only a minimum of breaks. The men need a day or more to recover before we begin this new march."

Stiger took a pull from his pipe and then blew a stream of smoke up into the air. He watched the smoke swirl and begin to climb for the canvas ceiling. Salt was right, of course. The men needed rest before another long march. Heck, Stiger himself needed rest. Still, morale was still high. The men could give him more and they would.

"Braddock and I are meeting again in the morning," Stiger said, "to finalize our plans for the days ahead. You will be joining us, of course. That will mean a day's rest before the army moves. I wish it were more…but speed, once again, is our friend."

"One day?" Salt almost seemed pained by the prospect of so short a rest for the men.

"One day is all I feel comfortable giving," Stiger said, "all I can afford to give."

"It will have to do, sir," Salt said.

Stiger did not reply, but instead took another pull on the pipe.

"I was informed Hux just arrived," Salt said. "He is seeing to his horse. He should be here shortly."

Stiger looked up at that and gave a nod. "Make sure the men have a free day tomorrow. No training, no work, and an extra ration of drink. They've more than earned it."

"Yes, sir."

"Very good," Stiger said. "Send Hux along when he's ready. I will meet with him alone."

"Yes, sir," Salt said and left the tent.

Stiger rubbed at his tired eyes. There was always so much that needed doing, so many decisions that had to be made. He'd almost forgotten what it was like to share a campfire by himself, with only the worries of a single company upon his mind.

Now, he had not only the legion but the empire and the world to worry about. He was in a battle with evil, and if he wasn't careful, the enemy would win. Stiger keenly felt the sands of time running out.

Ogg was right: His anger was building. He could feel it. Stiger had long since accepted his fate, his role in this, that he was gods blessed. But that didn't mean he had to like it or enjoy it. The fact that it all fell upon his shoulders and weighed him down...made him angry, at times terribly wrathful. But was that so bad? It was fueling his drive to end this madness on his terms and not the enemy's.

Or was it something else? The sword wasn't feeding it. Of that he was certain. Was it Dog? As he'd promised Ogg, it bore thinking on.

"Excuse me, sir," the guard said. "Prefect Hux here to see you, sir."

"Send him in."

Hux entered. The cavalry prefect was dusty and dirty from a long ride. Despite that, he looked to be in good spirits. Hux offered a salute, which Stiger waved away and then gestured toward the wine jar. "Would you care for some refreshment, Prefect? You look like you could use a drink."

"I do need one, sir," Hux said. "We ran out of wine ten days ago and I'm parched from the ride."

"Help yourself, then," Stiger said.

"Thank you, sir." Hux filled himself a mug of wine and drank deeply.

"That's right fine wine, sir," Hux said.

"Take a seat," Stiger said and gestured toward the stool Ogg had used.

"If you wouldn't mind, sir," Hux said, "I'd rather stand. I've been in the saddle all day. Stretching my legs a little feels good."

"Very well," Stiger said. "I've read your reports, which have been quite thorough. Fine work. You've done the legion great service."

"Thank you, sir," Hux said. "My boys have done most of the work, sir."

"Under your direction," Stiger said and then paused as he gathered his thoughts. "I'd like to hear your overall impressions from what you've seen over the last few weeks. I imagine you've covered some serious ground."

"I have, sir," Hux said. "I believe the enemy knows we're here, sir."

Stiger had not expected that direct response. "Have you taken any prisoners that have confirmed that?"

"Prisoners?" Hux said. "No, sir."

"Then how can you be sure?"

"They've destroyed all of the bridges they can find within seventy miles of their line of march, sir," Hux said. "They wouldn't have done that unless they had good cause and a fear of being pursued. And the confederacy has left very few garrisons with their own men. Those troops they did leave behind were second- or third-rate conscripts. The only garrisons in the South with any significant numbers are the rebels. They have just enough men to give them a little backbone." Hux stopped as if expecting Stiger to say something.

"Go on."

"Sir, they are headed for the coast with a single-minded purpose…but have destroyed whatever they can't take with them. So, sir, if I had make a guess…they know we are coming after them. How, I don't know, but I'd bet my next payday on it."

Stiger took a pull from his pipe and blew the smoke out. He suspected the same as well, and hearing it from one of his trusted lieutenants only reinforced that suspicion.

"I read your report on Aeda," Stiger said.

"It wasn't pretty, sir."

"Tell me about it," Stiger said. "I want to hear it in your own words."

"They took the city without a fight, sir," Hux said. "A few of the prisoners we grabbed confirmed this. The city surrendered with the understanding that all would be spared."

Hux fell silent and his gaze grew unfocused, as if reliving a terrible nightmare.

"And?"

"Well...the enemy can't be trusted. All of the bodies were outside the city, herded together. There were virtually no young men amongst the dead. If I had to guess, they were marched off as slaves. The old, infirm, and children... babies too were butchered. It was very organized and systematic. The dead were bound and lined up. Their throats were slit. There were too many bodies to bury, so we left them." Hux paused. "I've seen some pretty awful stuff in my time, but nothing like this."

"Is that all?" Stiger asked.

"No, sir," Hux said. "Many of the women were raped. There were also signs of torture before being put to death."

Stiger gave an unhappy grunt.

"They also crucified who we think were the imperial citizens. The surrounding towns and villages saw similar treatment. It's almost like they're intentionally emptying the land of its population. They take everything that is useful— food, animals, equipment. Whatever else that's left and they can't bring along is destroyed. As I said, I don't expect them to come back this way."

That supported the theory that the enemy was also looking to resupply themselves by sea. But wouldn't they have to come back if they wanted to get to Vrell and the World Gate? Perhaps, Stiger considered, they just wanted to make sure that there was no opposition for when they returned? That potentially told him the lengths his enemy would go.

"What I saw, sir," Hux said, "will haunt me for the remainder of my days. My boys are fairly riled up. They are in no mood to take prisoners, sir, and ever since Aeda it has been

an effort to get them to do so. I would expect the same sentiment to spread through the army as it advances, sir."

"I understand," Stiger fell silent for several moments.
He took a pull from his pipe as he considered what Hux had
reported. He looked back up. "I have a mission for you."

"Me and my boys are ready," Hux said. "What would you
have us do, sir?"

"You will lead a reconnaissance in force," Stiger said, "to
the city of Lorium."

"Lorium," Hux said. "Where the legions are holed up? Is
that where the army is going?"

"Yes," Stiger said. "If legionaries are still holding that
city, I plan on relieving them."

"Yes, sir," Hux said.

Stiger read the excitement in the other's eyes. Hux was
the right man for this job. "I need to know the size and com-
position of the enemy army besieging the city. Do you think
you can get me that information and return?"

"Yes, sir, I do."

"How many men will you need?" Stiger asked.

"At least two hundred of my troopers, sir," Hux said.

"So many?" Stiger was concerned about depleting the
army's protective screen.

"You asked how many of my boys I will need to do the
job, sir," Hux said. "More would be better, but that's what I
would consider the minimum. I would not want to deplete
the legion's screening force any more than it will be, sir."

"The minimum, huh?"

"We're going to have to bring a sizable force. That is, if
I'm to get through the enemy patrols. There will be fighting.
I will take one hundred with me...go in fast and hard, thor-
oughly eyeball Lorium and enemy army...then leg it. I will

keep the second half of the force a few miles back and wait-ing. With any luck, the enemy will get themselves organized and send a good number of their cavalry after us, to chase us off. We might be able to pull off an ambush while we are at it."

Stiger gave a nod of understanding. He understood a larger force would have a better chance of pulling off what he was asking Hux to do. He also wanted the job done right, and Hux was the finest commander of cavalry that Stiger had ever known.

"Take three hundred of your horse soldiers," Stiger said. "Do it right and bring back as many of our boys as you can. Also...if you can cut down a chunk of their cavalry...make that happen. I would deprive the enemy of as many of their eyes as possible."

"I will, sir."

Stiger took another pull on his pipe.

"You look as if you need some rest," Stiger said. "Come find me first thing in the morning. Before you depart, I would hear more on what you have seen."

"Yes, sir." Hux drained the rest of his wine and returned the empty mug to the table before moving for the door. He came to attention and saluted. "Thank you for the wine, sir," Hux said and then stepped out into the night.

His thoughts on what had been done to Aeda, Stiger took another puff on his pipe. It never got any easier. Whenever and wherever there was war, civilians suffered terribly. He had seen it all too often. It never got any easier.

"You look unhappy."

Taha'Leeth had entered the tent. He'd left orders with the guard that she was to be admitted without question whenever she wanted. He felt a thrill at seeing her. The unhappiness over Aeda and Menos lessened slightly.

"I am," Stiger said. "As you know, Menos is missing. Ogg tells me he may have died or left this world or gone far away. He does not know for sure. I'm worried."

"Left this world?" Taha'Leeth said. "That is not possible."

Stiger eyed her for a long moment.

"Ogg thinks there is a chance the other World Gate is still working," Stiger said.

She froze, staring at him incredulously. "That also is not possible. It was I who destroyed the Gate. There is no way anyone can use it."

"Then he must be dead," Stiger said and felt a wave of grief.

"I am sorry for your loss," Taha'Leeth said, "and saddened that such an ancient creature passed from this world."

Stiger felt his grief continue to well up. He fought it back.

"One day," Stiger said, "you will have to tell me how you did it, the destruction of the Gate."

"One day," Taha'Leeth agreed, "but not today. That is a story I do not enjoy telling."

Stiger felt his heart beat a little faster as she stepped nearer and reached down a hand to stroke his cheek.

"I did not think to tell you of the wyrm," Taha'Leeth said. "I really thought you knew."

Stiger gave a simple nod.

"It was never my intention to mislead you, my love," Taha'Leeth said, running a hand down his arm. "I ask you not to be angry with me."

"Well, there is nothing to be done about it now, and in truth I'm not sure it would have changed anything." Stiger paused. His concerns and worries had retreated a little with her presence. "I am not angry with you. Just being here... you have brightened my night."

She leaned down, kissing him on his forehead. Then she scowled slightly at the pipe. He thought it made her look more beautiful to him.

"That is a disgusting habit."

"One that I have come to enjoy," Stiger said. "Smoking the occasional pipe is one of my few vices."

"I would hear what other vices you have," she said, crossing her arms.

"I should think that obvious," Stiger said.

"Oh?"

"You, for one."

She laughed again and Stiger found the sound was quite pleasant. He enjoyed hearing her laugh. He could use more of that himself.

He grinned back at her and then his thoughts returned to Menos. He felt the grin fade from his face.

"I was prepared to ease your mind of your worries in other ways," Taha'Leeth said, "but I think you need a friend right now, more than a lover. How about we sit together for a while and talk?"

Stiger gave a nod. "I would like that, very much." His gaze went to the tent flap, wondering who would next arrive to demand some time.

"We won't be disturbed," Taha'Leeth said, spotting the look. "I told your guards no one is to disturb us until morning."

"You did, did you?"

She grabbed a stool and brought it next to his and sat down. Stiger held out his hand and she took it. Though it was rough and calloused, her hand felt warm. He loved holding her hand. She leaned her head against his shoulder. Stiger sucked in a breath through his nose and let it out slowly. She smelled faintly of roses. Despite his concerns and worries, he felt somewhat better. His thoughts returned to Menos and he suddenly chuckled.

"What is funny?" Taha'Leeth lifted her head off his shoulder and looked at him.

"We are," Stiger said.

"How so?"

"Well, you destroyed a World Gate," Stiger said, "and I sort of blew the top off a volcano. I am not sure which one is more impressive."

"You did what?" she asked.

"It was a pretty big explosion. You could see it for miles around. Pissed off a bunch of gnomes too. Boy did they want blood." He laughed at the memory.

"A volcano? How?"

"I didn't do it all by myself. I had some help," Stiger confessed.

"Menos?" Taha'Leeth tilted her head to the side. The movement reminded Stiger of Eli. "This I must hear."

"Are you sure you want to hear this?" Stiger asked. "It is rather a long story, though it is a funny one...unless you were one of those gnomes."

"I believe we both need a drink." Taha'Leeth stood and went to the wine. She poured them both a mug and returned. "I am very sure I want to hear this. Now, enough stalling. Start talking."

Stiger hesitated a moment, thinking with sadness on the fate of his friend. He took a sip of his wine and settled in to tell her the story.

EIGHTEEN

Stiger sat astride Nomad. He'd pulled the horse to a stop. Behind him, along the King's Highway, marched the legion. His horse shifted, taking several steps sideways to the left. Nomad was unsettled. Stiger absently tightened his grip on the reins and steadied his mount, then slapped his thigh in frustration.

The city of Aeda, tucked into the center of a wide valley, lay less than a mile downslope. It was nestled closely alongside a small river that was brownish in color. Aeda had never been the most beautiful of cities. When Stiger and Eli had passed through on their way to the Southern legions, he'd thought the city seedy and run down.

Once, long ago, Aeda had been the seat of power for a king. Now, it was a shadow of what it had once been. The stone walls that had surrounded the city had been pulled down. The city itself had been burned and thoroughly wrecked. All that remained were the shells of what had once been buildings and the dead.

Dog gave a soft whine.

"I know, boy," Stiger said, glancing down at the animal. Dog was looking in the direction of the city as well. "It's not quite fair, now, is it?"

There was no answer from Dog.

Stiger understood that in war there was no fairness. There never was.

The dead were lying in the fields that surrounded the city, masses of them. Flocks of vultures and ravens circled above, so many that they looked like a cloud of insects hovering around the city. An innumerable number of birds were on the ground too, feasting upon the rotting corpses. The ground seemed to almost undulate, like the surface of a lake on a stormy day.

Even this far removed, the sickly stench of death was strong on the air. It was not a pleasant fragrance and something Stiger had never become accustomed. Death mixed with the smell of smoke, which was also quite powerful, as the wind was blowing in their direction. It made him feel ill.

"Do you want to go down there, sir?" Lan asked.

The lieutenant and his troop were his escort for the day, as Stiger had decided to ride up the column of march and be seen by the men. He looked over at Lan. The lieutenant was grim-faced, as were his men. No one was enjoying what they were seeing. Stiger could not blame them.

Over the last three days, the road had passed by several villages and small towns. All had seen the same treatment as Aeda. An ugly mood had worked its way through the legion. It was one of the reasons he'd made an effort to make himself more visible. He wanted that anger directed and channeled toward the enemy. Whenever the opportunity presented itself, he'd spoken on paying the enemy back.

Stiger looked once more toward the city. He knew he'd never forget the sight. It was now forever seared into his memory. No matter how long he lived, what had been done here would be with him.

"We can go down there," Lan said, when Stiger did not immediately reply, "if you like, sir."

Stiger glanced over at the lieutenant. The bruises and cuts to his face had long since healed. His cheeks were red from the cold and his lips were chapped and cracked.

"No," Stiger said and touched his heels to Nomad's flanks. The horse started walking. "I don't need to go closer. I've seen enough death."

"Yes, sir." Lan appeared relieved as he nudged his horse into a walk. "Forward!" The lieutenant waved his hand forward for the rest of the troop to continue.

Ahead of them, on both sides of the road, were the bodies of imperial citizens who had been crucified. Every ten yards there were two more bodies, facing each other from across the road. Stiger had been told it continued that way for more than ten miles. The sight of the rotting bodies sickened him. Blood and gore had seeped down the wooden poles. Ravens and other birds had worried at the flesh until some of the figures were barely recognizable as once having been human.

"I think it would be a mercy to cut them down," Lan said as he rode alongside Stiger.

Stiger's voice when he replied was gruff. "They remain where they are."

"But, sir," Lan said, "it seems like the right thing to do."

"Lieutenant, we cannot take the time to care for the dead." Stiger gestured to a woman barely out of her teens who had been nailed to a cross. Her death must have been unimaginably hard. "She, like the rest of them, are beyond saving. One day, perhaps if there is time…we will come back and clean up. However, I will not slow the army…I dare not…for we must look to the living. Do you understand?"

Lan gave a miserable nod as they rode past two more bodies that had been crucified. One of them was a child, no older than seven. A man in Lan's troop retched at the sight, leaning over the side of his horse and spilling the contents of his stomach onto the dirt of the roadway.

They rode in silence after that, moving around a heavy wagon. In its bed was a large bolt thrower of gnome design. The oversized bolts, designed to kill a dragon, were strapped to the sides of the wagon. A group of gnomes rode in the wagon and a team of men, all auxiliaries, followed just behind. They were there to assist, for the machine could be set up quickly and operated from the wagon itself. Each cohort had at least one such bolt thrower wagon.

The gnomes swore the bolts would work and, in the past, machines like it had been used to take down smaller dragons, like wyrms. Having seen a dragon and fought one up close, Stiger wasn't so sure how effective they would be. Still, some protection was better than none, and he readily took what the gnomes offered.

They passed the wagon and rode along next to Eighth Cohort. Stiger had never heard such silence from marching men. It was as if they dared not speak, for it might wake the dead. But in truth, he knew they were grim and in an ugly mood.

He looked at two more bodies, both men in the middle years of their life. Stiger turned his gaze to the road ahead, lined with more of the dead. This was a sign. The enemy had intended to make a statement. He had no doubt it was meant for him and his men. Hux had been right. The enemy well knew they were coming.

It had also been meant to intimidate. And that's where the enemy had made a fatal mistake. They had misjudged the imperials. Instead of being frightened or intimidated, the murdering of innocent civilians had angered the army as a whole, and terribly so. Even the gnomes seemed upset.

Stiger could not have given his men better motivation as to why, day after day, they suffered through a brutal march. Each man would remember what they'd seen. He was sure of it.

The army had been marching north for ten long days. Stiger estimated they were covering a good fifteen to twenty miles a day. It was a brutal pace and grind, but one he and Braddock felt they needed to keep up.

Just five to six days away lay Lorium and the enemy. He'd not received a report from Hux yet on the enemy's strength but figured that would come any time. A battle would likely happen within the next week. That was good, for Aeda would be fresh to mind and the men would be looking to avenge themselves.

Stiger increased Nomad's pace, with Dog keeping up. After seeing the wreckage of the city, he wanted to ride for a bit and not just crawl along the column. He turned the horse off the road and out into a field that buttressed up against the highway and increased his pace even more. Lan and his troop easily kept up, following a few yards behind.

The countryside around Aeda was gentle and rolling. It had been dotted with farms and plantations, but all that was left were ruins and ashes. The land was empty of people. Stiger found that incredibly depressing. It fueled his anger, more than the sword ever had.

He continued until they were miles from the road. Only then did he slow Nomad to a walk. The grass was long and flowed gently with the breeze. Nomad bent his head and took a swipe at the grass. There were no ruins nearby, nothing that hinted at the destruction that had been wrought upon the region. The ever-present smell of death and smoke was gone. It seemed like a peaceful enough spot.

Stiger pulled Nomad to a stop. He slid off his horse and down into the tall grass, which came up almost to his knees. He took a deep breath and looked around a moment, then knelt and bowed his head in prayer. Dog padded over and sat down by his side.

Behind him, he heard the jingle and chink of armor as Lan dismounted. Then a moment later the entire troop slid off their horses. Stiger looked up. He was surprised to see the men kneeling with him in the grass. Their eyes were upon him.

"So be it," Stiger whispered to himself and then addressed himself to the men. "Let us pray for the souls of the departed."

They bowed their heads respectfully.

"High Father," Stiger said in a strong tone, "what was done to the people of this region was wrong and barbaric. There is no excuse for it. We ask that you take the souls of the departed into your arms, ease their suffering, and let them know peace in the afterlife." Stiger paused, thinking on what he desired to say next. It needed to be inspiring, for word of what happened here would spread quickly through-out the army. "We, the legion...the army...will be your sword of justice, your spear of righteousness as we move forward, seeking to right this terrible wrong. We will be your holy shield...for those in our homeland who are unable to pro-tect themselves." He paused briefly. "In your name we pray."

"In your name we pray," the men said in unison.

Stiger stood and, with him, the men stood as well. They were grim-faced, solemn. Stiger glanced up at the sky. An eagle circled high above, almost directly overhead. Was it a sign from the High Father? He returned his attention to the men. They were all staring skyward. It was clear they were thinking the same thing.

Without another word, he mounted back up, settled himself into the saddle, and nudged nomad back into a walk. His escort followed. Dog raced ahead, disappearing into a small stand of trees.

Eventually, Stiger turned his horse back in the direction of the road. Feeling the need to be diverted by conversation, he motioned for Lan to join him.

"What are your thoughts, Lieutenant?" Stiger asked as they passed by a burned-out farm. Two rotting corpses lay in the farmyard. Animals had gotten at the remains and spread them out a little. The stench was awful, as was the sight. Stiger was suddenly reminded of Sarai's burned body at their farm. He felt a sudden heat within his breast and, with it, his free hand found the pommel of his sword. The tingle raced up his arm. Stiger almost jumped in the saddle, for he'd not felt the sensation for some time, years even. Had he imagined it?

"If they would do this here, sir," Lan said, "then they will do it to Vrell and home. No one will be safe...until they are stopped."

Stiger thought on Lan's new wife back in Vrell. He was sure the lieutenant feared for her safety, especially after all they had seen.

"Agreed," Stiger said and touched the sword hilt again, at first almost tentatively. There was no tingle, no sensation. Stiger felt himself scowl. It seemed he'd imagined it. "It's one of the reasons why we must do everything within our power to stop them, to bring this to an end."

Stiger's thoughts shifted away from the sword. He was tired of reacting to the enemy. Ever since he'd been sent to Vrell, he'd been in reaction mode…whether it was Castor or Valoor through the Cyphan. When he'd made the decision to bring the Thirteenth back with him to the present, he'd decided to change the dynamic and break the cycle.

He was now pursuing the enemy's advance into imperial territory, and in a way, it felt like he was once again playing to their tune. That bothered him immensely. But at the same time, he understood the dynamic had already been changed. The cycle had been broken. He was no longer playing by their rules. Though they did not know it yet, they were playing by his.

At some point, the enemy would need to break the siege at Lorium and turn to face him. That was when he'd give them an education. He looked over at Lan.

"Doing this…" Stiger gestured at another farm they were approaching. It too had been burned. "Our enemy made a fateful mistake. They don't know the anger that they've awoken amongst the men, nor what's coming for them."

"No, sir," Lan said, "they most certainly do not."

It was later in the same day. Cresting a rise, Stiger could see for miles in almost any direction. The column of march, as far as the eye could see, snaked out to the front and behind. The army, from the van to the rearguard, stretched for over a hundred miles. Stiger knew that from the daily reports he received.

He was walking with Taha'Leeth and Dog. Ruga and his century were spread out around him protectively. Aver'Mons was walking with Ruga a handful of yards behind them. Both were engaged in conversation and had been talking in an animated manner for over an hour. To their front was a dwarven company composed of heavy infantry. To their rear was the vanguard of the legion. Today, the honor of leading the legion's march had gone to Tenth Cohort. Eli was with his father and the elven infantry.

The gods only knew what Therik was up to. Stiger had not seen the orc all day. Therik and Braddock had dined together. He supposed both had spent their time drinking late into the night, so it was possible Therik was still with Braddock.

Stiger glanced over at Taha'Leeth, marveling once again at her stunning beauty. She'd tied her hair back into a single braid. Under the sunlight, she looked radiant, strong, confident. Her bow was slung over her back, along with a tightly bound bundle of arrows. She carried a pack on her back as well.

"You need to be less obvious," she said, catching his look. She leaned in close. "What will your men think if they see you staring all the time?"

"They already know."

"You do not say!" Taha'Leeth shot him a scandalized look. Of course, she was aware the men knew of their relationship. Salt had told him it was the talk of the legion. Apparently, many of the men were quite happy for him. Stiger was abruptly reminded of Eli's counsel. He glanced back at Ruga and saw Aver'Mons's gaze on him. The elf quickly looked away when their eyes met.

"I don't think Aver'Mons approves," Stiger said.

"He might not," Taha'Leeth said, without glancing back. "He is loyal, and we have spoken. We have nothing to fear from him. There will be no trouble from that quarter."

"So, you agree we have something to fear?" Stiger asked. "People who will disapprove and try to take some action?"

"I do," Taha'Leeth said. "Most will simply make their displeasure known in other ways."

"It's not enough that we have to worry about the enemy and dark gods, but now our own people."

"Yes," Taha'Leeth said. "It is sad. Most people do not like change, especially elves. My people go out of their way to resist the change in things. It, sadly, is a failing of our race."

"This is more than simply disliking change," Stiger said, becoming heated. What with Aeda, it had been an emotional day. He'd been the target of assassination attempts in the past. It was a fact of life in imperial politics. But he still was having difficulty with the possibility that one of his people would seek to harm the woman he had come to love and hold dear. "So much is at stake."

"People don't all think the same way," Taha'Leeth said. "Some have trouble seeing what is right or even understanding the stakes you speak of. Fewer even are those who can comprehend what we really face or the consequences of their own actions."

Stiger knew truth when he heard it. In fact, he understood exactly what she was talking about. He'd experienced it himself. He was frustrated because he did not know how to defuse the problem. Once again, his happiness, along with the success of everything he was working toward, was at risk, and added with all his other headaches, it made him downright angry. She reached over and laid a hand upon his forearm.

"It will all work out fine in the end," Taha'Leeth said. "You will see. Have faith."

"I do," Stiger said.

"As do I. Between us, my god and yours, we have great faith."

She appeared quite earnest and he considered that she had a very good point. There was much more at work, and sometimes it was easy to forget.

"You are correct," Stiger said.

"I am," Taha'Leeth said and punched him lightly on the arm. "And don't you forget it."

Stiger let out a laugh.

She shot him a grin, and for a time, they walked in silence.

"I would have expected your people to begin arriving," Stiger said. "We have yet to see any."

She gave a slight scowl. It clearly had been on her mind too. "I do not know what holds them up. I am beginning to worry."

"Me too," Stiger said and then, having regretted bringing it up, he sought to divert her attention. "How many years will we have together?"

"Assuming we survive the coming days?" Taha'Leeth asked.

Stiger gave a nod.

"Too many to count with all your fingers and toes," she said, "presuming you can count that high."

He gave another laugh, feeling his mood lighten. "I pray that throughout the years, you continue to make me laugh."

"I do too."

"I'll settle for happiness."

"Good," Taha'Leeth said. "How about I begin in earnest now, giving you the happiness you desire. After such a depressing day, would you like some good news?"

He looked over at her. She was looking back at him intently. Her eyes were nearly shining with intensity.

He gave a nod. "I could use some good news."

"I am carrying our baby."

Stiger almost stumbled and came to a complete stop. He wasn't quite sure he'd heard correctly.

"What?" Stiger asked. "What did you just say?"

She gave him a confirming nod and rested her hand upon her belly, which showed no bulge whatsoever.

"What? How? Are you sure?"

Taha'Leeth gave him a funny look. "Your father did explain how these things work, did he not?"

"We were never really that close," Stiger said as he stared at her in disbelief. "Really? We're gonna have a baby?"

She gave another nod, her eyes beginning to brim with tears. Stiger was suddenly overcome with emotion. He reached out to her and pulled her close, hugging her tight.

"Sir," Ruga said, stepping up to them, along with Aver'Mons. There was concern in the centurion's eyes. "Is everything all right? We're beginning to hold up the march."

Stiger looked over at the centurion, confused, then beyond him to see Tenth Cohort stopped. The senior centurion was looking at him curiously.

"Sir?"

"It seems," Stiger said, turning his gaze back to Taha'Leeth, "I am to be a father."

Stiger noticed that Aver'Mons seemed stunned. The elf took a step back, his gaze going to Taha'Leeth.

"Well," Ruga said, "isn't that something. I guess you will have to make an honest girl out of her now, sir."

"I guess so."

Ruga turned to his men. "The legate is going to be a father."

The century gave a cheer.

"I love you," Stiger said to Taha'Leeth.

"And I you," Taha'Leeth said. "Together we will make a new beginning."

Tenth Cohort cheered as word was passed back to them. It was a hearty cheer.

"The entire legion will know about it soon enough, sir," Ruga said with a grin. "After all that we saw this day, some good news will be more than welcome. Congratulations, sir."

Stiger turned his gaze back to Taha'Leeth.

"I am going to be a father."

"And a good one you will make too," she said.

NINETEEN

Braddock, Cragg, Eli, Salt, Tenya'Far, and Taha'Leeth were in Stiger's command tent. It was late into the night, with Tenya'Far and Braddock having traveled hours forward for this meeting. They were gathered around a large table and had been studying a map. Lamps lit the tent in a yellowish glow. The legion had already bedded down for the night, and for the most part, the camp beyond was silent.

"It looks like keeping up this grueling pace has worked, sir," Salt said, glancing up from the map. "We've gotten real close, and without them budging too. It's been a grind for the men, but they're up for a fight."

"I cannot help but agree," Stiger said. "I did not think we would make it this far without them turning to face us."

It pleased Stiger greatly, especially considering they were just two days from Lorium. The enemy army engaged with besieging the city had not moved, at least not yet.

The map had been drawn by one of Hux's men and detailed the siege of the city, laying out the enemy's dispositions and defensive works. It even went so far as to mark their supply depots and animal pens. The map and accompanying report had arrived the day before.

To keep those within from attempting a breakout, the enemy had completely ringed the city with an earthen wall.

The notation on the map indicated this wall was capped by a stout barricade and protected with a series of trenches. The map also marked the enemy's artillery positions.

The note Hux had written that accompanied the report indicated the enemy had seven large stone throwers and at least thirty smaller machines. The larger machines were concentrated in two specific areas, facing the south and east walls. The artillery was actively hammering at the city's walls, working to reduce them. It appeared they had successfully holed and then collapsed a portion of the south wall. Hux reported that, with the amount of enemy dead both before and inside the breach, they had failed in an attempt to storm the city.

The enemy had shifted their focus and were now actively engaged in working to open multiple gaps in the wall. Hux felt that the work on the walls would be completed within the next two weeks. The more breaches the enemy created, the greater the chance of successfully storming the city.

Curiously, two wyrms had been taken down and somehow killed. The positions of their corpses were also marked on the map. Stiger found it incredible that the legions had found a way to down the dragons.

Had they done it with bolt throwers? It gave him hope that Cragg's machines would work. He also considered that it was possible it had been the work of the wizard the emperor had mentioned in his letter.

Stiger turned his attention to Braddock, who was stroking his braided beard and looking down at the map. The thane wore a well-cut tunic, though he was dusty from the road and looked weary.

"Your thoughts?" Stiger asked the thane.

The thane looked up briefly and then back down at the map.

"Our cavalry patrols have pushed more than seventy miles to the east, in the direction of Asti," Braddock said, gesturing down at the map, "and are actively watching the road. We've seen no sign or even a hint that there are any other enemy forces within easy marching distance. I believe it is as Salt has said, we've succeeded beyond our imaginings. At this point, should the enemy break off the siege and move to face us, it will be done with haste, which will be to our advantage. And we know for a fact that we will outnumber them."

"Not by very much," Eli cautioned. "Any sort of battle will still be hard fought. We should not take our numerical superiority for granted."

"You are right," Stiger said. "This will likely prove to be a real test for us."

Braddock gave a slow nod. "One, I am certain, we will pass."

"We must not forget the enemy is aware of our presence," Tenya'Far said. "Ever since Aeda, their cavalry scouts have been spotted directly observing our column of march."

"True," Stiger said. "Our cavalry screen has seen several sharp engagements."

"That is a clear sign," Braddock said, "that they seek more information on our strength. By now they should have a good picture of our numbers."

"And yet"—Tenya'Far, in a mannerism very much like his son, cocked his head to the side—"I find it strange they've not broken the siege and either marched against us or away."

"Agreed," Taha'Leeth breathed quietly. "The enemy should have made some move. I wonder what they are waiting for."

"I hate to say it, sir, and tempt Fortuna," Salt said, "but things are going well, sir."

Stiger gave a nod. He thought so too, and that worried him. It was almost as if the enemy thought they had nothing to fear from them. And perhaps they had a right to think that way.

Earlier in the day, the army had marched past a battlefield that was weeks old. It had clearly been the spot where the emperor's army had been broken. Stiger figured at least forty thousand men had been killed, perhaps more.

Though the scouts had described the battlefield in detail… Stiger found when he arrived, it had not prepared him for the horrific nature of the battle's aftermath. And he wasn't even sure it could be rightly called a battle, for what had occurred had clearly been very one-sided.

What had been truly shocking were the neat, almost orderly lines of charred bodies. Formed up and ready to face the enemy, men by the thousands had been burned down where they'd stood in line. The fire had been so intense, it had melted and fused armor with bone. In some places, the fires had burned so hot, the bodies had been turned to ash and the men's armor had run like water. None of those poor bastards had stood a chance.

While in the past, Stiger had seen such things before. But that experience with just one wyrm could not compare to the scale of the slaughter he'd seen on this battlefield. It told Stiger that multiple dragons had been used in the breaking of the army. He could imagine nothing less would be able to shatter, and rout a force led by General Treim in such a manner.

The legions would have been unprepared for any such attack, and he was sure the appearance of the dragons had come as a complete surprise. Nowhere in Hux's report had he mentioned the enemy having any live dragons at Lorium, only the two that had fallen. Where there were two, Stiger knew, there were likely more.

He rubbed his jaw and glanced at Cragg. The little gnome seemed to fidget constantly, as if, like a small child after getting a treat, he had too much energy to contain. Unlike the emperor's broken army, at least, theirs now had some protection, even if it was limited.

From the battle site, they had found a continual trail of rotting bodies alongside the road to Lorium. Though there was no telling how many men had simply run off, there had clearly been some sort of organized retreat and pursuit. He had not enjoyed anything he'd seen and neither had the men.

"I don't like it," Stiger said. "I just don't like it. Now that they are aware of our presence, there is just no good reason to remain at Lorium and continue the siege. They risk being trapped between the city and our army. We also know they have no fortifications facing outward, so there's no good reason to continue to sit there and do nothing."

"Perhaps," Eli said, "they are setting us up for a trap, or they just don't consider us a threat."

"I think a trap is likely," Braddock said, "with a dragon or two. They will intend to do to us what they did to your emperor's legions."

"We give dragon surprise," Cragg said, speaking up. The gnome gave a nasty little laugh. "Good surprise. We poison bolts. Yes, yes...dragons be very surprised."

"You poisoned the bolts?" Braddock asked Cragg in Dwarven. "What poison did you use? Tell me, what works against a dragon?"

"I no tell," Cragg replied in Dwarven. "It is our secret. Just know poison is strong enough to take down wyrm. We've done it before."

"You what?" Braddock asked. "When?"

Cragg did not reply.

"You and I will be speaking of this later," Braddock said, "kluge."

Cragg gave a tiny shrug of his shoulders.

"It could be as Braddock says, or they might be having difficulty deciding what to do," Salt said. "On one hand, they have an army boxed up in the city, and on the other, a second army is closing in on them. The enemy general might not know what to do exactly."

"Good point," Stiger said. "But we can't expect such indecision to continue for much longer. Eventually he will have to make a decision."

"Maybe they will use a dragon," Ogg said, "maybe not. Perhaps they will sit still until we get to Lorium...perhaps not. There is no telling what the enemy is thinking at this point. We must proceed as we believe best and not over-think things."

"You said"—Stiger turned to Ogg—"that you could detect the enemy's dragons, correct?"

"I can," Ogg said. "There are some to the north and others to the east. They have more than one wyrm. I do not know how close they are or their actual number. It is sort of a general thing."

"That's not very helpful," Braddock said.

"No, it's not," Ogg replied acidly. "If you can find a wizard who can do better, My Thane, then do so."

Braddock's cheeks flushed. He was about to reply, when Nepturus stepped into the tent.

"Excuse me, sir," Nepturus said. He held a dispatch in his hand. "I knew you would want to see this. It just came in from Prefect Hux. The messenger said it was of the utmost importance."

Stiger took the dispatch and opened it, scanning the contents. The dispatch was very brief. His heart quickened. He read it a second time and then set it down on the table.

"Is the messenger still here?" Stiger asked his clerk.

"Yes, sir," Nepturus said. "He's half-dead with exhaustion. He brought several remounts and, I am told, rode straight through from near Lorium."

"Send him in, would you?"

"Yes, sir." Nepturus retreated.

"I've just received an update from Hux," Stiger said. "The enemy has broken off their siege and are now marching."

"To meet us?" Braddock asked.

"Yes," Stiger said. "It seems they've made up their mind and intend to give battle."

There was a long moment of silence.

"Well." Braddock rubbed his hands together. "It's about time. Finally, a proper fight."

"Trooper Jagus, sir," Nepturus said, reentering the tent. With him was the messenger. The trooper was covered in dust and looked like he was ready to drop. Despite his exhaustion, Jagus appeared awed and nervous by those gathered before him in the tent. He offered Stiger a salute.

"Do you know the contents of this dispatch?" Stiger asked, gesturing at the table.

"I do, sir," Jagus said. "I received it directly from Prefect Hux's own hand, sir."

"Did you personally see the enemy army marching?" Stiger asked.

"No, sir," Jagus said. "However, I did speak to the prefect himself. He eyeballed the enemy's column of march, sir. He said there are at least seventy thousand on the move and they look well organized. They've completely broken off their siege of the city and are taking everything with them. That even includes their baggage train and camp followers. They have also burned their siege engines."

"When did they march, son?" Salt asked.

"This morning, before dawn, sir."

"At this point, we're likely a day's march away from each other," Braddock said, "maybe less."

"The prefect said they were making good time, sir."

"What else can you tell us?" Stiger asked, turning back to the trooper. "Were any dragons seen?"

"Dragons?" the trooper asked. "No, sir. We've not seen any live ones…only those that were dead in the fields before the city."

"Perhaps that's all they had?" Braddock suggested, looking over to Ogg.

"It's not," Ogg said. "They have more of the beasts. You need to trust my word on this, my thane."

"Good, good," Cragg said, enthusiastically. The gnome was so excited to see his dragon-killing bolt throwers in action, he was almost hopping. "We shoot and kill dragons. Good…good, yes?"

Stiger ignored the gnome.

"There was a nasty fight with the enemy's cavalry, sir," the trooper added. "It happened the day before the enemy marched, sir…late afternoon and into evening. It was as if they were trying to push us back and away from the city and the King's Highway. The prefect set an ambush. We gave them a good drubbing, sir…cut them up pretty good. After that, what was left of their cavalry pulled back."

Stiger glanced down at the dispatch. Hux had mentioned nothing of a fight, but it was good news all the same. A formal report would likely follow at some point. He'd sent Jagus to report on the critical information. Stiger figured the cavalry fight was the enemy attempting to push his eyes back and steal a march on them, only Hux had likely been expecting such a move.

Jagus abruptly swayed on his feet and almost fell. Tenya'Far moved forward and swiftly caught his arm and helped to steady him.

"Sorry, sir," Jagus said, pulling himself back to attention. "I've ridden straight through. I did not stop to eat or rest. The prefect told me to get to you as quick as I could."

"We thank you for your news and your effort." Stiger looked over at his clerk. "Nepturus, get him some food and a place to rest, will you?"

"Yes, sir," the clerk said and helped the legionary out of the tent.

"Well," Stiger said, "we have a battle to plan."

"We do," Salt said and stepped over to another table where he retrieved a map. He returned and laid the map down over the one Hux had provided. This new map detailed the South and included Lorium.

"Do we continue the advance to meet the enemy?" Stiger asked. "Or find what good ground we can and wait for them to come to us?"

"With all this rolling country," Braddock said, "there is no good ground to be had, other than the occasional rise. I say we march and meet them."

"Our marching column stretches for over a hundred miles," Tenya'Far pointed out and traced a line on the map, back down King's Highway. "Each night, we have three different encampments spread out over thirty to forty miles of road. We need to begin concentrating the army, and soon."

"That means a half day's march for tomorrow, then, maybe less," Salt said. "We will also need to begin pulling in our cavalry. We've been using them hard. I think we'll want to give them what little rest we can before we go into battle."

"There is no doubt we will need them during the battle." Stiger turned to his camp prefect. "Salt, see that orders are cut to Hux as soon as we are done here. He will still need to keep scouts out to shadow the enemy's line of march, but I want the bulk of his boys back with us."

"I will, sir."

"And if they have wyrms?" Eli asked.

"We use our dragon killers," Braddock said and waved a hand toward Cragg. "We put his boys to the test and hope they come through for us."

"We do job. No worry," Cragg said.

"With you gnomes," Braddock said, "I always worry."

"Bah." Cragg waved a dismissive hand. "You no worry."

"The emperor could be there, in Lorium, sir," Salt said. "Shouldn't we try to send word? Especially considering the enemy's lifted their siege."

"I doubt there's time to get word to Lorium," Stiger said. "Any battle will likely be long over by the time our messenger could arrive. They will be unable to assist us, even if they are not already on short rations and half-starved."

"I still think we should make the attempt, sir," Salt said. "They may be able to profit off of knowing we're out here."

"You're right," Stiger said. "I will write them later tonight."

"Thank you, sir," Salt said.

"The emperor may be in Lorium," Ogg said, "but at least we know the Key is not there."

"How so?" Braddock asked.

"If the Key to the World Gate was there," Ogg said, "the Cyphan would have torn Lorium apart to get at it. They would not be marching for the coast with the bulk of their army. Instead, they split their armies and settled for leaving the remains of the imperial army inside the city. My guess is the army sieging Lorium is meant to bottle up the legionaries and contain them there. At least long enough for the army that went east to defeat whatever other forces the empire has or can throw together."

"It all comes down to the Key," Stiger said.

"The Key is the heart of the matter," Ogg said, "for the present anyway."

"Shame you could not get it in the past and bring it back with you," Braddock said to Stiger, "like you did with the Thirteenth."

"That would have altered our history," Ogg said, "or at least changed some things we would not want altered." The wizard waved a hand in Stiger's direction. "Thoggle would have cautioned him on doing something like that. Am I right?"

"He did," Stiger said.

Ogg abruptly stiffened as he looked to the entrance of the tent. The wizard's hand clutching his staff tightened. He sucked in a startled breath. Stiger realized something was wrong.

"So," Eli said, having not noticed the wizard's reaction. "If the emperor doesn't have the Key with him or did not bring it south, where is it?"

"It is hidden in the heart of the capital," a new voice said from the entrance of the tent, "at least I believe it to be."

Stiger blinked and turned in utter astonishment, not quite believing his eyes. "You're not dead."

Menos had entered the tent. He gazed around at those gathered for a long moment.

"You bastard," Ogg hissed.

"I am very much alive." The noctalum gestured toward Ogg. "I imagine I gave the wizard quite the scare." He turned his gaze to Stiger. "Maybe even you too?"

"Bloody fool," Ogg spat at the noctalum. "Scare? You bastard. It's about time you decided to return. In my weakened state, this army could have been destroyed while you were out wandering around. Did you go sightseeing?"

The elves recovered from their shock at the noctalum's appearance. All three bowed their heads respectfully. Menos ignored them. He appeared amused by the wizard.

"Where were you?" Stiger asked, having also recovered from his surprise. He felt his anger burn hot at his friend, for being absent so long. At the same time, there was an immense feeling of relief.

"I was here and there," Menos said. "I was not sightseeing. I can tell you the enemy is certainly aware of this army. They are marching to meet you."

"We know," Stiger said. "We were just discussing that."

"They have two flights of wyrms at their disposal, and within easy reach too, just to the north," Menos said. "Eight wyrms in total."

"Gods," Salt breathed. "Eight dragons?"

"Oh good," Cragg said, rubbing his little hands together in eager anticipation. "Good...good."

Stiger turned to Salt. "You had to tempt Fortuna, didn't you?"

"Eight dragons?" Salt asked. "Sir, I saw what one was capable of doing with my own eyes…that one you took down before Old City. How can we withstand eight? Even with him on our side?"

"I believe," Menos said, before Stiger could answer, "when they bring you to battle, they intend to hit you with their wyrms. It will be a repeat of what they did to the emperor's legions a few weeks back. I spoke to several survivors. It was a rather one-sided fight. I would expect the enemy to be overconfident, since it worked the first time."

Stiger could well imagine. Before Vrell, he had thought dragons were creatures of myth and legend. Now, he knew differently.

"There are too many for you to deal with, right?" Salt asked Menos.

"Alone," Menos said, "you would be correct. Even with Currose, were she healthy, there are too many."

Stiger felt a wave of intense frustration wash over him. He rubbed the back of his neck and stared down at the rug, thoughts racing. Even with the gnomes and a noctalum, the enemy's advantage in dragons would see their army crushed and scattered.

"What about the sertalum?" Stiger asked, looking back up and fearing that Menos might have more bad news. "Is she coming, too?"

"She is keeping her distance, as of now," Menos said. "I do not believe she is planning on interfering."

"Well," Stiger said, "that is good."

"At least," Menos added, "not at present anyway. She might become involved later."

Stiger eyed the noctalum for a long moment, then stepped over to a side table where a pitcher of wine sat with a handful of mugs. He poured himself a healthy drink and drank it down in one go. Then, he turned back. The tent had fallen silent, with all eyes on the noctalum. Only Cragg looked excited by the prospect of what was coming.

"You went for help," Stiger said as he put the empty mug back down on the table. "Didn't you? That's why you disappeared for so long. You decided we needed help against the enemy's wyrms."

"I did," Menos said and shook a long, thin finger at Stiger. "Thoggle was right about you not being so stupid."

Stiger wondered on where Menos had gone for help.

"The other World Gate is still functioning, isn't it?" It was a gut feeling, but Stiger felt it the right one. "You went there. And traveled to another world. Didn't you?"

"Again," Menos said, "you impress me."

"That's impossible," Taha'Leeth said, looking between them. "I already told you, I saw to it that Gate was destroyed."

Menos gave a cold laugh.

"Fool elf." The noctalum's tone was condescending. "It was the noctalum and sertalum who built the World Gates. You only damaged it and then dropped it beneath a sea. Did it not occur to you the Gate could be repaired?"

"It's open?" Ogg asked, thoroughly aghast. "The Gate to Yarro is open? How long has it been open? Why would you do that?"

"Yes, it is active and open." Menos sounded pleased with himself. "But, even now, it is very hard to access." The noctalum paused. "Only Currose and myself can get to the Gate, let alone use it." Menos gave a thin smile. "I was thinking of offering that information to the sertalum…as a way…to ensure she does not interfere with us."

"What do you mean?" Ogg demanded. "You would trust her? Trust the noctalum's age-old enemy?"

"Trust her? Of course not," Menos scoffed. "However, I can offer her an escape from this backwater. If she agrees, it would make things easier for us in the long term. Who knows, she might even help us, if she wants off Istros bad enough."

"You will do no such thing," Ogg hissed, stamping the bottom of his staff on the rug. "I will not allow it. She might return from Yarro with reinforcement."

"I don't think that likely," Menos said and chuckled darkly. "Not now anyway."

"Why not?" Taha'Leeth asked. "Yarro was nearly overrun with our enemy when we fled through the Gate."

"Your enemy at the time was the Vass," Menos said. "Am I right on that point?"

Taha'Leeth gave a slow nod. "They are still the enemy, just as the Cyphan are."

"Well," Menos said, "Yarro is firmly in their hands."

"And yet you would still open the Gate?" Taha'Leeth hissed. "The sertalum are aligned to the Vass."

"She will not work with the Vass," Menos said, "and they won't work with her. I don't believe you need to worry about that, not anymore."

"Why did you bother going to Yarro?" Stiger asked. "I thought you said the Vass were across the ocean."

"I did," Menos said. "It was quicker to travel to Yarro than hunt down the Vass on Istros…quicker than flying halfway around this world."

"There are Vass on this world?" Taha'Leeth said, in near horror.

"There are," Tenya'Far said. "A handful came through the World Gate with us when we fled Tanis. They were part of a splinter group and fought with us, but still we did not trust them. Once the Gate was sealed they went their own way. We have not seen them since." The elf paused and turned his attention from Taha'Leeth to Menos. "How can you be certain the sertalum will not work with the Vass?"

"It seems," Menos said, "when it comes to the Vass on Yarro, their alignment has shifted somewhat."

"Shifted?" Tenya'Far said. "How so?"

"Who are the Vass?" Salt asked.

Taha'Leeth pointed an accusing finger at Menos. "You cut a deal with them, didn't you?"

"I negotiated for two knights of the Vass, no less, a few flights of taltalum," Menos admitted, "and some of their infantry."

"Taltalum?" Stiger asked. "Those are the dragons you mentioned before when we talked?"

Menos gave a nod. "They will be enough to counter eight wyrms, with my help, of course."

"What?" Cragg almost shouted. It came out as a high-pitched squeak. "No. We shoot, kill dragons!"

"I can't believe I am hearing this," Taha'Leeth said in Elven to Tenya'Far. "There are Vass on Istros and he wants more to come."

Eli's father became visibly enraged, his face flushing with color. He took a half-step toward Menos. "You are a fool, noctalum. Now that you have repaired the World Gate and invited them to this world, the Vass will stay and claim it for their own. All we fight for will be lost in the end. How could you do this to us? Why would you do it?"

"No," Menos said, sounding certain. His tone grew cold and menacing. "I have worked hard to make this happen. They will not stay, and I am no fool. Best watch yourself with me, elf."

"I don't understand," Salt said. "Who are the Vass?"

"They are an ancient race," Taha'Leeth answered, heat in her tone. "A warrior people and a sworn enemy of ours. They make the Cyphan look quite tame by comparison."

"They are not an enemy anymore," Menos said and walked over to the pitcher of wine. He poured himself a drink and turned back to face them. "They want nothing to do with Istros."

"I find that hard to believe," Ogg said. "The Vass are not to be trusted. With this I am in agreement with the elves. I believe you made a bad decision here."

"Believe what you wish," Menos said and sipped at his wine. "Despite our past differences, I bargained with them and we struck a deal. I saw no other way."

"That was a mistake of colossal proportions," Taha'Leeth said. "There is a reason why people never make bargains with the Vass. In the end, you always end up paying more than you want. Tell me, noctalum, what fair deal did you strike?"

Stiger shared a glance with Braddock. The thane did not look terribly pleased either. It seemed the Vass were quite a terrible people.

"I told them of the Vass who were trapped upon this world," Menos said quietly. "They agreed to help us. That was, if I allowed them access to the Gate. Once everything is settled, they will retrieve their people and go. I am quite certain that the Vass on Istros want off just as badly as the sertalum does. Istros has always been a sort of backwater world."

Stiger thought Menos looked rather smug.

"Just like that?" Tenya'Far asked. "You may have traded one enemy for another, noctalum."

"Not this time," Menos said. "There are a few other things of value I gave them. Besides, for good or bad, the deal is done and only Currose and I have access to the World Gate. They know this…so in a way you might say they are our hostages. If they do not behave, they are stuck on Istros and we kill them." Menos took another sip from his wine and looked over to Stiger. "Cunning, right?"

"That is easier said than done," Taha'Leeth said.

"We will see." Menos turned his attention to Braddock and Stiger. "I assume you intend on bringing the enemy to battle?"

"We do," Braddock confirmed.

"Good. When you manage that, the Vass and I will keep the enemy's wyrms busy," Menos said. "It will be up to you to break the confederacy's army. Think you can manage that?"

"We will have to," Stiger said. "Losing is not an option."

"I will not fight alongside a Vass," Tenya'Far said, "not again, not ever."

"You will, Father," Eli said.

Tenya'Far's gaze snapped to his son.

"You gave your word, along with the warden's, to fight by their side"—Eli gestured toward Stiger and Braddock—"and fight you will."

Tenya'Far looked as if he wanted to shout at his son. His cheeks flushed with color. Stiger had never seen an elf, other than Eli, get so upset. It was an interesting turn of events.

Eli's father took a deep breath and let it out, calming himself. A moment later, it was as if nothing untoward had ever happened. "My son is quite correct. I did give my word and I will honor it. I will fight by your side, just as I said... even if it is alongside a Vass."

"And I took your side," Taha'Leeth said to Stiger. "I will be by your side no matter how difficult or disagreeable it becomes."

"This is quite good wine," Menos said, having taken a sip, and then drained his mug. He returned the empty mug to the table. "I missed valley wine." He paused, as if something had just occurred to him. "Oh, you might be interested to know...your emperor is in Lorium."

"We'd heard that. How do you know for certain?" Stiger asked.

"I walked its streets, listened and spoke to those within," Menos said. "I assure you, he is there. Though I understand he was injured in the recent fighting when the enemy attempted to storm the city."

"Badly?" Stiger asked, alarmed and suddenly worried for his childhood friend.

"I do not know," Menos said, "and I did not have time to find out. The people I spoke with were more concerned with the hostile army besieging the city and the stones being thrown at the walls. Some of those stones made the ground shake. It was all very impressive."

"Did you go east at all?" Stiger asked, curious as to the enemy's army there.

"As far as I dared," Menos said. "The enemy has more wyrms protecting their main army that's marching to the coast. That army numbers over two hundred thousand. Oh, and for added cheer, another army is coming up from the south. I do not know its strength, but I believe it to be much smaller. They are currently being ferried across the Narrow

Sea. I had considered sinking a few of their ships, but I was pressed for time, so I did not bother and continued on."

Stiger pinched the bridge of his nose.

"What was that about Fortuna?" Eli asked Salt.

The camp prefect did not reply.

Could it get any worse? Stiger asked himself. He knew his task would not be easy, but could it really get worse? He took a deep breath and calmed himself. They now had the Vass on their side. That was something. He wasn't quite sure if that was a mixed blessing or not. Only time would tell. But it seemed the enemy's dragons might not be as bad a threat as they had thought. He brightened at that prospect.

"The enemy is coming," Stiger said, addressing them all. "They think they have a surprise in store for us, with their wyrms. We now have a surprise for them. We worry about what's coming our way and what is before us. We focus on one problem at a time. We deal with that problem. The enemy army marching to us is the first problem. The rest can wait until after we've dealt with it."

"That's why I like you, Stiger," Menos said. "You never, ever give up."

"If I did," Stiger said, with a glance over at Cragg, "you'd still be a worshipped pet."

Menos grinned at that and Stiger grinned back.

Ogg barked out a harsh laugh. The wizard laughed so hard, he almost choked. When he came up for air, he leaned heavily upon his staff. "And here I didn't think noctalum had a sense of humor. You like this human? You truly like him? Hah! Now, that is a hoot."

"Very funny, dwarf." Menos flashed a thin smile at Ogg, then sobered and turned to Stiger. "One other thing."

"What more bad news do you have for us?" Stiger asked, almost dreading what was coming.

"I wouldn't call it bad news, exactly," Menos said. "When I was in Mal'Zeel, your—"

"You went all the way to Mal'Zeel?" Stiger asked, thoroughly astonished. "You covered a lot of ground."

"Well," Menos said, "when I found out the Key wasn't in Lorium, I went searching for it. I thought I might be able to get it before the enemy and save us some trouble."

"I could have told you it wasn't in Lorium," Ogg said, "had you bothered to consult me."

Menos ignored the wizard.

"Did you find it?" Stiger asked hopefully.

"No," Menos said, "and believe me, I looked."

Stiger wondered where the Key was hidden. If the emperor was in Lorium, he would surely know. Over the years, the Key had become one of the emperor's symbols of office. But that was a problem to be concerned with later. First, they needed to defeat the army marching their way.

"As I was saying before I was interrupted," Menos said, "I learned your father has been put in command of the legions to the east."

"My father?" Stiger asked. He had not expected that. He knew he should not be surprised by it, but still he found that he was.

"When the emperor's legions were shattered, it seems the senate, in desperation, recalled him from his forced retirement. They've raised several new legions and pulled in others from the borders that did not march south with the emperor. They are busy fortifying Mal'Zeel and preparing for the confederacy's arrival."

"Now isn't that interesting," Eli said. "Two Stigers in the field. Who would have thought that? Not I."

"This is good news, yes?" Taha'Leeth asked, looking to Stiger.

"There is good news and then there is good news," Eli said, in a slightly mocking tone. "Isn't there, Ben?"

Stiger shot Eli an unhappy look and just shook his head in shocked disbelief.

TWENTY

Wake...

W *ake...*
Stiger's eyes snapped open. At the foot of his cot, a solitary clay lamp burned on a small table. When he'd fallen asleep, he had forgotten to extinguish the lonely flame. The tent, for the most part, was darkened and heavily shadowed.

Taha'Leeth was pressed firmly against him. Outside, the encampment was deathly quiet. Stiger had been dreaming about the sword and that it had been speaking to him again. The weapon lay on the rug, next to his cot and within easy reach.

He had no idea what time it was, but figured it was early. In the morning, the legion would march for at least a half day so that the rest of the army could catch up and the consolidation could begin. The day after would likely see a battle. Eyes watering, he yawned again. Gods, he was exhausted, run down, and just plain weary. It had been a long and hard march from Vrell.

It was cold and the blanket was doing little to add much warmth. Stiger pulled Taha'Leeth in closer and closed his eyes. As usual, her body radiated heat. She shifted and snuggled against him. Stiger closed his eyes, breathed in deeply, and prepared to return to sleep.

Wake...

His eyes snapped open again. Something was wrong. He could feel it, almost as if the wrongness was on the air itself and the danger was close at hand. And he'd not been dreaming.

As quietly as he could, he disentangled himself from Taha'Leeth and reached down for his sword. His hand found the hilt, and as it did, the tingle ran through him as a rush of intense power. The darkness in the tent lightened a tad and his exhaustion fled, as if it had never been.

He felt alive, alert, and fully awake. The last vestiges of sleep had been thrust aside. He had no time to marvel, for he sensed movement inside the tent. Someone was close.

Stiger ripped the sword free of the scabbard and it exploded into blue flame. He swung back around, jostling Taha'Leeth as he did it. She protested indignantly.

Danger...

The sword hissed the word in his mind, and with it, Stiger saw three figures inside his tent moving toward them. They had swords drawn. There was no time. He roughly shoved Taha'Leeth off the cot. She cried out and landed hard on the rug-covered ground.

A sword plunged into the cot where she'd been a heartbeat before and inches from his stomach. Stiger swung and cut down with his sword on the assassin's arm with all his strength. The blade flared with fire, slicing cleanly through the arm as if it were hot butter. The blade sizzled loudly. Stiger felt the hilt grow warm in his hand. Like a puppet with its strings cut, the attacker immediately dropped.

He threw his blanket aside and rolled off the cot and into a crouch, attempting to protect Taha'Leeth. Instead, he tripped over her as she worked to get up. Stiger nearly went down himself.

One of the assassins rushed him. Stiger ducked a sword strike that came lightning fast for his head. He brought his sword up and blocked. The tent rang with the clash of steel. He counter-jabbed.

With reflexes that were incredible, the attacker dodged backward and away. Outside, Stiger could hear the harsh clash of swords and the cry of alarm. He stabbed out again. The attacker blocked, and steel rang once again inside the tent. In the cold air, the repeated blows stung his hand painfully. Stiger paid it no mind and blocked another strike.

Then Taha'Leeth was on her feet and struggling with the other assailant. Out of the corner of his eye, he saw her grappling desperately with her opponent. She was weaponless. He was not.

Stiger had no more time for thought. His own opponent lunged forward, launching a flurry of strikes. Stiger blocked them, grudgingly giving ground, his sword licking blue flame on the air as he swung it about in a desperate bid to keep the enemy's blade away.

Stiger backed into the table that had been at the foot of his cot, knocking it over, and almost fell. There was a crack and a sudden flaring of light within the tent as the lamp shattered. The spilled oil caught fire. Stiger felt the heat of the flame close against his back.

At that moment, Taha'Leeth cried out in terrible agony. He knew with chilling certainty she'd been wounded. His rage surged. The sword exploded brilliantly. Combined with the fire from the lamp, the tent was fully lit in an almost blinding light. Startled, Stiger's attacker drew back a pace, shielding his eyes from the sudden brightness.

"Sovereign," a voice in Elven gasped. There was horror in it. "Forgive me."

"Garen'Teh." Taha'Leeth's voice was strained and barely audible. She seemed just as stunned. "Why?"

Stiger's opponent looked over in absolute horror at Taha'Leeth. Enraged beyond measure, Stiger lunged forward, jabbing his opponent in the chest. His sword sank deeply, and easily, sizzling as it went in. The attacker dropped to the ground, stone-dead, his life force stolen by Rarokan. The blood boiled off the blade as it came free. Outside the tent, the sound of fighting intensified and, along with it, there was a vicious growling that could only have come from Dog.

Rage beating within his breast, Stiger turned for the last assassin and found him on the floor. He'd dropped his sword and was cradling Taha'Leeth in his arms gently, as if he were holding a baby. Tears were in his eyes and streamed down his cheeks. Stiger stumbled to a stop and realized with shock the assassin was an elf.

He glanced at the other two who he'd killed. They also were elves. The sword dimmed, the flames licking along the blade growing smaller as his rage and anger retreated. Then, he saw the dagger sticking out of Taha'Leeth's right shoulder and the blood soaking the rug under her, turning it a dark color. The heat returned in a terrible fury. With it, the blade surged in power, the blue flames growing intense. He advanced.

"No." Taha'Leeth held her hand out toward him. Her voice was strained and the hand shook, trembling feebly. Stiger stopped. "No. Do not kill him. I beg you. He serves me."

"Serves you," Stiger growled. "He just tried to kill you."

"Forgive me, Sovereign," Garen'Teh begged, fairly sobbing over her. "I did not know it was you. I swear it. We were sent to kill the human leader named Stiger. We did not know you were here."

Outside the tent, the fighting died off. Dog burst through the entrance flap. His hair stood on end and his muzzle was bloody. He bared his teeth at the elf, gore dripping to the rug, and growled in a menacing tone that promised blood.

"Dog," Stiger snapped. "Hold."

The growling ceased.

Sensing the threat was over, Stiger shoved the elf aside and knelt beside Taha'Leeth. The dagger had cut deep, but it had also opened a large gash around four inches long. He could see exposed bone. She was bleeding badly, so much so that the blood-soaked rug wet his knees. Her eyes on him, she reached up a trembling hand and caressed his cheek tenderly. Her touch was cold, chill, and it frightened Stiger more than he cared to admit.

"My love." Taha'Leeth's voice was weak. She struggled to draw a breath. It rattled in her throat. She glanced over at Garen'Teh. "Do...not...blame him."

"No," Stiger said, feeling a terrible dread steal over him. "No...no...no!"

Men rushed into the tent, along with Ruga. Two legionaries, each gripping an arm, dragged Garen'Teh back and away as Dog nosed his way forward to Taha'Leeth. He whined. Her eyes shifted to the sad-looking animal and she smiled faintly.

"Naverum...look after...him," Taha'Leeth whispered to Dog.

Dog gave a whine.

"Sir, are you all right?" Ruga asked, then he saw Taha'Leeth. He turned to one of his men. "Send for a surgeon. Hurry, man."

The soldier raced out of the tent.

Taha'Leeth struggled to suck in a breath and coughed, spitting up blood. She was incredibly pale. Stiger wiped the blood away from her lips. She was cold to his touch. He felt desperate to help her, to get the dagger out.

"I fear I am leaving you, my love," Taha'Leeth whispered.

"No," Stiger said. He could tell the strength was failing her. "Don't talk like that. A surgeon is on the way."

"I want to stay." Taha'Leeth began shivering. "But I feel…"

"You are not dying on me," Stiger said insistently as he took hold of the dagger. "This is going to hurt, but I need to put pressure on the wound and try to stop the bleeding. I can't do that with the dagger in. Do you understand?"

She gave a weak nod and then her eyes fluttered closed as she lost consciousness. Stiger, as gently as he could and doing his best to not cause more damage, removed the blade. Blood fountained up, shocking him with the amount of it. He put his palm on the wound and pressed hard, attempting to stanch the flow.

With his other hand, he checked her pulse and found it weakening, for she did not seem to be breathing. He leaned forward, placing his cheek to her lips, and found her breathing shallow and barely perceptible.

"No!" Stiger shouted. Tears of loss pricked his eyes. She was slipping away from him. He looked over at Ruga, who was gazing back with raw grief in his eyes. "Where is that surgeon?"

"He's coming, sir."

"Well, make him come faster." Stiger turned back to Taha'Leeth. "Not again. Oh, please…not again."

Stiger pressed down harder on the wound. Desperate, he recalled what had happened with Therik in Forkham's

Valley. He had helped Father Thomas heal the former king. Could he do it on his own? He did not know, but there was only one way to find out. Closing his eyes, he reached out.

"High Father," Stiger called in desperation, "help me heal her, please."

Stiger felt the fire within him that was his connection with the High Father grow white hot. It burned and surged through his hand keeping pressure on the wound and into her. Taha'Leeth gasped and her eyes opened, looking wildly about. She arched her back, as if in incredible pain, and cried out. Then, inexplicably, the power left him as quickly as it had come. She went limp.

"No," Stiger said, knowing the surge in power was not enough to fully heal. "That can't be it. Give me more. Please, I beg you."

Inexplicably, there was no response. He removed his hand and saw the wound was still there, but the blood wasn't flowing as badly. She was very pale. Had he done anything to help? Or was it that she'd simply bled out too much? He'd not healed her, that was for sure, but he prayed that perhaps whatever had been done had been enough. Stiger felt helpless. He did not know quite what to do.

"Sir," Ruga said, shaking him by the shoulder. "The tent's on fire. We need to get out of here."

Stiger looked up and around. The back wall of the tent was fully engulfed in flame and the tent was filling with smoke. The heat from the blaze was intense. It would only be moments before the entire tent was afire.

Ruga sheathed his sword and reached down, removing Stiger's hands. Stiger resisted at first, but the centurion was firm. "Let me have her, sir. I will remove her from the tent.

I'll take good care of her, sir. I promise. I will get her right to the surgeon."

Stiger gave a miserable nod. Ruga scooped Taha'Leeth up into his arms and swiftly carried her from the tent. Stiger stood and picked up his sword from where he dropped it. The old familiar tingle raced up his arm. Dog, to his side, gave a whine and nudged Stiger's arm with his head, as if to say it was time to go.

Two men were still in the tent with him, looking nervously at the growing fire. The smoke was becoming thick and choking. Stiger calmly went over to his cot, retrieved the lacquered scabbard, and sheathed the sword. Though he acted calm, he felt no such thing. Anger, rage, and utter shock at what had happened warred within him. It did not seem quite real. He stepped to his overturned cot and reached down, retrieving his boots.

"Grab my armor, cloak and helmet." Stiger's voice was harsh. "And get out of the bloody tent before it burns down around us."

"Yes, sir," one of the men said and the two of them did as ordered.

They ducked out of the tent, with Stiger following. Outside, the air was fresh and cold. It was almost a shock, for the tent had grown hot from the fire. There were armed men everywhere, along with several bodies lying haphazardly about. Stiger counted six of his personal guard down. They were dead. The sight of them sickened him and kept the anger burning.

Two others were wounded. These men were being treated by several legionaries. One of the two had taken a bad leg wound. A tourniquet was being tied around the thigh. He was crying out in pain as the work was done.

Stiger saw two additional bodies. Both were elves and they, too, were dead. One had been badly mauled, likely Dog's work. The elves were dressed as rangers and had clearly not gone down easily. Garen'Teh and another elf, who was injured, were under guard. The sight of the prisoners fueled Stiger's rage to the point where it demanded blood.

Then he spotted Taha'Leeth. She had been laid on the ground, ten yards from the burning tent. A surgeon was kneeling next to her, examining her wound, as was Venthus. They had removed her tunic. The surgeon directed an assistant to put pressure on the wound while he reached in a leather bag for a bandage. Stiger moved over, watching helplessly as the surgeon began bandaging the wound.

"How is she?" Stiger asked.

"Difficult to tell, sir," the surgeon said. "I've never worked on an elf before and she's lost quite a lot of blood. But she's still breathing."

"She's carrying my child," Stiger said.

"Ah...yes, sir," the surgeon said with a quick glance up before returning to the task at hand. "I will do all that I can."

Venthus stood. "I will go with him, master. I too will do all I can to help. You have my word on that."

Stiger gave a nod and found himself more assured by Venthus's presence than the surgeon's. Two men arrived carrying a stretcher. He watched as Taha'Leeth was gently lifted onto the stretcher.

Behind him, his tent burned furiously. Salt and Eli appeared, both looking like they had been freshly woken. Eli came to a stop at the sight of the elves. Then his friend saw Taha'Leeth and he froze. Salt continued up to Stiger.

"Are you all right, sir?" Salt asked. The prefect began examining Stiger, checking for injury. Stiger glanced down and saw that his arms, chest, and legs were covered in blood.

"None of the blood's mine," Stiger assured the prefect. "It's all Taha'Leeth's."

"Yes, sir," Salt said. He glanced around at her. "I am sure the surgeon will do all that can be done."

Stiger said nothing as he watched them carry Taha'Leeth away, with Venthus following closely after.

"I don't know how they got in without being seen," Salt said as his eyes fell upon the prisoners. "I just don't."

"They are elven rangers." Stiger's anger returned and it surged like a terrible storm. It was an effort to keep it contained. His gaze shifted to the prisoners. "What is difficult for us is doable for them."

Eli stepped nearer.

"I am sorry," Eli said and rested a hand upon Stiger's shoulder. There were tears in his eyes. "Truly."

"So am I," Stiger said, feeling the anger give way to gut-wrenching grief. Anger returned a heartbeat later. He turned around toward the prisoners. Eli followed his look.

"Her people, I presume?" Eli said.

Stiger did not bother to respond. Instead, he walked over to the two prisoners. Eli followed as someone called urgently for Salt's attention.

Weapons drawn, six guards stood around the prisoners. One of the prisoners was wounded on his right arm and he had a nasty bruise forming on the right temple. Both elves had their arms tied behind their backs and had been forced to kneel on the ground. They silently watched him approach. Garen'Teh looked miserable. Stiger did not feel sorry for him, not in the slightest.

"Why would you do this?" Stiger asked them in Elven. "Why? When she pledged your people to our cause?"

Both elves shared a look.

"It is true," Eli said. "Your people are freed. No longer are you slaves. This is the work of Tanithe."

"You are not of our people," Garen'Teh said. It was more of a statement than an accusation.

"But I am," Aver'Mons said as he stepped up to them. "Eli'Far speaks the truth."

"Aver'Mons," Garen'Teh said. "How?"

"The sovereign sent messengers back," Aver'Mons said, "to bring our people north and quit serving the Cyphan. Why did you not come when she called?"

"We did not know," Garen'Teh said, anguish plain in his voice. "I tell you. No such word reached us."

"We heard nothing," the other elf said. "We were told only that the sovereign had gone with the army to Vrell and that contact had been lost."

Stiger's anger was burning hot. He was looking for an excuse to kill the prisoners, but in truth Garen'Teh was making it hard. The rational part of Stiger's mind knew that no amount of killing would save Taha'Leeth at this point. It likely wouldn't make him feel better either. The gut-wrenching feeling returned. He was losing the woman he loved and these elves were the cause of it. Despite that, he felt himself scowl, the scar on his cheek pulling tight. He looked over at Aver'Mons. "Is that possible?"

"Anything is possible," the elf responded.

"Who sent you?" Stiger asked.

"Veers," Aver'Mons said, "didn't he?"

Garen'Teh nodded. "It is as you say. The overlord sent us. We were to murder the leadership of this army. We have been watching you for the last few days as you marched north, learning all that we could."

Stiger grew cold. They weren't just targeting him. He turned and looked back at Salt, who was speaking with a messenger. The man was one of Hux's troopers.

"Veers is an overlord," Aver'Mons said. "He is a direct servant of Valoor, much like you are of the High Father."

Stiger's thoughts raced as he barely listened to Aver'Mons. Tenya'Far and Braddock were at risk.

"Salt," Stiger called.

The prefect looked over.

"Send word to Braddock and Tenya'Far as soon as you can. Warn them of a possible attack, like this one."

"Aye, sir," Salt said, though Stiger thought the camp prefect appeared distracted as he listened to the messenger. "Soon as I am done here, sir."

"It is too late," Garen'Teh said, drawing Stiger's attention. "They will have struck by now. We were to hit all three camps simultaneously."

"You would kill your own?" Eli hissed. "You would kill fellow elves? That is prohibited by Tanithe. Have you no shame?"

"No longer," came the reply from the wounded elf. "What shame we had was stripped from us when we became enslaved. Though we regret doing so, we will kill kin. We live to serve."

"Even now?" Aver'Mons asked bitterly. "After you've heard the truth. Even now do you serve?"

There was a long moment of silence, then Garen'Teh shook his head. "No longer. But my life is forfeit for injuring the sovereign."

"Sir," Salt said, stepping over and drawing Stiger away a few paces. Eli joined them. Salt lowered his voice. "You need to read this, sir. It just came in." Salt held a dispatch in his hand, which he handed over. The camp prefect did not wait for Stiger to start reading. "The enemy never stopped for the night. They continued marching, sir. Enemy cavalry is less than five miles away. Come morning, the entire enemy army will be knocking on our door."

Stiger began reading, feeling numb at what was happening. Taha'Leeth had likely been dealt a mortal wound. Now he was faced with the enemy arriving on their doorstep, just hours from now. Worse, the army wasn't concentrated yet.

"What time is it?" Stiger asked.

"A little after three bells, sir," Salt said. "Even if Menos can keep the enemy's dragons off us, we're gonna bear the brunt of any fighting. That is, until the rest of the army can come up. We're in trouble."

"Agreed," Stiger said and thought for a long moment. The enemy wanted a fight. So be it. He would give them one. He'd made his decision. They would fight. "Wake the legion. Let's get the men fed, with a hot meal in their bellies, and by dawn be prepared for battle." Stiger paused. "There is a small rise a quarter mile north of us. It's almost tall enough to be a ridge. I saw it yesterday afternoon, while I was riding around the perimeter. It is the best ground around for miles. The road cuts right through it. We will form the legion up behind the rise and just out of view. Understand?"

"Yes, sir."

"What should we do with them?" Salt asked and gestured at the two prisoners.

Stiger turned his attention back to the two elves. He could feel the power surging from the sword, the anger and hate flowing forth almost like a tangible thing. The intensity of it was surprising.

Feed them to me... I hunger.

Stiger took a deep breath. It seemed Rarokan was not as dead as he'd thought. The bond was just as strong as ever. *I am very much here, and before this day is done...there will be a great deal of killing. Feed me.*

"Sir?" Salt asked.

"Treat his wound." Stiger gestured at the injured elf. "Keep them under guard. If Taha'Leeth lives, she can decide their fate."

"And if she dies?" Eli asked.

"They will too."

TWENTY-ONE

S tiger sat on a stool before a low campfire. Eli had taken a seat on another stool, just across the fire from him. Dog was lying by Stiger's feet. The fire crackled softly, sending a thin trail of smoke swirling upward.

Though the temperature was above freezing, the day had dawned cold and was far from comfortable. Stiger glanced skyward sourly. Like a rumbling cavalry charge, thunder sounded off in the distance. Ominous storm clouds had moved in after daybreak, casting a darkened atmosphere over the world below. What with the assassination attempt, the day had already started out a miserable affair. Clearly, it seemed Fortuna had decided to make it worse.

Thunder grumbled again.

The heat from the fire drove the cold air back, just enough to warm hands and feet. Wrapped in his bearskin cloak, Stiger was moderately warm and comfortable. For the most part, he had been lost in his thoughts as he sat with Eli.

Two large open pavilions had been pitched ten yards away for his field headquarters. Men came and went at a determined pace, while the clerks worked diligently inside at camp tables.

Stiger's personal guard stood at a respectful distance. They had created a bubble around him. After the attempted assassination, Salt had doubled the legate's guard. Ruga's men, along with another century, looked grim-faced and ready for anything. Ruga stood with them.

Stiger needed a shave. The whiskers were beginning to itch, almost to distraction. He scratched at his neck.

The legion was forming up behind the rise where he intended to hold and give battle. The nearest formation was less than forty yards away. The process of forming up into a line of battle was time-consuming, and the legion had been at it for the past two hours.

The last cohorts were being guided into position by their officers and liaisons from headquarters. As each cohort moved into position in the order he and Salt had come up with, they began aligning and dressing themselves upon one another to create an unbroken line.

With banners and standards to the front, Stiger's cohorts looked sharp, almost as if they were on parade. Officers moved up and down the ranks, checking equipment and speaking with their men, doing their level best to prepare them for the coming battle.

The legion coming together was a grand sight, something that never failed to impress. Even with his worries about Taha'Leeth, Stiger could not help but feel a little awestruck at the force he commanded.

He picked up a stick from the ground and poked at the fire, shifting the logs around so they would better burn and perhaps shed more warmth. Sparks flew up into the air, but the blaze did not grow.

"Excuse me, sir."

Stiger looked up to find a messenger. "Camp Prefect Oney asked that I inform you the enemy's main body is less than a half mile distant. The enemy's cavalry is in sight. Ours are keeping theirs honest, sir."

"Does the prefect require my presence?" Stiger asked.

"No, sir," the messenger said. "He just asked me to pass along the report."

"Thank you," Stiger said. "Dismissed."

The messenger saluted and left.

"It won't be long now," Eli said.

"They will be here soon enough," Stiger said, "but that does not mean the battle will begin straight on. Likely we will do some standing around waiting on them."

Stiger glanced over at the legion once more. From one end to the other, his line of battle stretched out for almost a half mile. Several tents had been erected behind the center of the line. These were for the surgeons, doctors, and the inevitable flood of wounded.

With the weather looking like it would soon turn for the worse, Stiger had wanted to provide what comfort they could manage for the injured. Sadly, the few tents that had been set up would likely prove woefully inadequate.

Stiger's centurions were also under orders to allow no able-bodied man to help the wounded until after the fight had concluded. It was a harsh order, but it was necessary. The wounded would have to fend for themselves, for shortly, every sword would be needed.

Those unfortunate enough to become injured in the fighting would either wait until the battle was over, lying where they had fallen, or manage to get themselves back to the surgeons. Many would succumb to their injuries long before help could arrive. Stiger felt it disagreeable, but there was nothing to be done about it.

Since they had had some warning and the encampment was not far off, supplies of water and precooked rations had also been moved forward. There would be no telling how long they would be kept waiting by the enemy. The men could find themselves standing in battle formation for hours before any actual fighting began. That in and of itself was not only stressful, but tiring.

Having food and water available would help. At such a time, though many would likely find it difficult to eat, the centurions would see to it that they did.

Stiger rubbed at his tired eyes. He'd worked with Salt to lay out the line of battle, designate reserves, emplace the cavalry, and just generally strategize. There had been no time to dig fortifications. Had they bothered to do so, the terrain was so open, the enemy would easily be able to side-step them. Consequently, this would be a straight-up fight.

Messengers had been sent to the other camps, asking the dwarves and elves to march as soon as practical. By Stiger's estimation, those messengers should have already arrived. But there had not been time for them to return with word or news. With any luck, his allies were already marching to his aid.

Stiger dug up a tuft of winter-browned grass with his boot. He knew not whether Tenya'Far or Braddock lived. He hoped and prayed they did. If either had been assassinated, he did not know what effect that would have on their subordinates giving the order to march to his relief. What chaos would be caused by their demise? Would they hesitate? If they did, that could easily prove catastrophic to the legion's survival.

Thunder rumbled again, this time sounding a little closer.

"I thought this was supposed to be the dry season," Eli said. "Didn't you tell me that?"

"At least it won't be snow," Stiger said.

"Fighting a battle in the rain does not sound like much fun."

"Fighting a battle in any type of weather is no fun," Stiger said, "even on a breezy spring day. Killing is killing and it's an ugly business no matter the season."

Eli looked over at Stiger and tilted his head to the side. There was a concerned look to his eyes.

"Though we've never got on, I find myself worried for my father," Eli said.

"I am sure he's fine. I imagine sneaking into a legionary camp is one thing, doing the same to an elven encampment is something altogether different. It's Braddock I am concerned about."

"There is some truth to that," Eli said. "It bothers me that Taha'Leeth's people would willingly kill kin. I am having difficulty understanding."

"I understand only too well," Stiger said. "Humans have been killing each other for a long time."

"Not elves," Eli said, sounding slightly distressed. "It is one of the worst transgressions. Remember, we cherish life."

Stiger gave an absent nod. Though they cherished life, as Eli said, he knew elves to be extremely efficient killers. It had been a miracle Stiger had survived the assassination attempt. Had it not been for Rarokan's intervention, both he and Taha'Leeth would likely be dead.

He turned his gaze back to the fire and poked at it again with the stick. He was terribly worried about Taha'Leeth. Once he had received word the surgeon and Venthus were finished working on her, he'd stopped by the sick tents to get an update. They were unable to give him one, other than what they had done treatment-wise. Her wound had been cleaned, sown up, and bandaged.

When he'd seen her, she had been unconscious and terribly pale, a result of the loss of so much blood. Venthus had both insisted and assured him he would not leave her side until Stiger returned.

"Do what you must. No matter what happens," Venthus had said, "I will protect her life with my own."

There had been nothing for Stiger to do, nothing that could help anyway. So, he'd thrown himself into his work at preparing the legion for battle. Now that he'd done all that he could, Stiger had ordered a fire made for himself and Eli.

He'd thought about returning to the encampment and visiting Taha'Leeth, but then disregarded that idea. With the enemy so close at hand, he could not afford to leave the legion. He would not risk the potential effect it might have on morale.

In a few hours, there would be a battle. It was likely to be the most difficult and trying fight he had ever faced. The enemy had stolen a march and surprised him. That irritated Stiger.

They would be fighting by themselves. With the numbers he had on hand, he did not know if he could even hold long enough for reinforcement to arrive. It all depended on how long it took the enemy to fully bring their own army to bear upon him, or really when the actual fighting began.

It was in Stiger's advantage to delay the start of a battle. But he very much doubted they would wait that long before striking at him. His isolation was the reason they had stolen a march. The enemy general would be looking to take advantage of that.

If he confined himself to the defensive walls of the encampment, he would have difficulty coordinating with Braddock's dwarves when they arrived and, for that matter, linking up with him. The enemy might bottle the legion up with just enough combat power to make a breakout a costly affair.

He had thought about a withdrawal but had disregarded that idea. He felt he could not withdraw without affecting the morale of the legion. After weeks of marching, it might be viewed by the men as fleeing before the enemy. He could not have that.

No, he must stand and fight. His men were well trained and ready. They had seen what the Cyphan had done to the population of the South. And now, they knew what had happened to Taha'Leeth, how the enemy had struck in the dead of night with assassins. Getting past them and attacking their legate really stung the legion's pride. A pulse of simmering anger could be felt upon the line. In Stiger's estimation, the men wanted payback.

"We've come a long way," Eli said, looking up from the fire and breaking the long silence between them.

"All the way from Vrell," Stiger agreed.

"I meant you and I," Eli said. "We have seen a lot, done more than most."

"I did my best to keep things exciting for you. I think you might agree."

Eli pulled his canteen from his pack, which sat on the ground to his right. Next to the pack lay a leather-wrapped bundle of arrows and his bow. Eli unstopped the canteen and took a drink.

The elf swallowed a mouthful of water. "It helped pass the time."

Stiger gave a disbelieving grunt.

"I could use a little more excitement," Eli said, returning his gaze back to the flames as he set the canteen down on the ground next to his stool.

Stiger chuckled and found it felt good to laugh, just a little. The banter was an old game between them. Still, he knew his friend was attempting to distract him, to lighten his mood…if only for a little while. He was grateful for that and for Eli's company. Looking over at his friend, he realized that something remained unresolved between them.

"Eli"—Stiger cleared his throat—"I want to thank you."

"For what?" Eli asked, looking up from the fire.

"For your friendship," Stiger said, "for everything over the years…especially for what you did after my lashing. I would not be the man I am today without you."

Eli looked over at him with a funny, almost embarrassed expression.

"I should be the one thanking you," Eli said after a long moment.

"Oh?" That surprised Stiger.

"You have given my people hope," Eli said.

"Hope?" Stiger asked, confused. "How?"

"Yes, hope," Eli affirmed. "They may not realize it yet… but had you not taken up the mantle of the High Father, my people would still be sitting at home, shutting the world out. Even now, they would have been deliberately ignoring all that goes on, pretending our forests were all that mattered. Because of you, the warden felt compelled to act. Now, we are once again an active participant in events. It's hard to ignore things that way."

Stiger said nothing for a long moment as he absorbed what Eli had just told him. He decided he would refuse to be deterred or sidetracked. "I meant what I said, Eli. I owe you a great deal."

"You do." Eli flashed him a grin. "You can pay me back with a little more excitement, okay?"

"Excitement," Stiger said, "is something I've never craved. I believe I have told you that on more than one occasion."

"You say that," Eli said, "but we both know that's not true. Otherwise you would have gone into another profession, like basket weaving or something."

Stiger laughed again, then sobered. "You know, I almost became a farmer."

Dog picked his head up and growled softly. Stiger glanced over to see someone was approaching. He stiffened as he realized who it was. Eli followed his gaze and hastily stood. Stiger's guard moved to stop the newcomer, a woman.

"It's all right," Stiger called, before there could be an issue. "Let her through."

The guards moved aside. Stiger came to his feet. As she approached their fire, Eli bowed respectfully to the woman, who was in the prime of her life. She was tall and very attractive. She had a regal bearing and wore a shimmering silver dress that seemed out of place on such a dreary day.

Her hair was silver, perhaps almost with a metallic cast to it. With her almond-shaped eyes, pointed ears, and the vigor of youthfulness without aging, she had the look of an elf, but Stiger knew she was anything but.

She was so graceful, she seemed to glide toward them, her long dress whispering softly over the winter-browned grass. Stiger had once before seen her in this form. But he had not expected to see her again so soon.

"Currose," Stiger greeted, "it is good to see you well. I thought you were injured and had decided to remain in Old City."

The noctalum came to a stop before them and brought the palm of her hand to her stomach. "I am still healing, inside. It will be many months before I fully recover. Still, despite his objections, I could not leave my mate to face what he will this day. Even in a weakened state I had to come. You understand this, yes?"

"I do," Stiger said and then beckoned toward a free stool. "Would you care to join us and share our fire?"

"Thank you," Currose said, stepping up to the fire. "That is quite gracious of you." She held out her hands and warmed them over the fire. "When I take this form, I always feel chilled. How do you stay warm wearing only a tunic and cloak, let alone something as flimsy as this dress?"

"I suppose," Stiger said, thinking it was a good question, "you sort of get used to it."

"I don't see how," Currose said.

"Stay in that form long enough and you might just begin to understand," Eli said.

"I don't believe I care to," Currose replied as she rubbed her hands together before the fire. "It takes effort to maintain this form and, as I said, it's terribly uncomfortable. Besides, I've never much enjoyed shape-shifting, not like my mate, who loves to wander and meddle with mortals." She shot Stiger a meaningful look. "Over the long years, such behavior has led to a problem or two."

"You cannot still blame me for that," Stiger said. "The whole thing with the volcano was hardly my fault."

"So you and my mate keep telling me," Currose said. "However, I wasn't referring to that specific incident."

"Oh," Stiger said, "right."

Raising a delicate eyebrow, Currose took a seat on the free stool, sitting between the two of them. Eli looked from her to Stiger with extreme curiosity as he sat down too. Stiger returned to his stool.

"What of the World Gate?" Stiger asked, hoping to change the subject. Eli had no business knowing the history Currose was hinting at. It would require an explanation of events he was unwilling to go into. Thoggle had specifically warned him against doing so.

"What of it?" Currose leaned forward toward the fire and held out her hands again. "The World Gate is useless to anyone now. There's not a wizard on this world with the stored *Will* required to open or manipulate it...not anymore. The only way that Gate is opening is with the Key. And then, the doorway to Tanis cannot be unlocked for some months to come. With the dwarves guarding the Gate, I feel it perfectly safe."

Stiger was not too sure about that, but he did not feel like contradicting her. On the eve of battle, this was no time for a disagreement. What was done, was done. He would address it later.

"I did leave a few, shall we say, surprises behind," Currose said, "in the event I am mistaken in my assumptions."

"Surprises?" Eli asked.

"Nasty surprises," Currose said and then looked back to Stiger. "Besides, even in my weakened state, you have greater need for me here this day, considering all that you face."

"I cannot disagree with that," Stiger said. "I think before all is said and done, I will need all the help I can get."

"I, for one," Eli said, "am grateful for your presence, noble lady."

Currose gave a slight nod of her head. She turned her attention to Dog, who was looking at her. She studied him for a moment, then turned back to Stiger.

"I see you've kept that ragged pet of yours," Currose said.

"You know as well as I, he is no pet," Stiger said.

Currose gave an amused grunt. Dog, as if bored, lay back down again and rolled onto his side.

"I have seen Taha'Leeth," Currose said. "Before coming to see you, I visited the sick tent."

Stiger sat up straight.

"Venthus is with her. But I am certain you already know that. He and the surgeon did what they could," Currose said. "She is not out of danger…yet…but that elf is strong. Her *Will* is very powerful…very powerful. This is no promise, but I believe she will recover." The noctalum paused, as if thinking on what she wanted to say next. "I did not want to alarm them with my presence. Your surgeons thought I was one of their assistants. To improve her chances at survival, I lent her some of my own *Will*. It should be enough to see her through the worst of it."

Stiger let out a relieved breath, intensely grateful. He had not expected this from Currose. She'd always been cool to him, cold even. "I…I don't know how to thank you."

"You can thank me by seeing this mess through to the end," Currose said. "My small efforts will mean little to her life if you are not successful in this confrontation."

Stiger gave a nod. "I thank you just the same. She has become quite important to me."

"I did not understand why you kept that black paladin around," Currose said, changing the subject. "I was quite opposed to it."

Eli looked over at Stiger. It was clear he was wondering who Currose was referring to. Stiger had no intention of telling him. That also was something Thoggle had cautioned him about.

"And now?" Stiger asked. She fully had his attention. It had been a bone of contention between them before he went into stasis.

"Now, I do," Currose said. "That does not mean I approve, but I understand."

"I figured as much," Stiger said.

They fell into an uncomfortable silence.

"Taha'Leeth is expecting," Stiger said after a few heartbeats.

"I know," Currose said. "This is another reason why I came."

Stiger hesitated before asking what he badly wished to know. He was almost afraid to ask. A feeling of dread settled over him. "Will the baby survive?"

"That is difficult to say," Currose said. "Taha'Leeth was gravely injured. She lost a great deal of blood and that may have affected the baby. Only time will tell. If it is meant to be, it will be. If not..."

Stiger turned his gaze into the fire, feeling wretched. His thoughts shifted to the future. A baby had been part of that future. He poked almost despondently at the fire with the stick, sending a shower of sparks up into the air.

"They will keep coming," Stiger said, "and won't stop."

"Unless they are stopped first," Currose said. "That is the struggle and why we are here. Their objective is the end game, control of the Gate. They will do anything to achieve that goal...anything. There are times we must do the same, no matter how distasteful."

"I understand," Stiger said.

"Do you?"

"I do," Stiger said, and then something occurred to him. "Menos sent you, didn't he?"

"He did."

"Where is he?"

"Nearby," Currose said, "and waiting."

"With the Vass and other dragons?" Stiger asked.

"Yes," Currose said. "When the time comes, we shall be ready. You need not concern yourself with the enemy's wyrms. I assure you, they will have other things to focus on than your army."

"Good," Stiger said.

"I thought you would be pleased with that news," Currose said.

"I am very pleased. Now, I just need to figure out how to hold until reinforcement arrives. Heck, I don't even know if they are coming."

"They are," Currose said. "Menos asked me to pass that along. The dwarves and elves are marching."

"He's sure?" Stiger felt immense relief at hearing that. "But will they get here in time?"

"He's sure, yes. He sent one of the taltalum to see," Currose said. "Whether or not they arrive in time to save your legion, I do not know."

TWENTY-TWO

Stiger ducked out of his headquarters tent and strode over to Beck, the legion's Eagle-bearer. Beck had been standing with the Eagle and its accompanying guard, just off to the side of the field headquarters. On Stiger's orders, Beck had been waiting for him. Eli followed a few steps after, as did Dog. Stiger's personal guard, who had been waiting outside headquarters, fell in around him, creating a protective bubble.

Legionary standard-bearers usually were issued a wolf's pelt, but one had not been available. However, Beck was now wearing a tiger's pelt. The day before he'd not had it.

"There's something different about you, Beck," Stiger said, glancing over at the Eagle guard. An entire century from First Cohort had the honor of protecting the Eagle. Each man was a hard-charging veteran, willing to readily sacrifice their own lives in defense of the Eagle. The Eagle represented not only the legion's honor, but the empire's as well.

"Can't imagine what that is, sir," Beck replied with a straight face. He absently straightened the tiger pelt, of which the tiger's face sat over his helmet.

"Where'd you get that?" Stiger asked. It wasn't the Eighty-Fifth's tiger pelt. Stiger's old company was formed up with First Cohort less than twenty yards away as his reserve. He could see the company's standard, still draped with the tiger pelt that had adorned Captain Aveeno's throne in Castle Vrell.

"One of the dwarves delivered it," Beck answered. "Said it was a gift from Thane Braddock. Somehow the Thane found out about our tradition. He did not have a wolf pelt, but he did have a tiger's pelt and sent it over. It arrived last night and the camp prefect gave it to me, sir."

"Might as well call the Thirteenth the Tiger's Legion," Eli said.

Stiger shot his friend a scowl.

"I already have a company named after me," Stiger said. "I don't think I need to add a legion to that."

"Do you approve, sir?" Beck asked. It was clear he was exceptionally proud of the new pelt, as it distinguished him from the rest of the legion. The post of bearing the legion's honor was an important one, and the pelt was more than appropriate in Stiger's estimation.

"I do," Stiger said, then sobered and got down to business. "After I deploy the legion, you stick with me today. Wherever I go, you go too, unless I tell you otherwise. It is going to be a hard day. The men must see me with the Eagle. Even if I go forward to fight, you follow. Our example will give the rest of the legion courage. Understand?"

"Yes, sir." Beck tightened his grip on the staff. "I will be right there with you, sir, and I won't let anything happen to the Eagle."

"Good." With one more glance at the tiger's pelt, he turned away toward a group of the legion's senior officers who were clustered about Salt. Stiger had asked that his senior officers be assembled. He had wanted to address them personally, before the battle began. Therik also stood with the officers.

He started over, leaving Beck behind. Eli and Dog went with him. From his officers, as he neared, Stiger sensed the grim tension that was common on the eve of battle. It was born of the uncertainty of what the next few hours would bring. He felt it himself, as did everyone else in the legion to one degree or another.

"Sir," Salt said as he joined them. The camp prefect offered a smart salute for the gathered officers. "As requested, they're all here, sir."

Stiger motioned for the officers to gather around him. They did so in a half-circle, Therik amongst them. Unlike the others, the orc looked eager for what was coming.

"Gentlemen," Stiger said, "the enemy is just over that rise, about a quarter mile distant. As we speak, they are forming a line of battle. Only a portion of their army has arrived. In a few moments, we will deploy the legion to the top of the rise, hill, whatever you want to call it. That rise is ours. It belongs to us and will remain imperial property. We own it. The enemy wants to take it from us. Under no circumstances will they dislodge us from the summit. Is that understood?"

"Yes, sir," came the unified chorus from his senior officers.

He paused, meeting their gazes. It was important he projected confidence, strength, and a sense that he was in control. They would feed off that.

"Last night," Stiger said, "the enemy struck in a cowardly manner. They did so to kill me, because they have doubts about the outcome of the coming battle. That said, they stole a march on us, and now our allies are marching to our aid. They will arrive over the next few hours. When exactly, I do not know. But they are coming. That's what matters. So, we will hold until they get here…we must hold, gentlemen…and in doing so, we will make those bastards out there bleed. They will pay a steep price for testing our lines. We will hold until the rest of our army arrives. Then we will throw them back. That is our job this day, and make no mistake…it will be a hard one."

"We will hold, sir," Salt said.

"Aye, sir," Nantus added firmly. "We will be immovable as a stone wall."

"You can count on First Cohort, sir," Sabinus said, glancing around at the cohort commanders, "just as I am sure you can rely on the rest of the legion."

"I know I can," Stiger said, and he knew it to be true. His officers and men would give it their all. "The last few weeks have been grueling to say the least. The march getting here has been hard and long, with few breaks. I am proud of each of you and of the legion. I feel blessed to have your trust and I am personally honored to lead you."

A distant massed cheer reached them. Stiger turned toward the rise, just yards away. From its top, he could see cavalry scouts, whose job it was to watch the enemy. The shout had come from that direction. The rise wasn't much, but it meant he and his men would have the good ground.

"Gentlemen," Stiger said as a second massed cheer rang on the air, "the enemy seems to be in fine spirits. If there were any doubts amongst you, it appears we're going to have a fight today."

The group chuckled politely. It was a poor jest, but at times like this, any attempt at levity was generally welcomed.

"You have your orders. I just want to add a few things and then get you right back to your cohorts. Once we move the legion forward, have your men stand easy until otherwise ordered. They can even take a load off and sit. There is no telling how long the enemy will make us wait before they decide to give battle."

"That's the army, sir," Katurus said, "always waiting for someone else to do their job, just so you can do yours."

There was another round of chuckling. It wasn't the first time Stiger had heard such sentiments. Waiting was part of every legionary's life, whether that be officer or enlisted.

"While the men wait," Stiger continued, "make sure at some point your boys eat and stay watered. As the day wears on, be sure, if circumstances permit, to take advantage of the water and food stores that have been moved up."

Thunder rumbled loudly, much closer than before. It was as if the gods were grumbling their discontent. Stiger wondered if it was a bad omen. He hoped not.

"I don't think keeping them watered will be a problem, sir," Quintus said with a glance skyward. "We're all gonna be wet in short order."

"Likely so," Stiger said and then returned to the matter at hand. "The enemy's marched through the night. They are tired and in need of rest. At best, they have precooked rations; at worst, they have none and perhaps little water. Our men will be going into battle both fed and rested." Stiger pointed toward the rise. "That said, when their entire army deploys, we will be seriously outnumbered." There was some shifting of feet at that. "That's not the worst of it. They also have dragons."

The officers shared concerned looks. All of them had seen at least one dragon in action. He doubted any would ever forget that.

"You all saw the battle site and what happened to the emperor's legions," Stiger said. "They were burned down where they stood. Our enemy surprised the legions with a weapon they were unprepared to face and counter. That will not be happening with us."

Stiger paused, once again taking the time to meet the gazes of his senior officers before continuing.

"We have dragons, too," Stiger said.

That caused a stir.

"We do, sir?" Vargus asked. "As in more than one?"

"More than one," Stiger said. "Sian Tane has brought more than enough friends to neutralize the enemy's dragons and keep them off us. But that still does not mean the fight ahead will be an easy one. We cannot count on any help from our dragons in defeating the enemy's soldiers. We will have to defeat that army out there the old-fashioned way, with sword, spear, and shield."

"Excuse me, sir," Nantus said, "but where are our dragons? I don't see them."

"Hidden just out of view," Stiger said. "When we need them, they will come. Count on that. You must make sure the men know the enemy's dragons should not pose a threat to us. When they appear, we must maintain not only the integrity of our line, but also our discipline. We cannot afford a general panic. If one formation breaks and runs, it will prove our undoing. You need to understand that and so do your junior officers. No matter what, we must keep good order, even if you must kill a man who loses his head as an example to others."

There were grim and hard looks from his officers at that. Sometimes such examples had to be made. Usually they occurred during desperate moments, such as in the heat of battle. That they happened did not mean anyone had to enjoy it. But all present understood the necessity of maintaining discipline.

"Without discipline," Salt said, his tone hard as rock, "the legion is nothing. Do what you think best."

Thunder rumbled again. Stiger felt a raindrop on his arm.

"We lose this battle," Stiger said, "and it could mean the end of the empire. We must hold until our allies arrive. When our entire army is up and online, we will have the advantage in numbers. Until then, make no mistake, this will be a difficult and desperate fight. Discipline, grit, order, and maintaining the line will see us through the day."

"Sir," Nantus asked, "where will you be, in the event we need you?"

"Look for the Eagle," Stiger said, pointing at Beck. "Wherever that Eagle is on the field, I will be there. Should you have need for any reason, send word immediately." Stiger paused again as Nantus nodded his understanding. "Any questions so far?"

No one voiced any.

"Very good." Stiger paused again and looked around the assembled officers. He felt a fondness for them, almost as a father would for his children. "This legion and her auxiliary cohorts are the best the empire has to offer. Each of you are its beating heart. Without your direction and leadership, the legion would be nothing. You set the example by which your men will follow. Always remember that."

Stiger fell silent for a prolonged moment to allow that to sink in.

"Before the sun sets, the Cyphan will learn the truth of how tough an imperial legion can be." Stiger paused as he swung his gaze around his gathered officers. "Now, gentlemen, see to your commands, and good luck."

The officers saluted and broke up. Sabinus remained behind with Salt and Eli. So too did Therik. The orc was wearing the armor that had been made for him. Though it sort of looked like legionary armor, he still stuck out like a sore thumb.

"Good speech," Therik said. "You brought a tear to my eye."

Ignoring the orc, Stiger looked over at his primus pilus in question, wondering why he'd remained.

"Sir," Sabinus said, without any preamble, "may I ask why First Cohort does not have a place on the line? Why are we in reserve? I would think the auxiliary cohorts would be better suited for that task."

Stiger knew that he should have expected this conversation. First Cohort was the go-to cohort for the legion. It had the highest ratio of long-service veterans. Not only that, the cohort was double the strength of the other formations. When he needed to plug a hole, pull a cohort back to rest, or reinforce a section of the line, the First would likely get the job, followed by the Eighty-Fifth.

"Sabinus," Stiger said, "this is likely to be a very hard and protracted fight. I know I will need my best at some point. That is why you are in reserve. I can't afford to have your boys used up and spent when I need them most. Wherever the greatest need will be...that is where you will be going. That's why I am holding you and the Eighty-Fifth in reserve. Understand?"

"Yes, sir, I do," Sabinus said and gave a firm nod. "Thank you for the explanation, sir."

"Good," Stiger said, "tell your boys that, will you? Make sure they understand and they're ready when I call upon them."

"I will, sir, and we will be ready for your call." Sabinus saluted.

Stiger returned the salute and then held out his hand to the centurion. "Good luck."

"Thank you, and good luck to you too, sir." Sabinus shook firmly and then moved off.

Stiger turned to Salt, but as he did, pounding hooves drew his attention. One of the scouts was racing down the rise, his horse tearing up chunks of the browned grass as he made a beeline for Stiger.

"Sir." The trooper saluted as he hastily pulled his horse to a stop. "The enemy is moving forward two formations. It looks like they mean to take the rise. The rest of their line is staying put."

"Salt," Stiger said, turning to the prefect, "it's time. Sound the call to form up."

"Yes, sir." Salt looked over to a legionary who had been standing a few feet off with a horn. "You heard the legate. Blow the call to form up."

The legionary brought the horn to his lips and blew the call. As he blew the horn a second time, it began to rain in a steady drizzle. It was as if the horn call had given the sky permission to let loose. Stiger glanced up at the sky unhappily. The clouds above were thick and angry-looking.

Almost immediately after the second call ceased, officers across the legion began shouting for their men to pull themselves together and form up into ranks.

"Eli," Stiger said, "let's go see the enemy, shall we?"

"After you," Eli said, then grinned at Stiger, suddenly very pleased with himself. He held out a hand, palm upward, in the direction of the rise. "Be my guest."

Stiger was about to turn away, but then stopped and looked back at his friend.

"How long have you been saving that one?"

"Since Larensus," Eli admitted.

"Outside that tavern?" Stiger asked, thinking back. "What was that place called again?"

"The Nag," Eli said.

Stiger recalled the tavern's owners, the Powels, and their little girl. Her name was Adera and she'd been a thin wisp of a girl with a threadbare dress. Stiger remembered her as a kind soul. He decided she must not be so little these days, for that had been over ten years back.

It seemed like a different lifetime, almost. He'd been through so much since then, but what had occurred in Larensus with Prefect Hans, one of Avaya's servants, had proven to be a dark foretoken of what was to come. Only, back then he'd not known it yet.

"Well," Stiger said, "I think we left that town a better place than how we found it."

"We did some good," Eli said.

"That we did," Stiger said, then glanced up the rise. "Right...enough stalling. Let's go see the enemy."

With Eli at his side and Dog trailing, Stiger turned and started up the rise. Therik joined them. It wasn't much of a climb. The slope was just enough to conceal his army. He knew that enemy scouts had already reported their presence. It was why the enemy had fallen out of a column of march and deployed into a line of battle.

So, in truth, there was not much to hide. The show he was about to put on was designed to impress the enemy soldiers, not their commander. At the crest, one of Stiger's mounted scouts glanced over in their direction, but then returned his attention outward toward the enemy.

Beyond the small rise, the rolling grasslands spread out, wide, open, and nearly flat. Like a sword scar, the King's Highway cut right through the grasslands. The enemy had deployed at least ten thousand men in a long line about a quarter of a mile off. The road ran almost straight through the center of their line.

Two formations that had been organized into thick rectangular blocks with ranks five deep were moving forward at a steady pace, crossing the space between the enemy's line and the rise Stiger was on. He figured there were two thousand men in each formation.

Lightning slashed across the sky in a blinding flash that left an afterimage on Stiger's vision. A thunder crack followed mere heartbeats later, sounding like a hammer strike on a blacksmith's forge.

Hux and the bulk of the cavalry were off to the left about four hundred yards away. The prefect had formed his horse soldiers up on the crest of the hill and into a long double-ranked line. They were facing off against a like number of mounted troops to the right of the enemy's line.

The two cavalry wings were simply watching each other, with several hundred yards of open space between them. They were waiting for the other to make a move. That suited Stiger just fine. He did not need to force an action before he had more of the army up and was reinforced. He was more than content to allow things to drag on.

Dog growled, low, menacing, and long, as he stared at the enemy.

"Dog," Stiger said. "Quiet."

Dog ceased his growling.

Stiger surveyed the scene, impressed by all that he saw of the enemy. He figured those already deployed outnumbered him, and suddenly his force seemed small by comparison. More concerning was what was directly behind the enemy's battle line, on the King's Highway.

A long column of enemy formations could be seen marching forward toward the enemy's line. The column of march stretched out for as far as the eye could see, disappearing into the distance and rain. The sight of it made him feel ill and suddenly had him questioning the wisdom of his battle plan.

Still, it was one of the reasons why he'd chosen to give battle rather than sit behind the encampment's fortifications. It would take time, hours at best, for the entire enemy army to deploy. That hopefully would give the dwarves and elves time to come up and reinforce him, evening the odds. He would need to hold until then.

He glanced behind him and past the assembled legion. All he could see was his fortified encampment. Beyond that, along the King's Highway traveling south, there was only open road. There were no marching columns in view.

"That is a lot of men," Ruga said in a near whisper.

Stiger looked over at the centurion. His bodyguard had spread out around him. Ruga stood a few paces off. Though the centurion had made the comment to himself, Stiger could not help but agree.

Stiger glanced back at the legion's marching encampment. If needed and pressed hard enough, they would fall back upon the safety of the encampment's walls, but Stiger did not want to do that. It would mean giving up any possibility of maneuver, which might prove important when Braddock's dwarves arrived.

"The time for withdrawal is over," Therik said, having caught his look and mistaken it. "It is too late to march back to link up with the dwarves. You are committed to battle and must now stand and fight."

Stiger nodded and, without correcting Therik to his thinking, turned his gaze back to the battlefield. The two armies were coming together at a spot with no name. The spot was unremarkable, just an open grassy field. After today, at the cost of several thousand lives, this place would likely get a name. The only question was, who would get to name it, the empire or the confederacy?

"This is good ground," Stiger said to Eli, studying the small grassy rise, which he intended to hold. "To get at us, the enemy needs to climb a little. Granted, it's not all that high, but it will do. This position is perfect for javelin work. I sure wish we had some artillery though, a few dozen bolt throwers...but I guess you can't have everything."

The artillery was at the far end of the army's line of march. Lagging well behind, it had never managed to catch up.

"All we have are a few of those gnome-made dragon bolt throwers," Eli said and pointed behind them. "They fire up, not down."

The gnomes who had marched with the legion were driving their wagons out of the encampment and toward the rise. Each wagon carried a dragon-killing bolt thrower. With Menos and the other dragons nearby, he seriously doubted they would get to use them as they had intended. The gnomes would have to settle for disappointment.

Thunder growled off in the distance again, and with it, Stiger felt his anger begin to boil. He returned his gaze to the enemy. There was a good chance these bastards before him had a hand in what happened to Aeda and the surrounding countryside. More importantly, they were intent on crushing the empire.

Somewhere out there was Veers. At least, he hoped Veers was down there with the army. The man was responsible for Taha'Leeth's condition, and Stiger intended to make him pay. The wrath raged within him greater than the grumbling thunder. He would make them all pay.

Stiger's hand came to rest on his sword hilt. The tingle raced up from his palm and was gone in a flash. The tiredness he'd felt from lack of a full night's sleep vanished. The gloomy day became brighter and the colors around him grew more vivid.

We will make them all suffer.

"Yes, we will," Stiger said to Rarokan, then looked over at Eli. "What do you think?"

"Do you really want me to answer?" Eli asked, gazing outward at the enemy's battle line. The elf had paled considerably.

The rain picked up from a cold drizzle to a near steady downpour. Stiger rubbed the back of his neck. He was already becoming soaked. He had a feeling it was going to be a long day.

"I do," Stiger said. "Tell me what you are thinking."

"I think…we're in trouble," Eli said. "Truth be told, I wish I were elsewhere about now."

Stiger looked over at Eli and blinked, thoroughly astonished. The anger and rage retreated a little, but it roiled just beneath the surface.

"What?" Eli asked with an innocent expression.

"Weren't you the one who started tagging along with me because you wanted me to find you some trouble and excitement?" Stiger gestured outward toward the enemy. "I found it."

Eli sucked in a breath. "Ben, there is trouble and then there is trouble."

"Well, I've gone and done it then," Stiger said. "I've finally found more trouble and excitement than you can handle."

"You have," Eli admitted. "I give you permission to no longer trouble yourself at trying so hard on my behalf."

"It's a little late for that," Stiger said and returned his gaze to the enemy.

The two of them fell silent for a few heartbeats.

"The grass will grow taller here next year," Eli said somberly. "It always grows better the year after a battle."

Stiger knew that to be true.

The two formations were continuing to advance and were now less than three hundred yards away. Both formations gave an enthusiastic cheer.

"It looks like there won't be any attempt to parley," Therik said. "They want blood."

"Blood and bodies make good fertilizer," Eli said.

"Right," Stiger said at that cheery thought, then half turned, looking back down the hill from the crest. Lightning slashed the sky again. The thunder crack came a mere heartbeat after. It seemed to shake the ground. "Salt."

"Sir?" The camp prefect had partially climbed the rise behind them and was only a few yards away. With him stood the legionary with the horn, Beck with the Eagle, and the Eagle guard. A dozen yards behind waited a group of ten dismounted horsemen. They were his messenger corps for the coming fight. Like the Eagle, they would follow him around the battlefield, only the messengers would hold back from any fighting. Their job would be to run orders from him to the cohort commanders. Such measures would keep him in touch with each cohort. It would help him better manage and fight the legion.

"Would you be kind enough to give the order to advance up the rise?" Stiger called.

Salt nodded to the legionary, who then blew his horn.

"Forward," Salt shouted. The command was picked up and down the line by the cohort commanders. "March."

The legion began to march up the rise. Within moments they crested and came in view of the enemy. With their shields held before them and marching in neat, orderly ranks, they must have appeared to be an armored wall springing up from the ground. Stiger felt his heart swell with pride at the sight of the legion looking so sharp, even as the rain poured down around them. They were fine boys, all of them.

"Legion, halt," Salt shouted in a clear voice that, but for the rain, could surely have been heard across the way by the enemy. The legionary with the horn blew the call to halt. The cohorts dutifully ground to a stop. The cohort commanders began aligning and dressing their formations again, so the battle line was unbroken and straight as an arrow.

"They look good," Therik said.

"That they do," Stiger agreed.

A terrible cry rent the air. Stiger turned his attention back to the enemy as everyone stilled. Another savage cry sounded.

The wyrms had arrived.

Like a flock of harmless geese, the dragons were flying in a V-shaped formation and had just emerged from the clouds behind the enemy's line. Stiger counted eight of the massive beasts, all jet-black in color. They circled over their army a couple of times and then, as one, with their wings extended, began gliding downward toward the ground. As they neared, each gave several powerful flaps to slow the rate of their descent. They landed a short way behind the enemy line of battle. Stiger could feel the vibration in the ground through his boots as each massive monster touched down.

One of the wyrms stretched out its neck and raised its head into the air. It gave a deafening screech, then shot a gout of flame upward into the rain. It was an impressive display and Stiger felt a tickle of fear run through him.

"Now," Eli said, "I think would be a good time for Menos to make an appearance."

Stiger could not disagree.

TWENTY-THREE

"That one, there." Stiger pointed at the officer he wanted, less than ten yards away. "Behind the first rank, off to the right. See him? I think, by his rich-looking armor, he's a company commander or better."

"I do." Eli had an arrow nocked in his bow and was tracking the target. The rain was coming down in a steady downpour, making such a shot a difficult one.

"Take him down," Stiger said.

Eli released, and less than a heartbeat later, the arrow, perfectly placed, punched through the enemy officer's collar, a hair above where his armor ended. The power of the strike drove the officer backward and out of sight.

With the press of the bodies struggling against the legionary line, he was likely being trampled to death by his own men. Eli calmly nocked an arrow as Stiger scanned for another officer.

The sound of thunder cracked loudly overhead.

"There's another." Stiger pointed at a man he thought to be a junior officer. His armor was just a little better-looking than the rest. He was pacing behind the first rank of the enemy's line, shouting orders, encouragements. It would be a tricky shot, as this one was moving. "Think you can take him?"

Eli did not bother to respond. He aimed, following the target with his bow, and then released. As he did, the officer stumbled over something unseen. The arrow snapped by his head and struck a man in the rank behind. The arrow hammered into chest armor and bounced off with an audible crack.

"You missed." Stiger looked over at his friend.

Eli had already nocked another arrow and released. As he straightened up, the junior officer took this arrow in the neck. The arrow had gone halfway through and emerged out the back side. Mortally wounded, with eyes impossibly wide, he reached out a hand and attempted to tug the missile out. All he managed to do was worsen the wound. Blood fountained from his mouth and sprayed out into the air from where the arrowhead had emerged. Then his knees gave out and he sank from view.

Eli lowered his bow and looked over at Stiger. "Occasionally, I do miss, Ben."

Stiger scanned the fighting to their front. He could see no more officers within easy range. They had taken down four in rapid succession. Satisfied, Stiger took several steps back up the rise to get a better view of the fight. Eli followed. He was tempted to move to a different location and start afresh, but then he spied Therik standing with Salt and he made his way over, joining them. Beck, carrying the Eagle, trailed behind, as did Stiger's protection detail and the Eagle guard. It was quite a procession.

He turned back and studied the fight. The struggle had been going on for almost an hour. The enemy had attacked with just the two formations that had started across the field. Only three of Stiger's cohorts were engaged with them, Second, Third, and Fifth. The rest of his line remained where they had formed up, watching the fight unfold.

"They still have not moved." Therik nodded toward the enemy's main body across the field.

Stiger looked beyond the fight to his front. The enemy's main line had not budged. They stood there, like the rest of Stiger's battle line, simply watching the fight. While the struggle had been going on, fresh enemy formations had continued arriving. Even now, a new company was moving into position on the enemy's extreme left flank, extending the line there. Stiger figured the enemy had now brought up at least fifteen thousand men.

Behind the line, the enemy's wyrms sat and, like the rest, watched. Stiger could not fathom why the enemy's main body had not yet gone forward in strength or, for that matter, their dragons.

"We're holding just fine, sir," Salt said. "They're not making any progress against us. That said, these they sent forward are good quality."

"I agree," Stiger said, "they are well-trained and disciplined."

Stiger looked to the left and then right. The fighting along his own line was happening just to the right of his center. He had resisted the temptation to send two cohorts to flank the formations attacking him. Had he made such a move, he judged the enemy across the field might have started forward. If that happened, it likely would have proven difficult his get the cohorts back into line before the main body arrived. That might have been what the enemy was hoping and waiting for. But Stiger did not think so.

"They are certainly not second-rate," Stiger added. "I'd not consider them fodder for the grind."

"No, sir," Salt agreed.

"A test then?" Therik asked.

"Of our quality?" Stiger asked, glancing over. "I seriously doubt it. With the dragons out there, there's no reason to waste good men like this. At least none that I can think of."

Stiger turned around and looked to the south, searching the road. It was still empty. He had not expected reinforcement yet, but he could still hope. Couldn't he?

"We're holding easily enough," Salt said, "and giving more than we're getting."

Stiger had to agree with that too. Though the enemy were good quality, his men were chewing up the two formations. He studied the enemy directly to his front. They were not quite light infantry, but close. Perhaps they might be considered medium infantry, more than anything else, if there was such a thing.

The enemy's soldiers wore simple chainmail shirts and basic helmets. They carried small rounded shields, which could not provide as much protection as their legionary counterparts, and they used long swords, which were proving difficult to wield within the press of the line.

As he studied the action, a whistle was blown by Centurion Nantus. The first rank was changed out, with the second rank stepping forward to take their place. It had been smartly done.

Stiger figured that since the fight had begun, the enemy thus far engaged had lost about a third of their number. A steady stream of wounded were working their way back across the field toward their own lines. They were paying a steep price for testing the legion's mettle.

"I don't like it," Stiger said. "I don't enjoy seeing good men wasted like this for no purpose."

"There is a purpose," Therik said. "We just don't know the thinking behind it. They might want to keep us busy while they bring up more of their army."

Stiger said nothing, but he conceded that Therik might be right.

"Why not use their dragons, then?" Stiger asked the orc and gestured across the field. "Why prolong this?"

Therik gave Stiger a shrug of his shoulders.

"Why give up the siege of Lorium when you have so many dragons?" Eli asked. "They could have hit us along the line of march at any time."

Stiger glanced over at Eli and felt his friend was more than correct. It left him feeling disagreeable, for he did not understand what the enemy was hoping to gain. He blew out an unhappy breath.

"Whatever their reasoning," Stiger said, "we will keep murdering them for the present."

"We could give them a little shove, sir," Salt said. "Speed up the murdering, if you will. I would not want to tire our boys out too soon, especially before the enemy decides to send more of their number forward."

Stiger considered that. He could keep things going as they were, essentially prolonging the fight and dragging things out. That would, as Salt said, wear down his men. Was that the enemy's purpose? If so, why bother? No, he decided that could not be it, especially with their dragons sitting across the field. This must be some test by the enemy. Pushing back against the two formations trying his line would speed things up considerably. There was only one outcome to the fight that was now raging, and that was the breaking of the enemy directly before him. It was a foregone conclusion. The question now was timing.

"You're right," Stiger said. "Do it. Once the enemy gives up the fight and breaks, I don't want our boys chasing them all the way across the field. That would make them easy prey for cavalry."

"Aye, sir. I will pass along that order." Salt turned and made his way over to the messengers. He spoke with three of them, and then released them to hurry forward in search of the senior centurions of all three cohorts.

"Done, sir," Salt said as he returned. "We can expect them to push forward momentarily."

Sure enough, within moments, Second Cohort abruptly changed out its front rank, then, with their officers shouting orders, the entire formation gave a mighty push forward.

The enemy's first rank was immediately put under great pressure as the legionaries put their shoulders into the effort. The enemy tried to shove back, but to no avail. The sound of the fight increased with intensity as men cried out, shouted, cursed, and struggled against each other.

Stiger could hear the agonized screams of the enemy in the first rank, who were literally being crushed against the legion's shields, and the foreign shouting of the rank behind them as they tried in vain to push back at the legionaries.

Fifth Cohort pushed forward next, and a heartbeat later, Third shoved their way at the enemy. Caught completely by surprise, the enemy to their front began immediately giving ground. With all three shoving their way forward, there was no stopping them. The legionaries had the momentum.

The steady advance continued. Each cohort on their own shoved, taking the proscribed half-step forward, hammering their shields into the enemy. Then, the shields would inevitably scrape aside and the gladius, the deadly legionary short swords, jabbed outward. Screams followed.

The shields would lock back in place and the senior officer of the cohort would give the order for the next push so that the effort was unified. This was why the legion trained hard and repeatedly. The advance and subsequent killing were efficient, brutal, almost machine-like.

Stiger stood silently and watched it all. The enemy were wasting good infantry and he did not know why. That bothered him. His men were murdering the bastards. Though they were the enemy, it still angered him no less.

Kill them...kill them all.

The sword fed him a sudden surge of hate, anger, and rage. It was almost enough to make him draw the blade and join the fighting himself. Stiger physically restrained himself and turned his attention inward, as Menos had taught him.

Enough from you!

Stiger pushed back against Rarokan. He felt the surge from the sword diminish and then recede to a mere trickle. He needed to keep his head and focus on the fight at hand. If it came to needing to join the line and making an example or doing his part, he would, but not until then.

He felt a sullenness from the sword, but also a grudging understanding.

Stiger returned his attention to the battle and continued to watch it develop. The enemy were being actively pushed backward, manhandled by the legion. They gave up five yards, then ten. A trail of bodies and wounded were left in their wake. Very few were legionaries, which Stiger thought encouraging.

Abruptly, the formation on the right thoroughly crumbled and collapsed. Its organization came apart. Keeping their lines for the most part, the legionaries surged forward as the enemy in mass gave up more ground. The enemy soldiers did not immediately run or flee. They fought as individuals or in small groups, struggling to fight back. It was ugly and brutal. The legionaries cut the enemy down in great numbers. The second formation fell apart a few moments later, and with it, the remains of both formations completely broke. Leaving their dead and wounded behind, they fled back across the field as fast as they could run.

The entire legion gave a hearty cheer as the legionaries of the three engaged cohorts finally broke ranks and chased after the enemy. But with their officers shouting and cursing them, they did not get very far. Within short order, they slowly began to return to the ranks and reform.

"Sir," Salt said, "as long as the enemy don't advance their main line, I think we can spare a few men to help our wounded back to the surgeons."

"See to it," Stiger said, giving a nod. "Let's get those we can some care while we have the time to do so."

Salt called for another messenger and passed along instructions. As he did, a slow, steady, methodical beat rose up from the enemy ranks. Hundreds of drums began pounding out a steady rhythm that was ominous and menacing and clearly intended to intimidate. It went on and on. It told Stiger the enemy was coming. They were clearly working themselves up.

Stiger turned and saw Severus join them. The tribune had been working at headquarters. Stiger motioned him over.

"Kindly send a runner to Prefect Hux," Stiger said. "Confirm his understanding that whatever the enemy cavalry does, he is to shadow them. If practical and without undue risk, take any action he sees fit. Is that understood?"

"Yes, sir," Severus said and stepped back to the messengers. Within a matter of moments, a rider was galloping down the line for the cavalry wing.

The cohorts to his front that had just been engaged had almost finished pulling themselves back into a semblance of order. Centurions and optios were moving down the ranks of men, checking them over.

Stiger turned his attention back to the enemy. They had not moved. The drumbeat had continued unabated. His eyes shifted to his own lines. He got the sense his men seemed a little unsettled. No matter how disciplined and ready for battle, Stiger understood morale could be a fickle beast. He looked back on the messengers and came to a decision. He turned and jogged over.

"I need both of your horses," Stiger said and pointed to two men who were holding the reins of their mounts. He looked back and called, "Beck. Grab a horse, man."

"A horse, sir?" Beck hustled over.

"You can ride, can't you?" Stiger asked. "I seem to remember you can. Am I mistaken?"

"Yes, sir...ah no, sir," Beck said. "I can ride."

"Well, then, grab a horse and bring the Eagle," Stiger said.

"We're going for a ride, sir?" Beck asked, blinking. "Now?"

"We're gonna give the men something to fight for."

"Yes, sir," Beck said.

"Sir." Ruga had followed him over and was clearly alarmed by what Stiger was intending. "If you don't mind me asking, what are you doing?"

"I don't mind you asking," Stiger said. "I am going for a short ride."

"But, sir," Ruga protested and then looked to the messengers, clearly thinking to requisition a horse for himself.

Lightning flashed across the sky.

"Don't worry. I am not putting myself in any danger," Stiger said, before Ruga could request a horse of his own. "We're going to put on a show for the men. Remain here. I will be back soon enough. That is an order, Centurion."

"Yes, sir," Ruga said, sounding none too happy.

Eli walked up. "Don't do anything stupid, will you?"

"And here," Stiger said, "I thought you knew me."

"I do," Eli said and stepped back as Stiger grabbed the reins of the horse from the messenger and pulled himself up onto its back. He took a moment to get comfortable in the saddle. With the cold rain, he was completely soaked through. Complete comfort under the current conditions was simply unattainable. Everyone was miserable.

Beck handed the Eagle to the messenger and took the reins. With less ease than Stiger, he mounted up. When he was settled in the saddle, he took the Eagle in one hand, while holding the reins of his horse in the other.

"All set, sir," Beck said.

The rain had begun to come down harder. Stiger rode his horse over to Salt, with Beck following. "I am going to give the men some backbone."

"Yes, sir," Salt said, though his expression appeared worried.

Stiger led Beck forward and through the ranks. The men stepped aside for them and then they had to pick their way through the field of dead, dying, and wounded, until they were out before the assembled legion.

The sky flashed again, lighting up the clouds, which had crowded tightly together. Thunder rumbled a few moments later. Stiger had considered a speech, but then disregarded the idea. It was raining too hard to be heard very far. Instead, he began riding down the line, with Beck following. Stiger pulled Rarokan out from its scabbard and held the sword up into the air for the men to see. The sword burst into blue fire that, despite the downpour, could not be extinguished.

All the while, the enemy's drums continued to beat, seeming to make the air throb with their cadence. He kicked the horse into a gallop and glanced back to make sure Beck was following. The men of the nearest cohort let out a hearty cheer. The cheer was quickly picked up by every cohort. The cheering became so loud and exuberant that it drowned out the drums.

Stiger felt a fierce pride in his men. They had marched for weeks, endured terrible discomfort and hardship just to get here, and they were assembled to fight a battle under the worst of conditions. They were the best soldiers in the world. By the gods, he loved them.

He rode to the end of the line and then back, clear over to the other end. Stiger turned his horse around and rode slowly back along the line to his original position and there he brought his horse to a stop. He faced the enemy and waved his sword in the air for show. The men continued to cheer themselves hoarse and he allowed them to do it.

Throughout it all, the enemy had not moved.

Over the cheering, Stiger could no longer hear the drums. He considered making another ride for good measure. Then, one of the wyrms stood and shook itself, unfurling its wings. The dragon craned its neck and let out a piercing screech that silenced the cheering of his men.

A terrible silence settled across the field. Even the enemy's drums had stopped.

The other wyrms began standing and unfurling their wings. The first leapt into the air. One by one, the others followed. The beating of their wings against the air could be heard clearly across the field. It sounded more ominous and menacing than the drums ever could. The dragons began circling higher and higher as they climbed up toward the clouds. Another dragon gave an ear-piercing screech.

Stiger shivered at the awesome display of power. He recalled the dragon he'd personally killed and the terrible fear that it had instilled within him. Before he'd brought it down, the beast had exacted a dreadful toll on his legionaries.

With nervousness, Stiger's horse danced sideways. He tightened his hold on the reins as more of the dragons began to screech and roar. It was a hideous sound, and with it, the horse became more unsettled, almost to the point of panic. Rather than risk being thrown, Stiger sheathed his sword and slid out of the saddle. Beck did the same, but his horse panicked as his feet touched the ground and ripped the reins free. The horse galloped out into the open, running between the two armies. Stiger released the reins of his horse. Freed, it too galloped off, bucking wildly as it did.

The dragons circled over the enemy's army. Stiger understood they were gaining height from which to dive down and attack the legion. It was only a matter of moments before that happened. He glanced back at the legion and hoped the gnomes were ready. But what could stand against such might? Surely not a handful of their bolt throwers.

There was a new sound, a deep, malevolent roar that made the cries from the wyrms pale by comparison. Two large dragons, clearly not wyrms, emerged from the clouds above. One was green and the other a fiery red. Their wings were tucked back against their sides as they dove for the ground with terrific speed. At the last moment, both unfurled their wings and flapped hard, slowing their speed. Legs extended, both touched down in the middle of the field between the two armies. The ground shook as they landed.

It happened so quick that, had they attacked, there would've been no time to react.

Two figures in black cloaks were riding upon the backs of the dragons. Stiger had not noticed them before and was astonished to realize each dragon had a saddle. Both figures climbed quickly to the ground and then, without hesitation, the two dragons took to the air once again, leaping upward into the sky.

Stiger looked over at the enemy's wyrms. Where a moment before they had been steadily circling and gaining altitude, now they were frantically beating at the air, angling toward the clouds. Incredibly, they appeared to be fleeing.

There was another angry roar that put every other dragon cry before it to shame. It was so loud that Stiger clapped both hands to the sides of his helmet. An even larger dragon, black in color, emerged above them from the clouds. Stiger almost grinned at the sight.

It was Sian Tane.

A second dragon, just as large, followed right behind. It was Currose. Both of the noctalum were diving on the wyrms, who became almost frantic in their effort to escape, wheeling and twisting about, like pigeons fleeing a falcon.

A bolt of what looked like lightning flashed and shot forth from Sian Tane. It struck one of the wyrms square on the back. There was a sickening sizzling sound. The wyrm cried out in agony, then went limp. The creature fell from the sky and crashed into the ground behind the enemy's line. The impact threw up a great spray of dirt and mud into the air. The ground once again shook violently from the impact.

Four more dragons came into view, diving through the clouds after the wyrms. These were colored brilliantly in red, green, blue, and yellow. Suddenly, it seemed, between the wyrms and the newcomers, there were dragons everywhere in the sky, screaming, roaring, or crying out in pain. Flame shot across the sky, as did lightning bolts.

Almost as quickly as it had begun, the wyrms were gone, lost from view. Some seeking escape had climbed up into the clouds. Others dove for the ground and flew away as fast as they could. Both noctalum followed after those that had fled upward and into the clouds.

The red and green dragons that had landed were in pursuit of a wyrm that had flown off into the distance. In heartbeats, they too were gone. The rest of the dragons flew back up into the rain clouds.

The clouds flashed from lightning and then from orange flame. There was a crack, a terrible screech of pain, followed by an abrupt silence. A lifeless wyrm, twisting in a lazy spiral, emerged from the clouds as it fell from the sky. Several heartbeats later, it crashed down with a sickening thud amongst the enemy's cavalry. Dozens of their horse soldiers were crushed. Even more were thrown into the air, both animals and their riders, from the violence of the impact.

There was a shocked moment of silence that followed. Screams from the wounded could be heard across the field. Then, there were more flashes in the clouds, along with thunderclaps, cracks, and bangs. Almost every eye on the field turned their gazes skyward again. It continued for a few moments, before silence once again returned.

The legion gave out a mighty cheer. It was one filled with intense relief.

Stiger blew out a relieved breath himself. Menos and Currose had come through. Now, he only had to contend with the enemy's army, and they likely had been shocked to their core by what had just happened.

He turned his attention to the two figures who had dismounted from the dragons. They were striding confidently toward him. Though they walked on two legs and had two arms, their gait was a strange sort of loping walk that was most definitely not human. Both wore chest armor that was painted a jet black. It matched their cloaks, which trailed slightly on the ground behind them. Mail shirts under the armor dropped down to just above their knees.

They did not have shields, but both carried long swords that were strapped to their backs. There was a certain menace about them and how they moved that concerned Stiger. It was almost predatory. But it was their faces that got his attention, for they were not human...but tiger-like. They were, for lack of a better word, tiger men.

"Are you Stiger?" one of the tiger men asked, baring his long canines. It came out almost as part growl, with an animalistic feel to the tone. Stiger struggled not to take a step back as they towered over him. They were over eight feet tall and their arms and legs rippled with muscles covered with orange fur.

"I am," Stiger said, surprised they spoke Common.

"I am Lord Jeskix and this is Lord Arol. Menos sends his compliments."

"You are of the Vass?" Stiger asked.

"We are Knights of the Vass, human," Arol said in a disdainful tone, "and we come to fight at your side, Champion of the High Father."

The word Champion was said with a hint of distaste.

"Then you are most welcome," Stiger said, "for we will surely have a fight this day."

"That is what we live for," Jeskix said, with a glance toward the enemy army, "and why we've come." Jeskix looked back to Stiger. "There are just two of us now, but in the coming weeks, our soldiers will arrive. They are marching up from the South, and it is a good long way."

"How many?" Stiger asked.

"Enough," Jeskix said, and turned to look at the enemy across the field. "So, human, how do you plan on dealing with them?"

There was a challenge in the question.

Stiger tore his gaze from the Vass and returned his attention to the enemy. He studied them for a long moment. They seemed shaken up by what had happened. The neat ranks of the army were gone. His eyes snapped back to the cavalry, which was in great disarray because of the dragon having crashed in their midst.

There was an opportunity here, and he suspected it would not come again if he did not act quickly.

"Follow me." Stiger left the Vass and started jogging to where he'd left Salt. As he did, he glanced back. Like everyone else on the battlefield, Beck was standing there in near shock. "Come on, Beck. Move your ass, man."

The Eagle-bearer snapped out of his stunned disbelief at what he'd just witnessed and hustled to catch up. The rain had finally let up, returning to a miserable drizzle. Stiger jogged through the wounded and dead, then pushed his way through the ranks of Second Cohort. Everyone else seemed just as stunned and awed by what had happened. There was a sense of disbelief in the air.

"Salt," Stiger said as he came up. He turned and pointed at the enemy. "I want Hux and the cavalry to swing around to the enemy's right flank. Their cavalry has been devastated by what just happened. What's left is seriously shook up. If Hux moves quickly, he might be able to smash their cavalry and tear into the infantry on the enemy's right, rolling them up."

Salt blinked and turned his gaze to the legion's cavalry wing.

"Are you listening to me?" Stiger demanded.

"Yes, sir," Salt said and then pointed, "only I don't think we need to order Hux forward."

Stiger turned and saw his cavalry wing, organized into a long line, was already in motion. Hux, on his own initiative, had started his horse soldiers across the field. Lances held high, the legion's cavalry was moving at a slow trot, increasing by the moment, working their way steadily up to a full charge. He could hear the beginnings of the thunder from their hooves. Stiger turned his gaze to the enemy's cavalry. They seemed terribly disorganized. Many had dismounted and were busy helping injured comrades. They were oblivious to what was about to descend upon them.

"Right," Stiger said, but then noticed that Salt was distracted. He was staring at the Vass, as was everyone else, including Eli and Therik. The two knights had followed him and appeared far from impressed by all that they saw.

Dog growled deeply.

"Dog," Stiger snapped. "Stop that."

Dog ceased his growling but moved nearer Stiger and kept his gaze fixed on the Vass. The Vass, for their part, were now staring at the animal with what seemed intense interest.

Stiger gripped Salt's arm and shook his camp prefect slightly. "Salt, this is Lord Jeskix and Lord Arol of the Vass. These are the friends Menos mentioned. But right now, we need to focus on the job at hand, and that is breaking the enemy army."

"Yes, sir," Salt said, "sorry, sir."

"The legion will move forward to attack," Stiger said, turning to point at the enemy. "If you do not follow at any point, speak up."

"Of course, sir," Salt said, having regained his composure.

"We are going to aim for the right side of their line." Stiger pointed to the left side of the enemy's position. "Their right, not ours. As we move across the field, I want to shift the legion to the left, so that we aim our midpoint directly at the enemy's right flank. At that point there, where the dragon came down."

"You don't want to move the legion straight at the enemy?" Therik asked. "They seem rather disorganized. A straightforward approach may be all that's needed."

"No," Stiger said, feeling that was the wrong path to take. "Hux is moving for the right flank and the enemy's cavalry. We will exploit any success Hux has in causing a panic there on the right." Stiger pointed. "That's where we are going to put our pressure. When we arrive and drive forward, we should have three, maybe four cohorts uncovered on our extreme left flank. There should be no enemy before them. I want them to swing around like a door and hit the enemy from the side. At that point, our line will become L-shaped. If we act fast enough, we might just create a general panic."

"What of the right flank, sir?" Salt asked. "What's to stop the enemy from doing the same to us, flanking around to our side?"

"Nothing," Stiger said, "but our enemy is disorganized. If we don't press them, that won't last long. I am certain they are in shock over losing their dragons. Perhaps, with their wyrms, they didn't even think they would have a real fight today." Stiger paused and sucked in a breath as he thought on how to address Salt's concern. "To counter such an effort, as the line moves forward, we will swing the reserve, First Cohort and the Eighty-Fifth, to our right flank. They can extend the line on our right, while we see what success we can have with their left. Understand?"

"I do," Salt said, "and I like it."

"Then we need to get the legion moving," Stiger said, "before the enemy recovers."

"Yes, sir," Salt said. He turned, calling out, "Messengers. On me."

"Orc, elf, human, naverum, and noctalum all working together," Jeskix said to Arol. "Istros is a very strange world."

"And you haven't even met the rest of our allies," Eli said. "We have gnomes and dwarves too."

TWENTY-FOUR

B y the time the enemy cavalry realized what was happening, Hux's charge was almost upon them. Men on foot, who had been unhorsed or had dismounted to help their comrades, ran for their lives. Others, who had the presence of mind, grabbed the reins of their horses, mounted back up, and desperately attempted to gallop away to safety. Those who understood flight to be a futile effort and were caught directly in the path of the charging cavalry wing drew their weapons and bravely faced the charge, with the clear intent to sell their lives dearly.

As the distance closed to the last few yards, lances were lowered into the attack position, and with a tremendous crash, the wall of horses and men slammed into the enemy. The charge had been brought home with exceptional skill and determination. The wing's momentum carried them clear through the confused mass of what had once been the confederacy's cavalry. It only slowed up when the wing was more than thirty yards beyond the enemy's line.

In its wake, Hux had left utter destruction and carnage. Horses and bodies littered the ground behind them. Very few were left standing, and those that were appeared thoroughly dazed, shocked by what had just occurred. Stiger knew all cavalrymen lived for moments like this one, striking at and riding down a disorganized enemy.

The legion, having watched the charge, gave a hearty cheer. All infantry feared cavalry. Hux had finished the destruction of the enemy cavalry, and the men were heartened by it.

A horn blew from the legionary cavalry. Stiger recognized the call to reform. He watched as the troopers slowed their horses and began angling them to the left, away from the enemy. The legion's horse soldiers were following a rider, who was waving his sword in the air above his head. It was Hux. Just behind the prefect rode the cavalry's standard-bearer.

Stiger noted that most of his mounted wing no longer had their lances. They'd lost them when the charge had slammed home. Lances were typically one-use weapons. They were now down to swords. That was fine, for now the enemy no longer had any cavalry of their own. With his charge, Hux had just effectively swept it away.

"Forward…" Salt shouted in a loud call. He waited for the centurions up and down the line to pick it up and repeat it. "March."

The legion began moving forward, advancing across the field of browned grass. Stiger followed behind Second Cohort. With him were Salt, Therik, Eli, and the two Vass. Dog padded along at his side. Beck, with the Eagle guard and Ruga's century, followed a few paces behind. An auxiliary with a horn trailed after Salt. Then came Severus with the messengers. It was a large party, but for this battle, they were his command entourage.

Stiger looked down his line and the orderly ranks of men to the left and was satisfied with all that he saw. He looked to the right. Everything was in order. With the auxiliary cohorts he had nearly nine thousand men on the field. Nine thousand against at least fifteen thousand of the enemy. He hoped Braddock and Tenya'Far hurried their march, for he had a feeling he would need their help before the day was done.

Turning his attention to the enemy army, he studied them intently. They still appeared disordered, muddled by the shock of losing their dragons and then the cavalry. Officers could clearly be seen working to restore order. Stiger well knew some semblance of control would soon be established. It was only a matter of time, and Stiger did not intend to give them much.

Salt snapped orders and the auxiliary blew his horn, relaying the order to the rest of the legion. There was about ten yards of space between each cohort. This was intentional, as they closed in on the enemy, to allow them room to make the required adjustments to the angle of march. Obediently, the legion began angling its way across the field toward the enemy's right flank, each cohort making the adjustment in their line of march. Eventually, as they neared the confederacy's line, the legion would close up and form an unbroken armored wall.

The pace was steady, controlled, and maddeningly slow. Stiger wished he could speed things up. He recognized that doing so would not have been the wisest of decisions. Though the distance to the enemy's line was only a few hundred yards, moving at a quicker pace would only serve to fatigue his men. He could not have that. They would shortly need all their strength and energy, for outnumbered as they were, the coming fight would surely test them. Moving at a quicker pace would also affect the legion's organization, potentially adding disorder to his own ranks. Stiger was not prepared to sacrifice that either, and so he contented himself with a slow, steady advance.

Off to the left, Hux had reformed his cavalry wing on the fly and was swinging around and away from the enemy army in a slow walk. He had reorganized his cavalry into a long single line. The wing had almost completed its wheeling movement. As Hux swung it back around, the cavalry began picking up speed again as they turned back and began bearing down upon the enemy. The growing thunder of their hooves could be heard over the steady tramping of thousands of feet marching over the wet, grassy field.

A horn call came from the enemy army. The call was immediately repeated. It sounded urgent to Stiger's ears, almost desperate. The drums started again, first a few stuttering away and then more until it became a steady beat.

Hux drove his cavalry directly at the enemy's right flank. The thunder of the hooves grew in volume with their speed, drowning out the sound of the massed drums. The ground seemed to tremble.

Stiger found himself holding his breath. Feeling foolish, he let it out. The enemy's cavalry was gone. It had been completely destroyed, wiped away by Hux and his horse soldiers. There was no longer anything to stand in the prefect's way.

The infantry on the enemy's right flank was still disorganized, especially so after they had seen the legion's cavalry wipe out their own. The officers had been unable to fully reform their men, but they had made some progress.

After another horn call at Salt's prompting, the legion once again made a shift to the left.

The cavalry across the field galloped harder. The infantry, in their path on the confederacy's right flank, turned and attempted to form a hasty line facing the charge. Officers rushed about in a desperate bid to firm up the scratch line. Stiger saw no spears. Without spears, the infantry would be vulnerable to a charge.

The enemy began to shrink back and away. A few ran. Then more fled and finally the entire right flank was in flight, causing great confusion with the rest of the line as men pushed their way into and through formations that had yet to break.

The distance closed from thirty yards to twenty...

Ten...

Swords were readied, and as they were, the cavalry smashed into the mass of the confused enemy. It was incredible. Horses slammed men to the ground, rode them down, trampled them under their hooves. So great was their momentum, the cavalry charge punched forty yards into the mass of confused and fleeing infantry before slowing.

In all Stiger's years and experience, he had never seen the like. Hux and his boys had rolled up and disrupted almost an entire third of the enemy army, causing great confusion. Hundreds had been killed, injured, and maimed in their latest charge, perhaps even thousands.

A hearty cheer went up from the legion as the horse soldiers began laying about with their swords, hacking and slashing at the enemy, killing all they could. Men shouting, horses screaming...it was pure chaos.

The legion continued its advance, closing to within two hundred yards, then one hundred fifty. Stiger tore his gaze from the shattered remnants of the enemy's right flank and studied the rest of the confederacy's line. The left had been brought back into order and the center too. It was the right that had been thoroughly wrecked and the heart of the legion was driving directly at it. Stiger hoped to complete the destruction there.

"Salt," Stiger called, looking over, "take the right flank. Make sure First Cohort and the Eighty-Fifth are well-used and get into position. I do not want the enemy turning us on the right. I'm also keeping your man with the horn."

"Yes, sir," Salt said, "I'll take care of it."

"Holler if you need help," Stiger said.

"You know I will, sir," Salt said and began working his way over to the right, walking behind the line as it continued to advance.

"What's your name, son?" Stiger asked the auxiliary with the horn.

"Marus, sir."

"Good," Stiger said. "You stay close, understand?"

"Yes, sir," Marus said.

A legionary horn call to Stiger's front snapped his head around. Hux was seeking to pull the cavalry back and disengage. The enemy had clearly stiffened and begun to fight back. Stiger saw a horse go down as a group of infantry attacked. The cavalry was beginning to pay a price for fighting amongst masses of foot soldiers. Hux had clearly realized it was time to pull back and regroup. Stiger noted that, in the chaos, the wing had also become spread out, with many becoming isolated as fresh enemy companies of infantry pushed back.

The horn call sounded again, this time more insistent. At first it was a few and then it was many, but the cavalry began pulling their mounts around and galloping away from the vengeful infantry.

The legion was now less than one hundred yards from contact. Officers to the front of the enemy's line worked feverishly to get their men organized and prepared. Stiger looked to the left of his own line. The Tenth, Eighth, and Sixth Cohorts would be uncovered. There was no enemy to their front. He'd already sent them orders that once the legion reached the confederacy's line, they were to fold around on the enemy's flank and push hard into their side. Stiger intended to put the enemy's right flank under as much pressure as possible and thereby roll it up.

The distance narrowed to fifty yards.

The enemy to their front brought their shields up and drew swords. Stiger studied them critically. Unlike the enemy they'd already engaged, these were heavy infantry. They carried rectangular shields a littler smaller than the legion's and short swords. Their armor consisted of a chain mail shirt that went down to the knees and a helmet, complete with cheek guards. Black crests topped their helmets, making them appear taller and more imposing.

Though the enemy had managed to get two ranks in place on what remained of their right flank, their line was far from firm. It was also painfully thin when compared to the legion's five ranks. Behind their line, it was utter chaos, with men from companies that had broken and fled all mixed up. They were milling about in great confusion.

Stiger read near panic in the ranks ahead as his line closed the last few dozen yards. The enemy's right flank was still a relative mess. There was no sense of stability or firmness. A few of the men in the first rank began backing up as the distance closed to the last handful of yards. Officers shouted at them in a language foreign to Stiger, undoubtedly ordering them to stand firm.

Stiger turned to Marus. "Sound the call to halt."

Marus dutifully blew the call, two long blasts, followed by a short one.

The legion ground to a halt.

"First rank, ready javelins," Stiger ordered and nodded to Marus.

The call was blown. Centurions across the line repeated the order. The first rank took a step forward and prepared to throw. Across the way, orders were snapped and shields were brought up in preparation for what was to come.

"First rank," Stiger ordered. "Release."

Marus blew. A heartbeat later, the men in the front rank grunted as they threw. A wave of javelins arced up into the air and then crashed down amongst the enemy's two ranks with a loud clatter. The heavy iron-tipped weapons punched through shield and armor. Men cried out in pain as they were struck. Shields that had been penetrated were discarded, their protection rendered useless as the soft shafts of the heavy javelins bent and became almost impossible to remove quickly. Others began working on the shields, attempting vainly to remove the weapons.

Stiger was very pleased with the toss. It had been well made and had wreaked havoc amongst the enemy.

"All ranks," Stiger ordered, looking over at Marus and waiting for the call to be blown before ordering the second part. "Ready javelins."

The horn was sounded again. This time, all of the ranks spread out, with first rank taking another step forward and the last rank taking three steps back. The middle ranks spread out as well, to give themselves room to make their toss.

Stiger looked left and then right, checking to make certain all was ready.

"Release."

The horn blared his command again.

The javelins were released.

The deadly weapons arced up into the air before crashing down in a devastating wave upon the enemy. The result was what could only be described as near catastrophic. The first toss had deprived many of the enemy of their shields. Hundreds of men were hit by the second toss; even more shields were rendered useless.

"Close up ranks. Ready shields," came a shout to his front as a centurion in one of the front ranks made the call. "Draw swords."

Up and down the line ran the similar calls as the legion prepared for direct battle.

"Let's give it to them, boys," a centurion shouted.

"HAAH," the centurion's cohort shouted in reply.

"HAAH," another cohort shouted, "HAAH, HAAH."

The entire legion gave a massed, "HAAH."

Stiger thought it quite intimidating and so too did the remnants of the line facing him. Many of the survivors began to back up and look about. Discipline was failing.

"Advance," Stiger shouted, as loud as he could, deciding to forgo another horn call. It proved sufficient, for the legion, as an armored wall, started forward, resuming the steady step.

"We're gonna kill them all. What are we going to do?" a centurion somewhere to the front called.

"Kill," the men responded. "Kill, kill, kill."

Shield met shield in a crash as the two lines came together. Men grunted, shouted, and cursed. They pushed and shoved against one another as each line struggled for dominance. It wasn't a long contest, as the weight and numbers were on the legion's side. The enemy line, disorganized and lacking depth and strength, especially after the javelin toss, was shoved violently backward. That was when the killing machine began its work. Push, step, stab, and push again. The legion began efficiently butchering the enemy.

The confederacy's line gave up a foot, then five, then ten yards. The legion began to drive the enemy's right inward as it thinned even more. Stiger looked over to his left. His cohorts that were uncovered had begun to swing around nicely. Shortly they would be in position to drive into the enemy's flank, and unlike the cavalry, they would be staying.

The sound of fighting to his right intensified. Stiger looked and saw the enemy had pushed forward and was tightly engaged there. They were also attempting to advance forward. Salt was extending the line back and around to receive it, with the Eighty-Fifth on the extreme end of the line. Stiger's camp prefect appeared to have everything well in hand, at least for the moment.

Stiger returned his attention to the action at the front. His uncovered cohorts were completing their movement, and before they could become engaged, the enemy's line to his front broke.

Centurions and optios shouted, grabbed, and cursed at their men to keep them in ranks. The men, for the most part, responded, though a few did race after and chase down the nearest enemy.

"There's another line," Arol said. "They have formed a second line. See it?"

Stiger had been so focused on the fighting to the front, he'd not noticed the Vass come up next to him. Arol pointed, and sure enough the enemy had formed a new line along the road's boundary. It looked hastily formed. This line had wisely opened gaps, so those fleeing could pass through without carrying away the fresh soldiers in their panic.

"I would complete your turning movement," Arol said, "and advance with your army against this new line. It lacks in depth. If you strike quickly and hit them all at once, you may be able to overcome them too."

Stiger studied the new line and decided he was correct. He turned his gaze down the road. There were still enemy columns marching up, with the intent of joining the battle. Stiger found that very disagreeable. The enemy would be able to continue to feed fresh companies into the battle, while Stiger, at the moment, had no reinforcement.

Studying the columns marching south toward the battle, Stiger wanted to stop them, or at least interrupt any reinforcement long enough to rout the army before him. He turned around, looking for his cavalry, and spotted Hux busy reforming his troopers fifty yards away.

"Messenger," Stiger called, and a man came forward leading a horse. "Ride over there and kindly ask Prefect Hux to report to me."

"Yes, sir." The messenger mounted up and rode off.

Stiger glanced over to his left again. "Severus?"

The tribune, who had been with the messengers, stepped over.

"Grab a horse. I want you to ride down the line to the left," Stiger said. "Speak with each senior centurion. Order them to stop their cohorts when they are facing the King's Highway. Once each cohort is in position and aligned with the rest, I will give the order to advance. Only then, understand?"

"Yes, sir," Severus said.

Stiger turned away and back to the fight as the tribune left. Six of his cohorts were now uncovered on his left and swinging around to face the new line along the road. On the right, where his auxiliaries and the other four legionary cohorts were, the fighting was intense and hard. Despite that, Stiger's lines were still moving forward there, pushing the enemy roughly before them. The extreme flank to his right, which Salt had bent back around, seemed to be holding against the enemy's best efforts.

"The fight is going well," Therik said.

"It is far from over," Arol growled, "far from decided."

Stiger could only agree. The enemy had not completely collapsed, as he'd hoped. He'd essentially destroyed the enemy's right, but the rest of their army had fight left in them.

Hearing hooves, he turned to see Hux approaching. The prefect's horse and armor were splattered with dried blood and mud. Hux even had a deep gash along his chest armor and a cut on his cheek that bled freely.

"Sir," Hux said, pulling his horse to a stop. "You called?"

"I did," Stiger said. "Fine work with that charge."

"It was quite exhilarating."

"I can imagine," Stiger said. "I have another job for you."

"I thought you might, sir," Hux said. "We have at least one charge left, maybe another, and then our mounts will be spent. Where would you like us to go?"

"See those reinforcements?" Stiger pointed northward, along the King's Highway. "The enemy is bringing up fresh units."

"I see them, sir," Hux said. "I take it you'd like me to disrupt that effort?"

"I would," Stiger said. "Kindly do so, and the sooner the better."

"Very good, sir." Hux saluted before pulling his horse around and riding away back toward his men.

Stiger turned his attention back to the enemy. The battle on his right had become more intense. It seemed as if the enemy's resistance had stiffened considerably. His line was no longer advancing there. He looked to his left and saw the last of the cohorts moving into position and aligning themselves next to one another so there were no gaps in the new line. The movement took time, but there was no point in hurrying it. He would rather have it done right than rush things, which would serve to further fatigue his men. Finally, the movement was complete, and his line was ready. The muddy road was only twenty yards to their front. The legion's entire line was now bent at the middle, almost like a V.

"Marus, left flank, advance," Stiger said. "Sound it, son."

Marus blew his horn, and with it, Stiger's left flank began to go forward. Stiger and his entourage moved with them. Very quickly, the line was engaged. The enemy were armored differently than those they had previously faced and were equipped identically to those he had encountered back at Vrell. They held their line well, even with the legion pushing them hard.

"I believe these soldiers we face," Eli said, "are the slave soldiers we've heard much about. See the collars they wear?"

"I think the ones before must have been conscripts." Stiger waved a hand before him. "They are more determined than the last bunch, stubborn even."

"Slave soldiers who fight with a purpose and will. This world is already proving very interesting," Jeskix said, and then looked at Eli, "even without dwarves and gnomes. I am glad I came."

Stiger glanced over at the two Vass. Both were hulking individuals. Even Therik seemed small by comparison. In fact, the orc had been actively giving them space, as if the Vass unsettled him. Stiger turned his attention back to the battle. His entire line was now fully engaged.

The noise from the fight was deafening. Shouts, screams, cries, hammering of shield on shield, sword on shield...it blended into a terrific racket. Stiger's eyes swept the fighting. His centurions, along with the auxiliary prefects, were managing their cohorts, fighting them as they saw best.

Stiger would not interfere, unless he saw something that needed doing. And right now, there was nothing for him to do, other than watch. The temptation to do something was incredibly strong. Instead, he decided to walk behind the line and settle for observation. He started on the left side, working his way to the end of the line, before turning back and returning. Wherever he went, Beck with the Eagle followed, and so too did his entourage.

"How's it going, Kiel?" Stiger hollered at the senior centurion from Seventh Cohort. He wanted another's opinion.

"Tolerable, sir," Kiel responded from behind the first rank and made his way back to speak with Stiger. "This lot before us is good and determined, but my boys are holding them just fine."

That was high praise from the centurion.

"Anything you need?" Stiger asked.

"No, sir," Kiel said. "We're doing just fine."

Stiger's eyes had never left the fighting while the two of them talked. Both sides were evenly matched. He did not see a reason to begin the push yet. If he ordered it too soon, the effort might fail and he'd exhaust his men for naught. So, he allowed the contest of wills to continue.

"Very well," Stiger said, "carry on."

"Yes, sir." Kiel returned to his cohort.

The enemy formation before Seventh Cohort abruptly changed out their front rank. Stiger noted that it was well executed, and a sure sign they had drilled repeatedly in how to do it under the pressure of the line. The legions did the same. He did not find it surprising. It only served to confirm his men were facing off against professional soldiers.

Returning to his original position near the center, Stiger stopped and looked over the fighting to either side. It seemed intense, particularly on Salt's side of the line. Stiger wasn't sure how he could relieve it.

There was a distant rumbling to the far left. Hux was finally moving with the cavalry. The prefect had swung the cavalry wing out and around by about a half mile, well clear of the fighting, before starting back toward the road. His boys had worked up some speed and were now charging the road, aiming for one of the marching columns. Looking like toy figures, the cavalry went home, sweeping over the road like a tidal wave, driving all before it and washing away the column that had been there.

Hux had swept a good portion of the road clean. Once clear of the road, his cavalry began to swing back around for another go of it. With any luck, further reinforcements coming from the north would be forced to deploy farther up the road rather than risk receiving the same treatment. That would serve to seriously delay immediate reinforcement, meaning the enemy now had to fight out the battle with what they had on hand.

"Look there," Eli said and pointed, drawing Stiger's attention to the enemy's line.

It took Stiger a moment to realize what he was looking at. Just behind the line moved a man escorted by an entourage, very similar to Stiger's. There was even a standard-bearer. The top of the standard appeared to be a golden head, as opposed to an Eagle, but from this distance, Stiger was not so sure. He knew he was looking at the enemy's general. The man was moving down the line, just like Stiger had just done a short while before.

The enemy general wore armor that was silver and polished to a high sheen. Even on such a dreary and miserable day, he stood out from the rest. Stiger's opposite moved with a confidence born of being in command. He seemed calm and collected, just how a professional should be. He stopped when they were directly opposite and made a show of studying Stiger. Several of the general's staff were pointing at Stiger and his entourage.

"Your opponent," Therik said to Stiger. "He seems rather confident. I don't think he's heard of you."

"It's a long shot." Stiger looked over at Eli. "Think you can hit him?"

"I do," Eli replied and pulled his bow off his back. In a flash, he had an arrow nocked. He aimed and loosed. All the while, the general just stood there and watched Stiger. He showed no alarm. The arrow flew true, only to stop impossibly in midair before its intended target. The man did not even flinch, but eyed the suspended missile curiously.

A warrior in nondescript armor who had been standing just behind the general stepped forward. He grabbed the arrow out of the air and examined it briefly before dropping the spent missile to the ground. Then he pointed at Eli and wagged an index finger.

Stiger felt a loathing as his gaze settled on the man. It was such an intense feeling, it almost made him ill. He recognized it immediately, for he'd felt the same thing when he'd held Valoor's holy scripture weeks before. The man was some sort of a warrior priest in service to Valoor.

"A paladin," Arol said. "We will need to watch him. He could prove dangerous."

"Just what we need," Stiger said as he wondered if any of the men over there with the general was Veers. Just the thought of it fed his wrath.

The general turned to an aide and said something, then gestured vaguely at the legionary line. The aide walked calmly over to a man with a horn and spoke in his ear. The horn sounded a moment later.

Almost immediately, the enemy shoved forward against the legionaries. The men of the Thirteenth pushed back hard. The intensity of the fighting increased to new levels. Despite the noise, Stiger knew that very few men were being injured or killed. It was mainly a struggle of wills at this point. Only when one side broke would the real killing begin.

"How long can your men withstand this?" Arol asked, glancing over at Stiger.

"For a good while yet," Stiger said, not taking his eyes from the enemy general. "We have depth in the ranks. There is time yet."

"They outnumber you," Jeskix said.

"They do," Stiger admitted. "We have reinforcement coming."

"When will they get here?" Arol asked.

"We do not know," Therik admitted, before Stiger could speak.

"Is this true?" Jeskix asked.

Stiger gave a nod and waved a hand at the enemy. "They stole a march on us. The rest of the army is marching to our aid."

Stiger glanced at the road headed south. There was no one on it. The only ones left on the rise were the gnomes, who had parked their large bolt thrower wagons just past the crest of the hill. There was also a steady stream of walking wounded, who were working their way back to the surgeon's tents on the other side of the rise.

"If reinforcements do not arrive soon, you may want to begin thinking about withdrawal," Arol said, "before their superior numbers begin to tell. You have already badly mauled them. They may not be prepared to pursue you. If you can manage to successfully disengage, you may be able to preserve a part of this army until your reinforcement arrives."

Stiger shot an unhappy look to Arol.

"You can kill the messenger," Arol said, "but those soldiers are good quality and they outnumber you. It can only end one way, unless something unexpected happens or the dynamic is changed in some way."

"It was a good attempt," Jeskix said. "Another lesser army would have crumbled under the pressure you put them under. But these warriors before us have strength of will and heart. They are truly a worthy foe. There is no shame in a fighting withdrawal, especially in the face of probable defeat. But withdraw you must, and soon…otherwise it will cost more in blood should you delay."

Stiger turned his gaze back to the fighting. He wanted to tell them they were wrong. And yet, he knew the truth. Though he had shattered part of the enemy army, they had not succeeded in breaking it all.

Worse, the enemy had become quite stubborn. Essentially, his men were holding their own. They could do so for quite some time to come, but eventually, as Arol had said, superior numbers would tell.

By deploying Hux, he'd delayed reinforcement. The cavalry's mounts were likely close to tiring, if not already blown. Eventually fresh enemy formations would make it up to join the fight. Stiger keenly felt the frustration of his position. He did not have any good answers and saw no real solutions. After all of his efforts, he was staring at potential defeat.

If the dwarves were close, he might be able to hold until they arrived. Yet, if they were still hours away, his decision to attack would come back to bite him. The Vass were right. The enemy would eventually overwhelm and destroy the legion. Though there was still time, he began thinking of how to pull off a disengagement that allowed him to fall back to the encampment in good order, if that was even possible. If they could make it, they might be able to hold out until relief arrived. He turned to Therik.

"What do you think?"

"I—" Therik was cut off as something almost impossibly large shot by overhead.

It hammered into the enemy's line with a crash. Stiger blinked, at first not understanding what he was seeing. A large bolt had torn through several ranks of the enemy, physically ripping men apart. The bolt had impaled itself in the dirt. The end was quivering with unspent energy.

Another bolt hammered into the last two ranks of the enemy's line, about ten feet from the general. It threw up a spray of dirt and blood into the air, which showered the general's party. A blue sphere flashed to life around the general and the paladin. The dirt and mud slid off the sphere to the ground. Like smoke blown away on the wind, the blue sphere vanished.

"Priestly medicine," Therik said in disgust. "That priest of Castor, Cetrite, could do something similar."

Stiger turned in the direction the bolts had come from. He saw the gnomes jumping up and down on one of the wagons. They were slapping each other on the back and appeared to be laughing, as if what they had done was terribly hilarious.

On the second wagon that had fired, the gnomes there worked feverishly to reload their machine. He suddenly realized what they had done. The bolt throwers only fired up into the sky, but the sick little bastards had driven the wagons over the top of the rise and down a ways on the other side, angling the bolt throwers in such a way that they could fire their deadly dragon-killing bolts directly at the enemy.

Another bolt was fired from a third wagon, parked a few dozen yards off from the others. The wagon rocked violently as the missile was released, throwing a gnome from the back of the wagon to the ground.

Stiger tracked the large missile as it flew over him. The bolt hammered into the ground, just behind the ranks of men and into the middle of the general's entourage, killing one of his aides and injuring two others.

"They're firing on the general," Eli said.

"The little bastards are," Stiger said, "and I love them for it."

Yet another bolt hammered into the enemy's line, directly to the front, taking out five men. One moment they were standing in their ranks, waiting for their turn to be cycled to the press of the front rank, and the next they were gone...snatched away, as if by a god's hand. Those around them were showered in blood, gore, and body parts.

The unexpected assault had stunned the enemy directly before them. There was no defense against it. Shields would not even offer a sliver of protection.

Centurion Nantus, leading Fifth Cohort to the front, apparently sensed some weakness, for he ordered his men to push back at the enemy. Watching Fifth Cohort work, Stiger suddenly had an idea, and the more he thought on it, the more he liked it.

"Ruga," Stiger called the centurion over.

"Sir," Ruga said.

"Gather up your men, and those of the Eagle guard too. Form them into a wedge behind Nantus's cohort."

"What?" Ruga asked with alarm. "Sir, you can't be thinking of going into action yourself."

"See that general right over there"—Stiger pointed—"and the enemy's standard…? We're going for both. We will cut the head off the snake. It is the only way to end this."

"Are you serious, sir?" Ruga appeared horrified by the concept of Stiger risking himself.

"I am," Stiger said. "The Eagle will be going with us. That way, the entire legion will see what happens. We either sink or swim on this one, so let's make sure we swim, eh?"

"Sir," Ruga said, "I think that's an uncommonly bad idea. Let me go in your stead. The men need you here and safe. There's no need to take the risk yourself."

"No." Another bolt slashed into the enemy's ranks, taking eight men with it. Stiger knew he had to go himself. There was a paladin over there, and without Father Thomas, there was no real protection against his powers. This was something he had to do, and it had to be done quickly. Besides, he felt like it was the right thing to do. That paladin had to go. "Now, form the wedge. Hurry, man, before it's too late to act."

"Yes, sir." Ruga moved off, calling for his men and those of the Eagle guard.

"Messenger," Stiger shouted. One hurried over. Stiger tapped him on the chest and pulled him close so he could be heard clearly over the fighting. He did not want any mistakes. "You go and tell the gnomes that we are going to attack the enemy's general. Once we push forward, they are no longer to fire their bolts at him, or they might hit us. Understand?"

"What if they don't understand, sir?" the messenger asked. "Or they don't want to stop?"

"Take all of the messengers with you, then," Stiger said, "and make sure they don't bloody fire, even if you have to use your swords. Make them understand you're serious. Got that?"

"Yes, sir." The messenger rushed off.

Stiger turned to Eli and Therik. "I am not going to ask you to go with me."

"We're going," Eli said, before Stiger could continue.

"Do you think I'd let one of those slaves kill you? I only have the right." Therik thumped his chest armor hard. "None other but me has that honor. I thought you understood...one day, you are mine."

Stiger felt a surge of warmth fill him at their friendship. What he was about to attempt could well prove suicidal, and they were willingly going with him.

"We will join you as well." Jeskix drew his great sword, which was in truth the largest sword Stiger had ever seen, at least three times as long and thick as a gladius. The sword was beautifully crafted and maintained. The steel was polished to a high shine and glistened in the dull light. Jeskix flexed his powerful muscles and growled. "It has been long since I tested myself. Champion of the High Father, I thank you for this opportunity to once again prove myself on the field of battle against a worthy foe."

"Brother," Arol said as he too drew his sword. It was an identical blade. "Let us honor our ancestors this day, with blood."

"Right," Stiger said, and jogged forward. Another bolt flew overhead and hammered into the ground, just beyond the enemy's line. He glanced at the enemy general, who was standing there defiantly, studying the gnome bolt throwers on the rise, which, for the most part, were tucked safely behind Stiger's line. They would not be easy to get to.

And why not stand there defiantly? Stiger thought, eyes on the general. With the paladin's shield, he had nothing to fear. But then again, he did not know Stiger was coming for him.

"Nantus! Over here, man. Nantus." Stiger waved when he caught the centurion's attention.

"Sir." Nantus made his way back through the ranks and joined Stiger. "Those bolts are doing a lot of damage to the enemy to my front. I decided to shove the enemy a little. They gave and I feel like, if we push hard enough, we can knock them back, perhaps even crack their line here."

"We're gonna do just that," Stiger said. "You are going to push forward as hard as you possibly can. I want you to break the bastards. You saw their general?"

Nantus nodded. "Yes, sir, standing there as bold as can be."

"I'm going to be right behind you with the wedge." Stiger pointed at Ruga's century and the Eagle guard, which were forming up behind Fifth Cohort. "Once you shove the enemy back, open a gap and we'll move through your formation and go for their general and standard. You got that?"

"Aye, sir." Nantus grinned at the prospect of what Stiger was about to attempt. "I do. My boys will give you what you need, sir."

"Good," Stiger said, "get to it. Quickly, man."

Nantus jogged off, and as he did, Stiger walked back to the wedge that Ruga had formed. The men eyed him as he approached. They looked grim, for they knew they were going to be thrown into the thick of it.

"We're aiming for their general and standard," Stiger said, "just over that way. Fifth Cohort will open the way and we will charge through. We keep going 'til we get to both. The entire legion will be watching us do this... I know I can count on you all."

There were grim nods all around.

Their eyes shifted to the two Vass, who arrived with Therik, Eli, and Dog.

"We're all going," Stiger said, raising his voice so they could hear him clearly. "We're going to do something that is not only stupid, but will one day become a legend amongst the legions. It'll be something that, when you're old and toothless, you can all tell your grandchildren you were there, with me, when we took the enemy's standard and killed their general."

"Ready, sir?" Nantus hollered back.

Stiger looked round and gave a thumbs up.

"Push," Nantus roared, and his cohort shoved forward.

The noise at the front increased dramatically as the legionaries from Fifth Cohort gave it their all. Stiger tightened the straps to his helmet. He drew his sword. The tingle came as a rush and he felt a surge of rage. He welcomed it, for he knew he would need it.

Yet another bolt flew at the enemy. Stiger could hear the clatter and crash above the noise of the fight as it slammed into the enemy's ranks.

"I sure hope they stop shooting when we go forward," Eli said.

"You and me both," Therik said, with a glance back at the bolt throwers. "You don't think they will shoot at me, do you? Gnomes don't much like orcs."

"You don't say?" Stiger asked and suddenly grinned at the orc. "I never knew that."

Therik shot him a scowl.

"You are rather a big target," Eli said and then looked over at the Vass. "How do gnomes feel about you, Vass?"

Jeskix bared his canines at Eli, in what Stiger hoped was a grin. The knight held his sword ready in a two-handed grip, blade pointed skyward.

Fifth Cohort moved forward several steps as the enemy to their front gave ground. Then it grew from mere feet to yards. Ruga took the point position on the wedge and hefted his shield, sword held at the ready. He looked back at Stiger and received a nod.

"Forward, boys," Ruga said. The wedge moved forward with Stiger, Eli, Therik, Dog, Beck with the Eagle, and the two Vass in its center. They followed Fifth Cohort forward, stepping over the wounded and dead. Men jabbed downward with their swords at the enemy's wounded as they stepped over them. Better to be sure than risk a knife or sword stabbed into the leg or back.

"Get ready," Ruga yelled from the point position on the wedge. "They're opening the gap."

The enemy formation suddenly broke apart, like an egg cracked open at the center, and a wide gap formed as Nantus made room for them.

"Go," Nantus shouted back at them.

"Forward," Ruga roared, "forward...kill 'em!"

"Kill!" the legionaries in the wedge shouted. The wedge charged forward through the gap Fifth Cohort had created

and into the enemy, of which there was no longer any semblance of a coherent line. The wedge hammered into them,
battering them back and down with their shields. A quick
jab from a sword ensured any who went down stayed down.

"Close up ranks," Nantus shouted behind them as he
worked to reestablish the integrity of his line.

The legionaries with the wedge bashed with their shields
as they advanced deeper into the remnants of the enemy
formation. The charge slowed to a quick jog, then a walk,
as pressure to their front increased. Behind them, Nantus's
cohort gave a great cheer and pushed forward after them.

Enemy resistance to the front grew stiffer as they simply ran into more soldiers. The legionaries in the wedge
jabbed outward with their swords, taking man after man
down. Stiger saw a thin screen of men between him and the
enemy's general, who had turned and seemed surprised by
the effort to reach him. The slave soldiers fought back with
renewed effort as they realized Stiger's objective. The general's protective guard came forward and engaged them, putting intense pressure on the wedge, which became reshaped
into more of a half-circle.

Eli had his bow up. He loosed and, at close range, took
a man in the face. Before the body had even fallen, Eli had
another arrow nocked. He dropped a second man and then
a third. A group of the enemy charged the wedge and broke
the left side of it open when two men there were cut down in
rapid succession. Stiger stabbed with his sword at one of the
attackers. The blade flared to life and easily cut through the
armor as if it were parchment. The hilt grew warm in his hand.

Kill more... Kill them all...

Arol roared and threw himself at the enemy. He swung
his great sword from side to side, each swipe knocking an

enemy bodily aside or cutting through armor, flesh, and bone. Jeskix followed after him, roaring savagely as more enemy charged them. Dog launched himself through the air like a missile and onto an enemy soldier, growling viciously as he took the man down, ripping and tearing with his teeth.

Beck swung the butt end of the Eagle's standard like it was a long spear. He smacked a man in the helmet hard and drove him down to his knees. The Eagle-bearer then pulled back and jabbed with the butt, which had been sharpened to a fine point. It found purchase in the man's neck.

Stiger saw the general close at hand. He advanced, stabbing another man in the leg. This one screamed and went to a knee. Stiger punched him in the face and then threw him roughly aside. He stabbed another man, this one in the stomach, who cried out in agony and fell away, sobbing, and curled up into a ball. A heartbeat later, he was through, and only the general and the paladin remained before him.

The paladin drew a long, thin sword and prepared to approach. But the general held up a hand said something in a language Stiger did not understand. Instead, the paladin stopped, then took a step back and reluctantly sheathed his weapon. The general drew his sword. This close, Stiger could see the faint outlines of the protective sphere.

"You are mine," the general said, in heavily accented Common. He stepped toward Stiger and out of the protective sphere, which shimmered as he moved through it.

Stiger studied his opponent. He had a hard face that had been marred by battle. The left eye had been damaged, the pupil turned a milky white. The man's forearms were nicked and scarred from years of arms training and combat. Here before him was a fellow warrior, hardened by a life in service. Even if he was dedicated to an evil god and a regime focused on the destruction of the empire, Stiger could still respect him.

"No." Stiger pointed the tip of Rarokan at him. "You are mine."

The general threw his head back and laughed deeply, as if terribly amused. "I have heard much about you, Stiger."

"Oh?"

Though the fighting continued to rage, a sort of invisible bubble seemed to have formed about them as the combatants realized that the two leaders were going to engage in personal combat and left them to it.

"You have quite the reputation," the general said. "The man who was reborn, or so the prophesy says, if you believe such things."

Stiger felt chilled by the words, but remained silent.

"Your head should prove a nice trophy," the general said and grinned nastily at Stiger. He was missing several teeth that had been knocked out. "I promise, after I kill you... for years to come, I will honor you. I will make your skull into a goblet for wine. Yes, you and I shall drink many toasts together. It will be a great honor for you and shall continually remind everyone who lays eyes upon it of your bravery at facing me."

"Were I you," Stiger growled, "I wouldn't get ahead of yourself."

Stiger waved his flaming sword before the general and then abruptly lunged. The general blocked, and as he did, his own sword burst into flames. The flames were blue, just like Rarokan.

Each took a step back, studying the other.

"You think you are the only one with a magic sword?" the general asked and grinned again. "Mine is called the Biiken

Blade. Yours? Tell me its name, so that when I take it from your lifeless hand it shall receive the honor it deserves."

Stiger had grown tired of the banter. He was here to kill this man. And that was what he would do, whether the man had a magic sword or not. He launched himself at the general. They traded a flurry of blows, each one sending blue sparks flaring out into the air. Stiger felt his hand beginning to tingle from numbness caused by the repeated blows, but he kept on battling away, pressing the general for all he was worth.

The general proved a skilled fighter, and soon, despite being soaked through from the rain that had begun to drizzle once again, Stiger felt himself beginning to perspire and breathe heavily. The general's breath came fast and hard too. They seemed evenly matched.

Still, they fought on, while the battle raged around them. Stiger ignored it all and focused exclusively on his opponent, for he could not allow even the tiniest lapse of attention.

A sword strike almost connected with his arm. Stiger jumped back and dodged at the last moment. The general reversed, then stepped forward to follow up, but he stumbled over a body and almost fell.

Stiger lunged outward, aiming what he hoped was a killing blow. Rarokan connected with the general's chest armor. Shockingly, the sword did not penetrate but screeched loudly as it scraped across. Red magical flame erupted where the sword struck the armor. It flared brilliantly, and Stiger realized the general's armor was enchanted.

The general recovered quickly and brought his sword around to strike. With his free hand, Stiger hastily gripped the general's wrist to keep him from completing the strike.

The general managed to grab Stiger's sword hand too. Locked in each other's grip, they struggled against one another. Stiger attempted to break the hold on his wrist but found it too strong.

"And now," the general said, his face very close to Stiger's, "you die."

The general's blade flared with near blinding light.

Stiger heard Rarokan cry out in his mind and felt the mad wizard struggle against the wave of power from the other sword. The blue flame on Stiger's sword went out. He felt his connection with Rarokan break and a deathly coldness begin to steel its way down into his body from both hands.

Stiger knew that some dark power was overwhelming him and was seeking his soul. He could feel the tug as it was being pulled from his body. It was much the same way Rarokan took life. His soul was under assault. He struggled against it but felt himself losing the battle. A terrible fear began to steal over him. Without Rarokan, he knew he did not stand a chance.

Time abruptly seemed to stop.

The sword was never the weapon. It was only a tool. You, my Champion, were always the weapon. Use the gift I have bestowed upon you. Do not look away from the light but embrace it.

The voice rang like a bell in his head. Stiger blinked with surprise, the motion seeming to take forever to complete. Time began moving again.

Desperately, and cursing himself for not thinking of it before now, Stiger reached within himself to the connection he had with the High Father. Like a man dying of thirst, seeking water, he touched the light. It exploded into brilliance within him. He felt his fear give way to a calmness and basked in the feeling for a moment. Then, Stiger shoved back with the power and immediately the darkness was pushed back from whence it came. The grip on his soul snapped back and away.

The general's eyes went wide in shock as his own sword's fire went out. Stiger broke the general's grip with ease. He brought his sword hilt back and hammered it into his opponent's face. Stiger felt the general's nose crunch under the blow.

Thoroughly dazed, his opponent went down in the mud. The High Father's power was coursing through Stiger, and he felt energized by it. Stiger reached down with his free hand and picked the general up by his neck, as if he were a mere child's doll. He lifted the general, screaming and gagging, up into the air and sent the High Father's power surging into the man's body. The scream cut off as white light shot from the general's mouth, eyes, and ears. Thunder cracked from the released energy. The general went limp and, with him, the light died. Stiger tossed the lifeless husk of a body aside.

The power left him and suddenly he was terribly exhausted, almost beyond measure. Rarokan reignited with flame, but it was a shadow of what it had been. The sword fed him a small surge of energy and Stiger felt slightly better, but not quite recovered. He straightened and turned toward the paladin. The man had not moved. His narrowed eyes were fixed wholly upon Stiger.

"My master will not like this," the paladin said, with a look thrown to the general's body. He glanced around quickly then returned to him. Stiger found the paladin's eyes unnaturally black. They seemed to look directly into Stiger's soul, or tried to at any rate. "You have won this day, Champion."

"You are Veers," Stiger said, "aren't you?"

"I am Lord Veers. I see we have heard of one another. It is good to know one's opponent... one's enemy."

Stiger felt an intense surge of loathing overtake him. This was the man who had sent assassins to murder him while he slept. He was responsible for Taha'Leeth being gravely injured and threatening his unborn child's life. He took a step forward, murder in his heart. Stiger wanted nothing more than to end this blight upon the world that was Veers, a paladin of Valoor.

"Oh, I think not," Veers said, taking a step backward and away from Stiger. "This is not our time, Champion. The day will come when we meet in battle... a final battle. Today is not that day. Savor your victory. You have earned it. Savor it while it lasts, for all things are fleeting.... all things come to an end."

With that, Veers took another step back and smoke seemed to envelop him. Before Stiger's eyes, the smoke evaporated in a heartbeat. Veers was gone, vanished as if he'd never been. The rage surged. Stiger cried out his wrath to the world. His enemy had escaped.

The exhaustion returned abruptly, and with it, Stiger found it hard to maintain the rage. He blinked. The world around him swam. He staggered, almost falling. Gods, he was tired, so terribly tired. The sword fed him a little more energy and Stiger sucked in a grateful breath of relief as he was able to stand.

I am very weak, Rarokan said in his mind. *I cannot spare much more energy or sleep will once again take me. Be on guard, for you are still on a battlefield.*

Stiger glanced around, looking for a new threat. Instead, he saw the enemy standard being seized by Ruga and two other legionaries. They fought like madmen against the enemy's standard guard. Around them, the rest of the enemy soldiers had seen what happened between Stiger and their general or were just now learning of it. Apparently, they'd lost the will to fight and were running or turning to flee. It seemed infectious, for it began spreading to the nearest units.

Dog jumped on the back of a man who was in mid-run and took him violently to the ground. Eli, less than ten paces away, dispatched another with his daggers. The work was swift, efficient, and blindingly fast. Therik was engaged in personal battle with what looked to be a high-ranking officer. They traded several blows and then the orc kicked out with his hobnailed boot into his opponent's right knee. The officer cried out and went down in the mud. Therik drove his sword down into the man's exposed stomach, blade punching powerfully through the armor. He screamed horribly as the orc gave a savage and violent twist to the blade.

Jeskix and Arol had charged into a line of men that were still struggling against Nantus's cohort as it shoved its way forward. Between the two of them, they killed several of the enemy in rapid succession, wielding their two-handed swords as if they weighed nothing.

Stiger looked beyond the fight immediately around him and saw that elsewhere on the battlefield the legionary cohorts had pushed forward. It seemed that men all across the line had seen the Eagle go forward and, with it, Stiger. They must have been inspired, for the legion was driving the enemy back. They were essentially manhandling the enemy's line, and the sight of it filled Stiger with great pride.

There was a deep roar. Stiger looked up to see a red dragon diving down onto the battle. It was one of the ones that had come with the Vass. It flew over the enemy's line and breathed a stream of fire down upon them, burning men by the hundreds. Another dragon was right behind it, one of the noctalum. Which one it was, Stiger had no idea.

Roaring loudly, the noctalum landed in the middle of a mass of the enemy. The ground shook violently from the impact. Stiger almost lost his footing. Dozens, if not hundreds, of men were instantly crushed. The great dragon snapped its long tail around, hurling men into the air. It breathed fire, a long stream of it, burning all it touched. The violence of the attack was incredible, awesome to behold.

Where a short while before Stiger had seen defeat, now he saw victory. What had started with the death of their general and the fleeing of Veers was completed by the return of the dragons. The enemy army came apart and ran. Wrath sated, Stiger felt an intense relief fill him. He would win, and with it, the empire would be the one giving the battlefield a name, not the confederacy.

Incredibly, he had won.

Epilogue

Stiger climbed down off the dragon's back. He'd never been so cold, wet, and miserable in his life. The sun was just coming up, poking through the scattered clouds on the horizon. Though it was drizzling, the coming day promised a break in the rain.

Eli followed him down, jumping the last two feet to the ground. Two other dragons had landed with them, and off the backs of those creatures climbed Ruga with ten men, Stiger's protection detail for the day.

They were in a field, overlooking Lorium a few hundred yards away. The enemy's abandoned camp and siege line lay all about them. Legionaries from the city had been out in the camp, scavenging around. At the sight of the dragons, they had dropped what they were doing and run for the city.

Stiger glanced around at the detritus left by the enemy. They'd left a lot behind, including wagons, a scattering of tents, and some makeshift wooden buildings they'd constructed. There was trash and discarded equipment everywhere. They'd clearly moved with some haste when the decision had been made to march against the legion.

Turning his gaze to the city, Stiger took in the damage and suddenly felt exhausted. Though the walls still stood, barring a couple of breaches, much of the city was in ruins.

That much had been apparent from the air when they'd approached. The dragons had been unwilling to go closer and so they'd set down some distance away.

Stiger rubbed at tired eyes. The battle had taken place the day before. He was still worn out and had yet to have a full night's sleep. The remains of the enemy army had scattered, including a large chunk that had never made it to the battlefield. Without the wyrms for protection, the dragons had harried them onward.

Three hours after the battle had finished, the dwarves arrived in force. To say Braddock was pissed he'd missed it all was an understatement. But Stiger had not really cared. They had won. In the end, that was all that mattered.

After the battle Stiger had wanted to remain at Taha'Leeth's side. She hadn't awoken yet and that worried him terribly. Still, he felt he had to go personally to Lorium, especially if the emperor was here, and report as soon as possible. Salt had agreed and so Stiger had climbed up onto one of the dragons that had come with the Vass and off they'd gone.

Cold and wet, Stiger shivered.

The dragon, named Inex, blew fire upon an abandoned wagon the enemy had left behind. It burst into flames. The heat washed over him and felt more than welcome. He moved closer to it, warming himself. Eli joined him.

"Thank you," Stiger said to Inex.

You are welcome, human.

The dragon spoke in his mind.

"This feels good," Eli said, joining him, "very good."

The elf was just as wet as Stiger and looked quite miserable. Ruga and his men joined them too, all warming themselves. The flight had taken a little over an hour, but the wind had been brutally cold and cut to the bone. The rain had made matters worse than miserable.

"I thought I was going to catch my death," Ruga said and shivered.

A horn call sounded from the city. It was a recall, likely for those legionaries on the other side of the city who had not seen the dragons arrive. Clearly, those in Lorium thought they were the enemy.

"How many wyrms did you catch?" Stiger asked, thinking on the enemy's dragons.

Three, Inex said, sounding disappointed. *The rest fled.*

"And losses?"

None.

"Good," Stiger said.

Another recall sounded from the city.

"I think we've scared them a tad," Ruga said, eyeing Lorium. "I'm guessing they're changing their togas about now."

"Right," Stiger said. "I think it's time we got going. No sense in continuing to frighten them."

Hating to leave the fire, Stiger started for the city, with Eli at his side. Ruga's men formed a protective bubble around them. They made their way through the remains of the enemy's camp toward the city's main gate, which surprisingly remained open.

An entire company stood just inside the open gate as they neared. The legionary company was formed up and ready for battle. Their shields were held at the ready and swords had been drawn. Stiger noted the walls were manned as well, and not by a handful either, but by hundreds of men. Archers had bows nocked and were aiming downward at them. Bolt throwers were also visible.

"Halt and declare yourself," a captain, standing to the side of the company, shouted. Beside him stood a lieutenant. Both men appeared nervous.

Stiger came to a stop.

"We seem to keep having this problem," Eli said, looking over at Stiger. "Whether it's a fort, castle, whatever...they never want to let us in."

"Think they will arrest me?" Stiger asked, somewhat amused by his friend's comment, "like they did at Fort Covenant?"

"Well," Eli said, "if they do, I won't be able to help you this time. But I do know an entire legion that would tear this city apart to rescue you, including a couple of very large noctalum. In truth, they'd be stupid to try to detain you."

Stiger gave a grunt.

"I said," the captain repeated in a tone that was becoming irritated, "declare yourself."

"Impatient," Eli said, "isn't he?"

"Legate Bennulius Stiger," Ruga shouted, before Stiger could say anything. "Commander of the Thirteenth Legion and your bloody liberator. Show some manners."

Stiger glanced over at the centurion, amused.

"I did not like his tone, sir," Ruga said.

"That makes two of us, Centurion," Eli said.

The captain turned to the lieutenant and the two began an animated conversation amongst themselves that sounded quite heated.

"Who did you say?" a voice called down from the wall over the gate. Stiger thought he knew that voice.

"Legate Stiger," Ruga hollered back.

"Ben, is that you?" the voice asked.

Stiger searched the wall and recognized the man who went with the voice from amongst the legionaries lining the walls.

"General Treim," Stiger called back and held out his arms, "it's me, in the flesh."

"Let them in," General Treim called down from above, and a moment later, the general disappeared from the wall.

"Stand aside," the captain ordered to his company.

"Let's go," Stiger said and led his escort to the gate. The captain offered a salute, which Stiger made sure to return. All eyes were on him and Eli as they passed through the massive wooden gates and entered the city.

Inside, they found most of the buildings in view were missing roofs. The city smelled strongly of smoke. Some of the buildings had completely collapsed. The debris had been moved aside to clear the streets for passage. Still, it was a shock to see the destruction up close.

Men and women lined the streets, whispering amongst themselves, for word had begun to spread. General Treim appeared, along with Colonel Aetius. They pushed people aside and approached. Both looked haggard and half starved. Clearly the ordeal of holding the city had been a difficult one. Treim looked to have aged ten years since Stiger had last seen him, before riding south with Eli to join the Southern legions.

The general walked up to Stiger and eyed him for a long moment, then stepped forward and embraced him, like he was a long-lost son. He laughed as he did it. The move completely surprised Stiger and he suddenly felt embarrassed by the overt display of emotion.

"We received your letter," Treim said.

Stiger was about to ask what letter, then remembered Salt pressuring him to write one, alerting Lorium of their presence. He had done so and with the excitement had forgotten about it. The messenger had clearly gotten through.

"You know," Treim said, "there were days I cursed myself for sending you to the South, but I had my orders from the emperor."

Stiger had not known the emperor had intervened. He'd thought Treim had done it as a favor to Kromen.

"Only you would go south with just an elf and come back with an entire legion and allies to boot." Treim turned his attention to Eli. "And you…is he still getting you into trouble?"

"Most assuredly," Eli said. "So much so, we almost were not able to dig ourselves out of it yesterday."

"The army that besieged us?" Treim asked. "That's the trouble you speak of?"

"Routed and scattered to the winds," Stiger said. "Trouble no more. My legion is a day's march from here, along with the rest of the army."

Those standing nearby had been eagerly listening for news. They began whispering amongst themselves. A few cheered. Stiger could almost sense the excitement as it raced from person to person, along with the relief.

"You defeated them?" Aetius asked.

"I did," Stiger said. "We have about ten thousand prisoners too, though that's just an estimate at this point. I don't think anyone's bothered to do a proper count yet. We also bagged a few of their dragons. That's fewer we will have to deal with in the future."

"I see you have some of your own," Treim said and nodded through the gate at the three dragons waiting out in the field.

"Allies," Stiger said. "I will be happy to introduce you to them, once I've reported to the emperor. I understand he's here. He is, isn't he?"

Treim's face fell at that. He gave a slow nod.

"What's wrong?" Stiger asked.

"I know you two were friends and played together as children. I am sorry"—Treim paused—"to give you bad news. The emperor is dying."

"He was injured in battle," Aetius explained, "by a priest of Valoor. At great cost, the Praetorian Guard managed to rescue him, but by the time they got to him, the damage was done."

"He does not have much time," Treim said. "At least we can give him some good news before he crosses over. We can speak more after we see him. Come, let me take you to him. This way."

Treim led him into the city, through a tangle of dirty and debris-strewn streets. Most of the buildings had burned and were now only shells. The stench of fire was mixed strongly with that of death. People lined the street to watch, both legionaries and civilians. They whispered and pointed. All had the gaunt appearance of the famished. Their eyes were hard and deadened.

"It looks like it's been tough here," Stiger said to Treim.

"It was bad," Treim said. "After the defeat, we fell back here and were able to hold, just barely. They gave us a difficult time until we killed two of the enemy's dragons and wounded a third with bolt throwers. That's when they settled in for a siege."

"In truth, we would not have lasted much longer," Aetius said. "We're almost out of food. We have enough for a week, at best. All the dogs, cats, rats, and pigeons are gone. There isn't much left. Some have begun eating the dead."

Stiger gave a slow nod. Having lived through a siege, he'd experienced similar conditions. A protracted siege was not a simple stroll across the road. They tended to be hard and testing.

"Well, that's no longer a problem," Stiger said. "Last evening, my cavalry captured the enemy's supply train. It is a very large haul. How many are here?"

"Just over seven thousand men left from three different legions. Most are from Third Legion," Treim said. "We have about three hundred of the Praetorian Guard. There are also at least ten thousand civilians."

Stiger stopped. He had hoped for more. "That's all? That's all the fighting men you have?"

"We lost a lot of good boys," Aetius said. "The enemy's dragons tore us apart. We had no idea they had them. We barely made it to the shelter of this city ourselves."

"Well," Stiger said, "courtesy of the confederacy we have plenty of food for you all. As soon as I return, I will order the enemy's supply train brought to the city."

"I appreciate that," Treim said and they began walking again. The general led them to a large square before the ruins of a temple to the High Father. Much of the temple had collapsed, but some of the debris had been moved aside to clear a path. The general brought them to a pair of stairs that led down into an underground complex. He started down. As Stiger climbed down after him, it became apparent there was a catacomb system under the city. He was forced to cover his nose and breathe through his mouth as the stench of sickness and death hit him hard. At the bottom of the stairs, there were injured everywhere he looked. They had been laid out on the floor, wherever there was space.

"With the dragons," Aetius explained, "we've been living underground like animals. They've taken to flying up high, well above the range of our bolt throwers, and dropping large rocks on our heads, that and bundles of lit hay soaked with oil. It's burned more than half of the city. This is one of the sick houses for those about to pass on. It is one of the better accommodations. Some are living in the sewers."

Stiger gave an unhappy nod. He'd seen such places before, where those with mortal wounds could die in peace, usually with little to no care. Still, it bothered him that the leader of the empire was down here, spending his last hours living like a rat.

"This way," Treim said and led them down a hallway lit dimly by oil lamps to a room in the back. A man in officer's armor stood just outside the room, along with two of the praetorian guard. Stiger stopped as he recognized him.

"Captain Handi?" Stiger asked. "You were on General Kromen's staff."

"Tribune Handi," the man corrected. He appeared somewhat dazed, likely due to lack of food. Then his gaze focused on Stiger's face and a look of distaste came over him. "Captain Stiger."

"Legate Stiger," he corrected and deciding to waste no more time on the fool, stepped around him and into the room, following after Treim.

When they entered, Stiger saw it was a crypt of some kind. Between two sarcophaguses was a small cot with a little space on each side. On the cot lay a man with a stomach wound. He had been propped up on pillows. Bandages had been wrapped tightly about the stomach, but even so, blood had seeped through to stain the bandage a dark red.

Though he'd not seen him in over ten years, Stiger recognized his friend in the dim light. The emperor, Tioclesion, was covered in a sheen of sweat and was clearly in great pain, for his expression was not an easy one but twisted by agony and torment. Stomach wounds were the worst. Stiger had known men to linger for weeks before succumbing.

Next to the emperor was an elderly priest sitting upon a stool. The priest was holding the emperor's hand. He looked up as they entered.

"You came," the emperor said in a weak voice, clearly recognizing Stiger. "I knew you would."

Stiger removed his helmet and handed it to Ruga. He stepped over to the emperor and knelt by his side, feeling terrible sorrow, not only for his old friend, but also for his suffering. If only a paladin was nearby, the emperor could be healed.

Tioclesion removed his hand from the priest and held it out for Stiger to take. The hand was ice-cold. Stiger realized the emperor was fading, and fast. He would likely not last the day.

"I have been given my last rites," the emperor said, nodding to the priest. "Can you believe that, Ben? Me? Given last rights?"

"No," Stiger said, remembering the times the two of them had spent playing together as children in the palace, exploring all the nooks and crannies, and driving the servants mad with worry. Those had been happy days, when things had seemed simple...before the rebellion. "I don't want to believe it."

The emperor coughed and it was a weak, pathetic sound. Blood bubbled up to his lips. The priest reached forward with a stained cloth and gently wiped it away. Stiger took a deep breath through his nose and instantly regretted it. The air was quite foul.

He considered the emperor for a long moment... Perhaps, he thought, there was something he could do. He closed his eyes and bowed his head, prepared to ask the High Father's blessing for a healing. It had not worked on Taha'Leeth, but perhaps it might with the emperor, since he was a follower of the High Father and not Tanithe. He saw no harm in asking.

"I am beyond prayers, Ben," the emperor wheezed, misunderstanding Stiger's intent.

"He is beyond your abilities, Champion," the priest said.

Stiger looked over sharply at the priest.

"I've already done what I can," the priest said. "The wound is mortal and is cursed by Valoor's poison. I assure you a healing is quite impossible."

"You're a paladin," Stiger asked, though it came out more as a statement than a question.

"Father Restus," the emperor said weakly, struggling to get the words out. They were badly slurred. "Head of his order. If anyone could heal me, it would have been him." The emperor laughed. "I am beyond help. Remember... Ben...my father used to tell me that...he used to say I was beyond help. Well, now I really am. I guess...soon I will see him. Though I have no wish to ever see that bastard again."

"I am sorry," Stiger said to the emperor, and truly he was.

"Legate Stiger has defeated the enemy army that was besieging Lorium," Treim said.

"That pleases me," the emperor said and then laughed again. He almost immediately regretted it, as it caused him great pain. He gritted his teeth and moaned until the pain had passed, then calmed himself and took a few labored breaths before attempting speech again. "You have been busy."

"A little busy," Stiger admitted. "You should rest. We can talk more later, when you have the strength."

"We talk...now. Soon enough, I will have plenty of time for rest," the emperor wheezed. "Treim, Restus, can you hear me? I can't see you. It's gotten so dark in here."

Both were close at hand. Treim was standing just behind Stiger. The level of light had not changed since Stiger had entered the crypt.

"Yes," Treim answered for the both of them, "we can."

"That is good," the emperor said and took a deep breath. "Now...for my last command, for I feel myself slipping over to the shade. The ferryman is calling, beckoning me to pay his fee and cross the great river."

The emperor's gaze shifted to Stiger and he could read the fear of an impending death in his old friend's fading gaze. The hand tightened ever so slightly.

"Restus tells me you are the High Father's Champion, as was prophesized."

"I would dearly love to see that prophesy," Stiger said, looking over at the paladin. "Everyone, it seems, has seen it but me."

"You are descended from Karus himself," the emperor said, "an honor even my family cannot claim." The emperor coughed again, attempting to clear his lungs. It was a pathetic sound. "As prophesized, you have come to save the empire. Long ago, I was shown...shown...a vision... I did not want to believe... It was why when I came to the curule chair...I spared you and your family. The vision was his work."

Stiger felt himself go cold at the emperor's words. There was no doubt who he meant.

"The High Father showed me the truth..." The emperor coughed again. When he recovered, he managed to stir himself. He gripped Stiger's hand tightly. "I name you..." The emperor wheezed and struggled to suck in a breath. It seemed to take a tremendous effort. The emperor almost completely sat up, pulling himself closer to Stiger. "I name you, Ben, my successor. I have no heir. I never married. I...name...you." Then, he collapsed back onto the cot, a pleased smile upon his face. "There, I've gone and done it. I've cursed you, my friend...cursed you with the headache that is the senate and the empire...but it's what I was shown. You...are...meant...to be...emperor."

"What?" Stiger asked in shock, looking over at Restus. Had he heard correctly? Surely not. The paladin leaned forward and felt the emperor's neck. Stiger realized that the emperor's hand, which he was still holding, had gone slack.

"Oh, no," Stiger breathed.

Restus closed the emperor's eyes.

The paladin pulled a gold imperial talon from a pocket and placed it in the emperor's hand. He bowed his head in silent prayer, then looked over at Stiger.

"Long live the emperor," Restus breathed, after a slight hesitation. "Long live Emperor Stiger."

"No," Stiger gasped, letting go of the hand and looking toward Treim and Aetius. Behind them stood Ruga.

"Isn't that some shit," Ruga said, his eyes on his legate.

Stiger could not help but agree with the sentiment.

Rarokan laughed ominously in his mind.

"Long live Emperor Stiger," General Treim shouted out into the corridor.

Aetius joined in. "Long live the emperor."

Stiger could hear the call repeated as it spread outside the crypt.

General Treim and Aetius knelt as Stiger woodenly stood.

"Wait," Stiger said in growing alarm. It came out as a gasp. He suddenly recalled his conversation with Therik as they'd ridden up to Castle Vrell. Stiger had told the former king about the slave whose job it was to whisper in the victorious general's ear during the triumphant ride through the capital. Then his thoughts shifted to Taha'Leeth and how he'd changed. He was no longer mortal...but something else... Stiger felt a burst of panic. "This can't be. I can't be the emperor, not me...not with my family."

"It is meant to be," Treim said. "For better or worse, you are the emperor, and I swear upon my family's honor, my ancestors, and my life to serve you loyally."

"I swear as well," Aetius said, with a smile of pleasure on his face.

"It is fitting," Eli said.

"What do you mean it is fitting?" Stiger demanded. "This is bullshit. I am not cut out to be emperor."

"No one will dare lock you up now," Eli said. "I knew you would always make something of yourself."

"Very funny," Stiger said.

"You are the emperor, sir." Ruga saluted and then knelt. "I am honored to follow you."

"We don't kneel to our emperors," Stiger snapped, becoming irritated.

"No, sir," Ruga replied, "but you are doubly blessed, being the High Father's Champion and all."

"I will agree with that," Restus said. "He is gods blessed."

"Good gods," Stiger breathed in shock. "I never wanted this."

"No, sir," Ruga said, "that's why Eli's right. It's fitting that you should not want to be emperor. It's why me, my boys and the legion will follow you to the Seven Levels and back, sir."

Stiger glanced back on the corpse of his childhood friend and suddenly felt the need for fresh air. He had to clear his head and think, even if just for a moment. He brushed past everyone, left the room. He pushed by a visibly astonished Handi and the two praetorians, who had been standing in the way. Stiger made his way back up to the surface. The rest of his escort was out there, waiting, but so too were hundreds of civilians and legionaries. Word had spread about his arrival and defeat of the enemy army. Then had come word from the catacombs of the new emperor. Stiger stumbled to a stop, astonished to see so many gathered before the temple, filling the square.

"Long live the emperor," someone shouted, and then it was taken up as a chant by all. "Long live the emperor. Long live Emperor Stiger."

"Oh, shit," Stiger said to himself. "I am truly and thoroughly screwed."

The End

Interested in how Stiger began his military career? Read on.

For those who have not yet discovered the Tales of the Seventh series and how it all began with Stiger and Eli...I have included this two-chapter preview of *Stiger, Tales of the Seventh: Part One.*

Enjoy,
Marc

STIGER

Part One
Tales of the Seventh

ONE

"Ah, yes...the young Lieutenant Stiger. How can I help you?"

"Captain Bruta." Stiger offered a salute.

Bruta ignored the salute, turning back to his drink and companion. Corporal Varus, who had been following Stiger, stopped a few steps behind him. Stiger sensed the corporal was bored and longed to be somewhere else—really anywhere else—than with him, a junior lieutenant. Seven Levels, Stiger thought, I want to be anywhere but here at this supply depot.

Bruta looked up from the roughly cut wooden table he sat at with another officer and simply gazed at Stiger, an irritated expression on his pock-marked face. Both officers before Stiger were wearing their service tunics, which did not carry rank insignias or the trappings of office. The two had been sharing a drink. The other officer scowled at Stiger's presence before taking another pull from his cup.

A merchant had set up shop inside the rapidly growing supply depot, which sprawled around them. The merchant had clearly just arrived. He had yet to pitch his canopy to provide some shade from the early summer sun, but had managed to set out several rough tables and a few rickety-looking stools, at which several patrons were enjoying cheap, watered-down wine or ale.

Two slaves were busy digging holes for what Stiger presumed would be the canopy's support posts. The rolled-up canopy lay next to the merchant's heavy wagon loaded with wooden casks, amphorae, and crates. A third slave was slowly unloading the wagon.

Behind Bruta and his drinking companion, Stiger could see several auxiliaries on sentry duty slowly walking the walls, on the lookout for any approaching trouble—particularly the Rivan, with whom the empire was currently at war. Inside the depot, several crude wooden buildings, including a headquarters and barracks, had been raised, with a number of other structures in partial states of construction. The growing, fortified compound gave the impression the empire expected to be here for a long time to come.

Bruta said nothing for several uncomfortable and embarrassing seconds.

"I have been waiting much of the day," Stiger said. "I need…"

"Bruta, tell this pup to go on his way," the other officer said in a bored tone. He then looked up directly at Stiger. "Let us men drink in peace, boy."

Stiger bristled at this, but held his tongue. Not only were both officers senior to him, they were also much older. He had no idea who Bruta's companion was, but the man's age and manner alone told Stiger he was at least a captain. Stiger assumed that he was the prefect commanding the auxiliary cohort that had been stationed at this depot. There was no other reason for a senior officer other than Bruta to be here.

Stiger was still relatively new to serving with the Eagles, and he was unsure of himself. He had only recently arrived to take up his first military appointment as an infantry lieutenant serving in the Third Legion, Seventh Company. Stiger had discovered, to his disappointment, the legion's officer corps had been anything but welcoming. In fact, his fellow officers had been outright discourteous to the point of rudeness.

"Lieutenant," Bruta said, looking up with a scowl, "can't you see I am having a peaceful drink here with my friend, the prefect?"

"Yes, sir," Stiger conceded. "I can."

"Then why are you still bothering me?"

"I have orders from Captain Cethegus," Stiger said stiffly, "my commanding officer."

"Cethegus." Bruta barked out a laugh. "That fool deserves you, Stiger, you know that, don't you? An incompetent fool saddled with a traitor's son. Somehow, I find that fitting."

"Sir," Stiger said, struggling to contain his mounting anger. The accusation, however true, burned. Stiger glanced over at Varus, ashamed the corporal had heard the outright insult. Varus glanced quickly away. Perhaps Stiger should have left him with the rest of the escort like he had with Corporal Durus. He looked back to Bruta. "All I want is for my wagons to be loaded with the requisitioned supplies and then to be on my way."

Bruta took a pull from his drink. He sucked in a deep breath that turned into a heavy sigh. For a moment the supply officer said nothing and then turned his gaze slowly back up to Stiger.

"You and every other company from the Third wants something from me," Bruta said heavily. A fly buzzed around his drink. The captain shooed it away with a hand.

"My supply train is the only one present," Stiger said, becoming exasperated. He gestured with a helpless feeling over to the neatly organized stacks and piles of supplies just a few yards off. A number of slaves lounged about, doing no work under the hot midday sun. "Your slaves are doing nothing."

"Even slaves occasionally need rest," Bruta said with a barely concealed chuckle and smirk directed at the prefect.

"They are slaves," Stiger said, the helpless feeling growing more acute. He knew damn well the supply officer was toying with him, intentionally dragging his feet. It had been the same act each time Stiger had come to fetch supplies for his company.

"That is an exceptionally keen observation," Bruta's companion said sarcastically.

"I am expected back this evening," Stiger said, trying another approach. "If we do not get the wagons loaded soon, I will be unable to follow my orders."

"That's your problem." Bruta laughed openly, sparing Stiger a broad smile with a number of broken teeth. The man's nose had been shattered many times and was mashed off to the side slightly. Combined with the pox scars, Captain Bruta was one devastatingly ugly man. "My slaves need the rest."

"Then we shall load the wagon ourselves," Stiger said. "That way your slaves can get the rest they so well deserve."

"You will do nothing of the kind," Bruta barked. "I won't have your thieving men go near my supplies. No telling what they would take. No, Lieutenant, your men touch nothing."

Stiger was silent a moment as he considered the situation. Being treated abominably due to his name was something to which he had become accustomed in recent years.

Stiger had no friends or patrons in Third Legion. As such, he worked himself harder than anyone else, determined to let his actions speak for him. In essence, Stiger was struggling forward to make a name for himself, apart from the disgrace his father had inflicted upon the family.

Until this moment, Stiger had bit his tongue and taken whatever abuse had been thrown his way. Disgraced or not, his family was still powerful. Somehow they had managed to hold on to their senatorial seat, one of only a hundred. The man before him, an officer from a relatively minor house, was intentionally disrespecting him. It was an affront not only to his, but also his family's, honor. What little there was left.

Stiger knew he would be justified in challenging Bruta to a duel. However, he also understood such a challenge was impossible. General Secra, commander of the Third Legion, had prohibited all such contests of honor. It had been made clear that any officer issuing a challenge or participating in a duel would be harshly punished. Unfortunately, General Secra had recently sickened and died. Yet, even in death, the order stood, and Stiger was bound to obey.

The legion was waiting on its new temporary commander, General Treim, who was due to arrive any day. The emperor would eventually get around to selecting a permanent commander for the Third, who would in turn be approved by the senate. That would take months. With luck, General Treim would put such useless officers as Captain Bruta in their place. Until then, Stiger was completely helpless and at the mercy of this lazy, incompetent officer.

Prior to Stiger's arrival to take up his appointed posting, the Third had driven a small Rivan army from the frontier back into enemy territory. It had fought several pitched battles along the way. With the death of its general, the Third had been ordered to wait for a replacement. That had been two months ago. Accordingly, the legion had stopped its pursuit and now stood idle. Supply depots like this one had been erected all the way back to the frontier, with the intention of keeping the legion and a number of newly made garrisons supplied.

"Well then." Stiger let out an explosive breath and shifted his stance slightly. "When do you expect your slaves to be sufficiently rested and able to return to work?"

"That's hard to say." Bruta furrowed his brow in an exaggerated appearance of consideration. Bruta's drinking companion chuckled. "Perhaps in a day or two."

Stiger was silent as he thought things through. He was tired of feeling helpless. There was simply nothing he could do to influence the situation to his advantage…or was there? Stiger's eyes narrowed slightly. Bruta was a bully, inflicting petty cruelty on someone he thought was in an inferior position. Though the supply captain was higher in rank, Stiger could easily turn the tables on him. Bruta could be put in an inferior position. Stiger almost smiled but resisted the temptation. He would play Bruta's game, but change the terms.

"I guess there is nothing more I can reasonably do," Stiger said with a quick glance over at Varus, who was studying the ground at his feet and still looking very much like he desired to be anywhere but here. "You have tied my hands."

"I have, haven't I?" Bruta laughed openly as he took another gulp from his drink. It was a harsh barking laugh that Stiger found doglike, and it grated on his nerves, as did just about everything to do with this man. Bruta was a mockery of what a legionary officer should be.

At that moment, the merchant came around the corner of his wagon and suddenly provided Stiger a welcome interruption. Stiger beckoned for the man to come nearer.

It was hot. Stiger glanced up at the sun and wiped sweat from his brow with the side of his hand as the merchant made his way over.

"How may I help you, sir?" The merchant smiled. Filled with yellowed and rotten teeth, it was not a pleasant smile. The merchant had been working, and he quickly wiped a hand on his greasy apron. Stiger looked disdainfully on the man, wondering if he had ever heard of such a thing as a bath, or for that matter having his tunic and apron laundered. He stank of stale wine, ale, and sweat—all made worse by the heat of the day.

"What is your finest bottled wine?"

Stiger feared the response. They were in barbarian territory, hundreds of miles from civilization. There was likely nothing good to be had, and he suspected he would be forced to settle for some inferior vintage that was overly acidic. The thought of it almost made him cringe.

"I have several cases of red from Venney," the merchant said after considering the young officer before him. The merchant had made a quick study of the quality of Stiger's armor and had likely judged him to be of some means, which was why he had suggested such an expensive vintage. "Just came in on a caravan from Cress a few days ago."

"Venney?" Stiger asked him, surprised.

"Indeed, sir."

"How much?" Stiger was pleased that such high quality wine could be had, but also concerned with what he would have to pay.

"For you, young sir..." The merchant thought for a moment. "A half silver talon."

"That's robbery," Stiger scoffed. "I shall pay no more than a quarter."

"I could not accept less than a half," the man countered. "Alas, we are far from civilization, and such a fine vintage is difficult to come by."

"What is your name?" Stiger scratched at an itch on his arm.

"Trex, noble sir." The wine merchant bowed in a show of respect.

"Do you know Arrus the wine merchant?" Stiger asked him with a raised eyebrow. He had a feeling the man knew his competition. It was time to test it.

"I do," Trex said, the smile slipping from his face. It returned a moment later, a little forced. "He is most untrustworthy in his dealings."

"I have no doubt he is as dishonest as you say," Stiger said, and the wine merchant's smile became more genuine at that. "Yet, Arrus has set up shop with the Third's camp followers."

"He did?" Trex looked unhappy at such news.

"A few days ago, he sold me a similar vintage that was quite fine for a quarter talon." Stiger did not mention that the wine he had bought was not from Venney, but a half talon was highway robbery, even this far beyond the frontier. A quarter was high too, but it was to be expected, and Stiger considered it a reasonable price to pay.

The smile disappeared at that. "He did?"

Stiger nodded. "I would much rather do business with someone like you. Arrus is disagreeable, but his prices are better. I am sure you can see the position I am in."

The merchant looked agonized as he considered the possibility of losing business to a competitor and weighed that against potentially getting a better price from another noble of sufficient means at a later date.

"Very well," the merchant conceded and bowed his head. "A quarter then."

Stiger took out his purse and removed a quarter talon from it. He handed it over. "Have the case delivered to my detachment immediately." He paused and gestured with a hand. "We are on the other side of the depot over that way."

"I will, sir. Thank you for your patronage." Trex bowed and turned. He then stopped and looked back. "I hope you will seek me out for future purchases. May I have your name, noble sir?"

"Stiger."

The merchant froze. His eyes widened. Then he rapidly recovered. Trex bowed very respectfully, then bustled around to the other side of his wagon to see to the order. Stiger watched him disappear.

"You should have been a merchant, Stiger," Bruta grunted in amusement.

"Corporal Varus," Stiger snapped, ignoring Bruta and turning to the corporal.

"Sir?" Varus said, clearly surprised that he was being addressed.

"Have the men fall in and the mules hitched up," Stiger ordered. "We will leave as soon as my wine is delivered."

"Yes, sir." Varus saluted. He glanced briefly over at the supply captain and then back to Stiger before he turned to go.

"Leaving us?" Bruta asked, a surprised and mocking expression on his face. "So soon?"

"Yes, sir." Stiger turned back to the supply officer.

"Without your supplies?"

"I will report that I was unable to obtain the supplies the Seventh and the Tenth companies require to continue operations."

Bruta paused mid-drink and turned slowly to look over at the lieutenant. The man's eyes narrowed dangerously.

Stiger continued in a bored tone. "Captain Cethegus might not say anything, sir, but I am quite confident that Captain Lepidus will file a complaint." Stiger shrugged as if it were no concern of his.

Stiger knew the captain of the Tenth would be furious. Unlike Stiger's own captain, Lepidus was a stern, no-nonsense officer. He would either make the trip himself to see Bruta or would indeed put in a complaint. If that happened, command would likely wish to know why the supply captain had denied the properly requisitioned supplies. Stiger did not think it would get that far. He was betting Bruta would not allow it.

"Well then, I believe our business here is concluded. Good day, sir." Stiger snapped a smart salute and turned to Varus.

The corporal had stopped to watch the exchange and was looking on his lieutenant with a funny, almost amused expression.

"Wait," Bruta barked harshly, standing and pushing his stool back with a leg. It toppled over in the dry dirt. "You don't threaten me, you little shit, even if you are a Stiger."

Stiger turned back to Bruta with an innocent look. "I am truly sorry that you think that, sir. I assure you that was not my intention. I make no threats."

Bruta took a step toward him, hands flexing in anger. The man was not wearing his armor. He had on only his service tunic, and unlike many of the legion's frontline officers, he was overweight and going soft. This was likely the result of eating well, a perk of being in the supply branch.

Safe behind the walls of the depot, Bruta was also unarmed. Stiger, on the other hand, wore his segmented armor. He was armed with his short sword and dagger. Despite that, the supply officer towered over him, and Stiger questioned himself for a moment. Then he ground his teeth. The man was a petty bully, and Stiger had tired of his game. He was determined to see this through.

He stepped closer to Bruta, into the man's personal space. Jaw clenched, he was unafraid.

Stiger's father had paid some of the best tutors the empire had to teach his son how to fight. Though fresh to his posting and still unsure of himself, Stiger was in perfect shape. He was confident in his ability to defend himself, both armed and unarmed, especially against a soft supply-type like Bruta. His hand came to rest casually on the pommel of his sword.

"I am a Stiger, and I will report as I have said I would." Stiger allowed some of the anger he was feeling to seep into his tone. "I assure you, sir, I make no threats."

"You little shit," Bruta breathed. Stiger did not back down. He was unsure whether it would shortly come to blows, but he had taken enough grief from men like Bruta. However, beating a senior officer insensible would not advance his career. Stiger was beginning to regret his decision somewhat. Though he had to admit to himself that it felt good to goad this disagreeable man to anger.

Bruta glanced quickly over toward the officer he had been drinking with. The prefect, who outranked both of them, simply looked on but said nothing. Though likely from an influential family, the man's tunic was cut from inferior quality. He was probably of the equestrian class and had more sense than Bruta.

"Very well…" Bruta exhaled when it became clear the other officer would not back him up. He seemed to deflate. Stiger smelled the onion mixed with cheap wine on the man's breath.

The supply officer turned away and shouted for the overseer of the slaves, who had been sleeping nearby in the shade from a pile of stacked crates.

Bruta quivered with anger. "You will have your supplies, you bastard."

"Thank you, sir." Stiger saluted and restrained himself from smiling. He had won. It had been a minor victory, but it felt good nonetheless. He found Varus eying him with a trace of a grin. The corporal wisely said nothing as they made their way back to their wagons. Stiger noticed that the prefect's eyes followed him as he walked off.

"Make sure my wine arrives before we leave," Stiger said to the corporal.

"Yes, sir," Varus replied neutrally.

Two hours past noon, Stiger had his twelve heavy wagons fully loaded. The teamsters, all hired civilian contractors, looked on with bored expressions as Stiger's two files of legionaries formed up. One file, Corporal Varus's, would march to the front of the supply column, and the other, Corporal Durus's, to the rear, with a few men floating about the middle.

Sitting astride his horse, Stiger swatted at a fly as he waited impatiently for Corporal Varus, the senior corporal, to get the men organized. It seemed as if things were taking longer than they should. Seven Levels, Stiger thought with frustration, everything the army did took longer than it should. The men were moving slowly, and it infuriated him. Stiger stifled the urge to yell at Varus and instead forced himself to project the calm countenance of an officer in control.

In the sweltering heat of the afternoon, Stiger found even that difficult. He was hot, uncomfortable, and cooking in his armor. There was no breeze, only waves of heat that rolled down from above. The sooner they got moving, the sooner he would have some relief.

"All ready, sir," Varus reported finally.

"FOORWAAARD," Stiger hollered without a second's hesitation. "MAAAARCH."

Shields in their canvas coverings, short spears resting on shoulders, and helmets hanging from ties about their necks, the legionaries to the front of the column started moving, armor chinking and jangling. A few moments later, the lead wagon, with a snap of the teamster's whip and a braying of the mules, followed by an ungodly rattle, trundled forward.

"Join your file," Stiger said to Varus, who dutifully saluted and left at a jog. Stiger watched the corporal go and felt relief. He had difficulty tolerating the man's presence. Varus was big, even for a legionary. The corporal was brutish and uncouth. Though he could write and manipulate numbers, a requirement of his rank, he was fairly uneducated. Stiger found Varus dull and boorish company, certainly not fit for a proper conversation. Like the rest of the men, the mere presence of the corporal irritated Stiger immensely.

"Hup, my beauties," the teamster in the second wagon called loudly to his drowsing mules. A crack of the whip followed. "Hup now, hup."

The covered wagon, neatly stacked and piled high with supplies of all sorts, rattled forward, following the first. Stiger watched and waited with barely concealed patience. He hated supply escort duty, but it was what had been assigned to him. He had to see the duty through. There was no avoiding it. After the sixth wagon started rumbling out of the supply depot, he nudged his horse forward and into a walk. A bored-looking auxiliary guarding the gate offered a weak salute, which Stiger sullenly returned.

Stiger pulled his horse off of the dirt road and onto the grass. The supply depot had been constructed alongside the main road going north and into Rivan territory, in a grass-covered prairie that rolled with gentle hills. The depot sat atop one of the larger ones, tall enough that it provided a fairly good field of view in all directions.

To the north, Stiger could see a dark tree line in the distance. This marked the beginning of a small forest through which they would need to pass before the prairie continued for a number of miles farther. Then they would enter another wooded area. The North seemed replete with small forested patches. Stiger let out a slow, unhappy breath. At least the trees would provide some relief from the baking sun.

Stiger's horse whinnied, eager to be off. He patted his mount affectionately. Nomad was a good, solid animal. The horse was a parting gift from his father, and one of the few things that Stiger was grateful for from the old man. His commission in the legions was another gift from his father, who had paid the price to buy his son a lieutenant's commission. Though he could easily have afforded a captaincy, Stiger's father had started out his military service as a lieutenant and felt that was where his son's career should also begin. At first, Stiger had been elated with his rank. Then he'd arrived to take up his duties with the Third and been assigned to Seventh company.

Almost immediately, his fellow officers made it plain they disdained him for who he was, his father's son. They took every petty opportunity to snub him, acting as if they could barely tolerate his mere presence. Frequently, they played the game of pretending that he did not even exist. Senior officers were worse, demanding more from him duty-wise than other lieutenants. It was all very ungentlemanly and bothered him to distraction. This led Stiger, whenever possible, to actively avoid the company of his peers. The injustice of it pained him greatly.

Stiger's father had once been a great general, one of the more accomplished military leaders the empire had ever put in command of a field army. Stiger's family had been proud, powerful, and above reproach. That had lasted until the elder Stiger had backed the wrong son and the losing side in a civil war over succession to the throne. It had cost the family greatly and seen his father confined to his estate outside of Mal'Zeel, a prisoner in all but name these past five years. As punishment, many of the family estates and lands around the empire had been confiscated, but through some miracle, the family had managed to hang onto their senatorial seat. Stiger's older brother, his father's firstborn, now served in that capacity.

With no lands or titles to inherit, the younger Stiger had turned to the military, as his father once had. But where his father had been accepted and welcomed as a noble from a great house, Ben Stiger was shunned and cut out of camp society.

Stiger gripped the reins tightly with irritation. He found it terribly humiliating. It was so unfair. He was being judged on his father's merit and not his own. He slapped the palm of his hand on his thigh as Nomad continued to walk alongside the tail end of a wagon. All he wanted was to serve and win glory for himself and his house.

Upon joining the Third, Stiger had expected constant action and excitement. There was a war on. Instead, he suffered through boredom and a tedious existence that continually tested and frustrated him. Life in the legion was exceedingly boring, made worse by the attitude of his fellow officers.

Captain Cethegus was the worst. He seemed to resent Stiger even more than the rest. The captain was also a recent appointment. From the moment Stiger had arrived, the captain had not hesitated to let his feelings of disgust be known about having Stiger serve as his second-in-command. Cethegus had handed over to Stiger every shit job there was, including supply train escort duty.

The senior officers of the camp usually rotated the duty amongst the junior officers, but Stiger seemed to get stuck with it more often than not. There was nothing he could do about it, and so Stiger had privately resolved to do his duty to the best of his ability, no matter what injustice was heaped upon him. There would come a time, he vowed, that would see him treated for his ability and the glory he achieved on the battlefield. He would not be treated for who his father was. Each night, before he turned in, Stiger made a point to pray to the High Father, asking for the great god's assistance in sustaining him during this difficult time.

Stiger's mind drifted as they continued up the dry and dusty road that was little more than a track. They passed through the small forest he had seen from a distance, and beyond. The dirt road was nothing like the paved solid roads of the empire. Abandoned farm fields lined both sides of the road. They had become depressingly familiar, and though it had been many weeks, the barren fields still bore evidence of the scorch-and-burn tactics the Rivan army had employed as it pulled back before the might of Third Legion, stopping only long enough to occasionally counterpunch and offer battle.

A small, mean hut just off of the road to his left had been burned, leaving only a charred shell of rounded stakes and blackened foundation stones. What Stiger took to be a modest planting patch had also been scorched by fire. The enemy had burned everything for miles around. They had also driven their own people from their homes and marched them north. Nothing of value had been left behind, only desolation.

Once the war ended, life would return. These burnt and charred fields would be replanted. Before long, the empire would send imperial land agents and speculators. Soon thereafter, settlers would follow. It would only be a matter of time before this land became a new imperial province.

Stiger walked his horse around a large rut in the road. Even this sad track would be converted into an imperial road. As it had in other places, the empire would bring civilization, order, and law to these lands. A rich province filled with villages, towns, and cities would grow from the newfound order. Third Legion led that noble effort, and Stiger was proud to be part of it.

The Rivan were a determined foe, perhaps the most serious the empire had faced in centuries. Upon imperial decree, the legions had crossed the border in retaliation for repeated Rivan raids into the border provinces of the empire. The Third Legion was the empire's vanguard and spear point for the much larger imperial army, aimed at putting this dangerous enemy down. Four additional legions had been gathered. Now that the fighting season had arrived, they would soon follow the Third's advance north.

In the weeks and months ahead, Stiger understood keenly there was bound to be the opportunity to win glory. Thus, he would begin the hard work of wiping the stain from his name. The men of the Seventh, as foul, uncouth, and uneducated as they were, would help him achieve that. In Stiger's eye, they were no different than any other tool at his disposal.

The wagon Stiger was riding next to suddenly ground to a halt. He looked over at the teamster with an unhappy scowl, and then ahead. All of the wagons to the front had also stopped. They had entered another small forest, and the road bent around to the right and out of sight. Stiger could not see the cause. He spurred his horse forward and galloped up to the front. When he rounded the bend, Stiger pulled Nomad to a stop. Several hundred head of cattle were blocking much of the road ahead. Just beyond the cattle was a small river, which the road crossed in a narrow and shallow ford.

Drovers, along with as many as a dozen slaves, were busy beating the herd across the river. They yelled, called, and with long reed switches smacked the behinds and sides of the animals in an effort to move them across. Under the heat of the baking sun, the cattle desired nothing more than to drink when they reached the water's edge and seemed quite immoveable.

Stiger spared an exasperated glance up at the heavens and then down at the corporal, who was striding over. It seemed everything was conspiring to slow him down, which would not go over well with Captain Cethegus.

"Sir," Varus saluted, "cattle for the Third."

"I can see that," Stiger said irritably. "Do you suppose we can move them aside?"

"I don't think so, sir," Varus replied with a wary look at his lieutenant, almost as if he expected Stiger to give such an order.

"I suppose not," Stiger said, studying this side of the river as he wiped sweat from his forehead with the back of his arm. With the trees pressing in on both sides of the road, there was no room to move the wagons around the herd.

Stiger knew from repeated crossings of this river that the ford itself was quite narrow. On the other side of the river, the terrain opened up. It looked as if the opposite bank had at one time in the distant past been cultivated. There were the remains of a small barn—only the stone foundation and a couple of walls. The rest of the structure had collapsed in upon itself. The ruin was overgrown with brush, several young saplings sprouting from inside the decaying walls.

"Orders, sir?" Varus shifted uncomfortably in the heat. He, like the rest of the men and Stiger, was baking in his armor.

"Stand the men down," Stiger said, resigned to fate. "Might as well have them eat their rations and refill canteens."

"Ah, yes, sir," Varus said, and Stiger sensed the man seemed a little uncomfortable.

"You have something to say?" Stiger asked, looking down on the corporal from his horse. This was the first time he had been assigned Varus's file to help with escort duty. The other file was led by Corporal Durus, whom Stiger could stand less than Varus. "Say it, man."

"We are in enemy territory, sir," Varus said. "I recommend we set a watch and bring as many of the wagons up and together as possible in the event of trouble."

"The Rivan have retreated north," Stiger said.

"Their army has, sir," Varus said. Stiger noticed the corporal's careful tone. "They would only need a handful of men to strike at our supply trains."

Though he was in a sour mood, Stiger nodded slightly. What Varus said made sense. His military tutors had mentioned time and again that good officers listened to their sergeants and corporals. Uneducated and uncouth though he may be, there was no doubt in Stiger's mind that Varus knew his business of soldiering. If Varus was concerned, then perhaps Stiger should be as well.

Stiger glanced back down the road, narrowing his eyes against the brightness of the sun. There was just enough room along the road to double up the wagons side by side.

"Very well." Stiger let out an explosive breath and turned back to Varus. "Bring the wagons up as much as possible. Detail a watch and some men to refill canteens."

"Thank you, sir," Varus said, and Stiger noticed a look of relief on the corporal's face.

"Do we have any scouts with us?" Stiger asked.

"Yes, sir. One with each file."

"Send them out into the forest to look for evidence of the enemy." Stiger pulled out one of his own canteens from a saddlebag and unscrewed the top. Taking a deep pull of the warm, stale water, he looked unhappily at the mass of cattle ahead. "Might as well put the scouts to some use."

Varus was silent, and Stiger looked over at him.

"Anything else, Corporal?"

"No, sir."

"Good," Stiger said. "Dismissed."

Varus saluted and left to pass along Stiger's orders.

Stiger nudged his horse forward, skirting around the edge of the cattle moving upriver, away from the animals and their stench. The drovers shouted and cursed the animals as they prodded them toward the river crossing. So far, they had managed to get only a handful across. Stiger had a sneaking suspicion he had a long wait ahead. For a fleeting moment, Stiger considered ordering his men to hurry the animals across, but then dismissed the idea. His men had just marched several miles, and it was gods awful hot out. They needed a break, and this was as good a place as any to take one.

The river was shallow, anywhere from two to five feet deep, perhaps a little more, and slow moving. The water was clear. Stiger could see right down to the rock-studded bottom. Any fish that had been about had been driven away by the commotion of the cattle. They made an awful racket.

Stiger dismounted and led Nomad to the water's edge. Upstream from the crossing, he found a small tree to loop the reins loosely around. Nomad would be able to drink at will. Stiger drained his canteen in one swallow and then refilled it. He drank some of the cool river water and refilled the canteen again before returning it to a saddlebag. He then went and found a rock on the river's edge that was in the shade and sat down, his back against a tree that grew up right next to it.

Even in the shade it was hot, though the proximity to the water cooled the air somewhat. Stiger closed his eyes and dozed for a bit. After forty-five minutes, Varus reported that the scouts had found no evidence of the enemy. Stiger accepted the report, and then settled back in to wait.

It took over an hour and a half before the last of the cattle were splashing their way across the river. Stiger had impatiently mounted up and called his men to fall in as the last of the animals were driven over. The first wagon had rumbled off, but what should have been quick work turned into a painful nightmare.

The cattle had churned the soft river bottom into a morass of sucking and clinging mud. The wheels of the wagon almost immediately sank deeply into the river bottom and became stuck fast. Stiger considered unloading each wagon and carrying the supplies across, but that would have taken too much time. Instead it proved quicker for the men to push and pull each heavily loaded wagon across, straining with the effort as the river bottom tried its best to keep them from succeeding.

Stiger sat astride Nomad along the edge of the crossing and watched it all as the men worked, becoming muddy and weary. As he waited and fumed impatiently, Stiger glanced down at the dried mud and disturbed grass along the outer edges of the narrow ford. It was heavily marked with evidence of previous crossings. Since he had taken up his post with the Third, Stiger had made this crossing at least a dozen times without incident. Watching his men struggle to work each wagon across, Stiger realized that he had just learned something of importance about river crossings and the time they could suck up. He mentally filed it away.

"All lessons come with a price," Stiger said wryly as he recalled a saying his father had been fond of using.

TWO

Stiger crossed after the last wagon, Nomad splashing easily through the water and quickly across. The drovers had moved their herd to one of the abandoned farm fields away from the water's edge, allowing the animals a graze and themselves a well-earned break. The supply train was lined up along the road. The teamsters were clustered in small groups, playing dice or talking.

Stiger sourly surveyed his men, who, after their backbreaking work of moving the wagons across, looked extremely un-legionary-like. They were caked in mud and grim, and clearly tired. Stiger gazed up the road and was itching to be off. It was the middle of the afternoon, and he knew with certainty there was no way he would make it back to the legionary encampment this evening. The comfort of his cot would just have to wait. They would all be sleeping on their arms tonight. Worse, Stiger's captain would not be terribly pleased with his tardiness and would take it as another sign of his lieutenant's lack of competence.

"Varus," Stiger said when the corporal approached, just as muddy and bedraggled as his men. Varus had lent a hand at the backbreaking work of moving the heavy wagons across the river. "Have the men clean up before we march."

"Yes, sir," Varus replied, clearly not surprised by the order. He turned and called out to the men, who began moving back toward the river.

The added delay was unavoidable. The high standards of the legion had to be maintained. If a senior officer happened upon them in such a state, Stiger would find himself in serious trouble. And so, the men cleaned up while the heat of the day burned slowly away, and Stiger stewed about lost time. In the end, it took another forty minutes for the men to bathe in the river and tend to their kit.

By late afternoon, the supply train got back on the road. Stiger continued onward until dusk. He briefly considered pushing on through the darkness, but the road was poor and riddled with potholes. The risk to man, beast, and wagon was just too great.

He recalled a large open field just a few miles beyond the river. This, he felt, was a suitable place to make camp for the night. The field, like all of the others for miles around, had been burned by the enemy some weeks before. Stiger estimated that the campsite was roughly six hours from the main legionary encampment. With luck, he could be there by noon the next day.

Stiger had the wagons circled up just off the road. Fresh tufts of grass poked out from the charred remains of the field, though it no longer stank too badly of smoke. Varus sent men into a stand of trees to chop some wood, enough for several fires, while the rest of the men cleared space to lay their blankets and sleep. Despite the wagons being heaped high with supplies, the legionaries would subsist on their cold, pre-cooked rations. Stiger had made sure that they had left the legionary encampment with two days' worth of rations. The last two times he had made a supply run, Bruta had delayed him sufficiently so that what should have been a single day run turned into a day and a half.

Stiger tied up Nomad to one of the wagons and threw some hay down in front of his ever-greedy horse. Stiger's tutors had imparted a responsibility to care for his horse and equipment before he tended to his own needs. He had also been taught to rely upon himself to do the work and not servants or slaves, though many officers preferred to use the men as manservants. Stiger had that option available to him, but the lesson had taken and he was reluctant to rely upon another.

"Sir," Varus called.

Stiger had removed the horse's saddle and was brushing the animal down thoroughly. His armor, which he still wore, would come next.

"What is it?" Stiger called back, feeling weary from a long, hot day. Varus was on the other side of the camp, standing on one of the wagons and looking off into the distance.

"Riders emerging from the woods," Varus called back and pointed away from the road. "That way, sir."

Tiredness forgotten, Stiger hurried over to where the corporal was, climbed up the wagon, and stood on the driver's bench. There was a patch of forest around four hundred yards distant. A body of horsemen—of which Stiger quickly counted twenty—was emerging from the trees. The sun was setting in the direction of the riders. It was unclear whether they wore the red of the empire or the blue cloaks of the Rivan. Stiger very much hoped they wore the red.

"Get the men formed up," Stiger ordered curtly, suddenly feeling nervous and exposed. "Inside the wagon circle."

"Form up!" Varus roared. "Shields, helmets, and spears."

The men rapidly scrambled for their shields, protective canvas covers thrown aside as they drew them out. While the men assembled, Stiger glanced around. There was the work detail in the trees about fifty yards away, gathering wood.

"Send a runner to the wood detail," Stiger ordered Varus. "They are to remain hidden in the trees."

"What if we are attacked?" Varus asked.

Stiger shrugged, glancing back at the horsemen. "They are on their own then."

He did not think the detail could get back in time, should the riders decide to attack. They were safer staying put. Stiger had studied cavalry tactics. If the horsemen turned out to be the enemy, and were armed with lances and swords, Stiger's men would be relatively safe behind the wagons. After all, he outnumbered them. If, however, they were armed with bows, then it would be a different matter. The enemy horsemen would be able to stand off and pepper him with arrow shot, at least as long as the light lasted.

"Corvus," Varus called to one of the men. "Run to the wood-gathering detail and tell them to lay low until we know if that bunch are friendly."

"Yes, Corporal." Corvus, one of the youngest in the Seventh, set off. He slithered under one of the wagons and moments later was gone, dashing off toward the stand of trees where the detail of men worked, oblivious to the oncoming danger.

"They are moving toward us, sir," Varus said unnecessarily.

Stiger remained silent. He was frightened more than he cared to admit. He was concerned that, should he speak, he might betray his nerves and disgrace himself. So he said nothing and simply watched.

The riders formed up into a double column and slowly rode toward them. Stiger tried to remember if the Rivan employed horse archers but could not recall. He wished he had paid closer attention to his tutors. Then, Stiger saw the red cloaks of legion cavalry and the distinctive imperial standard being carried by one of the riders. He breathed out in relief as the troop of cavalry rode closer. They were from an allied auxiliary cohort.

"Stand the men down," Stiger said to Varus, his voice a little shaky.

"Stand down," Varus called.

"Lieutenant Fulvius," the commander of the troop introduced himself as he called for a halt some ten paces from the wagons, "of the Third Cogaron Cavalry Cohort."

"Lieutenant Stiger, of the Seventh Imperial Foot Company."

The lieutenant's eyes widened slightly before narrowing. "We're on patrol from an outpost fifteen miles from here." Fulvius gestured vaguely back the way he had come.

"Have you found anything?" Stiger asked. The Fulvius family was of the senatorial class. They were not exactly enemies of his house, but were not allies either. It was a gray area, and one of which Stiger was sure they were both well aware.

"We came across a path a few miles back that had evidence of a large body of horsemen moving through the area," Fulvius said. "The tracks looked fresh, perhaps a day or two old, but were headed north."

"I see," Stiger, said and then remembered his manners. "Would you care for a cup of wine?"

"Very kind of you," Fulvius said, inclining his head. He spared a glance behind him at the setting sun before turning back to Stiger. "Unfortunately, I am afraid I will have to pass. We were due back at sundown. Exploring those tracks took us farther afield than I anticipated."

"Another time then."

"Safe travels, Lieutenant," the cavalry officer said, nodded respectfully, and wheeled his horse around back the way he had come. His troop followed neatly after him. Stiger watched them for a few moments, then turned back to Varus.

"Let's get some fires going, and I think setting a double watch might be in order."

"Yes, sir," Varus said.

With the departure of the friendly cavalry, the men returned to the business of setting up camp. The wood-gathering detail returned with sufficient fuel to keep several fires going. And so, as the light died, the men settled in for the night. Stiger enjoyed some of the wine he had purchased, finding it quite good. It reminded him of the more comfortable life he had known back in Mal'Zeel. He was surprised that he actually felt a little homesick as he laid out his blanket near a fire that had been set for him.

The capital was an exciting place, with a much faster pace of life than the one he had seen with the legions so far. Entertainment was readily available, with the best being the chariot races, seconded only by the gladiatorial games. He had loved those sports.

Stiger took a long breath as he recollected better times. He missed the food, which was a sight better than the slop the legions provided. Most of all, though, Stiger missed his friends. He had a few, but treasured them nonetheless. Now, in service with Third Legion, he had no one else he could count on, save but himself. Stiger finished the wine he had been drinking and decided to turn in.

The night air brought on cooler temperatures, which was a relief, and Stiger wrapped himself up in his blanket. He used a rolled-up tunic for a pillow, shifted around until he found a comfortable position, and then closed his eyes and drifted off into sleep.

The night passed peacefully. Despite that, Stiger slept poorly, worrying about a possible attack and arriving overly late at the encampment next morning. He had left orders that he be woken well before dawn. After a quick, cold breakfast of precooked rations, Stiger had the supply train back on the road, creaking and clattering away as the first streaks of light brightened the sky. He was eager to return to the encampment, despite the dressing down that was surely waiting.

"Sir." A legionary drew his attention, pointing behind them. Stiger had been riding at the head of the column, alongside Varus's file. He turned in the saddle and looked backwards. The road was straight at this point, cutting through a small scrub forest that was beginning to encroach closely on the road.

Looking back, Stiger saw, to his consternation, that his wagons, one after another, were pulling off to the side and coming to a stop. Before stopping, the teamsters were driving their wagons into the scrub brush, at which the mules balked, leading to additional cracks of the whips interlaced with curses until they complied.

Stiger saw the reason a moment later. A double column of cavalry was coming up, with a carriage following closely behind. The cavalry and carriage were forced to wait for each wagon to slowly move aside.

"Get the men out of the road," Stiger snapped to Varus and also moved his horse aside as the troop and carriage approached.

"About bloody time," a cavalry lieutenant Stiger did not know barked angrily at him.

"Excuse me, sir?" Stiger asked, surprised at the open hostility. Though after the weeks of abuse from his peers, he knew he should not be too shocked at such treatment. Perhaps the other officer simply knew who he was and felt free to heap on the abuse.

"You heard me," the lieutenant said, drawing his horse up. The cavalry troop continued to ride by, horses hanging their heads in the heat. "You could have gotten off the road a little faster."

Stiger ground his teeth but said nothing. He turned to look as the carriage rattled by, catching a brief glance of an older man and a woman looking out at him. Then the carriage was past them, bouncing up the road, following after the escort troop of cavalry.

"Sir," Stiger directed himself to the cavalry lieutenant, who had remained behind. "If you would kindly get a move on, I would like to get my wagons back on the road and rolling."

The cavalry lieutenant shot Stiger a furious glance, dug his heels into his horse, and galloped off after the carriage. Stiger watched for a moment, thoroughly irritated, and then turned on Varus.

"Get the men bloody moving," Stiger fairly shouted at the corporal. He was angry, and embarrassed. Though he knew it was unfair, he was taking it out on Varus anyway.

"Yes, sir." Varus snapped to attention and saluted. He began to shout at the men to reform into a marching column.

Word was passed back down the supply train to move. Slowly, almost painfully, they got back on the road, crawling toward the main encampment of Third Legion.

Stiger kept his horse still as the supply train moved by him. He was in a thoroughly unpleasant mood and did not feel like sharing the road with anyone. Besides, none of the men were fit company for a nobleman. Before the end of the train reached him, he nudged Nomad into a walk and rode slightly behind, off to the side of one of the wagons.

An hour later, the road emerged into a rolling set of hills, the wagons slowly climbing and descending under the mounting heat of the day. The sun was almost directly overhead, and it was quite oppressive. Stiger took a quick drink from his canteen and then replaced it in his saddlebag as Nomad dutifully continued to plod along. The heat was so brutal that his horse hung its head as it clopped along, mile after mile. Stiger was considering calling for a break when a shout ahead drew his attention. The wagon he had been riding next to rumbled to an unexpected stop.

"Sir," the teamster called, having had word passed back to him. "You are needed up at the front."

Stiger kicked his horse into a trot and quickly made his way to the front of the supply train. Nomad did not seem terribly pleased at the increased pace and whinnied in protest. The lead wagon had stopped just short of the crest of another small hill. To the front of the wagon, Stiger found Varus organizing his file into a line of battle. The men had also discarded the canvas covers of their shields, an ominous sign that set Stiger's heart beating a little faster.

"What's going on?" Stiger demanded of Varus, who simply gestured to their front.

Stiger nudged Nomad forward a few steps to the crest of the hill and brought his horse to a stop. He found himself looking on the melee of battle. Down the other side of the hill was the carriage and cavalry troop that had passed them by earlier. They were under attack by a large force of cavalry, perhaps three hundred yards distant.

The cavalry wore the blue cloaks of the Rivan.

A good number of the defenders were down or had been unhorsed. The sounds of the fighting reached him clearly, and Stiger was surprised he had not heard it as he rode up.

"Looks to be around forty of the Rivan bastards," Varus grunted. Stiger did a quick count himself and found that the corporal was correct. Though in the chaos of the fight there appeared to be more. "They are pressing our boys hard, sir."

Stiger nodded in agreement, but was not really sure what he could do. His tutors had taught him infantry never attacked cavalry. It simply did not happen.

"Sir," Varus said, an urgent tone in his voice. "We need to help our boys."

"Right," Stiger said, the corporal's words jolting him into action. This was his chance to secure some of the glory he so craved and deserved. "Send word for the other file to come up at the double. We will take this file down and attack the enemy. As soon as the other file is up, they are to follow and engage. Understand me?"

"Yes, sir." Varus turned and spoke to a legionary who set his shield and spear down. The man immediately sprinted away toward the rear of the train.

Stiger glanced over his assault line, still hidden behind the crest of the hill. Twenty men organized into four ranks of five looked fairly insignificant. He then looked back down at the fight. He idly wondered if the disagreeable lieutenant he had encountered earlier was still alive.

"Corporal," Stiger said with sudden inspiration. "I want two ranks. That's all. Quickly now."

Varus reorganized the men into two ranks, which made the assault line look larger and—Stiger hoped— more intimidating. Once it was done, he unfastened his helmet from a tie on the saddle and put it on. Stiger secured the strap tightly and drew his sword. He looked back on his men. Each held a short spear and shield with grim expressions on their faces. He glanced back down at the fight. The enemy cavalry, engaged with the carriage's escort, were distracted. It wasn't like he was assaulting an organized and prepared formation. Stiger's appearance would hopefully surprise the enemy. The spears would serve well, Stiger hoped. If the opportunity came for a toss, where there was no risk of hitting friendly forces, he would take it.

"Sir," Varus drew his attention. "Would you care for one of the teamsters to hold your horse?"

Stiger studied the corporal for a moment. It was a gentle and subtle rebuke, which surprised him. Varus was right, he decided. He was an infantry officer, and in battle his place was afoot with his men. Stiger dismounted and beckoned for a man to take his horse. The man quickly led Nomad over to the nearest teamster and handed the reins up.

"Very good." Stiger used his free hand to check the tightness of the strap on his helmet. "Advance."

The line started forward and within five steps reached the crest. Then they were over it and on their way down the other side at a steady, measured pace.

"Seven Levels," one of the men breathed, seeing the action below for the first time.

"Quiet in the ranks," Varus barked. "Another word and I will personally make sure you will be up to your elbows in shit, mucking out the latrines after we make it back to camp tonight."

There were no more comments after that.

Stiger, studying the fight as they closed, estimated that about half of the friendly cavalry were down. Several had been unhorsed and fought afoot. Screams and the clash of sword on sword filled the air. Bodies littered the ground. Wounded crawled from the fight, while others writhed or thrashed about in agony. Horsemen wheeled around, trading blows. Horses whinnied and screamed.

Stiger saw the horses that had been pulling the carriage had both been cut down. An injured horse broke from the press and thundered away past Stiger and his men, a badly wounded Rivan cavalry trooper clinging desperately to its neck.

Stiger's nerves increased the closer they got.

This was his first fight.

He hands were sweaty on the hilt of his sword. His mouth was dry. Stiger suddenly found he was unprepared for the fight ahead. He offered a quick, silent prayer to the High Father, asking that the great god grant him glory this day. Stiger also prayed for strength. He begged that he not turn coward, for he really felt like doing nothing other than running.

What Stiger took to be an enemy officer abruptly pointed in their direction and shouted a number of orders. They had finally been seen. The enemy cavalry pressed their attack, clearly intent upon cutting the defenders down before Stiger and his men could intervene.

"At the double," Stiger shouted, understanding that he had to do something. It also occurred to him that as long as the enemy were focused on the carriage and its escort, the horsemen would not pose a threat to him and his men. The sooner they closed and joined the fight the better. "March!"

The pace increased, and the distance closed rapidly, armor jangling and chinking as the assault line closed on the enemy.

"Slow march!" Stiger called when they were fewer than ten paces from the enemy. "Close up."

The legionaries came back together in a solid line.

"Ready shields," Varus snapped. The shields thunked together.

Several of the enemy wheeled about and attempted to close on Stiger's legionaries. All they found was an impenetrable shield wall that bristled with short spears. The horses shied back, fighting against their riders' commands. A legionary lunged forward and jabbed out, found flesh. The horse screamed in agony. It reared up, dumping its blue-cloaked rider before the line of legionaries, then turned and ran madly in the other direction. The man died under a number of spear strikes.

Another horse was jabbed by multiple spears and went down, crushing the rider. Stiger stood off to the side of his line, slightly behind his men, as they coolly moved forward and into the fight. He was impressed by their calm and discipline, though he knew he should not be. They were mostly all hardened veterans with years of service behind them.

Stiger realized with an abrupt shock that he had left his shield back with the supply wagons. He cursed his stupidity as one of the enemy, seeing an officer off to the side of the legionary line, wheeled his horse about and drove forward, cavalry sword leveled for the kill.

Stiger crouched and made ready to spring aside, when one of his men at the end of the line casually stepped forward and drove his spear into the beast's chest. The force of the horse's momentum ripped the short spear from the legionary's hand as the horse collapsed to the earth, spilling the rider into the dirt. The legionary calmly drew his short sword and jabbed downward, killing the trooper before the man could even struggle to his feet. The legionary glanced over at Stiger and grinned before turning back to the action.

A strange-sounding horn blasted three short notes, then repeated again. The enemy cavalry immediately broke off the fight, pulling their horses around. They galloped away, making for a stand of trees some twenty yards to the left.

"Spears," Varus called to the men before Stiger could even think to give the order. "Release at will."

With grunts of effort, Stiger's men threw their spears. It was a ragged toss, but five of the deadly missiles found their mark, striking down horse and man alike. Stiger saw another wave of spears come down amidst the enemy a few heartbeats later. This toss had come from his second file, led by Corporal Durus, who had been at the rear of the supply train. They had just started down the hill.

Four more of the cavalry were struck down. One enemy trooper, whose horse was down, kicking about in the dirt on its side, stood and began dashing for the safety of the trees on foot. Another stood with an injured leg and began to limp painfully away.

"Send five men to dispatch the survivors," Stiger ordered Varus, gesturing with his sword at the horsemen who had been downed by the spear toss. An injured horse screamed and thrashed in the dirt. The animal's back legs no longer worked. "Also, kindly put the wounded beasts out of their misery."

"Yes, sir," Varus said.

Stiger watched the rest of the enemy cavalry make it into the trees and disappear. A few moments later they could be seen riding up a small hill beyond the trees and disappearing again over the top.

Stiger glanced around. None of his men appeared to have been injured or killed. He turned back to the carriage—a pile of bodies forming a ring around it. It was a right mess. Several of the cavalry escorts had dismounted and were moving amongst the bodies, putting any of the enemy they discovered alive out of their misery. A few were even searching the bodies for loot. A number of rider-less horses milled uncertainly about.

"You men," Stiger called to his men who were looking about at the carnage. "Gather up those horses."

At least the enemy's mounts were prizes of war. The legion would pay good money for them. The men would get a small portion, and so would Stiger. He received an allowance from his father, but that was barely enough to make ends meet. A little prize money would be more than welcome.

"You are not as slow as I had initially thought."

Stiger turned and saw the cavalry lieutenant he had met earlier approaching on foot. The lieutenant's armor and face were spattered with dried blood, but he looked unhurt. He flashed a good-natured grin at Stiger and offered his hand.

"Lieutenant Aquila Carbo at your service, sir."

Stiger took his hand and returned the grin. It was the first real respect he had been shown by a fellow officer since he had come north. The Carbos had once been allies of his house, but after his father's fall from grace, nothing was certain.

"Lieutenant Ben Stiger."

"Stiger you say?" Carbo asked, with raised eyebrows. "I was not aware there were any Stigers still serving." The lieutenant paused for a moment. "Lucky for me there are."

"Lucky," Stiger repeated quietly. He noticed that his hand had started to shake slightly. He placed it upon his sword hilt to keep the trembling from showing.

"I would like to apologize for my deplorable behavior earlier," Carbo said formally. "I trust you will forgive me?"

"Lieutenant Carbo," a firm voice called from behind, saving Stiger from having to respond. "Whom do we have to thank for our timely rescue?"

Carbo and Stiger turned. Another legionary officer, this one wearing the rich blue cloak of command, was striding confidently toward them. He also was splattered with blood and clearly had been involved in the fighting. Stiger stiffened to attention and offered a salute to the general.

"Enough of that, son," the senior officer said with a raised hand. "Today, I owe you my life, and for that I am grateful." The general paused and briefly surveyed the death around him. "Though, I would hazard we have a spy who tipped the enemy off…a nasty business, this. He will have to be found."

"General Treim," Carbo said. "May I introduce Lieutenant Ben Stiger."

"Stiger, eh?" the general asked, and Stiger realized that he was speaking with the new temporary commander of Third Legion.

"Yes, sir," Stiger said.

"You did well," General Treim said. "Are you in my legion?"

"Yes, sir," Stiger said. "Seventh Company."

"Excellent," Treim said. "I like men who can fight and are not afraid to pitch in. Carbo…how many men do you have left who can ride?"

Carbo glanced around and quickly counted. "Around eight, sir."

"Well, enough of this damned carriage," Treim said. "Get me a horse. We are only seven or eight miles from the encampment. We shall ride the rest of the way." The general paused and frowned. "The fact that the enemy moves so freely near our own encampment makes me wonder what our cavalry is doing."

"Yes, sir," Carbo said, and then hesitated. "What of Livia?"

"My daughter?" Treim turned back to the carriage, and then to Stiger. "Bring my carriage and my daughter to the encampment, son."

"Yes, sir," Stiger replied. "She will be safe with me, sir."

"I don't doubt it. Make sure you don't forget the carriage too. It was rather expensive and my daughter is fond of traveling in it."

"Sir." Stiger gestured toward the hill where the enemy had disappeared. "Are you certain about riding off? What if that bunch comes after you?"

"I rather doubt they will try," Treim said with a heavy breath. "After this, they have to know we will send out a force after them. Besides, we will ride hard for the encampment. They will not expect it. Yes, I think we shall be quite safe."

"Yes, sir," Stiger responded neutrally, not so sure he felt as confident. But it was not his place to question the decisions of his general.

Stiger watched as a cavalry trooper approached the coach and helped General Treim's daughter out. She wore a pale blue dress. Stiger was struck by her beauty and figured she was near his age in years. Livia had long blonde hair weaved into a single braid hanging down her back to her waist. Her green eyes looked on with distaste at the death and injury that had been wrought around the carriage.

"My dear," General Treim said. "See, I told you everything would be fine."

"Yes, Father," she said with a voice that was clear and fresh, though fluttered with an understandable nervous tremor. Stiger, in that moment, thought her very brave.

"This is Lieutenant Stiger," Treim introduced. "My daughter, Livia Domana."

"I am pleased to meet you," Stiger said, offering the girl a small bow. She did not share the same last name as Treim, which meant he had adopted her.

"Stiger?" She cast an interested look in his direction. "Stigers still serve the empire?"

"Yes, my lady," Stiger said, stiffly. "The emperor gave me his blessing personally."

"Lieutenant Stiger will see you safely to the encampment," Treim said. "I will ride ahead with Carbo. There is business I must attend to."

"But, Father," she said with an alarmed look. Stiger saw General Treim's face harden. She must have also seen it as well, for after a moment's hesitation, she bowed her head in acceptance, but not before glancing back at Stiger. Stiger realized that she desperately did not want her father to leave. Yet she would not embarrass him with a public protest either. She would endure as asked.

There was strength in this girl, he thought.

"You have my word of honor," Stiger said to reassure her, "that I will see you safely to the legionary encampment."

"Thank you, Lieutenant," she said, turning her beautiful green eyes upon him. "That will be a comfort."

Carbo led a horse over to Treim, who mounted with a smooth, practiced manner. He looked down upon Stiger and hesitated a moment.

"Mount up," Carbo called to those of his men who still could.

"Lieutenant," Treim said with a quick glance at his daughter and then around at the remains of the fight, which had centered around the carriage. "Make sure the wounded are cared for and brought back to the encampment. Also, bring back the dead."

"Of course, sir."

"I was friends with your father, you know," Treim said suddenly, which Stiger had not known. "I also fought against him."

Stiger said nothing, feeling he was on dangerous ground.

"If you are half the officer Marcus Stiger was, then I shall be pleased," the general continued, his new horse sidestepping nervously. The general tightened his grip on the reins and the horse stilled.

"Yes, sir," Stiger said, straightening.

"I shall be watching you, Stiger."

With that, the general kicked his horse forward into a trot and left Stiger with his daughter, and the aftermath of the fight, to deal with.

Care to be notified when the next book is released and receive updates from the author?
Join the newsletter mailing list at Marc's website:
http://www.MAEnovels.com
(Check out the forum)
Facebook: Marc Edelheit Author
Twitter: @MarcEdelheit

Printed in Great Britain
by Amazon

35977558R00333